KIWI SIN

KIWI SIN

NEW ZEALAND EVER AFTER, BOOK 5

ROSALIND JAMES

BELLBIRD PUBLISHING

© 2022 by Rosalind James

If it's better to marry than to burn, I was in trouble.

When you walk out of a cult with a driving license and the clothes on your back, you can face some challenges. How does a cooker work, and what do you cook on it? Is microwave pizza actually food, and how many times can you eat sausages before you never want to smell them again? And what do people put in all those bathroom drawers?

And, finally, how do you sort out the good and the bad of the place you've left and the place you've found and make your own way? How do you start over when half your family wants to recreate Mount Zion right here in Dunedin, New Zealand, and the other half wants to forget it?

And when you find the one and only woman you'll ever want to marry, what if everybody says no?

I'd been named after the archangel Gabriel. I was meant to know the truth and announce it to the world. So far, I wasn't even coming close.

Cover design by RL Design

www.gobookcoverdesign.com

❀ Created with Vellum

FAMILY TREE

(NAMES IN **BOLD** have left Mount Zion at start of book)
SAMUEL BROWN + MARY BROWN (both dec)

SON #1: THE PROPHET: STEADFAST PILGRIM (born Stanley Brown) (the founder) + MERCY PILGRIM (prev. Sarah Brown)

Grandson: VALOR PILGRIM

SON #2 (Steadfast's first convert): ELIJAH WORTHY (born Alvin Brown) + PROMISE WORTHY (prev. Pamela Brown)

ELIJAH'S SON #1: LOYAL WORTHY + BLESSING WORTHY (born Binita Kumar). They have 12 children:

- **DAISY (CHASTITY)** + GILEAD WARRIOR (div)
- **DORIAN (DUTIFUL)** + CHELSEA (not from Mount Zion)
- + 6 brothers
- **FRANKIE (FRUITFUL)** + GILEAD WARRIOR
- **ORIANA (OBEDIENCE)**
- **PRUDENCE (PRIYA)**

- DOVE

ELIJAH'S SON #2: **AARON WORTHY + CONSTANCE WORTHY.**

Constance's first husband died, leaving her with one son: **GABRIEL**

Constance & Aaron have 5 children together:

- **RAPHAEL + RADIANCE**
- **URIEL + GLORY** - - PATIENCE(Glory's younger sister)
- + 2 sisters
- **HARMONY**

Find a printable chart of the family tree here: https://rosalindjames.com/mount-zion-family-tree/

Some say the world will end in fire,
Some say in ice.
From what I've tasted of desire
I hold with those who favor fire.
But if it had to perish twice,
I think I know enough of hate
To say that for destruction ice
Is also great
And would suffice.

-- Robert Frost

1

RED DAWN

G*ABRIEL*

I knew that leaving Mount Zion meant walking into the world of the damned, and, if the Prophet was right, roasting in the burning fires of Hell. I just wasn't expecting it to happen so soon.

I didn't quite leave by choice, or not by any choice I could recall making. I was slow to speak and slow to act, because I thought things out before I made a move. Except on that day.

It was barely six o'clock, the gray dawn streaked with red, but I was up and dressed, working on some calculations for the new processing shed, which would hold the many different machines necessary to turn alpaca fleece into knitting wool. We were expanding our herd of Suri alpacas, and expanding the operation, too, because the Prophet always looked ahead. Mount Zion was prospering when most ventures failed, he told us often enough, because God smiles on the worthy and blesses their ventures. And if I wondered whether it was really because nobody here earned a wage, and forty years of families of twelve or fourteen or sixteen had expanded that free labor force in exponential fashion, I'd learnt not to ask that kind of question. Or any question. I kept myself to myself.

That was the problem with being chosen to help my father on the community's necessary business Outside, though. I saw things. And on that day, when I heard the noise from outside the gate, put down my pencil, and went out to investigate along with everybody else, I saw more.

Nobody visited Mount Zion. It was a closed community. "Sufficient unto itself," the Prophet liked to say. Not today.

The air was chilly and damp at dawn, and the kids were shivering as everyone stood silently to watch Fruitful Warrior, one of my almost-cousins, who'd run away from her husband but had been caught again, walk away from Mount Zion once more. Not in secret this time, and not without help. I held back Fruitful's husband, Gilead, as my dad entered a combination into the gate's locking mechanism that only he and the Prophet knew, and the steel frame slid slowly open with a grinding of metal. Fruitful, her face bruised from Gilead's blows, untied her cap and apron, dropped them on the ground, took off her heavy white shoes, pulled the pins out of her hair, and walked through that gate barefoot with her head held high, and Gilead's muscles tensed with violent effort under my hands.

I wanted him to break free. I wanted an excuse. Instead, I held him tighter, even though he was nearly fifteen years my senior and due my deference by every rule I'd ever learnt. I wished, with the hot rage of sin filling my chest, that I could hit him the same way he'd hit his seventeen-year-old wife. That I could hurt him. That I could use the strength I'd honed all my life and smash his face.

Violence is forbidden at Mount Zion. Violence between adult men, that is.

Anyway, Fruitful walked out, and the second she crossed the line, her sisters grabbed her and held on. That was Chastity, the eldest, who'd left long ago, plus the sister just younger than Fruitful, who'd run along with her weeks before.

Obedience, that was, sixteen years old, with her hair cut to just below her shoulders now and falling loose. She was wearing trousers and a shirt, the way women dressed Outside. Like a man, but Obedience would never look like a man.

The fella beside my cousin Chastity on the other side of that gate, who'd told us his name was Gray Tamatoa as if that would mean something, lifted a loud-hailer and announced, into the frozen shock of sudden change, "The rest of you have a choice, too. You're hard workers. Skilled laborers. There's a world of work out there, and it's waiting for people like you. I'm a builder in Dunedin, just down the road, but I was born in Wanaka, just like all of you. I've got good jobs going begging. Too much work, and not enough labor, so if any man here wants to give it a go, I'm willing to give him a try. All you have to do is step across the line. I've got people to help get you started, ready to hook you up with agencies and with churches that are waiting for you. They believe in God, too, just like you. They believe in goodness and compassion and service given from a willing heart, and they're there for you."

"Deceiver," the Prophet shouted. "Serpent." The voice we all had to listen to. The voice we all had to obey.

"Daisy has done it," Gray answered, talking back to the Prophet as nobody dared to do. "So has her brother." Oh. "Daisy" was Chastity, then. She'd changed her given name? You weren't allowed to do that. Names were given by the Prophet, except for my family, because my father had refused to allow our given names to be changed when the Prophet had decided on that. We'd taken the surname of the rest of my father's family, Worthy, but that was all. My brothers and I had been named for archangels, but those names had been my parents' choice, not the Prophet's.

Sometimes, rebellion sprouts from the smallest seed. Eventually, an acorn grows into an oak.

Gray went on, "There's money in your pocket, a fair day's wage for a fair day's work. There's a house of your own, eventually, and a good life for your daughters and your sons. All you have to do is step across the line."

I'd have done it right then, because even as my mind struggled to take it all in, my booted feet wanted to move. My brother Raphael, his wife Radiance, and their baby went first, though, because I was still holding Gilead. I handed him off to Regnum Standfast, who was young, but the only man I trusted to hold Gilead back, and followed my younger brother. Walking with my boots, not my mind. My mind was still thinking, *How can this be happening?* Nobody left Mount Zion, or almost nobody. Chastity and Dutiful had, because Chastity's twin was out there this morning, too, even though we'd been told they were both dead. That they'd left the community for Outside, all those years ago, and their sin had caught up with them, as the Lord would always smite the unworthy. Except that He hadn't, because here they both were, and Fruitful and Obedience, too. All outside the gate.

My parents followed me, bringing my youngest sister, Harmony, the only one not old enough to choose for herself, and that was the biggest surprise of all. My father was the Prophet's right hand. If he was leaving, could it be so wrong?

It felt wrong, and it didn't, as the Prophet's voice boomed out, sending us off to perdition to be devoured by snakes, tormented by demons with pitchforks, to spend eternity writhing in the fire the way he'd described at least once a week for as long as I could remember, the imagery so vivid I could feel my flesh blistering.

I walked out without a cent in my pockets, with nothing to offer except my willing hands. Not prepared a bit.

Did I walk away for myself? Probably. For my family? Possibly. For Obedience? No. That would be stupid, nothing but a dream.

When Gilead escaped Regnum Standfast's hold and charged through the gate, though, I was ready to hit him. That's how fast I descended into sin.

I was ready, but I didn't get the chance. Gray hit him first. Pity.

I RODE with a few blokes for the short journey down the hill into Wanaka. All of us who'd left today had made this trip before, to the doctor or the dentist. The world beyond Wanaka, though? My dad and I were the only ones who'd seen that, because I'd been helping him with his occasional trips to buy and sell and make arrangements, with me doing the driving and the loading and unloading, since I'd turned sixteen. I was clinging to that thought—that this wasn't quite as new to me—because unlike the others, I wasn't married, even though I was past the age for it, which meant I'd walked out alone.

Never mind. It's what Gray said. You know how to work, he's offering work, and he's a builder. Outside is full of people, and they don't get married for ages, so there has to be a way to live alone.

Driving up the hill, then, away from the center of the town, and stopping on a street of large buildings that had to be houses. "Single-family homes," they were called, and only a few people lived in each, enormous as they were and odd as that seemed.

The three other men in the car got out, so I did, too. Two of them were as tall and broad as me, and the third was taller. Highlanders players, they'd told me. I didn't have a clue what that was, but I didn't ask. I'd learnt that if I kept my mouth shut and my eyes and ears open, I'd eventually understand.

We were standing on the pavement, then, with about a hundred people, all milling about in an excited sort of way, talking about what had just happened, laughing or shocked or angry or all of those things together. Having emotions, and expressing them freely. They wore jackets against the chill, and I was in my shirtsleeves, my brown trousers, and the braces that held the trousers up. I was hungry, too, because I'd worked fourteen hours yesterday, taking advantage of the summer light, and it was time for breakfast.

I wasn't sure how I'd get breakfast. I knew no rules for this, except that breakfast would cost money I didn't have, and suddenly, I was nauseated. I breathed my way through it, telling myself, *There has to be a way*, and sure enough, within five minutes or so, Gray was taking charge again.

Parceling out the refugees, is the only way I can describe what happened next. Raphael and Radiance went with a couple who introduced themselves as Matiu and Poppy Te Mana and said they had an extra apartment in their house and would be glad of the company. My parents and Harmony went with Gray.

And me? So far, nothing, and the nausea was back again.

That was when a big, fit, tough-looking fella of forty-odd, who'd done some of his own talking through the loud-hailer back there and had an air of command I recognized, told me, "We have a granny flat. You're welcome to stay in it."

I didn't ask, *What's a granny flat?* I said, "Thank you. Until I get myself sorted." One thing I knew about Outside was that you did it yourself. It was like the drop of pond water we'd looked at under a microscope when I'd been at school, full of individual tiny things of different types called "single-celled organisms," moving around seemingly at random, intent on their own business, while I was used to being just one cell in a body.

"No rush," the man said. "Need a chat with anybody, or would you rather go?"

"Ready to go," I said, because I couldn't think of what I'd say to anyone. The only person I needed to talk to was Gray, and he was heading into one of the houses, a block of glass and steel unlike anything I'd ever seen before.

The man saw me watching and said, "I'll ring him later and ask him about you starting work, shall I?"

"Thanks," I said. "I'm Gabriel, by the way. Gabriel Worthy."

He put out a hand. "Drew Callahan." His eyes were gray, which was unusual, and he had some long-healed white scars on his forehead and around his eyes, and another one on his chin. He looked tough and felt quiet and calm, and I relaxed a bit. He asked, "You hungry?" and I relaxed a little more.

"Yeh," I said. "But I don't have money for food."

"I'll shout you food until you're earning," he said. "Let's go, then." And climbed up into the kind of car called an SUV. The seats seemed to be covered in leather, another thing I hadn't seen before, the instrument panel gleamed with electronics, and it was about as far from Mount Zion's small fleet of battered old farm utes as it was possible to be.

I climbed in, trying to scrape off my dirty boots along the way, but said, "I'll keep an account."

He set off down the hill, his movements assured and economical, and said, "No worries. I'm good for a few meals. Can't be bothered to keep track of all that anyway."

I had a little notebook and a stub of pencil in my pocket, as I always did. I pulled them out and said, "No need. I'll do it."

He braked to a stop at a sign, glanced over at the calculations I'd made this morning, and said, "Looks like heaps of maths. That what you do, then?"

"No," I said, feeling a bit embarrassed. "Just working out lumber, electric, that sort of thing, and a bit about the design."

"Hmm," he said. "In your head," and didn't say anything else until we'd stopped in town. "Takeaway OK?"

"Yeh," I said. "You'll have been up all night, though, I'm thinking." The Prophet had told us men outside were soft, but this man, though he was old enough to be a grandfather, didn't seem that way.

"Nah," he said. "I'm good. Hang on, then, and I'll be back with breakfast. Coffee?"

"Uh ..." I said. "I haven't had it." Coffee was an intoxicant, and a sin.

"Well," he said, "reckon it's time to try." And got out of the car.

SOME THINGS WERE THE SAME, I found. You felt better once you'd eaten, more settled. Drew didn't talk much, other than saying, "Three and a half hours to Dunedin."

"Fine," I said, because I had to say something, then looked out the window at not much at all and tried not to be overwhelmed by what I'd done, the yawning expanse of the unknown.

One moment, I was staring absently at the intersection ahead as we drove along beside Lake Dunstan. The next, I was shouting, "On your right!" at the top of my lungs.

It couldn't have taken Drew a half second to react, because even as I shouted it, as the car ahead made the right turn to the north toward Wanaka, swinging too wide, into the wrong lane, into *our* lane, Drew was slamming on the brake and driving straight off the road to the left, all the way onto the verge and nearly down the bank and into the water. I saw two horrified faces, mouths and eyes stretched, through the windscreen of the car as it flashed past, then heard the squeal of brakes as it slowed and swerved left, back into its own lane.

I hadn't even started to breathe again when another car, headed north too fast, was past us as well. Almost at the same moment I registered it, I heard the noise behind me. Loud and sudden and brutal, the sound of metal crunching into metal.

Drew said, *"Shit,"* punched a button for his hazard lights, and was stopped and out of the car, but I was faster. I hadn't had to hit the lights or turn off the car. I was sprinting, because the too-fast driver had hit the wrong-way driver from the rear. Even as the too-fast driver pulled to the side of the road, the wrong-way car was spinning down the highway in a sickening circle, then catching an edge of pavement and flipping. It rolled once, all the way around. Another half-roll, and it came to rest on its roof, rocking a little.

The other car had stopped, and somebody could be hurt in there, but I couldn't pay attention to that. I was running toward the crumpled rear of the wrong-way car, because I was smelling gas, and gas plus the kind of sparks you got when a car rolled on pavement ...

That meant fire.

Get in through the windows, I thought. The doors would be locked.

The driver, a youngish fella, was upside-down, still conscious, eyes wide. Drew was there, though. I could feel his presence behind me, so I kept running around the car to the other side.

A woman here. Dark hair, white face, upside down. I shouted, "Punch your seat belt! Punch it!" Drew wasn't shouting, because he was already hauling. The driver must have unclipped, but the passenger hadn't. She was fumbling for the latch, and I wasn't just smelling gas anymore. I was smelling smoke.

I didn't think. I crouched, and then I straightened. Right into the shattered window, grabbing for the shoulder harness and following it up, punching where the button would be.

The second it released, she fell straight down onto her head, but I wasn't worrying about that. I had my hands around her hips and was turning her awkwardly and hauling her out, legs first. She was tangled in the belt, and I pulled harder, the steep bank beside me not giving me enough space for the leverage I needed.

The smell was stronger now. Leaking gas. And smoke. Something catching.

I pulled like it was life and death, because it was, and she came loose. Her abdomen hit the edge of the window hard as I pulled her out upside-down by the legs, and she cried out.

The back of the car was burning, the flames licking toward us, but I had her mostly out, grabbing her around the middle now. It was a long way around there, and she was heavy.

Because she was pregnant.

The heat was a scorching thing. I could feel it on my cheeks, my arms. I was dragging her away from the bank that trapped us, around the front of the car. Then I had her in my arms, and I was running.

The blast like a furnace as the fire reached the gas tank and blew. A bloom of heat on my back, my legs, stinging hard, but I was striding like my legs could cover the world.

We were out.

We were free.

Escape.

2

THE WAGES OF SIN

G<small>ABRIEL</small>

By the time I lowered the woman to the grass, there were three more cars parked on the verge, and men running. One holding a handful of flares, running back toward Wanaka, the other waving his arms over his head at oncoming traffic in the other direction. Brave, but foolish. Drew, who had the driver of the burning car sitting propped against the bank, shouted to the arm-waving man, "Flares in the boot of my car, across the highway," and pointed, and the man ran for them.

I registered all that in a sort of compartment in my mind, a dispassionate corner that was taking stock, and then I was setting the woman down gently, beside her husband. I was afraid to look, afraid of what I'd see, but that dispassionate corner had me looking anyway, because it was necessary.

She wasn't crying. She was gasping, holding her belly, and I wanted to pray, but I didn't really know how. I knew about a vengeful God who punished sinners for their wickedness, and would punish me, too, for my sins today. God was probably punishing her right now, but that didn't feel right. What could she have done to deserve this? I didn't know how you asked for mercy, so I just crouched beside her and asked, "What hurts?"

"Susannah," the man said. "*Susannah.* Oh, my God. I'm sorry. I'm so sorry. I only forgot for a minute. How could it happen that fast?"

Drew said, "I've rung for the police and the ambos. They'll be here soon to check her out." He was still holding his phone, though, and now, he did some clicking around, waited a minute, then said, "Gray? Got the number of that doctor fella, Matiu? Read it out to me." Some more clicking, then he was saying, "That Matiu Te Mana? Drew Callahan here. Still in Wanaka, or on your way?" Another few seconds, and he said, "Come on as fast as you can, then. There's been an accident at the intersection with the Gibbston Highway. Got a pregnant woman here who needs attention, and some burns as well. Ambos on their way, but you'll be faster, and I want you to look at this lady." He rang off and told the woman, "There's help coming. An emergency doc, and the ambos. They'll take care of you, and the baby. What's hurting? Are you having contractions?"

She said, "I ... I don't know. I don't think so. I hit my belly hard on the window, though. It hurts. Is the baby ... do you think she ..."

Drew said, still calm as a glacial lake, "Pretty protected in there, with the amniotic fluid and all. Your body takes it in order to protect her, eh. I've got three kids myself, and I'm guessing you're doing a pretty fair job of that protection right now. How far gone are you?"

"Thirty ... thirty weeks," the woman gasped.

"We've been traveling," the man said. "Our honeymoon, before the baby. I've been driving on the left for two weeks! I wasn't even going that fast. I realized as soon as I made the turn, as soon as I saw you. It was only a second. How could it happen in a *second?*" He had hold of the woman now, and I thought about how many things could happen in a second.

You could turn your back on your home. You could hurt your family. You could burn down your life.

"American, are you, mate?" Drew asked. Still calm, but he was stepping behind me, checking out my back.

I said, "I'm fine. Stings a bit, that's all. Got a little hot there, maybe."

The woman focused on me, then. "You got me out," she said, her voice still jerky with shock. "You pulled me out. When the car was burning. You saved my life. My baby's life."

Well, this was embarrassing. "No worries," I said. "Anybody would've done the same."

"What's your name?" she asked. "Because I want to name the baby after you."

"Gabriel," I said. "But, ah …"

"An angel's name," she said. "Oh, my God. You're an angel. That's why you're so beautiful. You're an *angel.*"

"Archangel," Drew said, the corner of his mouth tugging upward as if he thought this was funny. It wasn't funny!

I said, "Pretty odd name, if the baby's a girl. And I'm not an angel, no worries. It's just a name." Now, my face was as hot as my back.

"Gabrielle," she said. "Sean, we're naming her Gabrielle. If she's all right. She has to be all right. He *saved* us. That has to mean something."

Her husband looked even more miserable. In fact, he was nearly crying. Here he was, thinking he'd nearly killed his wife and baby, and she wanted to name the baby after another bloke? Yeh, not too good. I didn't know much about naming babies—the Prophet did that, as I've mentioned—but I had a feeling this wasn't the best way. I said, "You'll want to name her after your husband, surely. What's your name, mate?"

"Sean," he said. "You're not getting a girl's name out of that. Her name's supposed to be Scarlett."

"Fire-wise," Drew said, "possibly problematic."

"What?" Sean stared at him. "And, yes, we're American.

We should've gotten a better car. I had an airbag, but why wasn't there one on the passenger side? Who'd rent out a car without a passenger airbag? How is that even legal?"

Drew said, "My wife's American, as it happens. She says it terrified her, learning to drive on the left. Where are you from, in the States?" Keeping them talking, keeping them calm, and possibly changing the subject. Good idea.

I said, "I'm going to check the other car." I didn't even know if anybody'd done that, and I didn't want to hear any more about this poor bloke having his baby named after me.

I jogged down the road, the sting on my back increasing, and found him. The bonnet was smashed and steam was coming out of the radiator, but the man, barely more than a boy, was sitting in the driver's seat, his hands still on the wheel, staring straight ahead as if he were about to drive it out of there. Shock, that would be. I crouched beside the window and asked, "All right, mate?"

He stared at me, his pupils dilated so far that his eyes looked black, and said, "Why the hell were they stopping in the road? What were they playing at? I couldn't stop fast enough, by the time I realized." The kind of bloke who hasn't seen enough things go wrong, who still didn't believe it had happened to him.

"American," I said. "Pulled into the wrong lane."

"Bloody Americans, Are they ..." He stared at the two of them, sitting on the verge. "She isn't pregnant, is she?"

"Yeh," I said. "Got any water?"

"What? No. Oh, my God. Is she all right?"

"I think so," I said. "Sit there until somebody comes, I guess."

A voice from behind me. "Do you realize that your shirt's scorched in back? And that half of it's burned away?"

"What?" I asked, turning.

It was a woman. Older, wearing jeans, her hair close-cropped. It was hard for me even to register her, and harder to categorize her. Women out here just looked so ... *different*. They spoke to you, for one thing, and *stared* at you. She said, "You've burned yourself. Hang on. I'm getting water."

They gave you orders, too.

Up ahead, Drew had the woman passenger leaning back against the grassy bank and had taken off his jacket to put over her, even though the car was still merrily burning away, heating the morning air and giving off the stink of burning metal. Shock again, making her cold. I thought, *We should put them into Drew's car,* and was about to go suggest it when the woman came back with a huge plastic bottle of water and said, "Take off your shirt."

I gaped at her. I couldn't comprehend this request. I said, "They need that water over there. That couple."

"Already took them a bottle. Unbutton your shirt and take it off. We need some cloth to cool those burns, and if we don't use your shirt, we'll have to use mine. I don't mind, but it might startle the animals and small children, eh. Come on, then. I don't have all day." She smiled cheerfully, and it was all, more and more, seeming like a dream.

I could never have imagined unbuttoning my shirt in front of a crowd, because there *was* a crowd here now, but I did it. I stripped off, and realized that it did indeed have some holes in it, or more like one big hole where the back had used to be, and that the singlet underneath was nothing but a rag. I watched the woman soak the pieces with the water from the bottle, after which she laid them over my back and tucked the edges under my braces. She said, "Good thing it was cotton. A synthetic would've melted, and you don't want that. You need to be sitting down with that on you, though. Or lying down, even better. Which one's your car? Let's get you into it, unless it's the burnt one."

I said, "I'm all right. Those others ..." I gestured at the couple up ahead, with Drew. "They're the ones hurt. The woman, especially."

"Looks like they've got somebody caring for them," she said. "Show me your car, because you're getting into it. Seems you were a hero, because I saw that happen. Time to sit down and let somebody else take a turn to be the hero for a while, and here I am volunteering, if only with water. Besides, you're going to draw a crowd of your own if we let you stand about here half-naked, looking like that. Like a film star, aren't you." And smiled again.

I breathed easier once the doctor turned up. He was the one who'd taken Raphael and Radiance, so there I was, with my brother again. Raphael looked bloody shocked to see me with my shirt off, as if I'd walked through the gates of Mount Zion and immediately descended into nakedness and sin, and for another confused moment, I wanted to laugh. My brain didn't know what direction to go here, and that was the truth.

The doctor told us that the pregnant woman seemed OK, so that was the worst thing set to rights. He smeared some stuff on my back and put dressings on, and the sting lessened. Pity I still didn't have a shirt, that people were still staring at me, and that I had to speak to the police like that when they arrived.

Eventually, the ambos came, and they put Susannah on a stretcher. She took my hand and kissed it when I said goodbye, which was possibly the most embarrassing thing to ever happen to me, but then the ambulance doors closed behind her and the husband, the towies got to work on the wrecks, and it was over.

And Drew and I drove on to Dunedin.

So, you see, I left Mount Zion, and I burned.

The wages of sin, possibly.

ORIANA

It was late afternoon by the time we drove back to

Dunedin. Honor, Gray's mum, had wanted us to spend the night, but Frankie had said, "I can't be this close to Mount Zion right now. I have to get out." Her eyes looked sunken in her bruised face, and she was moving stiffly, because she'd been whipped with Gilead's belt, so much harder than our dad did even in the worst of his anger. I'd seen the raised red wheals on her buttocks, her thighs, and they were awful.

I'd learnt things today that I'd never wanted to know, and I'd thought I knew all about Mount Zion. Maybe it was seeing it again after the contrast of being Outside all these weeks. Maybe it was seeing my dad again, the rage and contempt on his face, or, worse, seeing my mum, seeming to have shrunk even further into the tiny frame that declared her Indian heritage, all the expression wiped from her face, standing so small, holding Dove's hand. Dove, who was the youngest of us, who got scared sometimes like me, and who was years away from being able to leave.

Or maybe it was seeing our sister Prudence, halfway to the gate, standing straight, her arms at her sides, watching Frankie go. Not even fifteen, which meant more than a year before she'd be able to walk through the gates herself, and she had to know she'd be punished tonight. She'd got Frankie out when she'd been locked into Gilead's room, interfering between a husband and wife, and she'd pay the price for that. In the Punishment Hut, and worse.

Leaving them behind felt so bad.

I shivered, sitting in the warmth of the big ute behind Daisy and Gray, holding Frankie's hand. She was asleep, her head on a pillow squashed against the side window, and wearing clothes Daisy had brought for her from Dunedin, because this time, we hadn't burnt her cap and apron in Gray's firepit. We'd burnt her dress.

The clothes were soft things, because she hurt. She'd been given pain tablets in hospital, and she said they helped, but I wasn't sure what you did about the pain in your heart.

I wasn't tough, not like my sisters. Would I have risked what Prudence had to get Frankie out? I longed to think the answer was yes, but I wasn't one bit sure it was true.

A person could change, though, couldn't she? I'd left Mount Zion, and if I'd thought sometimes, in the dark hours before dawn when I couldn't sleep, that it would be easier just to go back there, not to have to make all these terrifying adjustments—well, today had shown me why that wasn't possible. What had happened to Frankie, and to Daisy before her, with Gilead—that was evil. The Prophet said evil was Outside, but I thought it was in that room where Gilead had locked Frankie, where he'd hurt her. In the dark, cold, stinking Punishment Hut, where both Daisy and Frankie had spent too many days and nights.

It couldn't be right to be treated like that just for wanting to be a person, and it couldn't be right to hurt the person you'd promised to love and cherish, either.

And my name wasn't Obedience anymore.

3

BEEFBURGERS

GABRIEL

When Drew announced, not even two hours out from the accident site, "Cup of tea, I reckon," then glanced at me, pulled to a stop outside a small, tidy building in a tiny settlement, and added, "and lunch," I balked.

Yesterday, I'd worked fourteen hours. Today, I'd worked none. I didn't need rest, I didn't need food, and I especially didn't need Drew paying for something else before I'd even got a chance to start work. When I did those runs with my dad, we took sandwiches and a thermos flask, but I'd seen the price lists in the windows of cafés. How many hours' pay would *two* of those meals amount to? I had no idea how much you got paid Outside.

"I'm not wearing a shirt," I pointed out. *And I don't know how to act*, I didn't say. That was the weakness talking, and the pain of those burns. Not too badly blistered, the doctor had said, so the pain shouldn't be bothering me, except that it was my entire back, and I'd had to rest at least some part of it against the seat. That must be it, because I *did* know how to act. I *had* been out all those times with my dad, and nobody had stared.

They'd stare at me if I wasn't wearing a *shirt.*

Drew said, "Easily fixed." He pulled off his own shirt, a flimsy, short-sleeved gray thing that provided wholly inadequate cover. It had a small triangle printed on the chest. *Adidas,* the lettering below it read. What were Adidas? He handed it over. "We're about the same size."

"I can't take your shirt," I said. This was awkward. More than awkward. Also, without the shirt, I could see that he was even more fit than I'd thought. Men Outside definitely weren't soft, or at least not all of them were, because Gray had looked this fit as well.

"Nah," Drew said. "I've got a jacket. And a hat. Good anyway, as it's started to rain. And that soft shirt will be easier on the burns." He pulled on the jacket and zipped it up. The hat wasn't much use for keeping rain off, because it had no brim at all other than in the front. Once he had it on, he climbed down from the car and said, "You coming, or planning to have a sook in the car? Nobody's going to bite, mate. Better eat now, while you have the chance of it, because once we get home, we'll be mobbed," and grinned at me as if nothing out of the way had happened.

I climbed out and dashed through the rain with him. No choice, though I still felt half-naked. I was showing nearly all of my arms, and the shirt was much too snug across the chest and shoulders for modesty.

Inside the café, things got odd. Not odd in the way I'd thought they would. Odd in a way I couldn't have imagined.

The place was bright, cheerful, and small, most of the tables occupied, and an older woman with a good-natured face standing behind a counter, the glass cabinets around her fairly bursting with food items, each individual thing prepared and ready for you to choose it. Whatever you liked.

Bacon and egg quiche with salad, one sign read, beneath a plate of fat pastry-clad wedges. *Cheese roll,* said another. *Carrot cake,* proclaimed a sign in a different cabinet. *Fruit custard tart.*

That one looked like something you'd get on a feast day, rich pastry piled high with fruit and cream. You could buy that kind of thing anytime here?

I was still staring at it when the woman said, "Lovely to see you, Drew. Not with the family today?"

"No," Drew said. "Here with my mate instead. He wants to try everything, I'm guessing, and small wonder, but we need to fill up fast. What d'you have that's good today?"

"Got some lovely beefburgers with chips," she said. "That should do the two of you pretty well."

"That'll definitely do," Drew said. "Cheers."

She spoke to a girl behind her, then turned around to ask, "Do you play rugby, then? Haven't seen you before, I don't think."

Oh. She was talking to me. I said, "Uh … pardon?" Now that I was standing, I was getting a bit lightheaded. Shivering as well, which was awkward.

Because I was cold. I'd got wet despite the running, and I was barely wearing a *shirt*.

"Nah," Drew said. "Though he looks it, eh. Just a mate." He reached for a glass bottle filled with what looked like water from a different cabinet, handed it to me along with two glasses, and said, "Find us a table, would you, and pour us some water? Sit down. I'll be there in a sec."

He'd noticed the shivering, then. I was embarrassed, but I hadn't been raised to argue, even though he'd pulled out his wallet and was paying again, and I didn't even know how much it was, so I could write it down. I did sit down, with my back well away from the chair, poured my water, sipped at it slowly, and tried not to be sick.

It wasn't even five minutes before the woman was at our table with two cups of tea and a pot, and I had to admit that the hot liquid felt good going down. I'd barely started drinking it, though, when a couple of boys of the littler sort came up to the table and the older one said, "'Scuse me."

"Hi," Drew said. "How're ya goin'?"

"Good," the older kid said. The younger one just stared at Drew, all round eyes and breathlessness. "But we wanted a selfie," the older kid said, "and our mum said we couldn't bother you when you're eating. You're not eating now, though, and she's in the toilet, but she took her phone, so ..."

"Ah," Drew said. "Found a loophole, did you? Got a pen?"

"Uh ..." The boys looked at each other, then back at him, and he said, "Tell you what. Go ask Janet, behind the counter there, to borrow one. Go quick, though, before your mum comes back."

They did, and when they came back, Drew scribbled something onto two paper napkins and handed one to each boy. He'd no sooner done it than another woman, as bold as the serving-woman even though she was younger, came rushing up and said, looking Drew right in the face, "I'm so sorry. I told them not to disturb you."

"No worries," Drew said. "Cheers." Then turned back to me as if nothing had happened and picked up his mug.

They wandered off, the boys practically jumping up and down with what looked like excitement, and I thought, *What?* "Is it a game?" I asked, despite my no-questions policy, maybe to distract myself from the shivering, and maybe because I didn't think there was any amount of looking and listening that would answer this. "Do people collect ..." I tried to think of a word. "Clues?" I finished.

"Something like that," he said. "Ah. Beefburgers. Cheers, Janet. Also—your pen." He handed it over, then told me, "Get that down you, and you'll feel better."

It was a sandwich. With some kind of beef in it, raw vegies, a fried egg, a couple of slabs of bacon, and a thick slice of pickled beetroot. Looked good, and mostly like things I recognized. Beside it was a pile of something else I knew about. Chips, those were, with tomato sauce. A treat I'd rarely had, and one that was making my mouth water now with the prospect of that crunchy/chewy potato taste, not to mention the salt.

Drew took a bite.

I froze.

He chewed, swallowed, then asked, "Problem? Is Mount Zion vegetarian, then? Never heard that. Sounds unlikely."

I thought, *Harden up. You know people Outside don't do this. Doesn't mean you can't.* Did I even want to? I didn't know. *Not doing it, though,* felt as naked as ... well, as standing about on the side of a roadway without my shirt on. I said, "Just a moment," then folded my hands, bent my head, closed my eyes, and muttered the prayer under my breath.

When I looked up again, half-afraid of what I'd see, Drew wasn't eating. He'd set his own sandwich down while I'd said the blessing, in fact. Now, he picked it up and took another bite, and didn't say anything else.

I ate all the chips. I also ate all of the sandwich thing. It was delicious.

People in the cafe held up their phones while we walked out. They talked amongst themselves, too. Excitedly. I was wearing a regular shirt, though, the same kind most of them had on. *Could* they tell? How?

I needed to learn how to fit in. I'd ask later, when I could summon the energy for it.

WHEN WE WERE in the car again and driving, I said, "You stop there often, then. With your family." I needed to make some kind of conversation, if only to distract myself from my back. It was against the seat no matter how I tried to position myself, and it was hurting more.

No, I needed to make conversation because he'd invited me to *live* with him. Or near him. In a "granny flat," whatever that was. Did that mean it had a granny in it? *His* granny?

I didn't know how to live Outside. What had I done?

I was breathing harder, so I focused. On the road, and on what he said next. "Yeh," he said. "Three kids, like I said. And a wife, of course."

"Oh," I said. "You're married? I thought people Outside just ..."

He shot a look at me, then smiled in a crooked sort of way. "Nah, married before our families and God and all, I'm afraid. Sorry to disappoint in the sin department. Anyway, I work in Dunedin, but we've got a place in Wanaka as well, so we're back and forth a fair bit. It's my holidays now, though, such as they are, and once the kids are done with their school term, we'll be up in Wanaka again for Christmas. The kids can never seem to make it all the way there without stopping for a wee and a feed, so hey presto—the café."

I did my best to take all that in. "You have two houses?" I asked cautiously. "That are just yours?"

He glanced over at me, then back at the road. "Holiday house. Pretty common."

I tried to digest that, but it wouldn't go down. "Holidays are days off work," I said, but after that, I had nothing.

"Let me guess," Drew said. "You don't have holidays—proper holidays—at Mount Zion. Don't even get a few weeks around Christmas to recover from the year? Or in winter, maybe, as it's farming? To go ... someplace else?"

"No," I said. "Who'd do the work? And where would we go?"

"Hmm," Drew said. "What do the kids do, then, when they're not in school?"

"Work," I said.

"Ah," he said, and that was all.

I didn't hear anything after that. Not to put too fine a point on it, I fell asleep, or at least into a doze. It wasn't what you'd call a comfortable sleep. More of a nightmarish one, to be honest. And when I woke up, that looked like a dream, too.

It was a house, I guessed. The Wanaka house we'd stood outside, the one that was Gray's, had been a cube, and this was ... a bigger cube, or a series of them, stacked in a sort of pattern. It was a towering structure, all white and windows, like nothing I'd ever imagined could be a residence for one family, or for four.

Drew said, "We'll have a look at your back first, then get you sorted in the flat. Come on," and climbed down.

I took a breath and followed him. My back was screaming now, but it wasn't the first time I'd been hurt, and anyway, there was too much strangeness here to get distracted by pain.

We didn't make it to the door before it opened and three kids came pelting out. Small, medium, and largish. The littler ones, who were girls, threw their arms around Drew's legs, while the boy just came close, upon which Drew threw an arm around *him*, even though the kid had to be nine or ten.

Somebody else came out of the door, then, a pretty woman with white-blond hair coiled at the back of her neck in a way I recognized. She was wearing shorts and a T-shirt, but I was already getting less shocked by women's clothes. Either the Devil whispering in my ear, or God deciding I'd had as much shock as I could endure for one day.

Or not, because she ran to Drew, then grabbed him around the neck and kissed him. Passionately, I guess you'd call it. In front of their kids. In front of *me*.

I'd never seen a kiss like that in my life. The closest I'd come had been when my parents were in bed and I was trying not to look, and these two were doing it in front of a stranger! I didn't know what to do, so I stared into the middle distance and tried harder not to notice. Not easy, when the people are a meter away.

The woman pulled back, finally, when I was wondering desperately if I should just get back into the car, and asked, "Where are you hurt?" Her eyes shadowed, worried. "You can still drive. How bad is it?"

"What?" he said. "I'm not hurt."

"Drew." She looked upset now, and she *sounded* upset. And, yeh—I'd also never seen a woman get upset at a man like this. "You asked me to get some large burn dressings. You told me that Gabriel was coming to stay, and to please get large burn dressings!"

"Did you get burned, Dad?" the boy asked.

"No," Drew said. "It wasn't for me, though. It was for Gabriel. Didn't I say?"

She had a hand at her face. "Oh. I'm so sorry, Gabriel, but —*Drew.* Why didn't you *text* me that?"

"Aw," he said. "Sorry, sweetheart. I was driving," and then kissed her *again*. When he pulled back, he was smiling. "I'm all good, see? Not getting myself hurt anymore, remember? Leaving that to the younger boys. Besides, I'd have thought you were immune from worry by now. And you got the dressings? Brilliant."

"Yes," she said. "*Despite* my worry, due to my husband deciding to assume I didn't love him enough *to* worry." She was smiling, though. "You're off the hook this time, but watch it, mister. Don't *scare* me like that."

He laughed, then said, "Let's go, Gabriel. We'll get your kit off and have a look. Some Panadol probably wouldn't come amiss, either. I'm guessing there's no drinking at Mount Zion. Pity. I'd say a beer or two, otherwise."

"Pardon?" I was starting to get a bit shaky again.

"Into the house," he said, his demeanor changing completely. "Need an arm to lean on?"

"No," I said, and then tried to make that be true.

A man was meant to be stoic and strong and in control of the situation. Unfortunately, none of that appeared to be happening.

Maybe tomorrow.

4

FISH OUT OF WATER

Gabriel

I'd known leaving would be a challenge. I just hadn't realized how much of a challenge.

That first night, I ate dinner with the family, telling myself, *They're not your family. You live alone now,* and went downstairs afterward. Ten minutes later, I was standing at a severely rectangular porcelain sink set into about a hectare of creamy stone benchtop and surrounded by more mirrors than I'd ever seen in my life, sponging myself off as best I could in an enormous bathroom that was just for one person. The shower would hurt too much on my back, was the reason for the sponging, not that I didn't know how to turn on a tap. I knew how to use a shower!

The "granny flat," it turned out, wasn't a granny anything. It was another whole house that I had all to myself, stuck onto the back of the series of cubes, with a separate bathroom that was all shiny surfaces and not a bit of concrete, containing an endless number of drawers that would hold ... what?

A razor and toothbrush, toothpaste and soap. Drew had found extras for me, and they'd about doubled my list of possessions. What else did people find to put in those drawers? What could there possibly be? I couldn't even imagine. Besides that, there was a stacked washer and dryer in here—at least, I assumed that was what they were—that were *also* just for one person, plus enough towels for a crew, both big and small versions, all of them about four times as thick and fluffy as any towel I'd ever seen. They were also resolutely, pristinely white, as if they'd never been used before. I used one of the little towels to dry off, trying not to dirty anything more than I had to, then walked through the kitchen, full of more mysterious appliances I had no clue how to use, and dressed in another of Drew's T-shirts and a pair of his undies, because I had nothing else to wear. I had no pajamas on, which was unthinkably immodest, but there was nobody here to see, so I guessed that was OK.

Not to mention that the undies themselves were shocking. They were short on the legs, low on the hips, and tight, so you could see all of me through them. I barely *fit* in them. They were also red. Drew had given me another pair, too, that were bright yellow and had palm trees and monkeys printed all over them. Both pairs had still been in their pack, and he'd said, "Don't laugh. Hannah bought them. Forwards wear black, I told her. Black boots, and black undies. If she wanted a man who wears red undies, reckon she should've picked somebody else."

He'd said it in front of her. That was the worst. I'd struggled for something to say and finally come up with, "Thanks," and Hannah had laughed and said, "It was worth a try. You've got that body, Drew, and you won't even decorate it this much for me? I'm a woman of few pleasures."

"Oh?" he'd said. "Sounds like I've got work to do, then." I didn't want to know what that meant.

The undies *were* immodest, then, which was a relief to know. Even though I was wearing them.

Hannah had put a loaf of bread, a stick of butter, a jar of jam, and a carton of milk into the fridge when she'd brought me down here. She'd also handed me a packet of tea, which was good, then given me a dozen eggs in a carton and told me, "We'll take you shopping tomorrow, but you'll need these to fuel you up for it, I'm guessing."

"I can't come and help," Jack had said, sounding disappointed. "Grace and I have school. Only Madeleine can go. It's a pity, because I'm good at shopping. I know where everything is. Usually, Mum and Dad give me some of the list, so it goes faster." All the kids had come down here with us, which made the place feel friendlier, not so shiny and empty.

"You are," Hannah said, resting a hand on Jack's head for a moment in a way that was, again, a little less alien. Also, having the kids here meant I wasn't alone with a woman. With somebody's *wife*. "Gabriel's going to be staying with us, so you'll have heaps of chances to help him."

"Only until I get my feet under me," I said. "It's very kind of you."

"It's nothing," she said. "Anybody would do the same." Which wasn't what I'd heard about Outside, but so far, nothing was.

I told myself that the pain from the burns would be better tomorrow, that I was just tired, and it would all get easier, and eventually tried to go to sleep on my stomach in an impossibly wide bed that should have held four or five kids, with the silence pressing on my ears and too much empty space around me. Totally exhausted, even though I'd worked not a bit today, and absolutely restless at the same time, as if my body was expecting to have to leap up again at any moment.

I tried to sleep, but I couldn't. I hurt, and my thoughts were too big and too dark. I got up again and went into the lounge.

A big black glass screen sat on a low cabinet. That would be a TV. Hannah had held up two separate box-type things full of buttons to be pushed and said, "This remote to turn it on and off and for the volume, and the other one's for Sky," and I'd thought, *What?*

So far, I was safe from the corrupting influence of television, because the only thing I managed to do was turn the thing on. After that, I pushed buttons and ended up with a fuzzy gray-and-black screen that I couldn't make go away, so I abandoned it for another day.

There were some books on a shelf near the TV—novels, I thought, because they seemed to be stories. I hadn't read many novels, and no worldly ones, but reading was one thing I *did* know how to do, so I took a look.

Most of them had names like "Final Notice" and "Red Dawn" and "The Hot Zone," and seemed to be, from the pictures on the covers and the first pages, about things exploding and people shooting each other. I'd had my fill of things exploding today, so I picked up a thinner book whose cover pictured a woman wearing jeans and boots. She was standing with her hip cocked and a thumb in her belt like a man, and the title was, *Arrest Me, Officer*. It looked like it might be funny, and possibly illustrative of actual real life Outside, beyond the wars and such. Homework, you could say.

I carried the book back to the bedroom, turned on the light that sat on the little table beside the bed, because you were apparently meant to lie about lazily here and would need light for it, lay on my stomach—yes, lazily—in my red undies, and started reading.

The book started out with a man riding a police horse at a gallop toward the woman, which seemed pretty reckless, and her tripping and nearly falling in a milling crowd, until he reached down and swung her up in front of him on the horse.

Huh. That seemed as improbable a scenario as the books about shooting and explosions. Also, if your job was working with animals, you'd surely know how to control your horse. The woman, whose name was Nikki, was quite rude to the bloke in a funny sort of way, though, and he didn't mind, so that was useful.

I was going along pretty well like that, forgetting to think about how I'd knocked the pins out from under myself and had burned myself fairly well in the process, which meant I probably wasn't going to be able to start work tomorrow the way I'd planned, when Nikki fell across the bloke's unmarked police car—his name was Roarke, which seemed odd, but what did I know?—as he was pulling out of something called a "stakeout"—these two people were the clumsiest couple I'd ever heard of—upon which he pulled her into the car to hide from the bad guys, or the other cops, and they ended up kissing. In his police car, which, again, didn't sound right, but ...

His mouth slanted down over hers. His hand was in her hair, and that mouth was a hungry thing. Demanding, and taking. She forgot about the rip in her jeans, because her hand was on the rock-hard muscle of his upper back, and she was falling against the door with him following her.

His hand inside her T-shirt now, his mouth at her neck. His voice, dark as smoke, in her ear. "We can't do this." And his hands telling a different story. His hands, and his talented, terrible mouth. Biting now. Sucking at her, like he couldn't get enough. And then his hand reached her breast, and the kiss changed to something else.

I tore my eyes from the book. What *was* this? I looked at the cover again. Same girl in her jeans and boots. The background was a big red heart, and the smaller print across the cover said, "A sexy, breezy, laugh-out-loud romp. Great fun!" – Alison Moriarty, *author of* Frankly Yours.

Great *fun?* It was pornography! I was reading pornography!

I read to the end of the chapter. Just to check.

5

DROWNING IN THE FLOOD

Oriana

On the last day of January, I wasn't enjoying being out in the fine weather, mucking out the chicken coop and mulching the fruit trees, harvesting the honey, making huge batches of jam, babysitting, or knitting hats and scarves to sell at the farmer's market, adding week by week to the account Daisy had helped me set up at KiwiBank. I wasn't even cooking dinner for the family and cleaning bathrooms the way I did every day, because most people didn't like cleaning, baths should be clean, and I didn't mind.

Instead, I was back in school.

My second chance to get this right, I told myself. *It can't be worse than it was before.* That would be my first six weeks or so at this school before the summer holidays had arrived. Those days had receded into a terror-blurred memory of walking into this huge, echoing old place every day with Frankie, dressed in our new uniforms, though they were at least a little familiar, with their long skirts and loose tops, the clunky shoes, the forbidding of makeup.

Walking in, and failing. Failing to understand. Failing to succeed. Failing to fit in.

Me, that is, not Frankie.

It hadn't really been starting school. It had been *restarting* school, because like Frankie and every other girl at Mount Zion, my schooling had ended as soon as I'd turned fifteen. That meant I was more than a year behind for my age, and going to school with younger girls. I'd told myself that first day, through my nerves, *Frankie's even worse off, because she's more than two years behind and still in Year 10 with me, even though she's seventeen.*

It hadn't turned out to be true, though, because Frankie was clever. She'd learnt to use a computer within days of leaving Mount Zion, and every minute she wasn't messing about with that, she was reading. She read *everything*. Novels, which were worldly, even though the ones she read were called "classics," and books about history and science, too.

And maths. She'd spent the entire school holidays "catching up" on maths, along with those other subjects, using books the teachers had lent her, and was starting Year 12 today instead of Year 11 like me.

"I have no choice but to skip Year 11," she'd told Daisy last week, when Daisy had commented on the way Frankie was rubbing her eyes at dinner after a day of scribbling in exercise books with a mechanical pencil, learning something called "quadratic equations," whatever those were, in addition to all the reading. "I'm nearly too old as it is, turning nineteen halfway into Year 13. That's *if* I can convince my teachers that I can do Year 12 work this year. I need all three of my NCEA levels in order to qualify for University, and that's going to take effort."

Daisy said, "Well, as I felt the same, I can't say much." Daisy was applying now to study as a nurse practitioner, on top of her work as an Emergency nurse and everything she was doing to help us. When *she'd* come out of Mount Zion, she'd had to work a cleaning job at night on top of her schooling in order to live. Which made me, as always, ashamed at how easy life was for me—or, rather, how *hard* life was for me, when I had it so easy.

For example, today. Here I was, doing nothing more difficult for money than looking after a few kids and weeding the vegie beds, starting Year 11, not trying to skip ahead to anything, just trying to survive. I was sitting in the back row in my first class, which was Biology, and hoping nobody would notice me. Not the other pupils, and, oh, please, not the teacher. Hence the back row.

The first bad thing happened when the teacher, whose name was Mr. Smith, started ticking off names. He went down his list of Emmas and Zoes and Jasmines, and the girls answered, sounding alert or happy or bored.

When I'd first started here, I'd looked around at the others during the calling-out of names and done my best to smile, thinking, *Which ones look like they might be my friend?* Based on those weeks, though, the answer was, "None of them."

I'd had friends at Mount Zion, always. My sisters, my girl cousins, my girl classmates. Girls had never just plain not *liked* me, because I was kind and didn't hurt people's feelings, but it wasn't like that here. Somehow, I seemed too different. Somehow, they knew.

Well, some of them probably *did* know. The teachers knew, Daisy had said, which was why Frankie and I had been admitted, even though we really didn't qualify, because the school was "selective." Which meant they only chose clever girls.

Like Frankie.

Twenty names called out. Twenty-five. And then the last one, as always, because my surname came at the end.

"Obedience Worthy?"

Shocked silence, and then somebody laughed and somebody else muttered. I put up my hand and said, "Present. But … can you please …" I faltered.

Daisy had told me to say this, had said it was all right. How could you correct a teacher, though?

"Yes?" the teacher asked. "Speak up. Time is money."

"Can you please call me Oriana?" I said. "That's my new name."

It felt like, once again, everybody could see through my school uniform, through my hair that was cut to just below my shoulders and pulled back at the sides, exactly like most of the other girls. Through my low socks and school shoes and all the way to the person beneath, in her long dress and huge apron, her knee-length hair knotted and hidden away under a cap, her ungroomed eyebrows and cludgy white trainers. To my absolute *other*-ness.

The voices were a buzz now. Mr. Smith said, "Well, you aren't the first person whose parents made an unfortunate choice on the birth certificate. Oriana it is."

He was one of those sarcastic teachers, it seemed. Sarcasm wasn't something you saw much at Mount Zion. He made a note, then said, "Less chat, please. We're going to start out today with an exam, just to maximize everyone's pleasure." More buzz, of the protesting sort, and he put up a hand for quiet. "This is how I find out where you are and what you know. Do your best on it, I'll survey the wreck of my hopes and dreams for the year, and we'll go from there." And passed out sets of stapled papers.

I got mine last. Back row, in the corner. All around me, girls had their heads down and their pencils moving. As for me? I held my pencil in one frozen hand and stared at the printed words.

Which of the following is FALSE about scientific theories?

That one, I could guess, because the last answer was, "They are firmly established and cannot be refuted." I'd spent most of my life hearing about how so-called scientific theories were wrong and *could* be refuted by the word of God, so that was the answer. I circled "E."

Which of the following is/are characteristics of living organisms?

(A) Organized structure. We were organized because we

were made by God, and God made things perfectly. That was true, then.

(B) Growth and reproduction. Obviously. Babies.

(C) Maintenance of homeostasis (stable systems).

(D) A and B

(E) A, B, and C

I had no idea what "homeostasis" was. "Stable systems"? What?

Wait. *Think.*

We'd learnt Latin at Mount Zion, because Latin and Greek were the root languages of Western civilization, which was the only real civilization. "Homo" meant the same, and "stasis" was like "stay." So that meant staying the same. Stable systems!

I'd got it! This wasn't too bad! People didn't stay the same, right? So that one was wrong. I circled *(D).*

Right. Next question.

What is the correct sequence of increasing organization in a human body?

A whole string of different words in different orders. Organelle, atom, molecule, cell, neutron, organ ... on and on.

I knew what cells were. Organs, too. I'd heard of molecules, and even atoms. Those were the smallest, right? I didn't know what "increasing organization" meant, though. Maybe smallest to largest, since organs were big? I didn't know what all the words *meant,* though. I skipped that one for now.

I turned the paper over and got an easy one.

How old is the earth?

(A) Ten thousand years

(B) One hundred thousand years

(C) One million years

(D) One billion years

(E) More than one billion years

The answer was (A), obviously. Everybody knew that.

After that, the questions got worse, because you actually

had to write your answers, and the words were swimming in front of my eyes now. My breath started coming too fast, and the sweat was popping out on my brow.

Focus. Try.

I did. I tried. I read the questions, read them again, and tried to think. I was only able to answer a few with confidence: the ones about the first humans and how the creatures had developed. On some of the others, I guessed what the answer might be, and on five or six of them, when I didn't even understand the question, I wrote, *I don't know.* I considered adding, *I'm sorry,* but teachers didn't want to hear you were sorry, not if you were meant to have done something and you hadn't.

It was finding out where we were, Mr. Smith had said. Well, where I was, was ... not very far along the path, apparently.

The rest of the day was more of the same. There were only two good parts: eating lunch with Frankie, during which time she had her head in a Chemistry book full of symbols—oh, no. That was worse than Biology! That was at least *words*—and P.E. I didn't know anything about sport, either, but I'd discovered during my first disastrous bout of schooling that I was stronger than most girls. They rode around in cars, and probably hadn't grown up cleaning for hours or carrying toddlers or working in the laundry. Besides, P.E. was swimming at the moment, and I knew how to swim. At least I didn't need to know the rules of some game I'd never heard of.

Maths was bad, because I *had* been babysitting and weeding the garden instead of catching up like Frankie had, which had clearly been a mistake. I'd have to ask Frankie to help me tonight, or maybe Gray would do it, if I made him a sweet for after dinner. Gray liked sweets. A thin pear tart, maybe. That was easy, because it took puff pastry, which you could buy in a shop, but it looked and tasted like it had taken effort. I could ...

For the rest of class, I thought about different fruits you

could use in a tart. I made it with pears after all in the end, because the pears were perfect right now. I mixed vanilla ice cream with cinnamon and made a caramel sauce to drizzle over the top, because caramel sauce made everything better. Gray *did* help me with my maths afterward, and Gray was more patient than Frankie. I understood a bit better after we'd finished, so maybe tomorrow would be easier.

When tomorrow came, I was in the same spot in the corner of the Biology classroom, trying to stay optimistic for Day 2 and pretending I didn't notice when somebody in a group of girls said, "Hi, Obedience," and they all laughed, and there was the teacher at the front of the room again with a stack of those stapled papers beside him.

He said it was just to find out what we know, I told myself. *It's all right that I don't know. I learnt the maths last night, after all. I'm not actually thick, I'm just not as clever as Frankie, but almost nobody's as clever as Frankie. I can learn.*

The teacher stood up there, silent, after the bell, and I could tell he was cross. He picked up a single set of papers from the top of the stack and said, "I must admit, I'm impressed. I don't think I've ever had a pupil go to the effort to get all but two questions absolutely wrong, out of forty. Impressive. Much as I appreciate a good joke, though, when I tell you that an exam is for practice, or for me to assess your knowledge, that doesn't mean it's your chance to have it on. I'm the only comedian in this classroom, is that clear?"

Some muttered "Yes, Sir's," and I thought, *At least I'm not the one in trouble.* Which was when he started reading off questions and answers, his tone getting more and more sarcastic, and I realized that the paper he was mocking was mine.

Everybody laughed. I stared down at my desk in shame and fear, extended my hands on the cold surface, and waited, trembling, for the flexible metal ruler to crack down hard on my palms.

It wasn't the pain I feared. It was the humiliation. I'd never been punished in school, and I'd hardly ever even been punished at home, because I knew how to behave, and I took care I did. Now, I didn't even know that. I'd got it all so wrong. How?

The blow didn't come, but when the teacher said, "Suppose you take over and explain to us, Oriana, how the dinosaurs became extinct, since you enjoy your joke," that was even worse.

I said, still looking down, hearing the tremble in my voice, "They drowned in the flood, sir," and everybody laughed. That was *right*, though. I knew it was right. I'd learnt it in Year One!

He said, "We can't hear you. Please project. And look at me when I'm speaking to you."

I was so frightened, my legs literally shook. I tried to look at him, but I couldn't. How could this be the rule, that you *had* to look at a man, to gaze into his face as if you were defying him? Your *teacher?*

I repeated, "They drowned in the flood, sir," and went on in desperation, "because they couldn't fit in the Ark." I hadn't said *which* flood. Maybe that was it.

More laughter, and my face was burning.

"Huh," he said. "I've always imagined the Ark had magical expanding properties in order to fit every species. Dinosaurs too big for God after all?"

I looked down again, felt my chin wobble, and didn't say anything, because I had no idea how I was meant to answer.

I wanted to ask Daisy, that night—or maybe Gray, who was kinder than any man I'd ever known—what I'd done wrong, but I didn't want to admit I'd got in trouble in school. In the life I knew, if somebody—always a boy, because girls knew better—got a hiding at school, they got another hiding at home. I knew Daisy wouldn't give hidings, and Gray would be horrified at the very idea, but surely *something* would happen to me when they found out.

Nobody said anything, though, so the teacher must not have told. *Write everything down*, I told myself that night, sitting at the table in the yurt across from Frankie, staring at the Biology textbook as my eyes blurred from the hot tears I was trying to hold back. *Read the textbooks twice over. Do the problems again at home instead of making special things for dinner.* And, most of all, *Figure out what the teacher wants you to say, and say that.* In that, it was no different from Mount Zion.

I could do this. I *had* to do this. Why else had Daisy got us out?

CHARCOAL EGGS

Gabriel

Things were going along better by the Monday that marked the start of my twelfth week working for Gray. When I climbed out of Drew's car at the jobsite, because he'd given me a lift this morning, I thought back to my first morning waking up Outside and realized that while I wasn't exactly a suave urbanite yet, I wasn't quite such a babe in the woods as I had been.

I'd woken that first day with the back hurting slightly less, which meant I'd be working soon. I healed fast, I was doing it again, and I didn't have to pay attention to pain. Some things, it seemed, didn't change. It was five-thirty, the time I'd been waking since I'd left school and started living in the unmarried men's dormitory, so that was another thing that hadn't changed. My body still knew how to wake up.

I listened, but heard nothing from the rest of the house. No feet overhead, no doors closing or toilets flushing. Five-thirty was too early, maybe, even though the sun had risen. I considered going outside and walking around the city to orient myself, but I didn't know when the family would wake up, or whether they'd want anything from me. So I used my four personal possessions—the toothbrush, toothpaste, soap, and razor—and got dressed, and after a bit, when all was still quiet, sat on the edge of the bed and finished the book. There was much more than kissing in it, it turned out. In fact, I was so engrossed, I forgot how hungry I was until I heard noises overhead at last. A cupboard door opening, a grinding sound, and those footsteps I'd been listening for.

They were making breakfast, which sounded like a very good idea. I'd made tea before my reading session with some experimenting—I wasn't sure how long you kept the bag in—and used the toaster to make four slices with butter and jam, so I wasn't as hungry as when I'd woken, but I was still pretty hungry. Fortunately, I'd fixed a toaster or two before and knew how they worked. Now, I went to the kitchen, opened the carton of eggs that stood on the benchtop, and looked around inside the cupboards—full of an immense number of mysterious items that I had no clue what to do with—until I found a pan.

You'd need a pan to cook anything. You couldn't just drop the food onto the cooker. That was obvious. I wasn't an idiot.

Right, then. I had a pan. I had the eggs. You'd crack them, obviously, because you didn't eat the shells. Crack them straight into the pan? Yes. They'd be flat, then. Fried, they called that, and it seemed like the easiest way, so I did it. Four eggs, filling the pan, looking flat. Looking especially flat, because I'd broken the yolks on two of them. The eggs I was served had always had the yolks intact. Better chickens, maybe, or better cracking technique.

Right. Time to cook. There was a sort of metal box set into the benchtop with a gray glass top and a door underneath. That had to be the cooker, because nothing else was, and when I opened the door, I recognized an oven. Again, because I'd helped my father fix two or three of them when something had gone wrong. Other than those occasions, I'd never been inside a kitchen, and definitely not while the ovens were actually in use. Women brought food out to the dining room in huge bowls and pans, but how it changed from bags of flour and potatoes, baskets of eggs and slabs of beef to become food—that was a mystery.

Think. Some cooking happened in ovens, and some happened on the top of the cooker, obviously, because kitchens had both. There were burners on top of a cooker, normally, like coils, that conducted electricity to radiate the heat that would warm the pots. I remembered seeing those, and I knew a reasonable amount about electricity, so that was all good and made sense. Except that the top of this box had no burners, and no markings at all except an outline drawn around the edge of the glass screen, and a smaller square in the bottom center with a name printed on it. It didn't mean anything to me, so it was probably whatever firm had made the cooker. The problem was—there were no coils, and there were also no controls.

Wait, though. There *had* to be controls somewhere, for the oven at least. The oven I'd fixed had had temperature markings, so it had a thermostat, and you needed to set it. I looked on the wall. A switch to turn on the power to the oven, because it said "oven" on it. I flipped that.

And nothing happened. I pressed all around the edge of the cooktop surface to see if something would slide out of a recess. It was the only thing I could think of. That, or maybe one of those boxes with buttons on it, like the ones for the TV. I didn't see anything like that, which was a good thing, because if that was what it took, I was probably going to end up with the cooking equivalent of black-and-white fuzz.

I pressed in the bottom square. A sudden chime sounded, so loud that I was surprised it didn't bring everybody running, and I jumped back. White letters were flashing on the glass, though.

Cooktop

Oven

That was all, but you were obviously meant to choose. How?

Pressing had turned the thing on. I pressed the word "Cooktop," and the letters went away, to be replaced by

1

+

−

Right. Now we were getting somewhere. I pushed the +. The thing was a cooker. You needed to increase the heat in order to cook.

A little illustration now, to the right of the symbols. A sort of wavy triangle. Oh. That would be a flame. Heat!

I pressed the + again and got two flames, pressed the − and was back to one, then kept going until the screen registered five flames. That seemed to be the maximum, because pushing the button again made nothing happen. Good. Hotter was better, surely.

I passed a hand over the surface. Nothing.

Maybe it took a while. I waited one minute, then two, then five. Still nothing.

I turned the wall switches off, then turned them on again, and started over with the pressing and *1* and so forth. Still no heat.

It was broken.

More noise upstairs. They'd be done with their breakfast, probably, and getting ready for their day.

I looked at my four eggs, sitting hopefully in their pan. Then I found a glass, poured the raw eggs carefully into it—they went in with a sort of *plop*—stirred them hard with a spoon until the remaining yolks broke, added some milk, stirred some more, and drank it down.

It wasn't delicious, but it was nourishment.

I was sitting on the bed again, starting to read one of the shooting-and-explosions books—it had been left here, so it was obviously the sort of thing people did read, and I needed more background information about life Outside than that you were apparently meant to lick a woman's private parts when you had relations, which was news—when I heard a knock at the door.

I put the shooting book down and went to answer it, and found Jack. He said, "We're leaving for school in about fifteen minutes. I walk with Grace, so she's safe. Mum says, first, do you want to walk to school with us so you can learn where you are, because you never know where you are unless you walk. She'll fix your dressings again afterward, she says. And second, do you want to go to the supermarket with her and Madeleine later, so you can make yourself food today, or would you rather eat with us for a while?"

I said, "I'll walk with you." I wanted to add, "I'd rather eat with you," but I didn't know what was right. Drew hadn't said, "Come live with my family," he'd said, "Come live in my granny flat." The granny flat had a kitchen. You were meant to cook for yourself in it, obviously. People Outside liked being separate. I said, "I should go to the supermarket. I don't have any money, though." It was easier to confess to a kid.

"She says not to worry about that," Jack said. "It's just until you're making money, she says. Anyway, my mum likes helping people." He had his father's gray eyes and his father's seriousness, young as he was. Those eyes had an observant look. A settled look. He was like me, maybe. He watched first, so he'd know.

"All right," I said. "I'm keeping an account, so I can pay your parents once I have a job."

"It's OK," Jack said. "They're pretty rich."

"Still. It's better to pay for yourself." That much, I knew.

Jack considered that. "Even if they have heaps of money? So you don't have to say thank you, maybe? Or feel bad that somebody had to do extra?"

"You still have to say thank you," I said. "They went out of their way to help. They shouldn't have to go *more* out of their way, unless it's to help somebody who could never pay."

"Like a kid," Jack said. "Or a really old person."

"Exactly," I said. "Also, I think the cooker here is broken."

"Really?" Jack headed over and pushed the buttons, the same way I had, and got the same thing.

Cooktop

Oven

He said, "It's working. You just have to press here to bring it up."

"After that," I said. "It doesn't heat up, the cooktop."

Jack did some more pressing and got the little flames, then looked at me and shrugged.

I said, "It doesn't get hot, though."

He reached into a cabinet and pulled out a pan, then set it on the glass top. There was a faint, high-pitched whirring noise, and he put a hand over the pan and said, "It's getting hot."

"Huh," I said, inspecting it. Yes, it was. "It didn't before."

"Did you have the pan on it?" he asked. "It only works if it has the pan on it. It cooks by magnets. If the pan isn't on it, there's nothing for the magnet to grab, so it doesn't start working. It's an induction cooker. In regular cooking, the element gets hot, and it transfers the heat to the pan, which is less efficient because you lose some heat when you transfer. That's called conduction, because of the transferring. In induction, the pan is where the heat starts, so you don't lose any. Also, it's safer, because there's no fire."

"Oh," I said, and felt stupid.

"I didn't know, either," he said. "My dad explained."

"Do you know how to cook things, too?" I asked.

"Not heaps of things," he said. "Mostly things in the microwave, and toast. I make my mum tea and toast sometimes. She's having another baby, and she needs those things while she's still lying down in order to get up in the morning if she's feeling sick. If my dad's not home, I bring it to her instead. He taught me. But I've watched my mum and dad cook, so maybe I know. I'm not sure. I don't really know if I know how until I try to do things."

I thought about my eggs in the glass. They'd been slimy. "D'you think you could help me later?" I asked. "Tonight?"

He studied me in the same way his father would have. Assessingly, I'd call that. "Don't you know how? Everybody knows how to use a cooker. Everybody who's grown up, anyway."

"Not me," I said. "Men don't do that where I was living, so I need to learn."

"Oh," he said. "OK." And grinned. He had all four adult teeth at the front, but was missing one of the canines. He'd be about nine, then. One thing I did know, and that was kids. Mount Zion grew heaps of things, but mainly, they grew kids.

I smiled with relief, put out a hand, and said, "It's a deal." We shook, he grinned some more, and I said, "We'd better start that walk to school, though. Wouldn't want you to get a hiding. They'd have to give it to me instead, eh, since it'd be my fault, and I'm too old. Embarrassing."

He didn't laugh, which showed that I wasn't much chop at Outside jokes. He said, "Why would I get a hiding? Fighting's not allowed."

"Not fighting," I said. "From your teacher."

He stared at me. "Your teacher can't *hit* you. Grownups aren't allowed to smack kids. It's against the law."

"No," I said.

"It is," he insisted. "Ask Mum. I'd get detention, that's all. And only if I was *very* late."

"Well," I said, "let's go, then, so that doesn't happen."

"Grace and I can explain more things on the way," he said kindly, "if you need to understand."

So, yes, when Hannah had taken me grocery shopping later that morning, *after* telling me to take off my shirt for her and changing my dressings, chaperoned only by a very young child, and we'd walked up and down endless aisles whose shelves were stacked high with packets and cans, almost none of which I recognized as anything I'd ever eaten before, and not even as food, other than the photos on the front, and I'd thought, *I need to choose things to eat, somehow, out of all this. And sort out how you cook them, or I'm going to starve*—I'd been able to keep the panic at bay, because I had a guide.

Until that evening, of course, when I decided to try the fried eggs again along with a couple of sausages. I set the pan on the glass cooker, as instructed, and the eggs cooked in about thirty seconds. And then I tried to take them out of the pan.

I ended up eating a messy, undelicious pile of rubbery egg-white slivers that were black on the bottom, mixed with chalky, overcooked bits of yolk and nearly raw sausages, then working for about an hour to chisel and scrub the burnt mess out of the pan, halfway through which process Jack came downstairs and told me I had to melt butter in the pan first so the eggs wouldn't stick, and maybe not cook them on five flames.

Oh.

"You've invented a new thing, though," he said encouragingly. "Charcoal eggs! Maybe you'll be famous for it!" And I had to laugh.

By the end of that first week, Jack had shown me which pans you used on the cooktop and which you put into the oven, which would be useful once I had a clue what I would put in those pans, and had demonstrated with the vacuum cleaner and the toilet brush, too. From Jack, I learnt that you cleaned your house every week if you wanted it to stay "nice enough for my Mum, I guess, because I never think it looks dirty when she says we have to clean it," and that boys cleaned, too, which was why he knew how. He taught me to use the dishwasher, though I didn't need it, because I usually ate standing up and out of the same bowl every time, which I washed afterward and put in the rack beside the sink. What was the point of sitting down if you didn't have anybody to talk to?

Jack had also shown me how the microwave worked and the easiest things to cook in it, none of which tasted very good, but they'd kept me alive so far. Then there was the bank—once I'd got my first pay packet, which seemed like a startling amount of money and probably wasn't—the EFTPOS reader at the shop, the very idea of a "debit card," and so much more. Jack had shopped for my phone with me, which had used up too much of the money in that pay packet, and he'd shown me how to use it, too.

I knew now how totally clueless I'd been, and I was the one who'd been out of Mount Zion before! I'd known how to read road signs, I'd been in a bank, and I'd ridden in a lift. I knew how to drive, and I even had a driving license. By Mount Zion standards, I was a dangerous sophisticate. By Dunedin standards, not so much.

In return for his guidance, I helped Jack use his dad's tools in an extremely well-equipped shed to make a gift for a girl at school he was desperately in love with. Which didn't seem like it could be allowed, but apparently was.

When he said, "It has to be a jewelry rack, because jewelry is what girls like," I was dubious. Unless I truly knew absolutely nothing, how much jewelry could a nine-year-old girl possess? But I helped him design it and coached him in fashioning the thing, then showed him how to sand it— for about three times as long as he thought necessary—before the two coats of varnish that he *also* thought were over the top.

"If a thing's worth doing," I told him, as my own dad had told me, "it's worth doing right."

When he ran down to my flat a few days later to announce with triumph that he'd given it to the girl—Serena—he also informed me that he was now her boyfriend. "So it worked!"

"What does that mean?" I asked. "Her boyfriend?" You see how useful it was to have somebody that you could ask these things of.

He said, "You hold hands on the playground and say she's your girlfriend."

"Oh." Yeh, nine-year-old romance was probably about my speed. Except that I'd never held hands. I'd read all the porn books from the bookshelf during the past weeks, though. There was heaps more to learn, clearly, and stuffing up there would be so much more embarrassing than fusing the eggs to the pan.

Last Friday, in a dramatic turn of events, Jack had come down for his usual evening visit, flopped into a chair, and said, "D'you want to watch *Wellington Paranormal* with me? Also, Serena and I broke up."

"Go ahead and switch it on," I said. "Because I've finished burning these sausages. You sad, then?" I knew about that now. The porno books were full of breaking up.

He shrugged. "Nah. Holding hands is boring." And punched the button on the remote. I knew the name now, and which buttons to push, too. It wasn't too much to learn after all. It was just too much to learn in one day.

They'd all taught me, in fact. Hannah, by tactfully taking me along on her shopping expeditions and making gentle suggestions of what I might need. And, of course, Drew, who'd taken me in at a moment's notice at six o'clock in the morning, and had gone with me at the end of my first day working for Gray to buy new clothes. "As you're a good size," he'd said, "and I know what will work for you."

When I'd objected to him paying for them, telling him, "I'll buy them once I get paid. It's only two more days," he'd said, "Mate. You've got one pair of trousers, two of my T-shirts, two pairs of undies, and two pairs of socks, and it's also two more days until Friday. If I don't buy you some clothes and Hannah doesn't get over her tactfulness and tell you to buy some deodorant and washing powder, not to mention finding you another pair of trousers to wear while you wash those, Gray's going to turf you out for smelling up the jobsite. You've already got a pong to you. Keep track in that notebook of yours and pay it back when you can, if you like." Which I'd done, and thought that people Outside didn't seem all that evil so far, and also that they certainly seemed to have enormous houses, not to mention heaps of money to throw about on clothes and toiletries and groceries for random strangers.

Now, *that* was more like what I'd heard. The Devil's wages.

ON THIS PARTICULAR JANUARY MORNING, six weeks into my Outside journey, Drew, who'd alternated with Hannah and Gray himself in transporting me to and from the jobsite thus far, braked to a stop in front of the rapidly rising steel framework that would eventually be student dormitories for the university. I thanked him and climbed out, and he stuck his head out of the window and said, "Forgot to tell you. Come upstairs for dinner tonight. We're doing racks of lamb, and we'll have too much otherwise."

I said, "Yes. Of course," with extreme gratitude—I was getting tired of sausages, even though I knew how to cook them all the way through now—and he gave a wave, said, "Six-thirty, then," and drove off.

I turned and nearly ran into the wall that was a big Samoan fella named Afoa, because he was standing stock-still, staring after the car. I said, "Nice, eh," a bit proud that I knew what it was: a Mercedes. Car makes were different, it turned out, and to my non-surprise, the most expensive ones were the best, especially if everybody knew they were expensive.

Afoa said, "Bloody hell. How do you know *him?*"

"What?" I asked. "He's my ... I live with him."

Afoa stared even harder. "He's married, though."

"I know he's married," I said.

Some more staring. "Maaate. You don't mean ..."

"What?" I asked. Why was this odd? "It's OK. I don't interfere with his wife." Wait. That sounded bad. "I mean," I hurried on, "I don't interfere in his life with his wife."

Yet more staring. I said, "I live in their granny flat. For now."

"Oh." His face changed, and laughed hugely, slapped me on the back with a force that threatened to buckle my knees, and said, "I try to be an open-minded fella, but Drew Callahan? Pardon, Sir Andrew? I was thinking, 'Nah, can't be,' and then thinking, 'Love is love, I guess,' and all that. And, I mean, Luke Armstrong. There's a surprise, if you like. But ..."

I had no idea what he was talking about. Which wasn't exactly a first in my life. I said, "They've both been very kind. Their kids as well," which was all I could think of.

"What's going on?" That was another bloke, whose name was Ollie.

Afoa said, "Got a dark horse here. Know whose granny flat he's living in? Sir Andrew bloody Callahan's, that's who. Who'd have thought it? What are you doing slumming around the place with us, mate?" he asked me.

"Uh ..." I said. "Because I know building, and Gray gave me a job. You know why. D'you know Drew, then?" My dad, my brother, and I were all working on this job, and unfortunately, every man here knew why. We hadn't said anything about Mount Zion, but the events of that morning had been shown on TV, and they'd caused a splash, apparently. Sometimes, it seemed like people Outside knew as much about each other as people at Mount Zion, at least if those people had been on TV.

"Mate," Ollie said, "you don't know?"

Two *more* blokes turned up now, and everybody was talking at once, until eventually, I got it. Drew was Sir Andrew Callahan, legendary former captain of the All Blacks, two-time

Rugby World Cup winner, current coach of the Highlanders, and national hero. I knew nothing about any of those things, or about rugby, either, how it was played or who did it. It was a game, that was all I knew, it was on television, and the blokes on the job tended to chat about it during morning smoko, especially about the Highlanders' chances in the upcoming season, which they disagreed about at a passionate level. From the way they were talking now, rugby was something very much akin to religion, blasphemous as that was, and so was Drew. Pardon, Sir Andrew.

I also learnt that Gray, my new boss, had been an All Black as well, and that it mattered.

"I didn't know all that," I said, wishing once again that I could hide the extent of my ignorance for a while, until I'd observed enough that I wouldn't constantly be showing it. "Drew offered me a place to stay until I find my feet, that's all. A granny flat that he and his wife weren't using. Kind of them."

"Wish somebody'd offer me a free granny flat in their posh house," Afoa said. "And a rugby contract while he was at it, eh."

"Maybe that's why he offered it," I said. "Because he knew I wouldn't know how to play rugby, or ask anything about it, either. It's all news to me."

The foreman appeared, then, and said, "Were you lot planning to join us in the safety meeting this morning, or is it too much trouble to interrupt your gossip session?" and put a welcome end to the chat.

When Drew came to collect me that evening, though, I said, climbing into the Mercedes once again, "I'm sorry that I didn't know your name. You could've told me. I know I've got heaps to learn." Trying not to be self-conscious about it, and failing. He and Hannah—Lady Callahan—had been that kind, and I'd been so impossibly rude.

"What are you talking about?" he asked.

"The title. Sir Andrew. And your wife's a Lady. I've been calling you the wrong things."

He laughed. "Nah, mate. Drew's OK." And never mentioned it again.

Also, the lamb chops were excellent. Drew and Hannah told me how to cook them, but unfortunately, they turned out to be much too dear for my budget, because I was saving every penny I could. Back to the sausages, then.

Goals, though. I'd learnt about goals, and I liked the idea.

Buying rack of lamb, and cooking it. Not feeling like an alien. And more independence. Another new concept, but Drew and Hannah and their kids weren't my family, and this was a temporary kindness, that was all.

Goals.

7

GUTS

Oriana

Things didn't get much better at school over the next month. I still ate lunch with Frankie, but now, Frankie had friends. Three of them, in fact. I suspected they were the cleverest girls in Year 12, because they talked endlessly about the world and its problems, and they seemed to know so much about all of it. At the moment, I was eating my sandwich, keeping my head down and listening, as usual, as a girl named Ivy said, "Because capitalism is a fatally flawed system of social organization, that's why, trying to sort us all into our slots as obedient little widgets for the Man. People are more complex than that, though, and their needs and contributions aren't just economic. *That's* the fatal flaw."

A blond girl named Petra answered, "There's merit to it, too, though." And at some scoffing, "There is! It does encourage people to strive. And why would you even worry about capitalism, when everybody around us is doing pretty much the opposite? Why do so few big ideas, so few big *entrepreneurs*, come out of New Zealand? Because everybody's so keen on their work/life balance, that's why, too busy thinking of going sailing at the weekend or having a barbecue with the family to start their tech company and actually *get* somewhere."

The one I privately thought of as "the snarky mutterer," but whose name was actually Kyra, muttered, "Peter Jackson," and Petra pointed a finger at her and said, "The exception that proves the rule. *Everybody* says 'Peter Jackson,' because there's just about nobody else! We're lazy here, is what we are, and women aren't any better than men. Where are the women at the top of our supposedly egalitarian society? Where are the female company directors? Where?"

"Well, there's the PM," Kyra said. "Game, set, and *match.*"

She high-fived with Ivy, and they all laughed, because it hadn't been a fight, even though it had sounded like one, an almost-shouting way of talking that I'd never heard women engaged in before. I'd never heard *men* engaged in it, for that matter, unless you counted the Prophet's nightly lectures. It wasn't fighting, Frankie had told me, it was a "passionate discussion of critical topics." She'd explained, "It's how important ideas get aired. It's how things finally change." It still sounded like arguing to me, and when they got worked up, it made my stomach hurt.

"But seriously," Ivy said, "and granted that New Zealand isn't as bad as some places, because we're a social democracy—"

"Democratic socialist, you mean," Petra said.

"Whatever," Ivy said. "How about the way capitalism devalues parenthood, how everybody's so focused on short-term gains, on *producing,* like GDP is the only measurement that matters, instead of focusing on keeping society going by, you know, actually *valuing* people having babies and raising children, putting their money where their mouth is? I'm surprised we're not growing them in test tubes and raising them in institutions. *So* much more efficient."

"Maybe that would be better," Frankie said. "To a point. If women didn't have to carry kids, or feed them from their bodies, there'd be no excuse for gender roles. On *either* side. People could just decide to raise kids, or not raise them, and there'd be no question that men should do half the raising. Which would make them not want so many, I guarantee it. Kids are heaps of work, and they can be pretty awful."

"Women aren't going to do that," Ivy said. "They *love* all that 'naturalness of motherhood' rubbish. Breastfeeding forever and all that. *You* know that, Frankie. You *lived* that! Mount Zion's the natural extension of the patriarchy, that's all. It's just more obvious. It's not *different.*"

They all thought Frankie was wonderful. "So strong," they said, and it was true. Frankie wasn't a freak like me. She was a *star.* She had all this anger, and it fueled her. Like Daisy, driving toward her goals, not allowing anything to get in her way, not letting anybody make her feel small.

"But why shouldn't women still want to have babies," I asked, somehow, "and feed them? Is that bad? We *did* put the babies in … in institutions, I guess, at Mount Zion, because the mum goes back to work after a couple of weeks, so a few women watch all the babies. Is that really better? I always thought—"

Frankie snapped, "We know what you've always thought. That's the point. Internalized misogyny."

"Bingo," Kyra muttered.

"Don't talk if you don't understand the point," Frankie said. "Especially if your entire existence is being the *anti*-point. Maybe you should go find your own friends, so you can talk about knitting and cooking and gardening and *babies.* Could you not be embarrassing, please?"

Everybody got quiet. I had a bite of sandwich in my mouth, and I couldn't swallow it. My mouth had gone dry, and my eyes were stinging. Frankie couldn't see that, at least, because she wasn't looking at me.

Kyra muttered, "Uh-oh. Sister drama."

Petra said, "Don't." To Kyra, or to Frankie, I couldn't tell, because I couldn't look.

I swallowed my bite of sandwich, somehow, and tried to think of something to say. I wanted to say, "You're right. I do need to go meet my friends," but they knew I didn't have any friends. So I just got up and left. I couldn't keep sitting there, not after that, even though I wanted to. It was the only place I could think of *to* sit.

If I'd been one of those strong women they always talked about, I'd have gone out and run three kilometers around the track, or stalked over to another table and studied my maths in preparation for my brilliant future.

I went and cried in the toilets instead. I only had my sister, but I was an embarrassment and she didn't want me. I couldn't go back to Mount Zion, but I couldn't stay here, either. I didn't belong at all.

AFTER THAT, I went to World History, because there was no choice. I could have said I was ill and gone home—I *felt* ill—but Daisy would ask why, and she'd be impatient if I told her, because Daisy *was* one of those strong women. Gray might understand, but if I talked to Gray, with his kind eyes and the way his voice got gentle when he thought you were weak, I'd start to cry, and once I started, I didn't think I'd be able to stop.

I needed to be strong, too. That was what everybody wanted from me. Gray was doing "more than any other man would do" as it was. I'd heard that too many times not to believe it. So I went to World History.

I'd thought it would be easier than Biology, because I'd learnt a long time ago about the pagan Greeks, and then the Romans, who'd tortured the Christian martyrs before abandoning their false idols once Emperor Constantine embraced the One True

Faith. I knew how the countries of Europe had brought civilization and salvation to the rest of the world, too, but the teacher didn't talk about those things at all, and everything she did say somehow seemed to be the opposite of what I knew.

She'd heard about Mount Zion, like all the teachers, except possibly Mr. Smith. He'd probably been thinking up sarcastic insults when Frankie's and my sad situation was being explained. Somebody must have alerted him eventually, because he didn't make fun of me anymore. He just sighed every time he called on me and I got the answer wrong, which was almost always. I could never think clearly when people were staring at me.

Ms. Roberts, the History teacher, may actually have been worse. After the second week of school, she'd asked to speak to me after class, then had perched at the edge of her desk, studying me as I stood there dreading whatever *this* would be. She'd said, "I understand your circumstances, Oriana, and that school is bound to be difficult for you, as far behind as you are. I'm not expecting perfection. I'm expecting progress. And History is a living subject. Examining our past is how we evaluate our present, and examination and evaluation require discussion. All of which is another way of saying that you really do have to participate in class, even if it's hard for you. What do you think is holding you back from doing that?"

"Nothing, miss," I said, because I couldn't think how to answer. *Because my body feels like it isn't allowed, because it was never allowed before? And because as soon as I participate, everybody will laugh?*

"There must be some reason," she said. "We're an inclusive school, an inclusive classroom. We celebrate differences here. You've lived a life nobody here can imagine, but it has parallels to so much of what we're talking about in here every day, not least the oppression of women throughout most of recorded history. I'd love you to bring that experience, *your* experience, to the class. You have so much to offer. You can help the other pupils understand in a way they couldn't, otherwise."

I wanted to say that offering up the rawest parts of myself for people to paw over wasn't going to be helpful to *me*, and would actually feel like being beaten with my father's belt again, but I hadn't been raised to argue, so I said, "Yes, miss."

Ms. Roberts sighed. Her sigh was less bad-tempered than Mr. Smith's, but it was basically the same thing. "I'm not asking you to hold forth in every class. I'm just asking you to speak up occasionally, especially if you don't understand something. I'll always welcome your questions, because not knowing something isn't anything to be ashamed of. Not *learning*, now—that's different, and you won't learn unless you ask. Hey?"

"Yes, miss," I said again, but privately thought, *I am not asking in front of everybody*. If that made me disobedient—well, you were supposed to be disobedient Outside! At least it seemed that way to me. I'd learnt to use a computer by now—no choice—and I'd discovered that you could find the answers to most questions just by typing the words into the search bar and reading what came up. *That* was what I was going to do when I didn't understand something. I might not be clever like Frankie, but I was clever enough for that..

Today, Ms. Roberts was talking about the idea of the "other," and, as usual, I was writing everything down and understanding about half of it. "When a country's having problems," she said, "maybe inflation or poverty or social unrest or even war, and the people are dissatisfied with their leaders and their lives, it can seem like an easy out to focus their attention instead on a perceived common enemy, or even better—a group of enemies, and get them to bond around that. An *historic* enemy is even better. We all feel virtuous, don't we, when we're united in righteous anger against people we perceive as evil? Who has an example for me?"

"The Christchurch mosque shootings," somebody said. A

girl named Aisha, who wore a headscarf and *did* participate in class.

"Excellent," Ms. Roberts said. "Both ways around, wouldn't you say?"

"Oh, I see," Aisha said, sitting up straighter. "Because the shooter was targeting a scapegoat—Muslims—because he'd been radicalized to hate them and blame them for everything, but the country afterward—"

"How everybody came together," another girl named Harper called out. It still startled me, the way pupils sometimes wouldn't even raise their hands or wait to be called on and just shouted out answers instead, but Ms. Roberts loved it.

"Expand," Ms. Roberts said.

"How they united against what *they* saw as evil," Harper said, "and doing that made everybody feel warm and fuzzy and close."

"And the Hollow-cost," a girl named Charlotte said. "Both ways again."

"The Hollow-cost is an excellent example," Ms. Roberts said. "In fact, you've managed to circle around to the place I wanted to go today, Charlotte." Charlotte beamed, because she loved being right, and Ms. Roberts went on, "I'd like to talk about that more today. About the Hollow-cost and the history behind it, because that idea didn't spring from nowhere."

Uh-oh. When she said, "I'd like to talk about that more," that meant it was the point of the lecture—why couldn't she just *say* the point, so I could write it down?—and it would be on the exam at the end of the year. The problem was, I didn't have a clue what she was talking about, and she was constantly veering away from the textbook, which was about "The Rise of the Nation-State" at this point in the class and no help at all, even though I'd read the chapter twice.

No, she went on and on about the Hollow-cost instead, and it was like she was talking in code. I waited as long as I could, hoping I'd pick up the thread again, then raised my hand. I didn't want to, but I did.

She looked pleased. "Yes, Oriana? You have a contribution?"

I asked, "Could you spell the Hollow-cost, please, miss, so I can look it up?"

"The Hollow-cost?" she asked in surprise. "You've never heard of it?"

Nothing to do, as the whole class either drew in a shocked breath or laughed, but say it. "No, miss."

"The Hollow-cost was the wholesale and deliberate mass murder of European Jews by the Nazis before and during World War II," she said. And wrote the word on the board for me, spelling it aloud with her usual extra-kindness, like I was delayed.

"Oh," I said. "Thank you. But I thought that wasn't going to happen until Armageddon."

More gasping and laughing. Ms. Roberts looked horrified, and I wanted to sink through the floor. Especially when she explained more about it, kindly still, and I started to cry. I tried not to, but it was so *horrible*.

I was sitting in the back, as usual, but everybody had turned around in their chairs to look at me. It was basically my worst nightmare. Ms. Roberts said, "Maybe you'd like to go to the toilet and collect yourself, Oriana. We can talk after school, if you like."

"She doesn't need to talk after school," Aisha said. "She just needs you lot to stop being such arseholes. How would she know? She spent her whole life in a cult! Everybody's heard that, but you keep badgering her anyway, laughing at her, until she's scared to say anything at all. You're talking about the other, about how people set up in-groups and out-groups, and how the in-group gangs up on the out-group to feel superior? How about what's happening here? How is this different from bullying me because I wear hijab?"

"Nobody bullies you because you wear hijab," Charlotte said piously. "We wouldn't."

"But it's all right to laugh at Oriana," Aisha flashed back. "Because she was raised with ideas you think are wrong."

"Well, they *are* wrong," drawled a sarcastic girl named Lucy, who was *also* in Biology with me and probably loved Mr. Smith's sense of humor. "People riding dinosaurs? I guess they don't give you much counter-programming at Mount Zion, though."

She was twisted around in her chair, talking to me as if we weren't in school, her expression expectant, as if I might entertain her some more with stories about Noah, and I said, "I'm not sure what that means."

"They don't expose you to different ideas, she means," Aisha said. "They don't explain the theory of evolution or carbon dating, they don't talk about rock layers, they just talk about God making the earth and all the creatures in six days, and then twist themselves into knots explaining dinosaurs and ice ages and all those rock layers. They teach you about Armageddon, but not about the Holocaust."

"Yes," I said.

"Relativity," Ms. Roberts said. She looked pleased as punch, somehow, even though, again, this was like no classroom I'd ever been in. "It's not just a physics concept. We all view the world in relation to our own background, our own point of view. It requires a higher power of thinking, and maybe disengaging our emotions, to turn around and examine the other person's point of view, but that's the only way change really happens, isn't it? That's the basis of diplomacy, after all—understanding what the other person believes, and what they want. What's the opposite of diplomacy?"

"War," I said. It was the first time I'd volunteered anything in this class, or in any class. It was just that I *had* learnt about wars in school. Mount Zion was very big on wars.

"Ah," Ms. Roberts said, a satisfied sound. "Explain."

"Well ..." I said, then faltered.

"Go on," Aisha said. She was smiling, but not in a mocking way. In a delighted way.

"Isn't war," I said, "not caring what the other person's point of view is? You try to get your way by force instead, because you're stronger, right? And diplomacy is trying to sort out what *both* sides want, and seeing if there's a way you can both be happy, or at least not fight. So it's the opposite."

"Possibly threatening them *with* war," Harper said. "Or just with consequences. Pointing out the downside to the conflict not being resolved."

"Like in families, Outside!" I said. "Mount Zion is more like war, and Outside is more like diplomacy."

Ms. Roberts was sitting on her desk now, the same as that first day. She was young and always wore trousers. "How?" she asked.

"Because at Mount Zion," I said, "women obey men because men are stronger, and they'll be hurt if they don't. And kids obey their parents and their teachers for the same reasons. It's always about obedience, not about ... about agreeing to follow the rules because the rules make sense. That was my name. Obedience." My face was hot now, but somehow, I was still talking. "But Outside, families don't work like that, and government doesn't, either. There's voting, instead of one person saying how things will be, and in families, there's ... well, there's a bit of voting there, too. Men don't *have* to care what their wives think, because they're still stronger, but it won't be very nice at home, maybe, if their wife is unhappy."

Harper said, "Not in the bedroom, it won't be," and everybody laughed, which made me flush more. "I'm not making fun of you," she told me. "Sorry. Just making a joke. My unfortunate habit."

"And you're not allowed to hit," I said, "which makes it different. You're not allowed to ... to punish your wife, or your kids, by beating them or not letting them eat or locking them up or anything like that. The same thing with the ... the society. You're not allowed to just kill people if they don't do what you say, even if you're stronger, so Parliament has to make laws instead and write down the rules people agree to."

The bell rang, and there was the usual rustle of papers and slamming of books. Ms. Roberts stood, put up a hand, and called out, "Wait."

Everybody quieted down, and she said, "I want to take a moment to thank Oriana for what she's shared today. Tomorrow, we can explore this topic more, but if you stop to think about it, she's taken us on a deep dive to the essence of representational governance, hasn't she? So thank you, Oriana, for your contribution and your honesty."

"And your guts," Aisha said. "Girl's got guts."

"Yes, she has," Ms. Roberts said. "Hold your head high, Oriana. You've earned it."

I cried in the toilets again, but not from misery this time. From something so much more complicated. Relief, and embarrassment, and maybe ...

Hope.

8

SHIFTING SANDS

GABRIEL

 January had turned to February, February had turned to March, and I'd been staying with Drew and Hannah for three months. My dad, mum, and youngest sister Harmony were moving on from Gray's caravan next week, and that wasn't the only change. Gray was training my dad to be a foreman, for one thing, which meant more money. That was how you could tell you were getting somewhere at work. They gave you more money.

 "We can't keep imposing on his hospitality, though," my dad had told me after work last Friday, when he'd been the one giving me a lift home. A lift, because he'd bought a car about two months in. My sister Harmony had gone out to sit in the little sedan every afternoon for the first week, and had borrowed the driving-license workbook from Mum the minute Mum passed the test for her Learner plates.

 Harmony wasn't even fifteen. She was going to be the best-prepared test-taker in the whole country by the time she got there.

 "Gray's Daisy's partner, though," I said, in the passenger

seat of said sedan. "I thought families did that, even here. Helped each other."

"That doesn't mean he wants all her family members on his doorstep," Dad said. "Also, your mum's found a job, and she's going to need the bus to get there. Gray's place is so far out, she'd be on the bus an hour each way."

"She has?" I digested that. It wasn't that surprising, actually, when I thought about it. Women at Mount Zion worked as much as men did. I just wasn't used to having their work seen as something you'd pay money for. "Doing what?"

"Working in a knitting shop," Dad said, "and teaching classes about it. They were quite excited to hire her, as she knows so much. Dyeing wools, doing the more complicated patterns, and all that, but she's got the patience to teach beginners, too, and doesn't mind how many hours she works. She came home from her interview practically dancing on a cloud." He sounded quite proud about all of it. My mum had been the lead for ages on the knitting rotation, and she'd also introduced hand-dyeing of the Suri alpaca knitting wool that fetched ultra-premium prices in the shops.

That was the sort of thing I knew. Ever since I'd got here, I'd been trying to remind myself of the things I did know, so I wouldn't focus so much on the world of things I didn't. I suspected I wasn't the only one who felt that way, standing on these shifting sands.

"She's already got heaps of ideas for things they could do," Dad went on, "and she hasn't even started yet. Reckon she'll end up running the place." Proud again, and not afraid to say it anymore. Mum and Dad didn't seem to have any mixed feelings about leaving Mount Zion, at least none they'd shared with me, other than that two of my sisters and my brother Uriel were still there.

"Don't women learn that sort of thing at home?" I asked.

"Apparently not," Dad said. "Good news for Mum, eh."

People thought there couldn't be love at Mount Zion,

because all the marriages were arranged by the Prophet, and you got no choice at all. But even a marriage like that could be good. Depended on the people, I reckoned. Especially on the man, in a place like that, and my dad was a good man.

We were at Drew's gates, so I hopped out and said, "Tell Mum congrats for me. Seriously, tell her ..." I paused. "That I'm proud of her. It feels good, earning a pay packet."

"It does," Dad said. "Just as good for a woman as a man, I reckon."

"Maybe even more," I said. "And thanks for the lift."

"See you tomorrow," Dad said, then turned the boxy twenty-year-old compact around with the competence he brought to everything he did and headed down the hill.

Hannah was outside when I got up to the house despite the chill in the air, weeding the flower borders with Madeleine and Grace helping. Well, Grace was helping a bit. Madeleine was mostly getting dirty.

When Hannah saw me, she sat back on her heels and smiled. Her belly was showing more now, but the rest of her looked thinner, her face tired. Drew was gone this week, because the rugby season was well underway, and that meant heaps of travel.

I said, "I'll do that. Just show me where you need it done."

"I don't mind," she said. "Being out in the fresh air feels good, and you've been working hard all day."

"Nah," I said. "Least I can do." I set down the backpack in which I'd carried my lunch and put my hand out for the cultivator.

She said, "You can help, then, and I'll appreciate it. Ten minutes more for me, because I need to start dinner. I'll tell you what. You finish weeding the front, and I'll feed you. Fair?"

"Fair," I agreed.

We weeded in silence for a while, other than Grace exclaiming over a worm and Madeleine deciding that the loamy earth might be chocolate cake, taking a taste to find out, and being sadly disappointed, with the emphasis on "sad." Finally, Hannah said, "Excuse me for asking, but is something bothering you?" and I wondered, as always, how she knew.

I said, "I think I need a car. And my own flat, of course, but I knew that. I can't keep getting lifts, though. My mum's got a job, and I'm thinking that once she's got her Restricted license, she'll want to drive my dad to work, then use the car to get to her own job."

"A job," Hannah said. "That's wonderful. And of course you don't need to move. We're happy having you here. The kids love it, especially Jack."

I said, "It was an offer until I got on my feet, and I'm on them." I didn't know much about Outside, but I was sure of this. "But I need a car as well, because Gray's got a new job coming up that's farther out, with no bus stop close by, and he wants me on it. So—a car, or a ute. A ute would be good."

"They're awfully expensive," Hannah said, "even used. A ute *and* a place of your own? That's so much cash outlay, unless you're buying the car on credit."

"What's that?" I asked.

"When the bank owns the car, and you pay it off slowly, with interest added to compensate the bank for their risk. Or, really, just because they can."

I thought about that. "It doesn't sound right. It sounds like moneylending."

"It is," Hannah said. "But there aren't many other choices. I'm not sure how you'd establish credit to get that loan, not without paying rent and utilities somewhere, at the very least."

It was a chicken-and-egg situation, you see. I needed a flat to get a car, if I did that "credit" thing, but if I got a flat, I wouldn't be able to afford a car. The problem was, I knew Hannah was probably right, and when Jack and I started to research it, I realized she was *definitely* right. I was nowhere close being able to afford both flat and car, hard as I was working to save. Not after three months, I wasn't. Not starting from nothing. And Gray had suggested I start doing evening study for a trades certification, "because if you've got one, I'll have to pay you more." The classes weren't exactly walking distance from Drew's place, though. It would be the bus plus the walk, but if I had to get a bus and then walk home from work, eat dinner, then walk and get *another* bus to class ... Well, no. The times didn't work. I needed a car.

"Plus," Jack pointed out, "you need furniture if you have a flat. You need chairs, and a table, and a bed, and dishes, and pots and pans, and a carpet, and a TV, and everything."

"You do?" I hadn't considered that. "Don't they come with all that?"

"No," he said. "I guess you could get a tent, though, and set it up on the floor. People sleep in tents all the time and eat sitting on the ground when they're camping, so that would work in a building, too. You wouldn't even have to worry about it raining! You could carry some tree stumps up to your flat for chairs, and you could buy camping dishes and a camping pan to cook in and a sleeping bag. And some hangers for your clothes, because there'll be a rod to hang them on in the closet. Then you wouldn't need any furniture at all. You could use a torch instead of having lamps, too. There's a kind of torch you wear on your head. That'd be efficient."

I said, "Might be easier just to make a table and stools and a bed. I know how to make furniture."

"You do?" Jack said. "I never heard of anybody making furniture."

"You learn heaps of things at Mount Zion," I said, "because they do everything for themselves."

"But it isn't nice," he said, "or you wouldn't have left. Mum told Dad it was awful. 'So horrible,' she said after that show was on TV, that one that you were on, where Gray

Tamatoa hit that guy. She said, 'I can't stand to think about it. That poor girl.' I don't know who the poor girl was, though."

"My cousin," I said. "Frankie. And, yeh, it wasn't the best. But some things ..." I paused.

"What?" Jack asked.

"Some things were good," I said. "Playing with my brothers and my cousins when we were young, all of us running and tumbling like a litter of puppies. Being outside every day, and caring for the animals. It's hours of work every day at Mount Zion, but there's a sort of peace to it, too, when you're working."

"But you're still working," Jack pointed out. "So that's the same."

I didn't know how to explain about fitting in, or about the taste of mountain air, how pure and cold it felt in your lungs. About working beside your brothers and your dad, doing the job you knew how to do and knowing you were doing it well, and going to sleep with the sound of quiet breathing all around you. I didn't know how to explain the way I felt now, waking in the night to the sound of the house ticking over and knowing there wasn't another heartbeat within twenty meters of mine, and nobody who knew me, who knew who I *was*, without me saying a word.

I didn't know how to explain, so I didn't. "Anyway," I said, "that's good to know, about the flat. A tent probably isn't necessary, because shelter's the one thing you do have, if it's a flat, but ... camping dishes, eh. That could work. I don't have a workshop anyway to make the furniture."

"You could buy things on TradeMe," Jack said. "But the camping idea would still be cheaper."

Right. That was no flat for now, then. I'd keep saving. But I needed a car.

That was why, on a Friday evening three weeks after my evening of research with Jack, I knocked at the kitchen door and asked Drew, who actually *was* home this weekend, "May I speak to you?"

"Come in." He took me to his office, where he waved me to a chair, sat behind the desk, and said, "Go."

I said, "I want to buy a ute, but I'd need to park it here. And I wanted to tell you that I'm saving for my own flat. You haven't asked yet, but I'm sure you're wondering."

He leaned back in his chair and studied me. "Hannah told me you'd spoken to her about it. We're happy to have you here, and it's barely been three months."

"You can't be happy about it," I said. "People Outside don't live like this. They pay rent."

Drew sighed. "I understand pride and paying your own way, but we don't need the money. Stay with us instead for now, and save for that place you want."

"With your wife, though," I tried to explain, then didn't know how to go on.

"Do you have feelings for my wife?" He didn't sound like you'd expect, though, and he didn't look like you'd expect, either, because the corner of his mouth was twitching again.

"No!" I said, then said it again more quietly. "No. But you must feel odd about it."

"Yeh," Drew said, "I got a pretty shocking view of your character when you risked your life to pull a pregnant woman from a burning car. But since I've got a pregnant wife and three kids myself and am gone from home too much, that view's worked for me. Also, not to get a big head about it, I've spent half my life evaluating men, and I'd like to think I'm a pretty fair hand at it by now. What would you do if the house caught fire some night while I was gone? If somebody tried to break in?"

"I'd do everything I could, of course. But any man would do the same."

"Nah, mate," Drew said. "They wouldn't. Get the car

problem solved, anyway, before you start planning to move out. You want to buy a ute, eh. That's going to take a loan."

"No. One of the fellas at the job is selling one. It's old, and it barely runs, needs just about everything. Only fit for scrap, the other fellas said, but that's why I can afford it. I've been saving."

"I noticed," Drew said. "Seeing as you've still got about five shirts. This would be the equivalent of the eventual shonky flat, then, with twelve generations of student filth under the burners and nasties growing amongst the bath tiles? You may want a car you don't actually have to push."

"I know how to fix a ute. An old one, at least, and this is an old one."

Drew raised his downward-slanting eyebrows. "Thought you were a builder at Mount Zion."

"I was. But I also know how to fix most things. The only problem is—I need a place to do it, and some tools. Gray's got everything, and my dad would help me during the times where you need an extra set of hands, but he's got a flat now and isn't living at Gray's place, so …"

"And Gray's your boss," Drew said. "Awkward to ask for the space and the tools when none of his other employees would."

"Yes," I said. "But I have even less claim on you than on Gray, and it can get noisy, fixing a car."

"Nah," Drew said. "What's it to me? Exactly how bad is this ute, though? Floorboards actually rusted through, or …"

"Not quite that bad," I said. "But close. Some rust patches. Sea air, eh."

"A project, then," he said. "Bring it on."

THAT WAS how I ended up spending every spare minute of the next weeks in Drew's garage, getting filthy under an ancient

Ford ute with the brakes worn down to bare metal and not much of that, only two cylinders sparking, a clogged fuel line, four bald tires, and a transmission that shifted with an audible *clunk*. After you held your breath and wondered whether it would shift at all, that is. Getting it back here from the jobsite had been a close-run thing.

It was also how Drew ended up under there a fair amount himself, because nobody seemed to have informed him that he was flash now, and a Sir shouldn't be spending his time off under disreputable utes. Jack was out there every second he could be as well, handing tools and asking questions, and I'd swear that both of them were as chuffed as I was on the day we got the motor turning over sweetly again and I took them for a ride.

"I own two things now," I told them when we were home again, standing back and admiring the low, tuned-up growl, since I couldn't bear to switch the motor off quite yet. "A driving license, and a ute. I know how to fix whatever else goes wrong with it, and if I have to, I can put a mattress down and sleep in the bed. Good as gold."

"You own more things than that," Jack said. "You have clothes and everything."

"You're right," I said. "Clothes, a pair of boots, a comb, a toothbrush, and a razor. I am a well-equipped man." It was silly to say, but I was riding high. Outside was all about independence, and finally, I had some.

After that, I installed some less-bald tires, banged out the worst of the dents with Jack's help, sanded and treated the patches of rust, spread primer around liberally, and then we were ready for new paint.

"What d'you reckon?" I asked them, once we'd finished with the priming and I was standing back and admiring my ute again. The paint, what there was of it under the patches of gray, was faded gold with an unbeautiful broad stripe of dirty white down the sides. "Paint it white all over, I'm thinking. Better visibility than black."

"It can't be *white*," Jack said. "It's a classic!"

Drew smiled, and I saw it. "It's not a classic," I said. "It's just old. What color are you thinking, then?"

"Red," Jack said with decision. "And shiny. Girls like red cars. If you had a shiny red ute, girls would ask you for a ride in it."

Drew laughed at that one, and I said, "Not sure girls will be falling all over me when I turn up in my 1979 ute, no matter what color I paint it. They'll see the inside, for one thing, if they ask me for a ride, and that'll end the romance pretty smartly."

"Seat covers," Drew said.

"No," Jack insisted, "because when you collected me from kapa haka on Saturday, Naomi Urquel said you were hot, and Andrea Norquist said you were *so* hot, and heaps of the other girls giggled. Naomi Urquel's the prettiest girl at school, and all the boys like her."

"We going to be making another jewelry rack, then?" I asked.

"No," Jack said. "I told you, holding hands is boring. I'm just saying that they think you're hot."

"Which would be excellent," I said, "if I were nine."

Jack sighed. "Older girls probably think so, too. I just don't *know* them, so I wouldn't hear. It was an *example*. And if you have a shiny red ute that's a classic, they'll really think you're hot."

"Unfortunately," Drew said, "every cop will probably think so, too. You get a car from the sponsor when you become an All Black. Those boys got the same memo, because their cars are always red or black, and they collect speeding tickets at a shocking rate. The cops see them coming and lick their lips. Of course, Gabriel doesn't speed."

"Not in this ute, I don't," I said. "Since it tops out at about a hundred and twenty, and it isn't too happy about that."

"Fair point," Drew said. "So not red, then?"

"Let's ask Mum," Jack said. "Girls are good at colors."

"I'll do that," I said, "then think about it for a few days, and then decide." On Sunday, we were doing a family lunch. It was at Gray's, as always, because nobody else had space, and it would be even more crowded than in the past, because two weeks after my parents had moved out of the caravan, my brother Uriel and his pregnant wife, Glory, had left Mount Zion, along with Glory's sister Patience, and now *they* were in the caravan. If Gray wanted to get rid of my family, he needed to get much tougher about the housing arrangements.

I'd buy those new seat covers now, I decided, no matter the hit to my bank balance, would clean every nook and cranny of the cab down to toothbrush-scrubbing level, and on Sunday, I'd drive to lunch and ... get an opinion. A woman's opinion, if girls were good at colors. I didn't know about that. At Mount Zion, everybody wore brown.

I could ask Daisy, for example, who'd be perfectly comfortable talking to me, and Harmony, since she was my sister. I could ask Radiance, too, since she was married to my brother, and that might make her feel safer. I wouldn't ask Glory or Patience unless they volunteered, since they hadn't been out very long and would probably have a hard time answering. I could ask Frankie, though, which would show them it was all right.

After all that, it would be perfectly natural to ask Oriana, wouldn't it?

Harden up, I told myself. If Jack could give a girl a jewelry rack, I could ask one what color I should paint my ute. It was one simple question. Anyway, I had to get over this. Oriana was too young for me, not quite seventeen yet. Well past time for marriage by Mount Zion standards, and normally about the age when the first pregnancy got obvious, but we weren't in Mount Zion anymore. Daisy would never allow it, and I worked for Gray. Besides, Oriana had left to find a future, and who knew what she wanted that future to be? She'd never said a word, or had she? I tried to remember. She was almost always the one cooking on the rare occasions when I saw her, and even when she was sitting down, she chatted as little as I did. Unless she wanted to be a cook, I had no clue.

Frankie, on the other hand, talked about careers all the time. About computer science and biotechnology and electrical engineering, and other jobs I'd never heard of. Database engineer. Full-stack developer. Biophysicist.

"Not many women in those jobs, are there?" my dad had asked her at last month's lunch. As usual, we were perched all over the place, anywhere we could find a spot. Yurts weren't very roomy by Outside standards, though they were cozy. A yurt was a flat *and* a tent. Huh.

"You're right," Frankie said, not lowering her eyes one centimeter. "That's one reason I'm interested. The pay, which is always better in male-dominated professions, and that employers treat you better in other ways, because you're valuable. I want to be valuable. Who knows? Maybe someday I'll be in charge."

"Fair enough," Dad said, "if you can take what the boys dish out along the way. Could be rough, eh."

"What, if they sexually harass me?" Frankie said, her eyes all but flashing, as they'd done so often since she'd got out. "They can try. Once. Because I will hurt them."

"Good on ya," Gray said, "but I reckon you'd be wise to try a complaint first. After that, once everybody's on notice?" He grinned. "Go for it." He told the rest of us, "Self-defense lessons."

"You taught her to hurt men," Dad said, his voice not exactly condemning, but not approving, either.

"Men who are trying to hurt her," Gray said, his eyes steely now.

Daisy said, "Gray didn't teach her, though he played the part of attack dummy. He's the best at that, because he's so fast, he's hard to hurt. But no. He didn't teach her. *I* taught her."

Raphael said, "You *tried* to hurt him?" Radiance offered a hesitant comment I didn't quite hear, Frankie's voice rose in response, sounding as if her very vocal cords were tightening, and beside me, I felt Oriana stiffening in the same way. She and I were perched with Harmony on bar stools in front of the kitchen bench.

"Did Daisy teach you, too?" I asked Oriana quietly.

"She offered," Oriana said. "But I ..." She stopped.

"What?" I asked.

She hesitated so long, I thought she wasn't going to answer. "I'll try again later. It's just that when violent things start to happen, I ... don't react right."

"How?" I pressed. "What's 'right,' anyway? You can run or fight, and there's no shame in choosing to run."

"But I don't do either one," she said. "I just sort of freeze, and my mind goes away, and after that, I feel shaky for ages. But I'll try again later," she assured me. "I don't want to be a coward."

That was all the time we had to talk, but it was better than the past times we'd done a lunch like this. I'd at least shared *words* with her, even though the words bothered me for days.

If she was afraid I'd think less of her for not wanting to learn to fight, though? On Sunday, I wouldn't wait until last to ask her about the ute. I'd ask her first. It would be better for her to think her opinion mattered, wouldn't it?

I was going to do it, and never mind that it wouldn't be easy, because she still wouldn't look me in the eye. That was because she went to a girls' school and lived with her sisters, and I worked with dozens of men. We both needed the practice.

Car colors. Neutral question. Perfect opportunity.

9

THE SIN OF PRIDE

Oriana

On a Sunday morning in late May, I could practically feel winter coming at the door when Daisy blew into the yurt with Gray and Xena, Gray's Labrador, on a swirl of cold wind. I was fixing two pans of hasselback potatoes, enough to feed fourteen, slicing agrias almost all the way through and as thin as I could, then brushing the slices with melted butter and garlic before baking them. They'd come out beautiful as fans, the outside of each wafer golden-crisp and the inside fluffy and starchy, perfect with the enormous pans of browned lamb chunks, parsnips, carrots, and onions that were already in the oven, cooking slowly and getting tender. Even more tender thanks to the entire bottle of red wine I'd stirred in there, which didn't taste sour and sharp when it was cooked with the meat like that.

Wine did something special to meat, because of chemistry. The tannins, Daisy had explained, softened the fat in the meat, which released more of the flavor, and the fat made the wine taste smoother and more like fruit. It would probably never be on an exam, but it was a thing I knew. Also, the alcohol cooked off, so it wasn't sinful.

I'd do green beans, too, at the last minute, and Aunt Constance was making the sweet, which was an apple custard crumble in shortcrust pastry. She'd taken some of Gray's Ballarat apples for it, because they were the most flavorful and went so tender when they cooked, and when she'd told me about the recipe, I'd wanted to be the one making that, too. The recipe said to use prepared custard, but it would taste so much better if you made it yourself, rich and creamy and vanilla-scented. I could also make extra for people to pour over their portions, and put it in the pretty little blown-glass pitcher I'd bought at the farmer's market last month, which I kept on the bedside table in my room. The first thing I'd bought just because I wanted it, even though I didn't need it. I was saving every dollar I could, but I'd wanted a pretty thing to look at, and to stick flowers in.

Do you want to do all that because you like to cook, or because you want to impress people? Especially Gabriel? It wouldn't make sense, because people didn't see cooking as impressive, and I tried not to think of Gabriel at all.

I'd read about "a schoolgirl crush" in a book. That must be what I had, because I *was* a schoolgirl now, even though I'd have been married for months in Mount Zion. And even though it was Gabriel, who wasn't just beautiful, he was strong and kind and quiet as well. On the day he'd left Mount Zion, he'd saved somebody who would've burnt to death otherwise. He'd burnt himself in the process, and had never said anything about it. Gray had found out because Gabriel hadn't been able to work much the first week, and had told the rest of us at the first of our monthly family lunches.

Gabriel hadn't said anything when Gray had told us. He'd looked down at his plate instead, because he was embarrassed, so clearly waiting until people stopped talking about it, not thinking that he was a hero.

Even if I *had* done the apple custard crumble as well as the rest of this dinner, it wasn't going to make me a hero. Cooking was my best skill, but it wasn't special. It was just something women did, like laundry and cleaning bathrooms and having babies.

Not everybody did it Outside, though, or they did it in fast ways that didn't taste very good, which meant that if you did it especially well, they noticed, and they thanked you for it and, possibly, *were* a bit impressed.

Pride goeth before destruction, and a haughty soul before a fall.

Was it so wrong, though, to be proud that you'd made something delicious to feed your family, if you *knew* that it wasn't pulling people out of burning cars and you weren't pretending it was? It wasn't as if I went around being proud of myself in a general way. I wasn't doing as badly in school now, but nobody was going to make me Head Girl anytime soon, or anytime *ever*.

Frankie was right. Cooking and gardening and babies. And cleaning bathrooms. That was what I had, not computer … engineering, or whatever it was. Frankie and I were on different paths, the kind that take you farther away from each other the longer you walk.

Things were a bit easier between the two of us now all the same, after that bad day when she'd told me to go away. She'd said on the bus home from school that afternoon, blurting the words out abruptly, as if she'd steeled herself to say them, "Petra says I was cruel. To you. That I was cruel to you."

"No," I'd said, knowing I was flushing, but trying to be cool and outspoken, like the people Frankie liked. "I know I'm … that you don't want me, not when you're with your clever friends. That I'm embarrassing. Sorry I didn't see." It was all I could manage, because my throat was closing again.

"You're not the thing that's embarrassing." She wasn't quite looking at me. She was looking straight ahead instead, her hands gripping her school backpack in her lap. "It wasn't really your fault. I don't want to seem like a … like a Mount Zion person, though. I don't want to be odd anymore."

"But you're not odd," I said. "You fit so much better than I do."

"I *am* odd," she said fiercely, in that "passionate discussion" way that made me flinch. "I'm married. Nobody else is married, and I've been married for almost two years! They all know I was beaten, too, and that Gilead had relations—" She broke off, then went on, her body tense, "That he raped me. They all heard. They all *saw*. I just want to forget all that, and I can't even change my name yet! The first day of school, when every teacher said, 'Fruitful Warrior,' and all the other girls stared and laughed, and then I saw somebody whisper about it, about who I was—"

"Me too," I said. "But you almost *can* change your name. It's only a little time until you're eighteen, and after that, nobody will ever know what your name used to be."

"But I'll still be married," she said. "It's so long until I won't be, and I *hate* it. I hate that he ... that he did all of that, and I have to carry it around with me. I want to be another person, somebody that didn't happen to."

"And if I'm there, you can't." The knowledge was a cold lump in my stomach, and she looked away and didn't say anything. "I won't sit with you anymore," I said, and it felt like something tearing off me. Like a piece of my skin, and I was trembling, my own fingers cold on my backpack. I'd slept in a room with my entire family all my life. I'd worked beside my sisters and my cousins every single day. Now, I kept getting more alone.

"You don't have to do that." She mumbled the words, though, and I could tell she didn't mean them. "I don't want to be cruel. I can't stand to think I'm like that, like Gilead, but I'm like that all the time with you and Daisy anyway. I see myself, I *hear* myself, but it's like I can't help it."

"Because we're there," I said. "Because we're *all* there, even if we're not all living at Gray's. Being odd. Being different."

Now, she looked at me. "Yes," she said, and that was all.

"What are you going to do?"

"I don't know." Her fingers were pleating the strap of her backpack now. "What can I do? Nothing. Get through it, I guess. I've got through things before. I've got through *everything* before."

"You could live someplace else, maybe," I said. "And go to a different school." I'd be alone at school then, but I'd felt alone today. I'd be alone in the yurt, too, not just alone in a bedroom, and that would be awful, but if I made her feel it was OK to go, that was something I *could* do.

I could pretend. For Frankie, I could.

She shook her head impatiently, and I felt the way I always did. Stupid, like I didn't understand. "I can't transfer," she said, "not in the middle of the year. And the teachers are helping me here, because they *do* know. I just want to be *done* with this, catch up on all my horrible gaps, go to university, and be like everybody else. Not with a weird name. Not married. Not …"

"Not with a family that keeps reminding everybody all over again." Because, yes, that happened. Whenever there was a story about Mount Zion, and it seemed like there were so many stories, they'd repeat it, with photos of Frankie's bruised face and details from the court case. "But it doesn't seem like it bothers Daisy," I said, "so maybe it gets better later on."

"In fourteen years, you mean," Frankie said. "I can't wait fourteen years."

"Maybe you can pretend it's already true," I said. "I thought it was. You seem so … so clever and cool and knowing what to say."

"I do?" For once, she didn't look decisive. She looked more the way I always felt.

"Yeh," I said. "You do. And if I don't sit with you, it'll be easier to pretend." Some more of that ripping skin, but the pain was less, like the skin was going numb.

"Then you won't have a friend, though," she said. "You left

with me. You came back for me. You're my *sister*."

My throat had closed some more, and the tears were welling up again, even though Frankie hated it when I cried. "I think I may have made a friend, though," I said. "Maybe she'll let me eat lunch with her." I knew it sounded pathetic, too hopeful, but Aisha had waved at me when she'd seen me after school, so maybe. Sometime.

Girl's got guts. She'd said that. About *me*.

"I know you don't have a friend," Frankie said. "I know you'll be alone."

I said, "I can eat alone. I've got guts."

"You don't have guts," she said. "Daisy has guts. I've got guts. You've never had guts. I'm not being cruel," she hurried on. "But you don't."

She pushed the button for our stop—we were almost the only ones left on here, out amidst the lifestyle blocks, out by the sea—and I stood up and moved into the aisle, grabbing for the bar to steady myself.

"I do, though," I said. I didn't know if I did or not, but I was tired of being scared, and tired of being lonely. If Frankie could pretend? So could I. "I have guts."

Now, I kept slicing into potatoes and told myself, *I may not be good at Biology, but I* am *good at cooking. Maybe I could be a nanny. That's a job.* Frankie looked up from where she was—of course—doing maths problems in an exercise book, and asked Daisy and Gray, "Where did you run?"

"Decided to swim instead," Daisy said, taking off her trainers as Gray grabbed a towel and began to rub Xena down. "Nothing clears the cobwebs after a night shift like a good long swim at the saltwater pool, especially if it's in the rain, except possibly a smoked salmon eggs bennie at the Long Dog café, which we also did. Swimming always makes me hungry."

"Getting fortified for this lunch, too," Gray said. "Have a sleep first, though, what d'you reckon? Even Superwoman has to sleep." He pulled Daisy in by the hips and kissed her mouth, but that didn't shock me anymore. That was tame, for them.

"Are you sure you're still OK with this?" Daisy asked, staying in his arms and not stepping back. "Fourteen people, some of them probably still in their caps and aprons? Keeps getting worse, eh. Not to mention my sister-in-law Chelsea, because she's bound to condescend to you again. You could give it a miss and go golfing instead."

"Chucking me out of my own house now?" Gray asked, but he was laughing. "Besides, it's raining, and it's going to rain more. I've had to work in the rain all my life, between rugby and building. I'm drawing the line at my leisure hours. Besides, whatever Oriana's making smells awesome, and I want some."

"As you paid for it," Daisy said.

"As *we* paid for it," he said. "Am I complaining?" He searched her face, then. "Something wrong?"

She shrugged. "No. Just tired. I'm going to take that nap. What do we have—three hours? That's time enough."

"Want company?" Gray asked.

She smiled. "Want to give me company?"

"You know I do."

The thing between Gray and Daisy—it always seemed like electricity, the same kind of tingle I got when I looked at Gabriel. *Was* that a crush? What was the difference? Maybe that the other person got the same charge. I didn't know much about electricity, but it had to go between things, didn't it? If you were the only one who felt it, it wasn't going to be lighting anything up. It just ran into the ground.

"We'll be at the house, then," Daisy said. "If you've got this, Oriana."

"I've got it," I said. "No worries."

10

SIGNALS, CROSSED

GABRIEL
The day wasn't going the way I'd hoped.

For one thing, Oriana was moving back and forth between cooktop, oven, and sink like a particularly industrious butterfly as Frankie continued to work away in an exercise book at the kitchen bench, my mum got out plates and cutlery, and Radiance and Glory served fizzy lemonade and tea. Daisy's twin, Dorian, was sitting on the couch, holding himself apart from the others along with his wife, Chelsea, who'd never lived at Mount Zion and always seemed like she was bursting to set everybody right. In fact, at this moment, Chelsea was feeding their baby and studying us as if we were her science project, which we probably were. Chelsea was a teacher, and in "graduate school," whatever that was. She had to write a thesis, apparently, and had announced at the last lunch that she was planning on studying "the effects of gender stereotypes on student achievement," which seemed ominous.

Take, for example, the way my dad was talking with Gray, Raphael, and Uriel about Gray's upcoming projects. Daisy was there, too, and my brothers kept looking at her oddly, clearly wondering why she'd joined them and wasn't ... doing whatever they thought she should be doing. As if she were going to learn their secrets.

Oh. Me? I was sitting on a stool at the kitchen bench. The idea had been to have a chat with Oriana, but as I've mentioned, that wasn't happening. Especially now that I'd been joined by my sister Harmony, as well as Patience, Glory's younger sister. Patience was barely sixteen, her wedding day already set when she'd walked out with her sister and brother-in-law. She'd been meant to marry the Prophet's grandson, Valor Pilgrim. He'd apparently been showing signs of wanting to leave himself, the Prophet had wanted to stop it happening, and she was the prettiest girl still at Mount Zion.

"Nothing binds you to Mount Zion like a wife and kids, he reckons," Uriel had told me the day our dad had brought them home. "At least that's how it looks, because he's marrying the girls off even younger now, the moment they turn sixteen, and the blokes as well. Barely twenty, some of them. We didn't give him a chance with Patience." Which was good. I hadn't liked Valor when we were kids. Maybe it was wrong to hold that against him, but I did anyway.

Now, Harmony said, "Can you show Patience and me the ute, Gabriel? Dad told me all about it, and I want to see."

I said, "I can if you like, though it's not much to look at." I tried to catch Oriana's eye, because I'd driven over here thinking about showing it to her, but she was arranging some spiny golden things on platters, then shoving them back into the oven, maybe to stay warm. They looked a bit like a photo I'd seen of pangolins, or possibly dinosaurs with their armored plates up, and definitely like no food I could remember eating. At any rate, she wasn't looking at me, and hadn't looked at me since I'd arrived, so I put on a jacket and went out into the rain with the girls, feeling a little stupid about my hopes for the day, not to mention the ridiculousness of showing off my still somewhat battered ute, gray primer and all.

Patience said, "It's so wonderful. Is it really yours? *All* yours?" She smiled in my direction, though not quite *at* me. She was cut from the same mold as Drew's wife, Hannah, with pale-blond hair and bright blue eyes and the kind of smile that sparkles, and she had a sort of infectious spirit, full of life and merriment. Patience was one of those girls that the unmarried men watched, because no rules about downcast eyes could entirely quell that life force, and all of them had hoped to be her husband.

I said, "It's not much, and it's not painted yet—I'm trying to work out the color—but yeh. It's taken a fair bit of effort to get it running sweetly again, but it's OK now."

"Can we see inside?" she asked, which was flattering, but then, she hadn't been inside many vehicles yet and wouldn't know how unimpressive this one was.

"Sure." I opened the passenger door and both girls climbed in, Patience first. At least they were out of the rain.

I could see them talking in there, examining dials and buttons, then Harmony opened the door and said, "Get in and show us, Gabriel."

I hesitated. The ute had a bench seat, but it wasn't close to the size of a couch. Harmony said, "Come *on*," and I thought, *We're not in Mount Zion anymore,* and climbed inside.

"Can you turn it on?" Patience asked, her shoulder touching mine, and when I did, feeling quite proud of the way the new heater blasted the air, asked, "What's that for?" and pointed at a dial below the speedometer.

"It's the odometer," Harmony said. "It tells you how many kilometers you've driven since the ute was new. It's an offense to turn the dial back so it looks like you've done fewer kilometers. You might do that if you wanted to sell it, because people would rather buy one that hasn't been used so hard. It must happen, because they put it in the driver's handbook."

"Oh," Patience said, with approximately nil interest. "What's this?" She reached all the way across me this time, and I tried to squeeze back against the seat but couldn't avoid her brushing against me. Her cheeks turned pink, at least the one ten centimeters from me did, and I thought, *She doesn't know what she's doing.* She was dressed fairly modestly still, but she'd had her hair cut and was wearing it down, like Harmony, and she was also wearing lipstick, I suspected. Betwixt and between, maybe with her family telling her one thing and her body and spirit driving her in another direction. I knew that feeling.

Wait until she discovered the public library and found the porn books.

"Sorry," I said, and turned the key to shut the engine down. "I think they're about to start lunch."

Oriana

The lamb dish was brilliant. Deep with flavor, thanks to the wine, and the meat so tender it nearly fell apart in your mouth. My potatoes were as good as always, too, but I was having trouble eating them.

I wasn't sitting at the benchtop today, ready to jump up and get anything needed from the kitchen. I was on the floor with my back against the wall instead, because there were no more seats. Gabriel was sitting on a stool at the benchtop with Daisy and Gray beside him, and Patience, Glory's sister, was standing halfway into the kitchen with her plate beside Gabriel's. Daisy and Gray were having a conversation, Patience was listening, and Gabriel wasn't. He had his head down and was eating.

He'd taken Patience out to see his ute earlier, though, and she was still with him. I wanted to see it, too, to ask him about it, to let him know, somehow, that I thought he'd done well to get it, and to hear how he'd fixed it, but how could I do it now without it being obvious that I wanted to talk to him? Or, worse, seeming like I was in some sort of competition with Patience?

That was what I was thinking when Frankie suddenly said, from the couch where she was sitting with Radiance and Glory and Chelsea, all of them squashed up together, "You all realize what's wrong with this seating arrangement, right?" When the others didn't seem to hear, she picked up her glass from the coffee table, rapped her spoon against it, and said, "May I say something, please?"

This time, they heard, because everybody stared at her.

Frankie said, "There are only two women eating at a table or benchtop here: Aunt Constance and Daisy. Six men eating with someplace to set their plates, and six women standing up, or on the couch with their plates in their laps, or sitting on the floor. And the one on the floor is the *cook.*"

"Yes," Uncle Aaron said. "And?" Raphael and Uriel, at the table with him, stopped chewing and stared at each other, and Dorian, who was sitting at the table, froze. As for me, I could hardly breathe. Frankie's tone was sharp, and I'd never heard a woman defying a man like this in my life. Especially not her *uncle.*

"That's not the way it works Outside," Frankie said. "If anything, *women* are the ones sitting in the best spots, especially pregnant women, and here's Glory, eight months pregnant, on a too-soft couch with her plate in her lap."

Glory, like me, sat frozen, not sure where to look or what to say.

"People come to New Zealand from other countries and keep their customs," Uncle Aaron finally said into the silence. "No reason we can't do the same."

Chelsea said, "Frankie's absolutely right. I'm surprised you sat at the table, Dorian, and left me here. What was your mindset when you did that? I understand peer pressure, but you *left* Mount Zion."

"It may be good for you to have a word here with your

sister, Daisy," Aunt Constance said calmly. I didn't know how she could be calm. I couldn't even eat anymore, the atmosphere had got so tense.

"What would I add?" Daisy was as cool as ever. "Seems to me that Frankie's doing well enough expressing her opinion, and I happen to agree with it."

"Gray?" Uncle Aaron asked. "You're the man of this house. If you think something shouldn't be said, you're well within your rights to cut it off."

Gray stood up. Not fast, and not slowly. Perfectly, the way Gray always did. He said, "Frankie's right, and I've been rude. Glory? Can I offer you a seat?"

"Oh." She didn't know where to look, it was clear. "No. I'm fine. Thank you."

"I insist," he said, and now, she looked truly miserable.

Daisy said, "I have a better seat for you here as well, Radiance, as you're my guest."

Gabriel said, "Yes." It was a bit loud, and now, everybody was staring at *him*. He said, "This isn't our home, and Frankie's right. Raphael and Uriel, get up and bring your plates."

It was a voice I'd never heard, and his younger brothers sat stunned for a minute and then, as he kept staring at them, did it. Uncle Aaron opened his mouth, then closed it again. Gabriel had a touch of color in his cheeks, but he said, "Radiance and Glory? Your seats are at the table. Help your wife up, Uriel."

Uncle Aaron said, "You're not in charge here, son," and *everybody* froze, the women half-up off the couch. All but Chelsea, who'd stood as soon as it had all started and was now changing places with Dorian. He, for his part, had jumped up like a scalded cat the moment she'd started talking.

Gray said, "If anyone's in charge, I reckon it's Daisy and me." Calmly again, because Gray was always calm. "And Gabriel's right. I'm exerting the privilege of a host and switching up the seating. And if you lot will rattle your dags doing it, I'll be grateful. Oriana's outdone herself today on this lamb and these potatoes, and I'd like to get back to eating all of it."

That was praise for my cooking, but Gray always did that, because he was polite that way, and he'd also told me that if you praised somebody for doing what you liked, they tended to do more of it. Diplomacy, not war. Nobody else, though, looked like my cooking was uppermost on their mind. I wasn't sure who looked more uncomfortable, in fact: the men, sitting on the low couch with their elbows banging into each other and their knees practically up to their ears, or the women, eating silently at the table, heads down.

To my surprise, Patience was the first one to say anything, once she'd swung around on the revolving stool Gabriel had vacated and was facing the others. What she said was, "I think Gabriel's right," which was bold of her, but then, she wasn't living with her parents anymore. "Isn't the whole point that we want to change? Why do you know so much about being Outside, though, Gabriel? Is it because you're not living with anybody else from Mount Zion?"

"Probably," he said. "No choice but to learn new ways."

Patience announced, "Gabriel's got a new ute, did everybody hear? All his own, because he bought it, and then he fixed it. It's brilliant, but he still needs to paint it. He was telling me about it earlier. I think blue," she told him in a confidential sort of tone. "That'll be prettiest."

She'd been Outside about three weeks, and she already knew how to talk to men better than I did! Women out here didn't impress men by their cooking skills. They were witty and forthright and didn't forget to wear makeup because they'd been in the kitchen all day. I looked down, because I couldn't bear to look up, and realized I was still wearing my apron. I'd completely forgotten to take it off. I'd made it myself, and it was yellow and had flowers on, but it was still an apron.

Gabriel said, "Oriana's still on the floor. I'll grab a chair from outside." And stood up to do it.

This was so embarrassing. Gray said, "You deserve to sit after cooking all this."

"Thanks," I said, taking the chair Gabriel had brought in and sinking back into my corner spot, wishing there were a discreet way to get rid of my apron.

"What color do you think I should paint the ute?" Gabriel asked, sliding down the wall to sit beside me without losing his grip on his plate. "All of you," he amended, and I flushed again and thought, *Of course he didn't mean me.*

"White's best," Raphael said. "More visible."

"That's what I said," Gabriel answered, "but I got told it was dull. Anyway, it's gold and white now, with some gray patches, and all of it's ugly. So not white, gray, or yellow, I reckon. It's old, though. Only so much better it's going to look."

It was more than Gabriel *ever* talked. Was that to turn the conversation after the awkwardness? Or was it for Patience? She was so pretty, and she'd been clever at school, almost as clever as Frankie. She was watching Gabriel, smiling, looking delighted, and now, she said, "I still say blue. *Bright* blue, and shiny."

"Mm," Gabriel said.

"May as well go for red, if you're determined to stand out," Uriel said. A little stiffly, and I didn't think he was relishing the couch, or the change. Had Glory been the one pushing to leave, then? "It's the Devil's color, but never mind."

"Red's good," Daisy agreed, as if she hadn't heard any of the undercurrents. "I prefer bright colors, myself. *Especially* red." As she was wearing a skinny tomato-red jumper today with her jeans, nobody would be too surprised by that.

"Oriana?" Gabriel asked. "What do you think?"

I wasn't sure how I even answered. He was being kind, I told myself, the same way he'd been about getting me a chair.

"Maybe green?" I asked. "A darker one, like the bush when you're in the shadows? It would still be pretty, but it's a bit quieter, maybe."

"I can help you paint it, Gabriel, whatever color it is," Patience said. "All I have to do until Glory's baby gets here is to go to school, so I have heaps of time. You could bring it over here, to Gray's, and we could spread a tarp on the ground so you don't get paint all over. If you have anything else that I could help with, too, you should ask. Or if Daisy does," she added. "If Oriana doesn't want to be the one cooking and cleaning all the time. I thought being Outside would mean having fun, but she's the same as at Mount Zion, always hanging out the washing or mopping the floor or sewing something. By hand, too, because she doesn't even have a sewing machine. She's basically Cinderella. Of course, at Mount Zion, that's just called 'Friday.'"

Gray said, "We're all grateful for Oriana's help, but you may be right that she does too much."

"Oh, no," I said, but then didn't know how to go on. "It's a very small yurt," I finally managed.

"Do you want a sewing machine?" Daisy asked.

"Of course not," I said. "I'm fine." I *did* want a sewing machine, but I didn't want anybody to buy me one. Gray and Daisy were doing enough. No, I was saving for it, along with everything else.

Aunt Constance said, "I've got apple custard crumble for a sweet. Oriana didn't have to cook this one, anyway."

Everybody *did* exclaim over the apple crumble, even though there was no thick, rich, vanilla-sweet homemade custard to pour over the top. And when Patience asked Gabriel if he'd take her for a ride in the ute, he said yes.

He asked if anybody else wanted to go, but I was doing the washing-up with Frankie at the time and wearing my apron. I thought about saying yes anyway, especially when he added, "Oriana?" That was an invitation, wasn't it? You wouldn't say somebody's name unless you really wanted to ask them.

I was about to answer when Aunt Constance said, "I'll go. I haven't even seen this famous ute yet. I can sit in the middle. No sin sitting too close to a woman if the woman's your mum, eh. It's not really on to go on a ride alone with a man," she told Patience, "no matter what you've heard. Your mum isn't here, but I am. This time, it's Gabriel, but who will it be next time? Not a good idea."

Gabriel said, "That'll be good, Mum. Cheers for lunch, Oriana. Best meal I've had in ages." But he left with Patience, and I didn't see him again.

I finished the washing-up.

I had to get over this.

11

BIRTHDAY WISHES

ORIANA

On a cold, sunny Wednesday in mid-June, Aisha turned to face me in her chair before the start of Biology and said, "I'm disappointed in you."

My head jerked up. "What? I'm sorry, what ..."

She laughed. "I keep waiting for you to invite me to your birthday, and you never do it. It's on *Sunday*. I invited you to *my* birthday, didn't I?"

"Yes," I said. "It was lovely." A family dinner, with savory dishes I'd never encountered and longed to know how to cook. I'd sat with her little brothers, her mum and dad, and her aunt and uncle and *their* kids, all of them singing a song to Aisha and then eating a yellow cake with raspberry filling and buttercream icing. The cake had had Aisha's name spelled out on the top in different-colored icing, and candles stuck into it. It wasn't as moist as when you got the time exactly right, but it was so pretty, and the candles were beautiful.

Afterward, I'd "slept over." Sleeping over was a thing, it seemed, though Aisha'd had to explain it to me. A *teenage* thing, which was what we were meant to be.

It was like time zones, when it was breakfast time to you

and the middle of the night to somebody else. In Mount Zion, I'd have been a woman for a year now, sleeping in my own room with my husband, getting ready to have a baby. Here, I'd be a child myself for years yet, because that was what "teenager" meant. That you weren't grown, and you weren't even expected to work.

"But why would you do that?" I'd asked Aisha. "Sleep over? If you have a bed at home?"

"Because it's more fun," she'd said. "Like having a sister to tell secrets to, in the dark. You never did that?"

"No. I *had* sisters to tell secrets to in the dark. And everybody had one bed. You'd have to swap, and that would be odd, sleeping with somebody else's family. You can't ..."

"Oh," she'd said. "You can't look at boys other than your brothers, and you're all in the same room. So *gross.*"

Now, she said, "So why haven't you invited me?"

I didn't know what to say. I finally stammered out, "I don't ... there won't ... I've never had a birthday like that. There isn't much ... any celebrating."

"Why not?" she asked. "People are people. Doesn't everybody want to make a big deal of their birthday? It's your special day!"

I had to think about it. "You aren't meant to be special at Mount Zion. It's a community. And anyway," I went on, trying to joke about it, the way other people joked about their lives, "with everybody eating together, it would be cake every day, and singing, too. There'd have to be a woman specially assigned just to make birthday cakes!"

Aisha said, "Right. Passing over the awfulness of Mount Zion—you've never had a proper birthday? *Ever?* Then I'm going to do it. I'm going to make you a birthday cake, and come over and eat it with you. That is, if you're allowed to invite me. I mean, you're not actually a prisoner or anything, just because you've never invited me before, when you've been at my house five times?"

I said, completely awkwardly, "It's my family's monthly lunch on Sunday, though. There'll be twelve people already." Just twelve, because Dorian had texted Daisy that he and Chelsea "couldn't make it." The stain of Mount Zion, was what that was. It was too different, too *wrong*, for Chelsea to witness, and she was married to Dorian! What would anybody else think?

Aisha said, "Won't your mum—wait, your sister, or whoever, cook for one more person if you ask? My mum always says one more doesn't matter. Especially if I bring the cake, though it'll have to be two cakes, probably, for thirteen people. I wish I knew how to make cake. I'll ask Mum to teach me. She'll faint with gratitude that I'm finally interested. I won't come if you don't want me, but—really? You don't want me?"

I said, "I'll be the one cooking dinner, but I can't just—"

"On your *birthday?*" Now, she was staring. "This story just keeps getting worse and worse."

Class started then, and we had to stop talking. I worried about it all day, and that night at dinner, which Daisy had cooked this time and which we were eating in the main house, I said, sliding into a break in the conversation—Frankie had been having a "passionate discussion" with Gray about labor standards, which I was barely following— "Excuse me. Gray?"

"Yes?" he asked. "Are you going to explain the unintended consequences of a higher minimum wage vis-à-vis the rising cost of childcare, contrasted with the benefit of lifting more of the population out of poverty?"

"Oh," I said. "No. It was a different question."

"Thank God," he said. "Let's have it."

"Do you think I could have a friend to lunch on Sunday?" I asked.

"You're the one cooking it," he said. "I'd say that gives you at least one invitation. Male friend or female friend?"

"I wouldn't—" I began to say in shock, then realized he

was joking and switched to, "Female friend, of course. My friend Aisha from school. She wants to bring—"

Daisy and Frankie were looking at me in surprise. Frankie said, "You want to bring her *here*? During family *lunch*? Aunt Constance and Radiance are still wearing long dresses! Radiance is still wearing her *cap*. Could it *be* any more humiliating to have somebody else witness?"

I said, "Aisha wears a hijab. So maybe it won't seem as odd."

Gray said, "This will be an interesting cultural exchange. You said she wanted to bring something. What kind of thing? A copy of the Koran? Testing Aaron's sophistication level, possibly."

"You realize," Daisy said, "that Muslims don't eat pork."

"They don't?" I set my spoon back into my bowl of pumpkin soup. "Oh. I was going to do a pork roast. I'll do meatballs instead, maybe, with beef and lamb, if those meats are OK. That would be easy. People ... men ... they like meatballs, don't they? With tomato sauce and pasta?"

"If you mean Gabriel," Gray said, "I reckon he'll be thrilled to eat whatever you cook. Got to be an improvement, especially now that he's on his own."

"Gabriel?" Frankie said. "Why? Oriana knows exactly one unmarried man—who's part of our whanau, by the way—so she must be mad for him? Give women a bit of credit. Even Oriana has outside interests."

I didn't pay any attention to that. Gray was teasing, that was all. He didn't know it could be true, so he didn't know it hurt. I said, "He's on his own?"

"Yeh," Gray said. "Got a new flat, because Drew's partner Hannah is having that baby soon, and his mum's coming down from the North Island to care for the kids. They told Gabriel he didn't have to go, but I reckon he felt that he'd be in the way. One of Drew's new young players was leaving his horrible flatshare, so there was a spot open, fortunately. Or unfortunately. Housing's a bugger."

"How d'you know it's horrible?" Daisy asked. "I did quite well on these paninis, by the way, considering that they're—well—sandwiches. It's the ham that does it. So fortunate that I'm not Muslim."

"Soup, too," Gray said. "No complaints. I'm like Gabriel, grateful for anybody cooking that isn't me. And the flat will be horrible because they're always horrible. Three blokes in a flat? One bathroom and one frying pan between them, and the grease practically dripping down the kitchen walls? How could it be anything else? But you said your friend wants to bring something, Oriana," he said, switching gears. "What is it?"

This was it. The ticklish part. I put my stockinged foot on Xena's chocolate-colored side for courage—she was lying between my chair and Gray's, as close to him as she could get—and said, "A cake. Well, cakes. It was her idea. She doesn't know how to bake one, though, so maybe I should have a backup sweet ready just in case. Something easy. A plum tart with custard? That's nice when it's cold outside."

Gray waited through all of that and had his mouth open to speak, but Daisy got in first. "Because it's your birthday on Sunday, and your friend thinks you should have a cake."

My face got hot, bang on cue. "I know we don't do that," I said, "but Aisha didn't understand. We don't have to sing that song or anything. She just thought it would be nice, and she wants to come over, and it's ..."

"It's better," Daisy said, "to have friends. To feel normal. I never thought of you inviting her here. I never did that. Living with Dorian in a one-bedroom apartment, eh. Completely weird, the two of us, sixteen years old and on our own. Oh—Gray? OK with you?"

"Of course," he said.

"Let's have her, then," Daisy said. "No reason we can't

have cake. No reason we can't sing the song, either. What do you think, Frankie? Should we start celebrating birthdays? This family's meant to be a democracy of sorts, so let's have your opinion."

Frankie said, "I don't mind. I know I'll be celebrating my eighteenth." It was ten days after mine, because we were almost exactly one year apart.

"We could celebrate both our birthdays on Sunday," I said, "as we'll have two cakes. But your birthday is the one that really matters, Frankie, because you get to change your name."

"Oriana's right," Gray said, "that we need birthdays. If anybody wants to sing to me on mine, I'll grin and bear it, and if Oriana wants to bake me a cake, I'll be more than happy to eat it. Carrot's my favorite. But I don't think we should combine them, because Frankie *will* be eighteen, and everybody needs their day."

"Gray and I are paying for that name change, Frankie," Daisy said. "The fees, and the witness. That's our birthday present to you. We could fill out the paperwork on your birthday, if you like, and file it. And that night, we'll have cake. *More* cake."

"Are we doing presents, then, from now on?" Frankie asked.

"No," I said fast. "I mean—for yours, yes, because you'll be eighteen, and that's special, but I don't need presents. It would be so awkward, with everybody coming. They barely have enough for themselves. I'd rather just have lunch, like usual."

"But with cake," Gray said.

"Well," I said, "cake's good."

Maybe Aisha would write my name on it. And bring those candles.

GABRIEL

I got ready for that lunch with my heart in my throat, wondering what I thought I was doing. I'd taken a shower, trying to feel cleaner than was possible in the flat I'd moved into barely a week ago. Now, I buttoned my shirt—I had a new one, a blue plaid in soft flannel, the first time I'd owned a shirt with a pattern—tucked it into my jeans, took a doubtful look in the age-spotted mirror, and headed out of the bathroom, then into my room for my phone and keys and wallet, because I had one of those now. I only had two things in it so far: my debit card and my driver's license. I had no idea what other blokes put in there to justify all those slots, but a man was meant to have a wallet, so I had one.

Jack had been wrong, though. I'd had to buy almost nothing for the flat. My room had come ready-furnished with a bed and bedside table left behind by the last occupant, my only contributions being some very odd bright-green patterned sheets and a purple duvet I'd bought off TradeMe.

"Purple's kind of a girl color, though," Jack had said doubtfully, peering at the screen on my phone.

"It is?" These things always eluded me. "The color of kings, eh."

"Maybe dark purple. This is light purple. I'm pretty sure it's a girl color. But it looks like the warmest duvet on here."

"I'm not going to care," I said. "I'll be asleep." And bought it. It did look a bit startling with the green sheets—they really were extraordinarily bright—but at least it was colorful. Cheerful, even, with sheets and duvet pulled up crisp and tight over the bed and the floor swept clean.

Now, Duncan, one of the new flatmates, grumbled, "You took long enough in the bath, mate. I was about to take a piss in the kitchen sink." He was bleary-eyed, his hair mussed and face unshaven, and he was wearing track pants and a T-shirt as if he'd just got out of bed, even though it was well past noon.

"Sorry," I said, and wondered with horror if that had been a joke. Surely he wouldn't do it.

Sadly, though, I had no illusions left. I was already cleaning the toilet every few days, because some things were more than a man could bear. I'd better add the kitchen sink.

Rowan, the other flatmate, a ginger, was lying on the flat's sole couch, which was green fabric and none too flash, even by my standards. You could call it "dirty," or you could go on and call it "filthy," and you wouldn't be far off. He lifted another extra-large spoonful of muesli to his mouth, wiped the milk out of his beard with the back of his hand, and said, "Don't mind him. He's having a sook because he didn't pull at the bar last night after working on it for about four hours. She gave him a kiss on the cheek, in the end, and walked out with her girlfriends." He laughed. "Loser."

Duncan said, "Got her number, though, didn't I. More than you did."

I didn't say anything. I pulled on my jacket and boots and headed down the two flights of stairs and out the front door.

In addition to not having had to buy much beyond the colorful bedclothes and an assortment of used towels which bore no resemblance to the thick, snowy-white things in Drew's granny flat, the new place had other benefits. It was in central Dunedin, which meant I could do most errands on foot or by bus and save on fuel, and I was improving my cleaning skills.

The state of the kitchen and bath had left me open-mouthed when I'd first seen the place. Duncan had rubbed his nose and said, "A bit untidy, sorry. We had a piss-up on Saturday night to celebrate Jocko getting his contract."

I'd thought, *Oh. OK. It was a party*, and had overlooked the beer bottles, pizza boxes, and something that I hoped was a pile of dirty washing and not a body. I'd signed the paper, then gone home and started collecting the purple duvet and so forth.

Barely a week after I'd signed, I was shaking hands with the whole Callahan family, including Hannah, which was progress on my part, saying my thanks and my goodbyes.

"I'll still be coming to your rugby games and all, when I can," I told Jack. "Still see you, eh. Almost the same."

"Not really," Jack said. "Not when you won't be there to play basketball and watch TV."

I didn't know what to say to that. I knew about being lonely.

Hannah said, "Gabriel's coming for dinner next Friday, remember. He'll be around." She looked more tired than ever today. Drew and Jack had been doing most of the heavy housework for the past couple of months, and when Drew was gone, I'd been coming up to help hoover and clean baths myself, but it was a good thing Drew's mum was coming next week, because I was a pretty poor substitute. I couldn't exactly provide dinner.

"If you need anything," I told all of them when my few belongings were in two carrier bags, "ring me." I put a hand on Jack's shoulder. "And I'll be ringing you, too, mate, when I need advice on shirts and washing powder and such."

He nodded, and I thought he was holding back the tears, so I got myself and my two bags into the ute and left.

Moving day.

Unfortunately, it turned out that the flat always looked like that. I spent nearly fifty dollars on cleaning products after moving in, and I had no idea how high they'd have let the dirty dishes pile up if I hadn't been washing them every night. On the other hand, my share of the rent was a hundred twenty-five a week, and my own place might have been twice that, if I could have found one at all.

When I'd missed living with a group of young blokes, though, I'd forgotten to remember that somebody else had cleaned the place.

Now, I turned the ute's nose toward Corstorphine and the

sea, heading for Oriana's seventeenth birthday. Gray had told me about it at work on Thursday, saying, "I know that birthdays aren't a thing at Mount Zion, and Oriana's a bit embarrassed about having it acknowledged, but I reckon it's good for those girls to feel special, if only for a day."

"Yeh," I said, wondering why he was telling me, of all people.

He said, "Could be getting some pushback from your dad and brothers, though. Maybe your mum as well."

"No worries," I said, getting the message. "I'll speak up."

He clapped a hand on my shoulder and said, "Good," then went back to work. And I was left to wonder—exactly why had he said it?

It didn't matter, though, because now, I had an excuse.

12

SEVENTEEN CANDLES

GABRIEL

We had another interesting moment with the seating at the very start that Sunday, when Raphael came into the house with a folding table, Uriel walked in with two folding chairs under each arm, and Dad came last with a simple wooden stool. They shoved all the furniture around until the two tables fit, though barely, and stuck the stool near the others at the breakfast bar as Gray looked on with a sort of blank expression that was oddly alarming. That he was holding his power in reserve, maybe, and could be hiding anger behind that calm.

"Room for eight now at the tables," my dad said, "four on the stools, and the rest on the couch. Constance found the table and chairs in an op shop yesterday, so here we are. Oriana and Patience can sit on the couch, as they're not married. Problem solved."

Gray looked at Daisy. She said, "He didn't ask me, either," her face doing the kind of shutting-down thing I was used to seeing on women's faces at Mount Zion, and I thought, *Something's wrong.*

All Gray said, though, was, "Cheers for bringing all that.

Since Daisy and I are hosting this gathering, though, it may be best if we decide on the seating arrangements."

My dad looked nothing but surprised. He was so used to being in charge, he forgot sometimes that Gray employed *him*. Also, I was starting to get the feeling that having your own place gave you more ... rights, or something. At Mount Zion, a man had dominion over his wife and children, but nobody owned their possessions. You got shifted every time somebody outgrew their family room, and it wouldn't have mattered anyway, as you didn't have anything but your clothes to move. Nobody outside the family came into your room, either, so the situation didn't arise.

Dad said, "Excuse me," maybe grasping some of that, but he didn't look happy about it. Meanwhile, Oriana's friend, Aisha, who had an even bolder eye than Patience and was wearing a head scarf that hid her hair, exactly like at Mount Zion, had her head on one side and was staring at each of us in turn, as interested as an archaeologist getting a rare glimpse into a primitive society. Only the hair-covering part was the same, apparently, because Aisha's gaze was nothing but direct.

We might be missing Chelsea today, but we weren't missing the astonished undercurrents. My brothers didn't look happy about Aisha's presence, and there was a sort of electricity in the room that felt like standing under a transformer. You moved on, because you didn't want to be shocked.

The moment passed once Daisy and Gray *did* determine the seating arrangements, though, and we ate dinner and exchanged news without further drama. My mum's new job, Patience about to start school, and the announcement that Radiance was looking after a couple of neighbor kids for extra money. After which Gray said, "Gabriel has a new flat as well," and I agreed that, yes, I did, tried to project something daring and glamorous, and didn't share the disgusting details.

Now, after we'd eaten pasta and meatballs in tomato sauce that, again, tasted totally unlike anything I'd ever managed to cook for myself, and had also been cooked once again by Oriana, Gray and Daisy were getting up from the couch and starting to collect plates. Most of the women jumped up the second it happened, including Oriana. Daisy said, "We're fine. You cooked on your birthday already. That's enough. Want to help with this, Frankie?"

Frankie, who along with Aisha *hadn't* jumped up, said, "Interesting that it's me you ask, and not one of the men."

Daisy said, "They're guests here," in a firm, even tone I imagined she'd practiced, and Frankie stood up with clear reluctance. I considered standing up myself and offering—I certainly knew how to do the washing-up by now, after all my practice—but I had a feeling that would cause another scene.

Instead, I watched Oriana. Not too difficult, since we were both eating at the benchtop today, with Patience and Aisha on my other side. The single people, I guessed, except Frankie, who existed in a sort of in-between space and had been sitting alone on the couch as if she didn't really want to be here. Oriana, on the other hand, was fizzing with excitement, and I thought, *Why?* Mentioning somebody's birthday wasn't usual, but it wasn't forbidden, and really, what was wrong with being given fewer chores to do on your birthday? Everybody would have one eventually and get their turn, right? Maybe considering yourself as special was wrong, but in comparison to everything else we'd adjusted to, it didn't seem that bad.

Frankie, still saying nothing, began loading the dishwasher, and Daisy and Gray disappeared, but came back a couple of minutes later holding cakes. Gray's had white icing and Daisy's had pink, and hers also had lighted pink candles stuck in. They were singing a song, and Aisha jumped up and joined in loudly as the rest of us looked at each other. I'd heard the song before, since a couple of the kids had had birthdays while I'd been staying with Drew, but it didn't seem like a good idea to sing it in front of my dad.

This was a change, you could say. Pure worldliness, creeping in under the doorjamb.

Daisy and Gray put the cakes on the benchtop in front of Oriana as the song ended. The one with the candles had her name written on it in shaky script along with a big "17," and Gray said, "Make a wish."

Oriana stared at the cake as if it contained every worldly delight and asked, "A wish?"

"A wish that you hope will come true, this next year," Gray said. "Then, if you wave all the candles out fast, you'll get your wish. That's the idea. I always blew them out, but Daisy says it's unhygienic, and I reckon she'd know. Oh, and it's a secret wish. If you tell, it won't come true."

Dad stood up and said, his voice no louder than usual but deadly serious, "We don't wish. We pray. I haven't said anything about the way you've let the girls cut their hair and wear tight trousers and all that makeup, Daisy. And Gray. I'll say it even if I'm working for you, because it needs to be said. I've thought that continuing their schooling is good, but I can't approve of putting a good girl like Oriana above herself. Seating her in the best spot, letting her sit idle, and now this, wishing for things for herself? Expecting them? It's spoiling her for marriage."

Daisy said, her eyes striking some sparks but her voice deliberately calm, "I don't agree, but I'm not going to argue about it here, in Gray's house."

"That's not yours to say," Dad said.

"It's exactly hers to say," Gray said. "Nobody but hers. Oriana's her sister."

"I'm her uncle," Dad said. "Constance is her aunt. The younger must be guided by the elder." His voice was even quieter now, the way he sounded when you knew you had to do what he said. That level of quiet had sobered me, and sometimes scared me, as a kid. My dad, in fact, did the same thing Gray did, and that calm mask was powerful.

Gray said to Daisy, speaking so low that I could barely hear it, "Are you sure this is the hill you want to die on?"

Daisy said, just as quietly, "Yes. Because I'm tired of this."

Gray said, "Then I'm right off your shoulder."

Daisy squeezed his hand, and I saw it, on the other side of the benchtop, but my parents probably couldn't. I'd seen enough open physical touch between couples by now not to be shocked—Drew and Hannah held each other every time they were close enough to do it, him with a hand on her lower back, her draping her legs over him as they lay together on the couch—but I doubted my dad had, and we didn't need another point of contention.

We had enough, because now, Daisy came out and said the worst thing.

"The critical point," she told Dad, "is that this is how Gray and I are celebrating Oriana's birthday, wishing and all. I don't see anything sinful about it. What's praying anyway but wishing, and thinking that if you wish exactly right, it'll come true?"

Frozen silence, was what this was. Or possibly a glimpse of the fires of Hell.

Dad said, his voice shaking a bit, "That's Satan's voice speaking, tempting you out of the right path. You endanger your immortal soul."

Daisy said, "Reckon I'll take my chances. Meanwhile, it's still Oriana's day. Make a wish," she told her.

Oriana said, all her happy expectancy gone, "I don't need to wish."

Dad said, "I can't countenance this," and went on to talk about sacrilege and so forth, but I wasn't listening, because the little candles on the cake were burnt nearly to the icing already. I asked Oriana, "Do you want to do the candles, and all the rest of it?"

"What?" she said. "Yes. Or I did. But if it's ..." She trailed off.

I said, quietly as I could, "Close your eyes and make a wish, then." She shot me a quick glance, and I smiled, though it was a little painful, and said, "It's all right." Even though every wish she could make would move her further away from me.

She closed her eyes, and her pretty face got serious. *More* serious, because Oriana had a face like Mary's, in all the pictures. Something I'd never tell my dad. She had a sort of serenity, when she was cooking or coming up from the garden carrying a trug, and the kind of happiness that comes out as more of a glow.

Now, she opened her eyes again and said, "I did it." Her cheeks were a bit flushed and, as usual, she wasn't quite looking at me.

I said, under the sound of Daisy and my dad having yet more words, "Wave the candles out, or whatever you do. That's the next part, right?"

"It was blowing them out, but I guess we're not supposed to."

"Let's try it together."

Oriana began waving her hands over the candles, which were nearly going out by themselves now, and the flames flickered. I added my own hands, and she looked at me and laughed. I laughed back, because we must've looked so silly, and finally, the tiny fires died.

Gray was saying, the same way Drew would have, like the kind of leader of men I wished I were, "I reckon we should expect to have some culture clashes, with everybody coming out of Mount Zion at different times, being on different tracks. But we're in my house today, and we're celebrating Oriana here in the normal way people do. If you don't want to participate, Daisy and I can't force you, but this won't be the last time you're faced with birthday candles and birthday wishes. Maybe it's not so bad to encounter them now, where we can talk about it."

Dad said, "One can be in the world without being of the world." His face sad now, and troubled.

Gray said, "Very true. On the other hand, I think this cake is ... what, Aisha?"

"One's chocolate," she said, "and the other's lemon. They probably aren't very good, since they were my first ones, so they may not be worth fighting about." Still looking expectant as a dog eyeing a bone, though.

"Please don't interfere in adults' business," my mum told her. Not nearly as harshly as a girl would have been reprimanded at Mount Zion, but Aisha still looked shocked.

"Again," Frankie said, because, yes, she was getting stuck into things, "not really yours to say, Aunt Constance. The rules are different Outside, and in this house, we're embracing the change."

Oriana stared at her cake, so clearly wishing this were over, and I'd had enough. I stood up and told her, "Come with me."

Oriana

I followed Gabriel out of the yurt and wanted to cry. Having a birthday, having a *cake*, had sounded so wonderful, and it was blowing everything up instead. I should never have suggested it. I should have—

Gabriel, though, helping me wave the candles out, laughing with me. He hadn't seemed to think it was awful to want to do it. He may not have laughed if he'd known what I wished, but he was never going to find out. Not because I believed my wish wouldn't come true if I told, because I already knew that, but because it would be so hideously embarrassing.

Aisha had seen all of that, though. Frankie was right. I shouldn't have invited her. What would she think now?

I didn't pay much attention to where we were going. I

assumed Gabriel was taking me out until the arguing died down. I wasn't expecting to end up at his ute. But ...

Wait.

I said, "You painted it green," and the warmth of it suffused me despite the chill of the day.

The ute was, in fact, dark green, exactly like I'd suggested, and polished to a shine. That shine said he was proud of it, didn't it? He *should* be proud. He'd just come out of Mount Zion, he was doing so well and had been so brave, getting his own place, and now, he had a ute!

If capitalism could be good as well as bad, why couldn't pride? What else was it, when your cake *did* turn out perfectly? It didn't mean other people had to say it. You could still feel the pleasure of it, and that pleasure pushed you to do even better, didn't it?

"Yeh," Gabriel said, "I did paint it green. I liked your idea best. I found I didn't much want my ute to shout, 'Look at me!' It's cold out here, though. Let's get in for a minute."

I did, which meant I was sitting beside him on the narrow bench seat, so aware of his presence, of the faintly soapy smell of him. I saw the faint dampness in his blond hair, too. He'd taken a shower before he'd come over, maybe, just like I'd taken one before people had arrived. I'd put on a bit of makeup, too, even though Aunt Constance's face always looked troubled when we wore it. So, yes, I was wearing lipstick, but I'd pulled my hair back, because hair in food wasn't anything like sanitary, and also ...

Well, yes. It was also in the low knot I'd worn since I was twelve, because I hated people looking at me disapprovingly. I knew it was weak. I knew I didn't have to obey anymore, but not doing it made everything so awful.

Gabriel's voice pulled me out of my thoughts. "Nice to be quiet a minute. That was awkward in there."

"Yeh," I said. "I shouldn't have suggested it. I didn't think it was so bad."

"It's not," he said. "It's a change, that's all. And I brought something for you. Thought it might be better to give it to you here, though, so we don't have another whole barney about it."

"Oh." I couldn't look at him. "That was kind, but I really didn't need presents. What—"

He'd brought me a gift? Really? How did you act if a man gave you a gift? Was it all right even to take it?

I needed to know.

That was when his phone rang.

13

CHANGE OF PLAN

G<small>ABRIEL</small>

I hesitated with one hand on the door handle. I needed to do this now. Oriana had looked so sad. She'd wanted a pretty cake with candles. How could that be wrong, especially for a girl who spent her life caring for everybody else?

The phone kept ringing. Only a few people knew my number, and most of them were in the house. Were blows being exchanged in there or something?

I had to check. I said, "Hang on," and looked.

Jack.

I let it ring, which felt odd, as if somebody were pulling at my collar. I said, "The box is in the bed, under the cover. Hang on," and climbed out to retrieve it.

My phone chirped with a voicemail, then rang again.

Jack.

I pushed the button and said, "I can't talk right now, mate. I'll ring you back in a couple of hours, how's that?"

He said, "Can you come help me?" His voice scared, uncertain.

My blood went cold. "What's wrong?" I asked. "Where are you?"

"I'm at home," he said. "But I think I need somebody to come help."

Oriana

When Gabriel got back into the cab of the ute, he didn't have anything with him. He also said, "I have to leave. I'm sorry."

It took me a moment to understand. "Oh. That ... that's all right." My face was on fire as I scrambled out of the ute.

"Wait," he said. "Oriana." I hesitated, then turned, wishing I could control my face. I'd been so stupid, hoping like that. He'd probably sensed, somehow, how I felt, and wanted to get away. He'd only been being kind, taking me out of the uncomfortable moment, and I should've known.

He passed a hand through his thick, shiny golden hair, which had grown long enough to touch his collar in back, and said, "I want to ..." He looked at the bed of the ute, where a tarp was tied down neatly over a lump of ... something, then back at me. "I want to give this to you, but I don't have time. It's an emergency."

"Oh," I said, feeling better but also wanting to weep, every part of me stretched too thin by this strange day. "I understand."

"It's Hannah," he said, as if I hadn't spoken, and I thought, *Hannah? Another girl?* and went back to "frozen dread" again.

"Drew's wife," he said. "The ones I've been staying with. The baby was coming, and Drew had to take her to hospital in a hurry. The neighbor who was meant to come at once hasn't turned up, and the kids—they haven't had lunch, and—"

Oh. *Hannah.* I'd met her, and the kids, on the day Frankie had been taken away. She was having another baby? I said, "The kids are alone? Of course you have to go, then. But—"

"What?" he said, all but bouncing on his toes. "Sorry, but I really do have to—"

I said, "I should come with you. I've met the kids before, actually, and they may remember me a bit. The little girl was still in nappies then. I can make lunch, and even dinner, if the parents will be in hospital. Her husband went with her to have the baby? Not her mum?"

"No," Gabriel said. "Outside, the dad stays in the room and all when the baby's coming."

That was so strange, I couldn't even process it, so I didn't try. "Then I'll come with you," I said. I was never sure of anything, but I was sure of this. "It could be overnight, and she—Hannah—will be so worried about them. I can help."

"OK," he said, looking harassed and unsure. "But we need to go right now."

I opened the door to the ute and climbed up. "Then let's go."

"You'll need to—" He wasn't getting in.

"No," I said. "It'll be an argument. An explanation. I'll text Daisy. She'll understand. Let's go."

Gabriel

The look of relief on Jack's face when he opened the door to us—I can't even describe that. I remembered how his dad had put his arm around him, that first day, and tried that. A quick pat on the shoulder, a quiet word, I reckoned.

"You did well, ringing me," I told him as Oriana went further into the house with the girls, saying something about lunch. "That was keeping your head, mate."

"I was scared, though," Jack said. "I didn't feel like I was keeping my head."

"That's why it's called 'keeping it,'" I said, closing the door behind me. "Because half of you wants to *lose* your head, but you're holding it on instead." I grinned, did another of those cuddle/pats, and he grinned back, finally. "Let me text your dad that we've got here," I said, "and that you're all in one piece, and then we'll have lunch and play some basketball."

Jack said, "Uh …"

I looked up. "What?"

"I didn't exactly tell him before," Jack said, "About Mrs. Chambers not coming."

"What?"

"I didn't want him to be worried," Jack said. "Madeleine was born really fast in a car, and my dad had to help. He was worried that this baby would get born in the car, too, and that's why he made Mum leave before Mrs. Chambers got here. He might be cross that I didn't tell him, though. Especially because the ambulance came, next door."

I could well imagine. "So you rang me."

"Yes. At first I thought I could do it by myself, because I showed you about cooking and laundry and learnt that I did know how to do heaps of things, but Madeleine was crying, and I got worried that I wouldn't be able to."

"You did the right thing," I said. "But I'm still going to text your dad and let him know Oriana and I are here instead."

"But what if he …" Jack said.

"Reckon he'll think you were resourceful," I said. "Resourceful's good. Means you can think of what to do on your own when there's a problem, and that's what you did. So —quick text, then lunch, and you and me doing the washing-up, *then* basketball."

"OK," he said. "It's going to rain, but Dad says a little rain never stops a sportsman."

"Too right," I said, somehow forgetting that I had exactly zero items of clothing in this house now. I only realized it when Jack and I came into the house again after our game, soaked to the skin. Oriana looked up from the puzzle she was doing with the girls and said, "Better go get in the shower,

Jack, and get warmed up and changed. Cocoa all round afterward, I'd say, and ... mm, maybe baking some cookies? What do we think about that idea?" as if it were the most normal thing in the world.

Then, of course, she looked at me and laughed.

I grinned back at her and said, "Yeh. Drew's about the same size as me, but I'm not good with going into his bedroom and looking out clothes. Feels like a step too far. Drip-dry, you reckon?"

"No," she said. "Go use the guest bath. Get your own shower, but drop your clothes outside the door first and I'll put them in the dryer. You can wrap up in a blanket until they're dry."

Grace said, "This is a baby puzzle. I want to do a hard puzzle."

Oriana said, "Just a minute. I need to talk to Gabriel first." She got to her feet, came over to me, and asked, her voice low, "Any news?"

"Yeh," I said. "Text. She had the baby. A boy. Drew asked if we could stay until later tonight, though, as Hannah's a bit rough still. You were right. The neighbor lady fell on the stairs and hit her head, by the way, rushing to get over here. Her husband didn't think about the kids, I guess, until later."

"Oh, what a pity," Oriana said. "I hope she's all right. We'll tell the kids about the baby during cocoa, don't you think? Now go take your shower, please, before you get everything even wetter."

At ten o'clock that evening, I heard a light step in the passage, then saw Oriana heading into Drew and Hannah's enormous, very comfortable family room. I'd hoovered this carpet quite a few times, but I'd definitely never sat alone here at night, and it felt a bit like trespassing.

Oriana said, "She's asleep again," then sat on the sectional couch beside me—well, technically beside me, as she was all the way at the other end—and asked, "What's happened?"

In the film, she meant. I said, "Same place. I paused it. I'll start it again."

This was the second time I'd done that, because Madeleine had woken crying twice now, calling for her mum, and I'd been more than glad of Oriana's presence. When I'd gone to take a quick look, she'd been sitting on the bed, stroking Madeleine's hair, crooning a lullaby that I remembered my mum singing to the younger kids.

> *"May thou sleep, may thou rest,*
> *May thy slumber be blessed.*
> *May thou sleep, may thou rest,*
> *May thy slumber be blessed."*

She had a sweet singing voice, soft and low and a little husky, and the little girl's face showed nothing but peace. Nothing but trust. I'd felt like an eavesdropper, watching them this way, but something in my chest had caught and twisted hard, and I hadn't been able to move until the song was over.

Ever since we'd got here, in fact, Oriana had taken quiet charge, organizing lunch for the kids, then asking the girls to show her their toys and getting down on the carpet and playing with them, making them feel like this was fun, like it was normal, while I took Jack outside to play basketball.

Now, I sat on the couch in my dry clothes, my stomach still pleasantly full from the shepherd's pie she'd cobbled together for dinner with no fuss and complete assurance, and looked at her. She was curled up against the end of the couch in the low light, watching the film, not looking at me. Then *really* not looking at me.

Oh.

The film had seemed all right from the description. "Romantic comedy," it was called, but then, that was what that first porno book I'd read had been called, too. We'd been watching for more than an hour, and nobody had even kissed anybody yet, so I'd relaxed. There had been heaps of what people called "flirting," which was pretty sexy, but not ... well, not having such an obvious effect on me. Now, though, the two people were kissing on the stairs of an office building, then kissing some more as the bloke opened the door to his apartment. They fell through the door, kissing still, then started to unbutton shirts, their own and the other person's, and the fella slammed the door, then got that last button undone on the girl's filmy shirt, pulled it out of the waistband of her skirt, and dropped it to the floor. All of it frantic, and the woman making some little noises in the back of her throat.

She was wearing a bra under that shirt. The kind of bra I'd never seen before, coming only halfway up her breasts, and my eyes were ... well, they couldn't have looked anywhere else, that was all. The bloke seemed to feel the same way, because he was holding her, kissing her, his hand sliding up her side to cup her there, seeming like he wanted to *eat* her.

Which he probably did. The eating thing had featured heavily in those books, if I haven't mentioned it.

I hoped Oriana wasn't looking at me, because there was no way to hide what was going on with me without actually crossing my hands over my groin. I glanced at her fast. She was sitting up straighter, her eyes fixed on the screen, her mouth a little open, and I'd swear she was breathing hard.

The two people were in bed now, kissing again. Close-ups of faces, his back, her shoulder, a big hand sliding down a slim torso. The man over the woman, and neither of them wearing anything on top. Oriana must have seen me glance at her, because now, she *did* look at me. Just for a second, and then she was looking away again fast.

I said, "Maybe—" Then had to stop and clear my throat. "Maybe not, eh." What would she think of me, choosing this, *watching* this? What would Daisy and Gray think of me, if they knew?

"Oh," she said. "Yes. Probably not. I, uh ... I don't usually ... I don't normally ..."

"Me neither," I said, and pressed the button to stop the film.

We sat there in silence for a minute, and then Oriana said, "Of course, now we won't know what happens."

"You're right," I said. "Not very satisfying. Maybe we should ..."

"Yes," she said. "Just so we'll know."

I pushed the button again.

When I finally turned the set off, I realized she'd fallen asleep sometime when I was doing that not-looking. Curled up tight, her head on the arm of the couch. Uncomfortable, that looked, and not nearly warm enough. I took the fuzzy blanket from the back of the couch and draped it over her, and she made a little noise and snuggled in closer, so I lifted her head carefully and slid a cushion under it.

There. That was better.

Asleep, she looked seventeen, or like the way people Outside viewed girls of seventeen. Her face unlined, her hand clutching the edge of the blanket, all of her curled up like a child. Today, though—

She hadn't been a child, had she? Taking charge of the kids the way she had, doing everything that had to be done, all of her calm and sure and ...

Happy.

Resourceful.

Wishful thinking, I told myself. *You know you can't ask. You know you can't hope.*

I knew better. I wouldn't ask, but I'd still hope. I wouldn't be able to help it.

14

POSSIBLY AWKWARD

ORIANA

I got to Biology, my first class, early the next morning, both drained and supercharged from the day before, not to mention the night. I hadn't had nearly as much sleep as usual, and I'd dreamed too much when I'd finally dropped off, but all the fatigue was doing was giving me a sort of a fizzing feeling in my blood, and in my ... in all sorts of parts of me.

Aisha's head went up when I came into the classroom, but she didn't smile. I slid into my seat and said, "Hi. Thanks again for the cake."

"You didn't even *eat* any," she said.

"Yes, I did. I ate a piece of each when I got home. The lemon was my favorite. It was lovely. You must have used real lemons, and heaps of butter. The glaze was excellent also."

"I don't want to talk about the *cake*."

"You just *said*—" I started, but she waved an imperious hand, and I subsided. "Then what?"

"Normally," she said, "when you invite somebody over, you don't *leave*. You especially don't leave them alone with your truly bizarre relations!"

"Oh. I thought you were interested. You *seemed* interested."

"When you were *there*. It was a fascinating sociological study when you were there. I thought I was about to be conscripted into the cult, and those were the people who *left*! What must the rest of them be like? And I thought *I* had an odd family. It was a good thing I knew Frankie a bit, that's all. I told myself that she'd help me escape. She's escaped from being kidnapped by the cult twice before. Third time's the charm, eh."

My face froze over. That's the only way I can think of to say it, the way it took an effort to make my mouth move so the words could come out. "That's not ..." I tried to say. "It's not ..."

"Oh." Aisha didn't look quite at me for once. "Sorry. That was awful, I guess. Being raped and all."

I nodded once, jerkily, then forced myself to say, "I texted you, though. It truly was an emergency. But I didn't think— I didn't know—" I broke off, because I didn't know how to go on.

She said, "Looked to me like you were bunking off, ditching the girlfriend for the hot guy. Not? That's not what *they* thought, because they raised merry hell when they realized you were both gone."

"They did?" Suddenly, I was more interested than uncomfortable. "Everybody was asleep when I got home last night," I tried to explain. "And Gray and Daisy didn't seem fussed this morning."

"*They* weren't the ones. Your aunt and uncle, mainly, but the other women looked pretty shocked, too, especially the one with the cap. Your uncle said, 'I'd never have believed it of Obedience. Fruitful, now ...' Seriously? Her name was *Fruitful?* Could it *be* more cringe? And then *Frankie* said, 'I'd what? Run off with a man? I thought it would be obvious that I'm not interested. I'll never be interested. I'm never getting married, and I'm never having kids.' *Very* combatively, and your uncle said, 'Speaking to me like that isn't acceptable,' and your ... what's Gray, exactly? Not your brother-in-law."

"No," I said. "He's just Gray."

"All I can say is, he must *really* love your sister. So *he* said, 'This is Frankie's home. She can speak up, eh, Daisy.' And after that, everyone was talking. Well, Gray and Daisy and Frankie and your uncle. The rest of them were just sitting there. The women all stared down at their hands, which I thought was odd. I mean, they didn't *move*. Just sort of shrank into themselves, at least until the baby started crying, and then they all went into the other room like it was an escape hatch. All five of them together, though I don't think Patience wanted to. She needs a new name. Trans people have dead names that you aren't allowed to use anymore. That's what all of you should have. Though you won't know about trans people either, I'm sure. Brace yourself for a shock, because I'm about to tell you."

"I know about trans people," I said. "That's a woman who was a man before, right? I have a friend who's that. Well, she's a bit my boss, but she's a friend, too. Iris. She lives at the bottom of the garden. She used to come to dinner with us more, but she doesn't like all the new people much, so I only see her when we're working now."

"I don't blame her a bit," Aisha said. "I can just imagine how *that* would go. And I got a lift home from Daisy, thanks for asking."

"Oh," I said. "Good. She's a very good driver. I have my Restricted license now, but I still can't—"

Aisha stared at me. "I don't *care* if she's a good driver. Are you *dense?* Wait, don't answer. All right, you don't know how odd it is to leave your guest to get home on her own, but I don't care. I want to *know*. Gabriel's about the best-looking man I've ever seen in my *life,* including in films. And his *body*. His thighs. His *shoulders*. So that was all? It *was* the emergency, not actually running off together?" She sighed. "Disappointing. But—wait. He's your cousin."

"Yes."

"Ick. But they're probably all marrying their cousins out there, I guess. It's a wonder you don't all have cleft palates or two heads."

On the one hand, I wanted the clock to move forward and Biology to start. On the other hand, I desperately wanted to keep talking about this. It was like excitement, but not comfortable excitement. I was getting familiar with the feeling, as I'd had it for most of two days now. "No," I said. "You can't marry your cousin, not your first cousin. That's why the Prophet's so careful with matching people. Uncle Aaron wasn't Gabriel's father, though. So he's a ... step-cousin, I guess. Not a relation, or not in the ... the past couple of generations."

"*Ohh.*" It was an *extremely* knowing syllable, and I knew I was blushing. "So it *was* ..."

"No," I said. "He just ... he took me outside because it was a bit awful, with the cake and all, and he had a gift for me. Which was kindness, that's all. And then he got that call, and—"

"Wait," she said. "I was just deciding he was gay, if he's not married yet, and he's so beautiful. I guess you'd have to be in the closet in Mount Zion. *Is* there a closet big enough in Mount Zion? Or you'd have to pretend, but how do you pretend, if you're meant to have all those kids?"

"He's not *gay,*" I said.

"How do you know?" she asked.

"I ..." I tried to think what to say. Which was when Mr. Smith called the class to order, and I didn't get to say anything.

LUNCHTIME, and Aisha slid in opposite me at our table and said, not bothering to ease into it, "He seems gay to me. Men like that, young ones, who are kind like that, especially if they're beautiful? That's usually because they're gay, at least according to my cousin who's at uni. Which would be a problem at my house, too," she went on, taking a giant bite of her sandwich, "but it's not a problem for me. Just a pity that kindness doesn't get passed down through the genes. Gay men can't reproduce together," she informed me when I must have looked puzzled.

"Obviously, I know that," I said.

"Oh," she said. "I thought you probably didn't know anything about sex. *I* don't exactly know how that actually works, gay sex. I've heard, but ... I can't imagine, really. Sounds so *uncomfortable.*"

"The family lives in one room at Mount Zion. And it's farming. Of course I know about sex. Dominant male alpacas will have sex with the younger males if you're not careful, so I even know about gay sex. I've *seen* gay sex. Well, in alpacas, and it *is* uncomfortable. Or more like painful." I was never cross, but I was cross now. "And Gabriel isn't gay. It doesn't matter that he's not married, because that's not his choice. I told you. It's the Prophet."

"Maybe the Prophet knows he's gay," she said. "And that's why."

"He's not *gay!*" I may have said it a little loudly, because some of the other girls at the table looked over. I lowered my voice. "I know he isn't, because we were watching a film last night, with a man and woman kissing and all, and he got ..."

"What?" Aisha asked.

"You know." I didn't know the word for it. "When their penis gets hard."

Her eyes widened, and then she choked on her sandwich. After she'd coughed a bit, she managed to say, "You *know* about that? You were raised in a cult! You go to a girls' school! *I've* never even seen that!"

"You haven't?" I tried to imagine how not. "What about when you've given your brother a bath?"

"I didn't do that. I'm not his mum. And it doesn't happen to *babies.*"

"Of course it does." I was never the person who knew, not if it wasn't about cooking or sewing or something. *Sewing. Pay attention.* "It happens to all boys," I said. "Even tiny babies. In their bath, especially, and anyway, when your brothers get up in the morning, you can see. Your dad, too."

"Your *dad?*" She looked literally horror-struck.

"Well, yeh. How do you think babies happen?"

She was shaking her head, then putting her forehead in her hand. "I'm rearranging my thoughts here," she informed me. "So was that awkward, when he got … that? Or is that just like, oh, haha, I notice you're enjoying the film? Because of the big families and farming and emphasis on reproduction and all? I actually have no idea which."

"Of course you don't *say* you noticed. You don't *look.* Well, you don't look at men anyway, but you *really* don't look at that. Except that I'm supposed to look at Gabriel, but I still can't, quite, so I don't look at his face, which is why I saw. But …"

"What was it like?" she asked.

Now I was the one staring. "Like?"

"I mean, is it really noticeable? Sort of big and pushing out their trousers? It can't be, though, or you'd see it all the time. You couldn't not notice *that.* Was his bigger than your brothers'? Well, if they're little brothers, obviously, but …"

I said, "I can't … compare. Sorry."

I should have been horribly embarrassed, and I was, but I also wanted to giggle like mad. In fact, a giggle did make its way out, Aisha's face cracked, too, and we were laughing like I hadn't done with anybody but my sisters. Hanging onto the table, nearly crying with it. Aisha gasped, "I think I just peed," and I laughed harder. The other girls at the table were definitely looking at us oddly now, but I didn't care.

When we were done wheezing and were wiping our eyes with napkins, Aisha said, "This is why it's good that we're not allowed to wear makeup. OK. You said he took you outside to give you a present, which is why I thought he *wasn't* gay. Just taking you outside ... how old is he, though?"

"I don't know. Twenty-four? Twenty-five? I'm not sure. He's the eldest, though."

"Oh. Forbidden love, then. A bit creepy for him to take you outside at all. No, *really* creepy. Pity, as he's really just incredibly hot. You're not meant to say that about predators, though. So tricky."

"He's not a *predator*. How? That's normal, his age. Radiance —the one in the cap—she's seventeen and has the baby, and Glory is *barely* seventeen. And their husbands are almost as old as Gabriel. It's normal."

"Maybe in the Bible," Aisha said. "Or in Yemen. So what was the present?"

I stopped wanting to giggle. The color flared up in my face, too. I could feel it. Aisha said, "What? You watched a sexy film, *and* he gave you a sexy gift, *and* he's about old enough to be your *dad*? Predator much?"

"He's not old enough to be my dad," I said, feeling cross again. "And it wasn't a sexy gift. It was the *best* gift."

"Was it scent? Or—wait. Jewelry? Was it a promise ring, with a vow to wait for you until he's thirty and you're finally old enough to be married?"

"You're just being silly. And it was better than that. It was the best present possible."

It had been this morning—very early this morning, that is. By the time Gabriel had driven me home, after a midnight arrival by a rumpled-looking Drew, I'd been both sleepy and agitated, as if my fur had been rubbed the wrong way. Now that it was over—the couch, the film, all of it—I didn't know what to make of it. I didn't know how to *be*.

Gabriel punched in the code for Gray's gate, rolled down

the drive in the ute, then just sat there. It was quite warm in the ute—he'd put in a good heater, he'd explained—but I shivered anyway. Neither of us had a jacket. We'd run off just that fast.

He must have noticed, because he said, "You're cold. I should let you go in."

"No." I wanted to go in, and I wanted to stay here. Desperately, on both counts. I didn't see how that could be true, and I also, unfortunately, couldn't think of anything to say. "I had a good time," I finally said. A girl had said that in a book I'd read, when she'd gone on a date. This wasn't a date, but it was the closest I could come.

He smiled ruefully and rubbed a hand over his jaw. I saw it, though I wasn't exactly looking. "You almost seemed like you did," he said. "Which is odd, maybe."

"No. It's the things I like. Cooking, and kids, and ... and being normal. At home. Normal at home. Even though 'home' isn't the same now."

"Yeh." He sighed. "I want to give you something. I'm a bit nervous about it. That's why I haven't done it yet, but I'll feel pretty foolish if I drive home with it still in the back of the ute."

I'd forgotten. I couldn't *believe* I'd forgotten. "Nobody's ever given me a gift before," I said, "other than Daisy buying us clothes and things when we left Mount Zion. I'll be happy, whatever it is. I won't know any better," I tried to joke.

He smiled, and his smile was so sweet, something happened in my insides. A sort of fluttering. I'd almost never seen Gabriel smile, because he was serious and quiet, like me. "You always say the things I think," he said. "About liking being normal at home and so forth. I've never given anyone a gift, either. Reckon I'd better get over myself and do it, or you'll be falling asleep on me again."

There. That had been a joke. I laughed, and he said, "Right, I'm doing it," and got out of the ute.

I sat there, tried to tell myself, *It's nothing. Or it's a kind thing, that's all.* But it didn't work.

He opened my door, and I jumped. "I realized," he said, "that I'd better carry it in for you. You can't really hold it in your lap and open it. Too heavy."

It felt like something out of a movie, walking up the ramp to the yurt in the dark behind him. Like the movie we'd watched. I opened the door as quietly as I could, wished and feared that he'd kiss me like in that movie, hoped desperately that Frankie wouldn't wake up, and kicked off my shoes. Gabriel seemed to understand, because he set the big box down on the floor—it did look heavy—and took off his own boots, then padded over to the table with me and set it on top.

It was wrapped in bright paper, like in a movie. The paper said *Happy Birthday* all over in different multicolored letters, and it was pink. I said, "You did paper." Keeping my voice down to a near-whisper.

"Yeh," he said back, just as low. "Paper's important, Jack said."

"Jack?" I asked, my hands on the box, not wanting to tear the paper off just yet, wanting to savor this moment. "You mean, *kid* Jack?"

He grinned, and this time, it looked sheepish. "My guide to Outside, because he doesn't laugh at me when I ask."

"Oh. I wondered how you knew so many things." I wanted to laugh myself, but that would wake Frankie, so I just smiled. "OK," I told him. "I'm opening it. Here I go."

A<small>ISHA HAD PICKED</small> up her sandwich again, but when I told her, she stopped with it halfway to her mouth and stared at me. "A *sewing* machine?"

"It isn't new, of course," I said, "but it's lovely. A Brother, and it came in a case. Gabriel said he'd had the lady show him that it worked, but if something was wrong after all, he'd fix it. He can fix anything. He fixed his ute, and ... anyway. I haven't had a chance to try it out, but I'm dying to, tonight."

"This is your romantic gift," Aisha said flatly. "A sewing machine. Did you *want* a sewing machine?"

"I wanted it so much."

"Lucky for him, then. One girl in a million, I reckon. How did he know?"

"Because I said I didn't want one."

"Oh," she said. "Well, that makes perfect sense."

"Yes," I said dreamily. "It does. If you pay attention."

15

AFTER-PARTY

G*abriel*

My dad said, when we were waiting for the safety meeting to begin on Monday morning—the Mount Zion crew tended to arrive early—"You decided to join us today after all, then."

"Pardon?" I looked at my brothers. They looked away.

"You seem confused about your loyalties," my dad said. "About your morals as well."

I didn't know what to say. My dad had almost never reprimanded me, because I'd never needed it. I wasn't impulsive, and I'd never been rebellious. I settled on, "How have I offended?"

"Taking Oriana out of the house," he said, "when we were in the midst of a family discussion about her behavior. Then taking her farther than that without asking permission. Your mum had just told Patience the week before in front of all of us that a girl doesn't ride in a car alone with a man, but you asked her to do exactly that. It's your job to lead, and instead, you led her astray."

I wanted to say, *I told Gray what was happening, though, and Oriana told Daisy*. I didn't, because it sounded like justification, like weakness. I thought hard about what to say instead. What I ended up with was, "I'm a grown man. Men make decisions. When Drew's family needed help, I made mine."

His face hardened, and my brothers looked stunned. Small wonder. I'd never expressed anything even close to that. Uriel could be hasty. Argumentative, even. Me? No.

"What's Oriana, though?" my dad said. "Not a grown man. A young girl."

"And Daisy's responsibility," I said. "Not ..." I wanted to say, "Not yours," but settled for, "And she's seventeen. Old enough to choose where to live as soon as she turned sixteen. That's what they do here, and that's the point, isn't it? Isn't it why we left? To have a choice?"

Now, my dad looked weary, and I felt a pang of guilt. He'd let us walk out, and then he'd come with us. He'd given us our freedom, and he'd given me so much more. Training. Guidance. An example. He said, his voice gentler, "You can't have it both ways, son. Either you're living by the rules laid down by God, or the rules of the world. Are you sure you want to follow this path?"

"Can't there be a ... a mixture?" I asked. *"Isn't* there a mixture? Mum's driving now. She's got a job. Daisy's living in Gray's house, having relations with him outside of marriage."

"Those things aren't the same in any way," he said. "And do you approve of what Daisy's doing, then? Does God? Should I let Harmony run off with any bloke she fancies, have relations with him outside marriage, have a bastard child, if that's what she wants? Should I stand back and let her endanger her immortal soul? Is that what you want for your sister, or for Oriana? Or for Patience?"

I'd have answered—somehow—but the meeting started, and afterward, there was no time for talk. Not until morning smoko.

I was sitting with the other blokes on my crew, my jacket zipped against the chill, half-listening to the banter and trying to calm the storm inside me, when my dad walked up and said, "Gabriel. A word."

"Uh-oh," Afoa said, giving his belly laugh. "Sounds ominous, bro."

I didn't answer. I just stood up, walked to my dad, and waited.

His face was somber, and I got an actual pain in my chest at how I was disappointing him. He said, "Let's sit." We perched on a bit of framing, and he finally went on. "I've been thinking. Talked to your mum last night as well, so you know. I'm not saying women can't have a say in their lives. That's why we left, because we both wanted a say in our lives. But the things happening at Gray's house … I can't approve. Not of Daisy, and not of Frankie. Not of Gray, for that matter. Far as I can see, he's got no plans to marry Daisy. What kind of love is that, when a man subjects a woman to the judgment of the world?"

"Is the world judging?" I had to ask.

My dad's sober eyes met mine. "Her family is. And so is God. It's not working out, all of us being employed by Gray, living on his land, having those family dinners at his house. He's the younger, and it's not his family, but in his house, with him handing out the pay, he has the final say. Those are the rules Outside, and by living here, we've chosen to abide by them, but that doesn't mean we have to put ourselves in that position." A pause, then. "Or subject ourselves to temptation. Can you honestly look at me and tell me you weren't tempted to sin yesterday?"

"No," I said. "I can't. But I can tell you that I didn't sin."

He sighed again, and it hurt me to cause my father pain. It hurt more, though, to hear what he said next. "Temptation is hard to resist. That's why it's called temptation. Oriana's a good girl. I understand you gave her a gift yesterday. Something we don't do. Something that singled her out. Do you want to hurt her?"

"No," I said.

"Then let her live her life." His dark eyes, so different from my own blue ones, were steady on mine. Not really my dad, and my dad all the way. "She's chosen to live by the world's rules, and maybe that's best for her, given what her sisters are doing. You're in neither one world nor the other here, though. Too old for her by the world's rules, and endangering her soul by God's. And do you imagine Gray will still employ you if you're pursuing her like this? A man of nearly twenty-five?"

I had no answer for that. He said, "I can tell you. He won't. It's not fair to him to put him in that position, as good as he's been to us. You aren't doing her any favors by anybody's rules, and you're hurting yourself as well. I can't let that happen to my family. You're my son in every way that matters, and I have to do what's best for you. For all of us."

I tried to imagine what that was, but I couldn't. *Not all of us quitting*, I thought. *Please*. Gray was a good employer. Where would we find a better? But how could I break with my dad? With my entire family? After I'd already left the only home I'd ever known? It was a panicky feeling. Rudderless.

Lost at sea.

Dad put me out of my suspense. "We owe him our gratitude, and our best effort on the job, too, as we'd owe any employer. And we owe him our distance, so he's not put in this spot again. From now on, there'll be no more family dinners. We'll all contribute to get Uriel and Glory their own housing, and your mum and I will take Patience. She can share a room with Harmony, and we can keep her from going the same way as Daisy. She's too pretty for the world and its temptations, and that spirit she has ... it could turn her willful, especially living with the two of them. She'll need a good husband to keep her on the right path. And you won't be alone with Oriana again."

I wanted to say, *No. I can't*. It was a sudden, sharp pain, like catching your hand on a nail and feeling the flesh rip. My dad looked at me some more, though, and asked again, "Do you want to hurt her?"

"No," I said, and swallowed.

I'd known the whole idea was impossible. I'd known it was wrong.

There was no choice.

Oriana

"What?" I was bleary-eyed from lack of sleep, aching to get to the sewing machine, longing to be alone and think about every detail of the day before, to live it over and over again in my mind. Instead, I'd come home, done my homework, and cooked dinner, telling myself, *You can wait. You know how to wait.* And had felt the pull of my thoughts as if they were a rope fastened to my chest. Now, I was sitting at the dinner table, listening to ... *what?*

Gray looked tired. "I only know what I'm telling all of you. That Aaron says I'll have the caravan back at the beginning of July, and that he doesn't think it's best for the dinners to continue."

"But ... why?" I asked.

Frankie looked up from where she'd been reading her Chemistry book while she ate—she seemed to look for everything she could possibly do to break Mount Zion rules—and said, "Obviously because we're too worldly and corrupting. Probably because you ran off with Gabriel, Oriana. Endangering his immortal soul, you temptress. As you *baby-sat.*"

"But I—" I tried to say, *I wouldn't. I didn't.* But I would have if I could, and I knew it. Last night, I'd wanted him to kiss me against the door the way we'd seen, to hold me like that.

To take off my clothes.

"That's probably not it," Daisy said, as matter-of-factly as always. "Oriana isn't much of a temptress. Probably just that

Uncle Aaron's realized he can't have things his way in Gray's house."

"Our house," Gray said.

"Well, no," Daisy said. "Yours. We both know it, and so does he. It's yours, and the firm's yours, and you have too much power. He didn't realize it at first, because he didn't know how things work, but now he does, and he's trying to draw some boundaries. Sensible, really, and I can't pretend that yesterday was fun. Only going to get worse, I imagine, as everybody finds their way, and do we need all that drama every month? Who'll be the first to crack? My money's on Uriel. He's got a rebellious look in his eye, and Glory and Patience *weren't* in long skirts yesterday, did you notice?"

"My money's on Patience," Frankie said. "Once she goes to school?" She slammed the edge of her hand onto the table with decision. "Crack city. *She's* not going to a girls' school. How long will it be before she turns up at the door here, asking for a room? Are you going to give it to her?"

"Of course I am," Daisy said serenely. "If Gray agrees."

Gray said, "I'll do whatever works."

"For Daisy," Frankie said.

"Yes," he said. "For Daisy."

Daisy and Gray did the washing-up. I went into my room, closed the door, and went to my desk. The white case sat where my schoolbooks normally stood, and I sat down, unbuckled the cover, lifted it off, and ran my hand over the sleek white machine. I plugged in the foot pedal and the power cord, and lifted the presser foot up and down. Then I found a bit of fabric, positioned it carefully, dropped the presser foot, and depressed the pedal.

No bobbin. No spool of thread. No needle. Just a turning, whirring machine, trying and failing to make something happen.

When the first tear fell on the white plastic, I released the fabric and used it to mop it up. I couldn't get salt water on my beautiful sewing machine that Gabriel had bought me with the money he'd saved, that he'd fastened down under a tarp against the weather, that he'd carried into the house for me. That he'd wrapped in pink *paper.* I'd folded the paper neatly and laid it beside the machine, and now, I stroked my hand over it. It was shiny, and slick, and so cheerful.

Happy Birthday, written all over it, because he'd wanted me to be happy. To have a present. To have a cake. To blow out candles.

He'd bought me *pink.*

When my throat closed, my chest heaved, and the sobs came, I buried my face in that scrap of fabric.

I'd brought shame on my family. I'd caused so much trouble. Daisy wouldn't say it, but Gray knew. That was why he'd looked so sad, and so tired. He'd done everything he could to help Daisy, to help *us,* and I'd ruined it, because I'd wanted too much. Because I'd wanted a birthday, and more than that. I'd wanted Gabriel, and somehow, they all knew.

I couldn't have him even if he'd wanted me, though, because I was too young.

I'd thought that, when we were out of Mount Zion, we could make our own rules, but there were always rules.

I couldn't sit anymore. I lay down on the bed on my stomach, held the pillow tight, and cried into it, so Frankie wouldn't hear. So Gray wouldn't hear. So Daisy wouldn't hear, after she'd risked everything—risked her *life*—to get us out.

I didn't know how to do things right. I tried and tried, but I could never seem to work out how to do this. How to go to school and like it. How to be with my family and stay in the background like I always had, like I was supposed to do, and not ask for things. It was like the needs just came out anyway, and everybody could see them.

I couldn't hurt Gray. I couldn't hurt my uncle and aunt, who'd always been so kind.

And, oh, how I couldn't hurt Gabriel.

16

ANOTHER BIRTHDAY

Oriana

Winter passed, like winter always did, and spring came. I never saw Gabriel now, and only heard anything of him and the rest from Gray. I told myself that it was for the best, and if I thought of him at night ... well, I knew pain. I'd left my mum and my sisters, my cousins and my friends and the life I'd known, and now, I'd left Gabriel, or he'd left me, or, more likely, there was nothing there to leave. I had to go on, because I couldn't go back, and besides—"pursuing your dreams" isn't exactly a value you're brought up with in Mount Zion. So I sewed myself new clothes on the machine he'd given me, grateful for the gift every time I used it, learning from my mistakes and discovering how to find inexpensive remnants of the beautiful fabrics I craved, just enough for a pair of flowing trousers or a soft shirt. I rode the bus to school with Frankie and watched lambs frolicking in the paddocks and new buds swelling on the trees, and, back at home again, helped Iris prune the fruit trees and prepare the beds for spring planting, clean the beehives and install new ones, and, most excitingly, shear our little herd of silken-fleeced Suri alpacas for the first time.

Cream, fawn, brown, black, and white, their fleece falling away to make blankets of fibers soft as cashmere, warmer than wool, with a luster that could only be compared to silk. We cleaned and combed the fleece into roving, then sent it to the processing mill and got it back as ... yarn. *Beautiful* yarn, which would yield garments with the most wonderful drape. Some of it, we sold at the market, giving Gray his share of the proceeds, Iris most of the rest, and measuring out a percentage for me. That last had been Gray's idea. He'd said, "It may be my land and my cash outlay, but it's your labor and your idea, and you deserve to profit from it." More money in my savings account.

Some of the yarn, though, I held back. I bought for a wholesale price I worked out with Gray, which he kindly advanced me against profits, because I had a plan.

People would pay so *much* for hand-knitted garments, I'd noticed from the other market stalls, if you were good enough at making them, if they were truly beautiful, if they could feel that they'd got a "find." The tourists would pay the most of all. They liked the small, easy pieces, without sizes, that they could pack into their luggage and give as gifts, and they liked them more if they heard the story behind them. I knew that, because I talked with them every Saturday as I sold them honey and jam, springtime rhubarb and asparagus, and the pale-green and blue Araucana eggs that were everybody's favorites. I noticed what they lingered over, and how excited they got about anything "authentic." They wanted to remember their time in New Zealand, and they wanted gifts to take home. So, one day in early October, I took a breath, told myself, *If it doesn't work, I'll sell the yarn instead,* and started my venture.

Every night, as spring warmed into summer, when Frankie was working out quadratic equations and chemistry problems in her exercise book from her favorite spot at the kitchen bench, I made us a pot of tea, sat in the chair that looked out at the soft light in the garden, and knitted luxurious scarves and hats and fingerless gloves with a mitten flap, experimenting with cables and ribbing and bands of colorwork and, best of all, lace. Black and gray and brown for men, but mostly, beautiful things for women. White and cream and fawn, because they were so lovely, but also something extra. I learnt to hand-dye the yarns and worked with colored pencils to find the shades I wanted, mixtures of reds and oranges, of soft pinks and peaches and creams. My favorite colorway, though, was a glorious melding of vibrant blues, greens, and purples that became my bestseller. There was that pride again, but surely, God couldn't hate your pride in working hard to make something beautiful from His gifts.

I tied each completed set into a bundle with rattan ribbons, put a sprig of dried lavender under the bow, and hand-lettered brown gift tags with my name and the name of the animal. Across the top, I wrote, *Lavender Hill Farm, Otago, New Zealand*, because that was the name Iris and I had given to our enterprise. All of it in dark blue ink, using a fountain pen and my best handwriting, so it looked authentic again. Personal, and special. My Mount Zion schooling had taught me beautiful handwriting. It was about the only thing that was actually useful.

I knitted at night, and I knitted more when it wasn't my turn to make dinner. I knitted on the bus, during my babysitting jobs, and before my classes, and I knitted at lunch, once I'd finished eating and cleaned my hands.

Aisha told me, the first day I brought my work in to school, "That's intensely odd of you," and I said, "But I *am* intensely odd. You already knew that. Besides, I can talk and knit at the same time," and kept on doing it. If Daisy could become a nurse practitioner, if Frankie could catch up two missed years of school and go to university, if even Aunt Constance could get a job, why couldn't I knit scarves? People Outside didn't think anything was worth doing unless other people paid money for it, and I wasn't going to make any money out of my biology knowledge.

Summer came, and two things happened. First, and most excitingly, three dams in our little alpaca herd gave birth to their crias. The first two births happened while I was at school, as everything I wanted to participate in seemed to do, but for the third, Iris came up to the yurt on a Sunday afternoon and got me.

The joy of watching the skinny little male emerge, all sticklike legs and an elongated tube of a body, with his coat of gorgeous chocolate brown, and the tenderness with which the new mum cleaned her baby ... it gave me gooseflesh. I cleaned up mum under Iris's direction, crooning soft words to her, telling her what a good job she'd done, carrying her baby for nearly a year, then giving birth to him so competently, her very first time. I watched to make sure she got rid of the afterbirth, too. Seeing the cria stagger over on his spindly legs to take his first drink, and the mum's nose nudging him along to the right spot was pure sweetness, and watching him frisk around, still wobbly as anything, with his five-days-older cousin made me laugh. So that was another good thing.

Oh, and I also made it through almost all of Year 11, somehow, and didn't look like failing anything. That was the second thing that happened. I was seventeen and a half, and it was over a year since I'd left Mount Zion.

And then there was the third thing. The warmth of summer was in the air on the early-December day that was my sister Prudence's sixteenth birthday. The day we headed to Mount Zion once more.

The holiday season was in full swing now. My second Christmas Outside. There's no feeling odder than driving through streets decorated with lights and wreaths and a gigantic, bearded figure called "Santa Claus"—the most blasphemous personage I'd ever seen, stuck up onto the outside of the Centre City Mall, beneath whose grinning visage shoppers were coming and going, carrying huge bags stuffed with things they probably didn't even need—and heading for a compound where Christmas was a workday, just a shortened one with an extra-good dinner with a sweet afterward, cooked by women who didn't get a shortened day at all.

This time, we hadn't brought an army. This time, Daisy and Gray and Frankie and I headed for Mount Zion's gate at nine o'clock on Sunday morning, after collecting Honor, Gray's mum, from Honor's house in Wanaka.

Frankie and Prudence and I would be staying in Wanaka over the summer holidays, working for Honor cleaning holiday houses, because Gray and Daisy were going to be moving back into the yurt once the holidays started, and the house wouldn't be available at all. It would be "remodeled" by a crew from Mount Zion, led by my uncle and including my cousins. All three of them. While I was here, in Wanaka. I didn't know whether they'd got Honor to offer those jobs on purpose, just in case I tried to see Gabriel again. They didn't realize that he'd never tried to see me, and that I'd long since realized he'd just been being kind.

Gray never said that was the reason, of course. He said the house was terrible and that it had to be fixed, even though it seemed like a palace to me, full of bedrooms, with a big bathroom and a kitchen twice as large as the one in the yurt, just for one person to cook in.

Whatever the case, it was past time for Gabriel to marry, and he was living in a flat now with other men, probably going on dates, or just having relations with girls after parties, since "dates" seemed to exist only in books, according to what I heard at Otago Girls. That was sad, because "dates" sounded so romantic, but the world didn't seem to be much like what books and films said. Gabriel hadn't seemed like he knew anything more about that than I did, but he wouldn't exactly share it with me if he did, would he? Men had needs. I didn't have to be sent off to Wanaka to know that.

Now, Frankie and I were riding in the back of the car, with Gray and Daisy in front, as we rounded the final curves that would take us to the gate of the compound. Frankie had got more stiff and still with every one of those curves, her hand like a block of ice in mine, and it was time to focus on her.

Daisy had asked, back at Honor's house, "Are you still sure you want to come, love? You can stay here instead, and welcome Prudence when she gets here. I've been back so many times, with all that sneaking in, and it won't bother me to go today. The first time I came back, though, it was awful. I felt like the Prophet could reach out his hand and pull me in again. I've never been more terrified."

"But you came back anyway," Frankie said. "If you could do that, in the middle of the night, with the electric fence and the dogs and all, I can go *once*, during the day, with everybody around me to keep me safe."

"I had to," Daisy said. "You don't. We're here to do it instead."

Gray didn't say anything. He just stood there, big and patient, and waited. Honor, though, said, "Sometimes it's good to face your fear, and the people who made you feel it. Makes you realize they don't have power over you anymore, eh. It'll hurt, though. No shame in not wanting to hurt."

Frankie lifted her chin, her eyes blazing and her face white, and said, "I want to go."

"Fair enough," Gray said. "We'll be beside you all the way."

Frankie's husband, Gilead, wasn't there anymore, because he'd been sent to prison back in August, but everybody at Mount Zion knew who'd put him there. Frankie, and Daisy, to whom he'd done it all first.

It was odder than anything else, Aisha had informed me, that my sisters had both been married to the same man, as soon as they'd turned sixteen. Daisy had run away and got a divorce, and Gilead's second wife had died in childbirth, so the Prophet had given Frankie to Gilead.

Aisha'd said, "That's the most disgusting thing I've ever heard of, and my family's from *Pakistan*." I'd had nothing to say in reply.

No army today, and no cameras. Just Gray and Honor and —the others.

Uncle Aaron and Aunt Constance were coming, too, and they had Gabriel with them. I hadn't seen him. I'd heard, that was all, and I'd tried hard to let it not matter. Raphael and Uriel hadn't wanted to come, and I imagined their wives had wanted to do it even less. The people who'd left over the past six months had told us how the Prophet had raged at them, had damned them when they'd announced their intentions to go. They were shaken even afterward, and said that heaps of others had changed their minds and decided to stay.

It's not fun, being told that you're damned. It's not fun to lose everything.

The most surprising departure had been of the Prophet's grandson, Valor Pilgrim. We'd all been shocked when Valor had walked out the gate, because like Uncle Aaron, he'd been one of the Prophet's favorites. He hadn't even announced beforehand that he was going. He'd just downed tools and walked out.

He wasn't here today for this latest confrontation, and who could blame him? I didn't want to be here myself, but I couldn't do anything else, not when Prudence was inside the gates still, and not when Frankie was coming. Somebody had to hold Frankie's hand, somebody who knew what she was feeling, what it was like.

Daisy, you're thinking, but Daisy was so competent, so confident, it was hard to be weak around her. Daisy had left first, and she'd left hardest, with no support at all, after being punished by her husband the first time she'd tried in a way I couldn't bear to think about. And yet she *had* come back, sneaking in every three months for years on end to inject birth control into arms in a storage shed, in the faint light of a torch, giving women a break from constant pregnancies.

I'd run from that shed myself. I'd run with my father chasing me, and I couldn't even imagine going back to face that again, let alone with the kind of resolute calm Daisy would be showing today. Her only regret was not being able to keep up the birth control. Instead, she and Gray and Uncle Aaron would appear outside the gates at nine o'clock on the first day of every month like clockwork, announcing their presence with a loud-hailer, then standing silent for an hour, ready to accept anybody who wanted to leave. Only nine more people had chosen to go since Uriel and Glory and Patience, but nine was a start.

I was thinking all that, and then I wasn't, because I was climbing down in front of that gate for the first time since I'd left, then taking Frankie's hand once again as she trembled.

Somebody moved up to stand on Frankie's other side, and it was Gabriel. He was the other one who'd come every time. When Uriel had walked out, he'd walked not just to his father, but to his elder brother, too.

I tried not to look at him, or to think about that, the solidity and the strength and the *kindness* of him, because if I thought about it, I got sad again. That was all right, though, because I could tell he wasn't looking at me.

He'd saved somebody's life on the day he'd walked out of Mount Zion. Me? I'd been *terrified* on my own leaving day. I'd been so far from pulling anybody out of a burning car. It had been all I could do to run! I certainly hadn't come up here each month with Daisy and Gray. I'd just have been terrified again. I was terrified now.

It was hard to believe it was really happening, that Prudence could really just walk out. I still remembered the look of her standing there, her arms at her sides, watching us go. That look, and the tears I'd seen on Dove's face, had haunted me for almost a year, but today, for Prudence, it would be over.

But, oh, how I wished we could take Dove, too. How I wished for my mother's arms around me, for her to be there when the work was done, the way she'd always been, small and quiet and loving us even when we weren't good. Most people only loved you when you did what they wanted, it seemed to me. My mum, though—she'd loved us no matter what, like we were still part of her body and she couldn't help it. She loved like an alpaca, steady and quiet and forever.

The loud-hailer, then, Uncle Aaron calling for Prudence to come out. Gray holding up his phone, recording. Frankie getting even more tense. And nobody answering. Nobody appearing.

It wasn't the first of the month. Maybe Prudence hadn't believed we'd come. Or maybe she'd been locked up to keep her here, the same way Frankie had.

What had the Prophet done? Or was it my father?

And what did we do now?

17

KITCHEN BREAK

G*abriel*

I was in two places at once, or maybe three. First—always—so aware of Oriana, whom I hadn't seen for months, that I'd got a lurch of the heart when she'd climbed out of the car, and more of one when she'd taken Frankie's hand. She hadn't even looked at me, though. That day at Drew's, there'd been a connection between us, a kind of warmth from her, and *with* her. When she'd opened the pink paper and seen the sewing machine, she'd stood stock-still, staring at it, then turned a shining face to me and asked, "How did you know?"

"You were sewing all the time, Patience said," I'd tried to explain, so absurdly happy to be the cause of that look. "And then you said you didn't need one, but you said it too fast, so I thought you did. That you might be thinking it was wrong to want something for yourself, the same way you thought it was wrong to want candles. I don't see how it can be wrong, not when you do so much for other people." I kept my voice down so as not to wake Frankie. It was oddly intimate, being with Oriana like this in the midnight-dark house, a single pool of light shining on the table. I felt the fatigue in her, but it was a relaxed kind of thing, a *together* kind of thing, the way you feel after a hard workday, sitting in the sun with your mates and letting your tired muscles rest.

"It's the most wonderful present," she said, her hands stroking over the machine. "You're ... you've been so wonderful today. All of today. Thank you."

In films, when the girl looked at the man like that, he'd put a hand on her face, bend his head, and kiss her. Gently, if she was a gentle person, if it was a tender moment like this one, the two of them floating on a pool of light in the quiet dark.

If she was a gentle person. A person he couldn't bear to scare, and couldn't bear to hurt.

Do you want to hurt her? My dad's voice, and he was right. She was seventeen, and she was on her own path.

And today, she wasn't looking at me.

Anyway, there was Frankie, too: the tension in her, and the fear. I had to pay attention to that. That was the point.

But Prudence wasn't coming to the gate, and she wanted to leave. Everybody knew that.

Prudence had been Frankie's closest sister in spirit, because they were alike. Independent. Outspoken. Bold at games, and brilliant at school. Unwomanly, the Prophet had said. You'd think he'd be glad to see them go. So why wasn't she coming out?

Gray was holding the loud-hailer now, calling, "Prudence Worthy? We're here for you. You're sixteen today. Free to go."

More silence, and then Daisy grabbed the loud-hailer and said, "Prudence. It's Daisy. We're all here. Me, and Frankie, and Oriana. We're all out, and we're happy. Come out and change your name. Come out and choose your life."

Nothing, and we were all staring at each other. Finally, I said, "How did you get over that electric fence, Daisy, when you left?"

"Pulled it down carefully," she said, "pinching the safe bits between my fingers, and staked it to the ground. At night, when nobody could see me."

"Then," I said, "let's do it now, and I'll go."

Did I want to? Absolutely not. Did I need to? Absolutely.

"You can't," Daisy said. "They'll call the police. You can be fined. You could get a record."

I looked at Gray. "Going to stop employing me if I have a record?"

"No," he said.

My dad said, "I'll go with you."

My mum said, "And so will I."

Movement from beyond Frankie, and Oriana said, controlling her voice with what I could tell was an effort, "I'll go. Prudence risked everything to get Frankie free, and I know she wanted to come. She's wanted to since she learnt Frankie and I were going. Frankie can't go inside. It's too hard. But I can."

She didn't look at me when she said it, and she didn't look at my dad, either. Even a year in, she still seemed to have trouble looking at men. She'd always been a bit timid, in fact. How could she be offering to do this?

Because love was more important than fear, that was why, and in Oriana, love would always win.

"No," Daisy said. "If anybody goes, it should be me."

"You'll do nothing but put their backs up," my dad said. "And you've got a position to lose."

"I don't," Gray said, "as I own the firm."

"You're an outsider," my dad said. "We're not. And I don't think you should come," he told my mum.

"You're not going in there without me," she said. My mum was normally quiet, like me, but when she was determined, there was no moving her. "You stay here, Oriana. You're very nearly a child."

"I'm not a child," Oriana said. "I'm seventeen." She was stiff with tension, but she was saying it. "I was past old enough to marry when I left, and that's not a child. I didn't have to leave. I chose to leave, and now I need to get my sister. If she needs persuading, I can persuade her."

"I want to go," Frankie said, "but I can't. I *can't.*" She was feeling how close Prudence was, I thought, and how locked away.

Gray said, "We should decide."

"We've decided," my dad said. "Constance and me, and Gabriel and Oriana." Not caring about our being together now, I noticed, but then, this wasn't exactly a romantic situation. "Take those videos with your phone that you do, Gray, showing us going in, and if we're not back in half an hour, call the police. I've got stakes in the boot we can use for the fence. Gabriel, come help me."

I got shocked once doing it, and it didn't feel good, but I'd been shocked before on this fence, out with the animals as a kid. When we had the wicked white webbing staked, my dad jumped across, and then my mum did, lifting her long skirts with one hand and leaping like a Valkyrie. I looked at Oriana and asked, "Ready?"

"Ready," she said. "I've done it before." She was terrified, I'd swear, but she was jumping, and then I was following after.

Across the bare ground of the deserted yard, the four of us, and I could feel the eyes on me. Oriana said, "We should check the Punishment Hut. That's the logical place."

"Two and two," my dad said. "More chance to get her, and less chance to get stopped. Your mum and I will check the dormitories and the school and the nursery, Gabriel. You and Oriana check the Punishment Hut and the laundry and kitchen. Those are the most likely, where she'd be in a group. If you find her, text us. If we get stopped, get out yourselves. You can't do any good from inside."

I looked at Oriana. "OK?"

She was nearly shaking, but she nodded. I said, "If they try to hold us, that's why we left the others outside the gate. Daisy and Gray know how to raise a stink. They've done it before, right?"

"Right," she said. "Let's go."

There was no point in sneaking. Everybody had to know we were here. Where were they, though?

We were past the milking shed, empty now, this long past dawn. Knocking at the rough boards of the Punishment Hut next door, calling out, then listening with an ear against the wood. The padlock was on the door, but it was always on.

Nothing.

Oriana said, "Laundry." Her voice had steadied, as if leaping across the fence had committed her. She led the way across the beaten earth, the scrubby grass, to a long, low outbuilding that I'd never been into, because washing was women's work, paused a moment with her hand on the door, then flung it open.

Nine or ten red-faced women inside looked up, frozen in the act of loading a washing machine, folding sheets, ironing men's shirts. Looked up for that instant, then dropped their eyes, because I was a man. I saw their horrified expressions, though, when they realized Oriana was wearing trousers.

I talked, not Oriana. They'd listen to me, and they'd answer me. They had to. I hated that it was true, but it was. I'd thought about what question to ask, and had decided against the obvious, "Where's Prudence Worthy? Where have they hidden her?" I'd make it an easier question to answer instead, which was why I said, "What roster is Prudence Worthy on today?"

The women looked at each other. Nobody very senior here, because laundry was one of the worst chores. I picked out Promise Truehope, who was married to my cousin Willing. I didn't think she was eighteen yet, and she looked much too pregnant for the heavy job she was doing. "Promise?" I asked. "What roster?"

"K-kitchen," she said. "With Mercy." And gulped.

Made sense. Mercy was the Prophet's wife, and in charge of the women. We turned to go, and the second the door closed behind us, Oriana was pulling out her phone, saying, "I'll text your dad. Then we need to run. They know we know now. We need to run."

"They can't tell anybody," I pointed out, but I was walking faster as Oriana's fingers flew. "They don't have phones."

Her fingers froze for a moment. "I forgot," she said. "I actually forgot." And then, "But we need to run anyway. This doesn't feel safe."

I felt it, too, the prickling at the back of my neck, on my arms. Some throwback to long-ago ancestors on the plains, I guessed, that awareness of the predator waiting. Watching. I said, "Then let's run," and we did. Oriana kept up, because she *was* in trousers, and we reached the kitchen just ahead of my parents.

We didn't stop and talk it over. Nothing to say. I burst through the door, and there Prudence was. Her face red and tear-streaked, her hands kneading an enormous ball of dough. She stood there and stared at us, then dropped her eyes like the other women.

Everybody but my Aunt Mercy. She snapped, "You're trespassing."

A stirring in the air behind us, and they were there, crowding through the door: a group of men, some of them holding tools. Not the Prophet, not this time. A younger group, a fitter group, and the man at their head was Loyal Worthy. Prudence's father, and Oriana's. He said, same as Aunt Mercy, "You're trespassing." His tone flat, his eyes hard, not a flicker of recognition in them for his daughter or his brother. "Get off our land."

"We're going," my dad said. "We're going now. Come on, Prudence."

The men took a step forward, blocking the exit. "She's not going," Loyal said.

My dad pulled out his phone, held it up, and hit a button. "I'm calling Daisy," he said. "You're being recorded, voice and video, and transmitted. False imprisonment, is what this is, and it's against the law."

Could you record a call like that? I had no idea. It sounded good, though.

"Outside laws," Loyal said with contempt. "Not God's laws."

As he said it, Oriana moved. Or she didn't exactly move. She *bolted.* Straight across the kitchen, grabbing Prudence's hand as she went. The two of them streaked across the building and out a far door.

Out into what, though? More men?

It was the same as the day I'd left. The same as the car. I didn't think. I ran. Through the women who were crowding around now, blocking my way. My arm went out to fend them off, but they didn't try to stop me. It wasn't in their makeup. They scattered instead. I heard running feet behind me and thought, *Come on, Mum and Dad. Come on.* I couldn't stop to look, though. I ran, and burst through the door to see Prudence and Oriana still running, too. Oriana with her sister's hand in hers, heading straight for the fence. The men were rushing to cut them off, but I was catching up, bellowing in a way I never had in my life.

"*Let them go!*" I shouted, even as I ran. Faster than I'd ever run before. Faster than I'd known I could. "*I'll kill the man who lays hands on them!*"

Somebody lunging, now. Not a cousin. Faithful Bright, who'd bullied the younger kids in school and was coming at me now with a hammer. I pivoted, grabbed his wrist, twisted his arm behind him, and took the hammer from his hand. It was easy. Faithful only knew how to hurt people smaller than him.

After that? I shoved him back into the others, raised the hammer over my head, registered my mum and dad running to join us, and told them, "Go. I'll come after."

My dad told my mum, "Go. *Run.*" Once she did, he raised

his voice and said, steady as a rock, "I'll have no bloodshed here today. This behavior is unworthy of God's grace, and it's unworthy of you. You'll step back now and let us go. You have no right to keep anyone here against their will."

I knew Gray and Daisy would still be filming, but he didn't bother telling them that. That wouldn't matter to them. It was a foreign concept, accountability to the world Outside. Instead, I watched my quiet father gather his energy into himself, then project it with an authority I'd only heard from the Prophet. "This is sin," he told them. "God is watching. Stand back and let us go. Stand back now."

He held them with his voice, his eyes. He told me, "Drop the hammer. You won't hurt this community, and they won't hurt you. This isn't the way."

I dropped it. No choice.

"We're walking to the fence," he told the group now. "We're leaving. Next time you try to hold somebody here who wants to leave, you'll answer to the police. Gilead is the only one in prison so far. Do the rest of you want to join him?"

"Treason," one of the men said.

"No," my dad said. "The truth. If you want to stay and give the Prophet your free labor and your obedience, that's your right. And anybody who wants to leave has the right to go, too. Man or woman. We're going now."

He set off for the fence, then, and I joined him. Not running. Walking. He muttered to me, "Don't look back. Keep going."

I did.

Scariest day of my life.

And what I'd give to have half my dad's mana.

SURPRISE PLAN

Oriana

Ten days later, everything changed again.

No, not what you're thinking. Gabriel didn't declare his awe at my incredible courage—at running away—or declare his love, either. We all got back in our cars, and that was that. He stood there with the door open before he got in, though, and looked back at me, and I held my breath. But then he got inside, and Uncle Aaron drove away.

And, yes, I had a roommate now. Prudence was sleeping with me, which was so much less lonely, but she was going shopping with Frankie, and buying the kinds of things Frankie wore. Tight jeans and bright shirts, skirts that didn't reach her knees, bras in different colors, and shoes with heels. She was also studying names, trying out different ones and asking us to call her by them. I kept forgetting and using the last one, or just saying "Prudence" by mistake, upon which she'd sigh and roll her eyes, and Frankie would laugh.

So, yes, that was a change, but not much of one, really, because I was still the same, stuck in between. I just had *three* sisters braver than I was now, instead of two.

No, the change happened while I was on a job search

website, looking to expand my babysitting client pool. I had a full driving license now, and there was no reason I couldn't babysit most evenings, once the outdoor chores were done and dinner was made. That was why I was on the site, and why I saw it.

Temporary Newborn Photography Assistant

Starts ASAP through 15 February, 24 December through 6 January excluded.

Full time

$22/hour

It was less than a week now until the school holidays, and the holidays didn't end until the last day of January. That wasn't exactly what the person wanted, but …

I clicked and read the rest.

Busy newborn photographer seeks fill-in assistant. M-F, 8:30 AM-5:30 PM

MUST have extensive experience with newborns, supreme emotional maturity, and a calm temperament. Safety is paramount!

Photography experience isn't necessary. Baby-handling experience is.

Please include cover letter with CV.

This is strictly a temporary job.

My heart was hammering all the way into my throat. I had no idea what a "newborn photographer" could possibly do—take photos of babies? All *day*? I loved babies, but how could taking their photos be a job?

Wait. You could look it up on the computer. I did that.

It was odd. It was odder than any odd thing I'd ever seen, and I'd seen heaps of odd things now. Babies in buckets, babies curled tightly into baskets, babies in *nests*. How could that be safe? It must be, though. The person had said, "Safety is paramount."

And babies were my favorite thing in the world. I knew it wasn't a good thing to be your favorite, not like maths or science or computers, but they were my favorite anyway.

All the same, I was pulling out an exercise book—it happened to be the one for Algebra, which was the exam I was meant to be revising for tonight—and starting to write.

I didn't exactly know what a "CV" was, to start with. I looked it up, and then I began, writing with my fountain pen instead of the computer, as usual, because I still thought better that way. I sat there for an hour, writing and scratching out, writing and scratching out. How did I explain where I'd got my "extensive experience with newborns"? If I said "Mount Zion," my email would hit the trash so fast, it may as well have never been opened. I'd learnt that from my babysitting experience. You said, "I have a large family, and I've been taking care of kids and helping at home since I was little." Full stop. Otherwise, they thought you were going to ... I wasn't even sure what. Preach a sermon? Indoctrinate their children? Kidnap them and take them to Mount Zion?

Also, did I have "supreme emotional maturity?" Probably not. I didn't even know what it *was*.

Finally, I just wrote:

Student, Otago Girls

and listed the work I'd done for money, since, as I've noted, people Outside mostly cared about things you did for money. So that was gardening, animal care, babysitting, and ...

And *Owner, Lavender Hill Farm Knitwear*. After some thought, I moved that line to the top, right under the "Student" part.

Owner. That sounded odd, but what else would you call it? It wasn't a lie, was it? Or was it? I wasn't sure. I left it for now.

Pity I hadn't cooked or cleaned for money yet, though. If only I'd already worked for Honor. One thing I'd noticed about girls Outside: most of them complained about doing what they called "gross things," and laundry and cleaning definitely counted. Wouldn't it make me look better that I didn't mind those things? Newborns meant heaps of dirty nappies, and surely, cleaning would be part of the job. You had to keep things spotless around little babies, who had no immune system yet and hadn't even had their jabs, and that would be the assistant's job, right?

Wait. *Honor.*

I sat there, my pen hovering over the exercise book, directly after having written,

Hello.

"Hello" seemed as good a place to start a letter as any, if you didn't know the person's name. Unfortunately, the realization was sinking in. I'd told Honor I'd work for her in Wanaka over the school holidays. I'd made a promise.

And Gray and Daisy were moving into the yurt as soon as Frankie and I left, because of that remodeling.

It wasn't possible.

I closed the exercise book, then opened it again, because ... algebra. Practice exam. I put down my fountain pen and picked up a pencil.

One equation. Two. Three.

I couldn't concentrate.

Babies in buckets. Surely you had to hold them so carefully, putting them in there, with a hand behind their head. You had to support their heads, because their necks were so fragile. The photographer had advertised on a student website. What if she got one of the girls from my school, who didn't like doing gross things and didn't know about babies' necks?

I put down my pencil and stood up.

I HESITATED outside the other house for a long minute. I'd never actually done this before—barged in on Gray and Daisy in Gray's house after they'd settled down for the evening. I wondered if I should text first. Or maybe I should walk in, the way I'd do at dinnertime?

No. Walking in would be wrong, when they weren't

expecting me. It would be almost as bad as walking into a family's room at Mount Zion. You didn't do that. I knocked. And then I waited.

Gray finally answered the door, looking alarmed, even though he must have known it wasn't a bad person, because Xena was wagging her tail and panting happily.

"Something wrong?" Gray was in rugby shorts and a T-shirt, and his feet were bare. His hair was rumpled, too.

Oh. He could've been in bed. *They* could've been in bed. I stepped back and said in confusion, "No. I'm fine." I looked at my phone. It was after nine o'clock! "Sorry. I'll come back tomorrow."

"No." He opened the door wider. "Come in. There's a problem, eh. For me, or for Daisy?"

"Oh." I considered that. "For … you? I think?"

"Fair enough." He closed the door behind me, took me into the lounge, sat on the couch, and, once I'd sat myself and Xena had thumped down at Gray's feet with a sigh, said, "Fire away." Gray was the most comforting person. He was big and tough and could handle anything, but he was gentle underneath.

Like Gabriel. Standing there at Mount Zion holding that hammer, telling me to run, but choosing pink paper for me, too, and putting his hand on Jack's shoulder to make him feel better.

Stop it.

I refocused and explained, and Gray said, "Hmm. I can see it's a quandary. Of course, you probably won't get the job, so there's that. Too young, eh."

"Oh." I hadn't even thought of that. How stupid. I was a schoolgirl. I was *seventeen*. Of course nobody would hire me to care for fragile newborns all day! I kept forgetting that I wasn't an adult anymore.

"No worries," he said. "You've got a work ethic I've never seen in anybody as young as you. Well, anybody but Daisy, and to be fair, I didn't actually see hers, just heard about it. Must be Mount Zion, eh. Reckon it's good for something. If you've lived in indentured servitude, anything else seems easy."

"Sorry, what?" I asked. "It wasn't ... whatever that is."

"You're right," he said. "Not indentured. No end date. Closer to slavery. But you want to apply anyway, just in case."

"I'd love to do that job, is all," I tried to explain.

"Even if you can't knit during it."

I wasn't sure if he was joking. "Of course I couldn't knit. It's tiny babies. Anyway, I knit at night. I won't be able to knit working for your mum, either. Never mind. This was stupid. I don't know what I was thinking."

I stood up to leave, and he said, "Hang on. Let's ring Mum."

"Won't she be angry if I tell her I'm thinking of not honoring my obligation?"

"You have no idea how many people don't honor their obligations. Let's ring her anyway." He did, and put the phone on speaker, and I sat there, trembling with the shame of what I wanted to ask, and waited for her answer.

It came after two rings. "Gray. Everything all right?"

"All good," he said. "But Oriana wants to apply for another job for over the school holidays, looking after newborn babies. She's sitting here with me now, worrying about it."

"I am," I spoke up. "But I won't do it, of course. I gave you my word." Just hearing Honor's voice, remembering all her kindness to Frankie and me when we'd come out of Mount Zion, so scared and knowing absolutely nothing, made my skin prickle with shame.

Honor said, "Looking after newborn babies is a treat, is it?"

"Yes," I said, because ... well, it was.

Honor said, "I've done this job for nearly forty years. If I got my knickers in a twist every time somebody didn't turn up or quit on me mid-shift, I'd have died of stress long since. Got two backpackers in today, a girl from Sweden and a boy from the States, looking for work. I don't get boys much, but he seems keen. Even cleaned before. One in a million, eh. Let's do this, then. You apply for the job, and give it a couple of days. If you haven't heard anything by then, you won't be hearing, and *then* you can commit to me. If you do hear—well, let them know you've got another offer, so you need to know fast. Fair enough?"

"Fair." I was so excited, I was fizzing. And then I was thumping down to earth again. "But ... I won't have a place to live. I keep forgetting that."

Honor said, "Rubbish. Gray and Daisy will be in one bedroom of the yurt. Got another one right next door."

I didn't know how to say, *But they'll be having relations.* I'd grown up with my parents having relations in the same *room,* and I'd never been embarrassed, but Outside—it was embarrassing, and the yurt's bedrooms didn't have walls that went to the ceiling. I'd been in this house sometimes, cooking or cleaning, and I'd *heard* them, even though they were upstairs! Also, Daisy sometimes got silent and felt sort of ... prickly when there were too many people around, especially Mount Zion people, and most especially her sisters. It was worse now, with Prudence here, and I could sense, as if Daisy had come out and said it, how much she was looking forward to those weeks with just her and Gray, not having to think about us, because we'd be with Honor.

Gray said, "The answer's obvious. Oriana lives in the caravan and goes to work. Independence, eh. Good for her. But possibly cook some dinners for us, still, Oriana, if you don't mind. This idea's sounding good to me."

"It is?" I wanted to. The caravan was like a tiny little house, everything in miniature. The beds folded out from the walls, one of them above the other, and the table had built-in benches. It was down in the garden, and waking up to birdsong and the clucking of chooks every day, amongst the flowers … it would be heavenly.

And the crew from Mount Zion would be remodeling the main house.

Stop it. It wasn't allowed, and I didn't do things that weren't allowed. And anyway, what was I going to do? Ask Gabriel if he'd kiss me like in that film? I'd die of mortification, and he probably would, too.

"There you are, then," Honor said. "Apply for the job. Good practice anyway, applying. Use me as a reference. I'm a bloody good reference, let me tell you. If you get to that point and I'm your reference, you'll get the job."

THE PHOTOGRAPHER, whose name was Laila Drake, rang me the next day.

I said, "Oh! I didn't think you'd call me," and then wished I could grab the words back. I'd gone on a bit, in my cover letter, about how much I loved working with kids, how I'd been trained in infant CPR and so forth. As much as I could, anyway, without coming out and saying, "I was fully responsible for up to five infants at a time in the Mount Zion nursery." You see how hard it was to write anything specific enough.

"What, because you're young?" Laila asked. "Or because you don't have the right experience?"

"I'm … I have the right experience," I somehow managed to say, wiping my palms on my overall legs and feeling glad she couldn't see me, with my sweaty hands and my probably beetroot-red face. "But I *am* young. I'm seventeen."

"Why did you apply?" she asked, which, again, wasn't the question I'd been expecting.

"Because I love babies." I tried to think what else to say, and couldn't.

"You realize this will be hard work," she said. "Not just cuddling a baby. It's cleaning as well, and it's an extremely responsible position."

"I know how to clean," I said, wishing again that I could just come out and *tell* her. "I—"

The phone wasn't in my hand anymore, because Iris had taken it. She said, "This the photography lady, then, calling about O?" I didn't hear what Laila said, but it couldn't have been much before Iris said, "Reckon you should ask me instead. She'll never tell you she's good. Probably because she doesn't know. In the garden with me right now, isn't she, weeding the vegie beds and mucking out the chicken coop and the alpacas' shelter, and in half an hour, she'll be up at the house, cooking dinner for her family and probably cleaning toilets as well. You won't do better. That's all I'm saying, and I shouldn't say that. Losing the best helper I've ever had, like as not, once you get your hands on her."

I'd been holding out my hand, whispering, *"Iris. It's an interview!"* with no results. Now, she listened a minute, then said, "Right," and handed the phone back to me.

"Hi," I said. "This is Oriana. Sorry about that. That was Iris. I didn't mean to—"

Laila said, "Reckon you'd better come and see me in person. Now I'm even *more* curious. Come ... oh, call it tomorrow."

"I have school." I knew it made me sound like a child, but there was no help for it.

"And I have babies to photograph," she said cheerfully. "Come after five o'clock. Be warned, there'll be children there still. A dog, too."

"That's OK," I said. "I like children. And dogs."

The weather was fine the next day when I found a carpark and began walking up the hill to the address I'd memorized, the breeze tugging at the gauzy, wide-legged, red-flowered trousers I'd sewn myself, with their wide tie belt. I checked to make sure my loose white T-shirt was still tucked into them and wondered again if I didn't look too frivolous. Daisy had said, "It's polished but casual. You're not applying for an office job," and I'd gone with that, because what did I know?

At five-thirty precisely, I stood on the doorstep of, oddly, a church, looking at a discreet brass sign screwed into the stone to the left of the enormous doors.

Laila Drake Photography

It looked so official.

I took a breath and rang the bell.

There *were* children. Girls. Two of them—twins, probably—aged about six, eating their tea in a shabby little lounge, overseen by a white dog with three legs whose hair fell in his eyes in a comical fashion. Laila, who was small and dark and neat and had a knot of hair as big as any in Mount Zion at the back of her head, said, "Let me show you the studio and explain what we do here."

The little girl with the shorter hair, whose name was Amira, said, "You have to be very careful with the babies, because they're just tiny. You can never, *ever* drop a baby."

"You're right," I said. "Newborns are fragile. You have to be very careful, and very clean."

Amira said, "Most people don't like to clean up babies, because they can have sticky poo on them, and it's very stinky, and sometimes it's *green*. They say they want Mummy's job, but then they don't want to do the washing and things. One lady said she couldn't bend down to get the props out because she had bad knees, but I think she was just too fat."

Yasmin, the quieter girl, said, "You aren't supposed to say that people are fat."

"I am if they *are* fat," Amira said.

"No," Laila said, but I could tell she was trying not to laugh. "Not even if they *are* fat. It's rude, eh, Oriana."

"Yes," I said, "and if you charge heaps of money to take photographs of people's babies, you have to be nice to them. I sell things at the farmer's market, and people buy more if you're nice to them. If you offer them a biscuit with honey on it, they're more likely to buy the honey. And if you smile and feel glad to see them, and *don't* tell them they're fat."

"It wasn't a *client*," Amira said. "It was just a *lady.*"

"Well," I said, "ladies who've just had babies are usually a bit fat, too. That's normal. They shouldn't have to feel bad about it. It's heaps of work, having a baby, and shrinking back's work, too."

"But the baby's *out* already," Amira said. "And—"

"Never mind," Laila said. "We can talk about it later. Come on, Oriana."

Through a door and into the studio, and Laila said, "I'll have a babysitter for the girls while they're on their holidays, so you won't have to wrangle Amira or tape her mouth shut so she doesn't call some poor woman fat, when she can still barely sit down from having pushed out a nine-pound bub four days ago."

"Kids say all sorts of things," I agreed. "I think that's why I like them." It was easy to talk to Laila, despite my earlier nerves. Maybe because she thought her kids were funny.

"Mm," she said. "You have brothers and sisters, then?"

"Yes," I said, then went ahead and added, "Eleven of them."

"*Eleven.*" She stared.

"Yes," I said, attempting to sound breezy. "Heaps of cousins as well. That's how I know about newborns. I come from a very, er, fertile family."

"Evidently," Laila said. "Why do you want this job, exactly?"

"Because it sounds like the best job in the world."

"Even with the sticky green poo."

I laughed. "Even so. I'd love to watch what you do. I'd love to help. I like to ... to be helpful to people. Cooking for them, and cleaning, and just ... *helping*. I know it's not what girls are meant to like, not maths or science or ..."

"Really?" Laila asked. "Not boys, or clothes?"

"Oh," I said. "No. Mostly, at my house, it's about liking serious things. I'm a bit odd, for my family. Now. For my family now."

I was entangling myself. Any minute now, I'd blurt out "Mount Zion," and the whole thing would be over. I *didn't* have an enormous knot of hair at my nape anymore, and I wasn't wearing a cap and apron, but I still felt like it.

Laila didn't seem to notice. She said, "School holidays begin next week. Could you start work on Monday morning?"

"Yes," I said. "But you said through February fifteenth. I'd help any way I could, even once I'm back at school, but I do have to go back. My sister says—" I snapped my mouth shut.

Laila put her head on one side and studied me. "Your sister says what?"

"That I have to go back. She had to work hard to get her schooling. She's a nurse. She thinks nothing's more important than going to school all the way through and passing all your NCEA levels so you can go to university. So I couldn't help you after February, not during the school day. I understand if that doesn't work for you," I hurried to add. "You shouldn't feel bad."

She was smiling. "I don't feel bad, no worries. And I'll give you a try anyway, shall I? Can you come on Sunday afternoon for a couple of hours so we can practice with a doll, and I can show you the props and explain?"

"You mean I have the job?" I couldn't believe it.

"What," she asked, "don't you want the job?"

"Yes." I laughed out loud. "*Yes.* Thank you. You won't be sorry. I promise."

"You know," she said, "I don't think I will."

So that was it. That, and Honor's reference. And, possibly,

Iris. I got the job—a full-time job, a *real* job, even if it was a short job—and I moved into the caravan with Prudence, while Frankie went to Wanaka to work for Honor and Gray and Daisy moved into the yurt. An all-Mount-Zion crew started work on the house, and I woke to the sound of their sledgehammers and the crash and clatter of lumber being tossed into a pile as they did their demolition. That was because they started before seven. I saw them sometimes when I came home, too, as they worked more hours than anybody did Outside. That was because they were trying to get Gray's house done fast, so Gray and Daisy could move into it at the end of the school holidays. Gray was hurrying the job along, I was pretty sure, for Daisy. He worked with the crew sometimes on Saturdays, and he checked in with them every morning, but Prudence and Daisy and I weren't allowed to look. "It's a surprise," he'd said.

For Daisy.

I caught a glimpse of Gabriel sometimes, on my way between caravan and car, and of the others, too. I waved, and they waved back, and that was all, maybe because I also caught glimpses of Uncle Aaron. And anyway, again … what else would I have done? Run up the steps, grabbed Gabriel's arm, and asked him to kiss me? Baked them cookies, like the most obvious girl in ObviousWorld? Asked Gabriel if he'd like me to sew him something?

Never mind. I spent my days holding babies, rocking babies, soothing babies, changing babies, and I loved it. On the third day, Laila sacked her babysitter, and then Prudence had a job, too, so that was even better.

Three days before Christmas, after my last day of work for Laila, I'd drive Prudence to Wanaka, and we'd work for Honor until New Year's Eve, when I had a longstanding appointment to babysit for Daisy's friend Matiu and his wife, Poppy.

"Because that's the worst of it," Honor had told me when I'd rung her to let her know I'd got the job. "Can't tell you how many Christmases I've been out there with the hoover and the toilet brush. Everybody's always got 'flu' on Christmas."

"I'd love to," I said, and meant it.

She laughed down the phone, a full, rich sound. "Nobody's ever told me *that* before. Not about working on Christmas Day."

"We can have a lovely tea afterward, though," I said. "Prudence and Frankie and I will cook it, and you can put your feet up, and it'll feel like ..."

"Like Christmas," she said, gently now. "With your mum."

I swallowed. "No. We never had Christmas like that. It'll feel a bit like home, that's all. At least ... a kind of home."

19

A HOLIDAY, NOT A HOLY DAY

Oriana

On New Year's Eve, Priya—hopefully the final name—and I were just back from Wanaka as scheduled after ten days' cleaning—some people were really surprisingly messy, and as for the bathrooms, I'd been glad for the rubber gloves Honor provided—with another satisfying chunk of money added to my bank account. Prudence, who'd spent most of what she'd earned on clothes, saying, "It's Christmas. You're *meant* to go shopping, and anyway, I did horrible cleaning for it. I'm going to find something to do for work someday that's clean. Perfectly clean. *Extremely* clean," was now officially (I hoped) Priya, though her brand-new passport still said "Prudence," just as mine said "Obedience." Frankie wasn't "Fruitful Warrior" anymore, but Priya and I still had to wait. Which meant that on the first day of Year 12, they'd be calling out "Obedience Worthy" again, and everybody would stare.

Never mind. Everybody probably knew already, and I'd handled more difficult things than that. Besides, in five months more, I'd be eighteen myself, and Oriana for real.

Priya's name was Sanskrit—Indian, like our mum—and meant "beloved," because she was. We'd come back for her because we loved her, though she could be a surprising person to love. Her once knee-length hair was cut in a sort of feathery way around her delicate face now, the shortest any of us had dared to go, and she'd spent that Christmas cleaning money on skin-tight jeans that she had to wriggle to put on, shirts you could see through, colored singlets to wear under the shirts, shorts that only came halfway down her thighs, and undies in red and black and bright pink.

She'd also bought some that were lace all over. They left marks on her bum afterward, which didn't look comfortable to me, but she'd said happily, "Having thin legs is good, though, Outside, and having a small bum is, too. You're prettier for Mount Zion, because they like that your bum's bigger, but there's nobody there to care except your husband. I'd rather be pretty to more people."

As I'd rather be pretty to as few people as possible—men here *looked* at you so much, especially on the bus—I didn't have much answer to that, other than, "You do look pretty."

Priya also wore makeup every day that took ages to put on, and was pretty disappointed to learn that she wouldn't be able to wear it at school, and that she'd be in a uniform again. At every turn, her answer seemed to be, "Do whatever is the opposite of Mount Zion." Like Frankie, only even more so.

Tonight, we weren't being pretty to anybody, unless you counted five kids under the age of eight. We were babysitting Poppy and Matiu's three kids, and, to my surprise, my employer Laila's twins as well. I hadn't realized Laila and Poppy knew each other. Poppy would've been a good reference, I guessed, except that she knew about Mount Zion, because Matiu did. So—not such a good reference.

Well, hopefully my one week of work for Laila was enough to overcome the "Mount Zion" hurdle, if that interesting fact came up.

Mount Zion hadn't prepared us for Biology, but it had for babysitting, which meant that Priya'd been able to earn money instantly, something she loved almost as much as red underwear and TV. We didn't have TV in the caravan, which Priya found extremely sad, but Poppy and Matiu not only had TV, they had one with a huge screen and all sorts of extra channels. We'd also make extra money tonight, with five kids, especially as Poppy and Matiu would be out late. New Year's Eve had never meant anything to me other than that the year changed, but it seemed to be an excuse for a party here.

A party wasn't a sweet being served after dinner and piano music and dancing amongst the married couples and unmarried girls. It was all the sinful things instead. Alcohol, and dancing with men you *weren't* married to, and, in the case of Laila, going to the party in something that looked like a nightdress, with your hair loose.

Even after a year, Outside could still surprise me. I'd never seen Laila with her hair down before. I'd definitely never seen her in her nightdress, because normally, she dressed about like me. But then, everything here was odd.

There was also something called "flirting," which was the most confusing idea of all. You glanced at the man, then looked down with a little smile. That was odder still, because it was what women did at Mount Zion, except that you never actually *looked*, you peeked. Everything at Mount Zion between men and women was wrong, I'd been told, yet this was, somehow, right. You were also meant to touch your hair, and that *was* different, because at Mount Zion, there would've been no point. Your hair was under a cap.

Oh. Wait. Girls *had* touched their caps. I remembered Radiance, who was barely older than me, doing that at dinner sometimes, before the Prophet had given her to Raphael. She'd glance in his direction, then look down and touch her cap as if she were straightening it. Radiance had very pretty hands. Had that been flirting?

Priya asked me now, a couple of hours after Laila, Poppy, and Matiu had left and when the kids were finally in bed,

"How late will they be gone, do you think? What if we can't stay awake until then? And how do people wake up on time in the morning after they go to parties?"

She didn't sound anxious. She just sounded interested. Priya always got her equilibrium back before I did. Even this palatial old house, high on a hill and looking out on Dunedin city, Otago Harbour, and the Otago Peninsula beyond, hadn't rocked her much for a girl who'd lived her entire life with no idea at all of "private spaces."

Your private space at Mount Zion wasn't three floors of enormous rooms with stone fireplaces and crystal chandeliers and rich, jewel-toned carpets, not to mention a kitchen that could have fed twenty. It was your bed cubicle, with its single drawer beneath for your extra set of clothes, your caps and aprons. Until you were married at sixteen, and your private space became your marital bed in the room assigned to you. Or not exactly, because you shared that with your husband. Your children's bed cubicles were added to that room, one by one, year after year.

There'd be beds then, and heaps of them. A table, too, though not for eating. And that was just about it. Laundry, cooking, dining, bathing, child-rearing, teaching? All of that was done in the communal space, and that space, like your room, was owned by Mount Zion. The very clothes in your drawer belonged to the community, and so did your work. You gave to the community, many hours a day and seven days a week, and in return, the community supported you.

I knew it was wrong, but it was so much simpler. And it was what I *knew*.

People thought the biggest shock, leaving Mount Zion and coming Outside, would be something like the clothes, or that you could marry the person you chose. In fact, the biggest shock was ... everything. Every day. The noise of the city, and the anonymity. Nobody watching you, but nobody knowing you or looking out for you, either. The completely foreign idea that you could have a house like this, or you could have no home at all, and that it was down to you to house yourself. The idea that you could choose how to behave, what to wear, what to do with your day, even your very name. The idea that a woman was equal to a man, and could speak freely to him. Could *disagree* with him. That she *should* speak freely to him. That she should *look* at him, and judge him.

Daisy and her twin, Dorian, seemed so easy with life Outside, it was hard to believe they'd ever been as rattled by it as I was. Daisy wasn't afraid of anything, while it seemed sometimes that I was afraid of *everything*. Including Poppy's house, and the idea that I could relax here, could even stretch out on one of the comfortable couches in the lounge and watch a movie instead of cleaning her bathrooms, because you weren't required to stay busy and productive Outside. That I should help myself to the endless amounts of food in the fridge, instead of giving it a good clean-out. There was, of course, no eating between meals at Mount Zion, not that it would have occurred to anybody but the boldest boys to try.

I knew that my favorite part of Outside should be exactly that. The freedom. Freedom to say what I liked, to look at whomever I pleased. To go to school and work in the garden at home—at Gray's, rather—or with the babies for Laila instead of filling my days with whatever rotation I'd been assigned to: cooking for hundreds in the kitchens, taking care of babies in the nursery, cleaning endless bathrooms. Or my least favorite: the drudgery that was a day spent in the enormous laundry, dragging heavy loads of cotton garments from washers to dryers, then ironing until my face was red, my hair curled into spirals under my cap, and the sweat soaked my dress under my apron.

Obedience was a value in Mount Zion. It was more than that. It was a *virtue*. And it was what I'd always been. Obedient, and safe in knowing I was.

I did like my job, and the babysitting, and the gardening, so much better than those chore rotations. The truth was, though, that the decisions Outside were endless. All day, every day, you were deciding, and often, you didn't even know what was the right thing to do. It was so *tiring*. Maybe that was why almost my favorite part of Outside, other than the babies and the animals and the garden, was still movies. Everything was perfect on the screen, not confusing and messy and involving so many choices that I didn't know how to make, and everybody *looked* perfect, too. I studied films like they were historical documents, searching for clues about how to look, how to act, how to *feel*.

Also, I could knit while I watched TV, which meant that I didn't feel like somebody would give me a hiding at any moment for being so useless. Just now, I was knitting something that I wouldn't sell. It was a blanket for Poppy's new baby, in a beautiful sage green with a ribbed edging made of a blend of white merino and angora. Buddy, Poppy's black-and-white dog, wasn't curled on the couch beside me, but only because he'd gone off to bed with Poppy's eldest, Hamish.

Dogs not only lived in the house here, they sometimes got on the furniture, too. I was only surprised they didn't sit at the table at mealtime. When I'd checked on the kids half an hour earlier, Buddy had raised his head from his spot curled up at the foot of Hamish's bed and tapped his tail at me as if to say, "Hello. Nice to see you. How're you going?" I could almost hear his squeaky little voice saying it, like an animal in a fairy-tale movie.

And then there was Priya, who'd pounced on the idea of trousers and red underthings like she really *was* the Jezebel the Prophet had warned us about, and who couldn't wait to start school again. At the moment, she was curled up on the couch in those jeans, watching a fairy-tale movie. *Cinderella*, because it was my favorite, and I was older and got to choose.

Even fairy-tale movies could be scary, which was why I loved *Cinderella* best. After *Beauty and the Beast* and *Frozen* both, I'd shivered in bed remembering the red glow of the wolves' eyes, their slinking bodies and snarls and the way they gathered themselves to spring. And the even worse thing: people being chased, and caught, and locked up. In cages, sometimes, alone and helpless.

I knew about people being chased and locked up. I didn't see how it could be fun to imagine, or fun to feel scared, either, but people Outside must love it, or why was it in every film? Then there were the other movies, the ones that *weren't* meant for kids, where people really *were* running from somebody who was chasing them and wanting to hurt them, or where they were taking off their clothes and sinning with people who weren't their husband or wife, in front of a camera. I tried not to watch those anymore, not since that night with Gabriel. It seemed too dangerous, stirring feelings I was trying not to have.

Priya didn't need to know about that, though. My older sisters knew I was timid, but with Priya, I could be the older one, the brave one, the one who knew things, Priya's comfort and guide at school. Now, I told her, "It's New Year's Eve, so the big part is at midnight. People dance and drink too much champagne and kiss each other like mad when the clock strikes midnight. Exactly like *Cinderella*, except it lasts longer, because you don't have to leave when the clock strikes, so they stay and stay. And they *don't* wake up early the next morning. People Outside don't have cows. Most of them don't even have chooks, and heaps of them don't have kids, because of birth control and ... and pursuing your dreams, and all that. They don't care about having meals at the right time, and at the weekend, they sleep as late as they like. They don't mind if you fall asleep, either, babysitting, if they stay out late."

I actually had no idea about New Year's Eve, of course, but it *seemed* like it would be *Cinderella*, with the dancing and midnight and all. As for the champagne and kissing, I'd seen it in a film that had New Year's Eve in it.

Fortunately, I *did* know about babysitting, because I still did as much of it as I possibly could, new job or no, knitting business or no. I wished I had the courage to tell Daisy, who'd gone to all this trouble to get us out so we could be educated and have all those choices, and who was so sure about everything, that I didn't like school. I loved my job, but it was temporary, and you couldn't support yourself all the way by gardening. Men did the heavy work here, exactly like Mount Zion, and for anything else, for growing flowers, or vegies, or growing an alpaca herd, you needed land. Land cost money, and I couldn't live with Daisy and Gray forever. That was another thing you didn't do, Outside: stay with your family once you were grown. So that was gardening out for me.

I wasn't clever, except maybe with my hands and with kids, and another year of struggling with things I'd never learnt, of being prodded to speak up after a lifetime of being told to be quiet, was so hard to face. And what came after it— yet another year of school, and then university? That felt impossible, and like such a waste, when I could be working.

I'll be doing it for Priya, I reminded myself, but it didn't help that much.

Priya was the one staring at me at the moment, though, and I tried to remember what we'd been talking about. Oh. New Year's Eve, and *Cinderella*. There was no television at Mount Zion, of course. No computers. No worldly picture books for kids, and no worldly music of the kind that everybody around me played on their headphones endlessly, so you couldn't talk to them even if you'd had the courage. Definitely no fairy tales, with rebellion against your parents and kisses to break the evil spell. When I'd first got out and learnt about all of that, it had felt like I'd see the Devil at any moment, prancing in on his woolly legs and his cloven hooves, grinning out of the black mask of his face as he came to join the festivities.

"You mean Poppy and … and Matiu will kiss each other?" Priya asked. "In *public?*"

"You've seen that already," I pointed out.

"Not with people with *families*. Not when they're not at home."

"Well, yeh, they will," I said. "And they haven't been married long. They lived in this house for nearly two years before being married, the same way Gray and Daisy are doing. Sleeping in the same bed and all, and making a baby. You don't have to be married, Outside, to have relations with somebody. You don't have to wait at all, and you can have relations with anybody." I tried to say it airily, the way Daisy did, but it didn't work.

"Oh," Priya said faintly. "I just thought Daisy was … fallen."

"No," I said. "It's normal here to kiss men. All different ones. Besides, Daisy says women have needs, too."

It wasn't often I felt worldly. This world went too fast for me, or I went too slowly for it. I just couldn't seem to adjust, and if it was normal to kiss all sorts of men, or boys, or even to hold their hands, I hadn't reached "normal" yet. It seemed normal for other people, though.

A voice piped up from the staircase. It was Olivia, Poppy's five-year-old daughter, saying, "Mummy and Matiu kiss all the time. *Everywhere.* Like this."

She danced into the room in her pink nightdress making kissing noises, and Laila's daughter Amira, who'd come downstairs with her, giggled and said, "No, they don't. Kissing is private!"

Olivia said, "It is *not.*"

"My grandad says it's private," Amira insisted. "When it's on TV. He switches the TV off and says it's private, and not for little girls to see."

"I bet your mum and dad kissed all the time, though," Olivia said. "When your dad wasn't dead."

"They did *not*," Amira said.

I had no idea what the rules really were, or if there were any at all. Kissing felt like it *should* be private, to me. When I saw it, especially on TV, I got all hot and prickly, like that night with Gabriel. Daisy did more than kiss Gray, too. She sat in his lap and put her hands on his body in front of us, and she hugged him on the street and kissed him in front of total strangers in a way I'd never imagined a woman could do, unless she *was* fallen.

Kissing, and relations, were things that happened in bed, under the blankets. I knew, because I'd grown up in that single room with my parents. Relations happened in the dark, and they were quiet, not with kissing in places besides your mouth, and definitely not with the noises I'd heard in films.

Maybe it wasn't real. Fairy tales weren't real, and neither was magic. Why would noisy relations be? Surely people didn't really do those things.

My mind tried to remember those sounds I'd heard from Gray and Daisy's bedroom, but I wouldn't let it. More of that hot, prickly feeling. Instead, I stood up. "I know one thing," I told the girls. "And that's that it's long past bedtime. What are you two doing awake?"

"We want to make popcorn," Olivia announced. "Because popcorn is for party nights, and this is a party night."

Amira said, "And I need to know if pirates are real, please. Mummy says Long John Silver isn't really real, except that he's our dog, so he's real that way, but Olivia says there are too pirates. If they're really real, I have to be ready so they don't get me if I go on a boat."

"You can't be *ready*," Olivia said. "Pirates have *swords*."

"But I could be very strong," Amira said, "and use karate."

"Do you know karate?" I asked, diverted in spite of myself.

"Not yet," she said. "That's why I have to be ready."

"No pirates in New Zealand," I said. "And what I *know* is that it's bedtime, so let's go." With kids, at least, I knew what I was doing, and these were stalling tactics all the way. I got a hand behind each of their backs and was shepherding them up the stairs when the doorbell rang, a shockingly loud peal in the nighttime quiet.

I hesitated, half up and half down the stairs. It was *night*. Did you answer the door at night? I didn't know the answer. Daisy and Gray had a locked gate and a system of cameras and alarms, because although they didn't say much about it, I knew they were still worried about the Prophet coming after us. Also, Gray was famous, something else I'd never heard of before. You got famous when you were on TV or in films, and he'd been a rugby star, before, and on TV every week. When you were famous, people bothered you, so you took precautions. Nobody rang Gray's doorbell unexpectedly.

The doorbell rang again, and I stared at Priya. Until Olivia said, "I'll answer it!" and ran around me down the stairs with Amira following her.

"Grab them!" I said to Priya. She wasn't quick enough, though, because Olivia had flung the door open.

It was Gabriel. In a blue work shirt, canvas trousers, and work boots, and with something that looked like a white singlet wrapped around his hand, which he was holding up above his head. Well, the singlet had been white once. Now, it was stained bright red.

He may have been looking at me. I couldn't tell, because I wasn't looking at *him*, other than at his hand. I knew I was *allowed* to look, but I couldn't, not after everything. I was grabbing the girls instead and telling Priya, "Go put them to bed."

She said, "You shouldn't ..." and I knew why. Even her lust for this new life wasn't up to inviting a man who wasn't our brother into a house where we were the only adults at home, but she also didn't know how to tell a man he wasn't allowed to come inside. Neither did I.

I probably shouldn't talk to him, not after what my uncle had said. But he was bleeding so *much*.

I said, "What did you do?"

"Came to see Matiu," he said. "I cut my hand a bit." His voice came out quiet and deep from his broad chest, so I was clearly the only one bothered by this. He needed a haircut, I thought, with another peek. At Mount Zion, women cut their husbands' hair, and mothers cut their unmarried sons', but Aunt Constance must not have seen him for a while, because it was getting long.

"Oh, no," I said. "How bad?"

"Dunno," he said. "Cut it on a can. Cooking is, uh ... still hard, but I'm trying to get better. I was trying to make sauce for noodles, like those meatballs you did, and I didn't realize it would be so sharp. The lid, I mean. And it won't stop bleeding."

He had hair on his chest, too. I could see it, because he wasn't wearing a singlet. It was probably what was wrapped around his hand. I was trying not to look at his face, but now I was seeing his bare chest!

"Shouldn't you have gone to hospital?" I asked. "Oh. Come in."

He didn't. "Thought Matiu could stitch me." There was a flush on his face, but I wasn't sure why. "I don't know how hospital, uh, works, quite. And I really am trying to learn, on the cooking. Buying takeaways gets too dear, and I'm a bit tired of those microwave things."

"Matiu's not here," I said. Then I took a breath and took the leap. "But you need to have that stitched. I'll drive you to hospital. How did you get here?"

"Drove," he said. "Stick shift, though. I don't think I can ..."

"No," I said. "You can't."

"But you can drive?" he asked.

How could he not know that? Well, Gray's work crews were all men. Gabriel's life, maybe, wasn't so different than it had been at Mount Zion. He worked hard all day, and it was the same kind of work. After work, he went home, also like Mount Zion. The difference was, I guessed, that once he got there, he had to take care of himself. But maybe he liked that.

I didn't know, because he'd never said. He'd always been quiet, but now, when I saw him at the house, he was silent. He'd been so brave on that day when we'd got Priya out, and he'd talked to me then, but that was different, I guessed.

Of course it was. Men Outside didn't spend time with teenage girls. It was different.

"Women drive here," I reminded him.

He turned red again. "I know. I hadn't seen you doing it, though, so I didn't think. Sorry." He shifted where he stood. "I shouldn't be here anyway. Not with you and Prudence here alone."

"Priya," I said.

The red intensified. "Sorry," he said again. "Priya."

"Come in," I repeated, "while I tell her I'm taking you."

"No," he said. "I'll wait out here for you."

How did Daisy and Poppy and Laila talk to men like it was nothing? How did they walk around with their hair and everything under their clothes so … so visible, and not want to hide?

I couldn't do this. I *couldn't*.

I said, "Hang on. Just a moment," and shut the door.

I knew how to drive. I knew how to pretend to be normal, too, the way people were normal here. I was in school. Girls' school, but still.

I could do this. It was an *emergency*. I had to.

20

DOWN TO YOU

GABRIEL

Oriana was winding her way down the steep, curving Dunedin streets to the hospital, driving competently but not very fast, without speaking to me. Without looking at me at all. I sat beside her, trying not to drip blood. Trying not to be woozy from blood.

I'd put her in a bad position, I realized now. Having to leave the kids alone with her sister, who was just out of Mount Zion and didn't know anything.

I should've done something else. Phoned my dad, probably, once I'd realized Matiu wasn't home.

I'd been tired, maybe, and careless. Sleep wasn't always easy. My flatmates were uni students, and their upside-down schedule would put bats to shame. Beyond that, I spent as many waking hours as I could manage working, picking up all the overtime Gray would permit, and I was taking classes as well for my trades certificate. The hours people normally worked here weren't enough to make a man really tired—eight hours a day and two days off every week, when I was used to ten hours, or even twelve, and not many days off at all—and besides, I needed to save money.

No reason not to work anyway, because when I got home, there were the flatmates, the washing-up, and the green couch. Once I closed my bedroom door, it was just me, and it had never been just me. When I'd moved out of my parents' room at sixteen, I'd moved straight into the unmarried men's dormitory to live with my cousins and the rest of them, who might as well be my cousins, I knew them that well.

That wasn't what I wanted now, though. It wasn't what I was missing. I didn't want to joke and laugh and wrestle, or even to be quiet while the others did all that. Somehow, what I missed was what I'd never had. A wife.

I'd be twenty-five next month, and I didn't want to be alone anymore. I wanted to strip off my clothes the minute I walked through the door and shower off the dirt of the day, because she didn't like me dirty. I wanted to eat dinner beside her, at a table I'd built for her out of the kind of wood she liked best, sanding the top and legs down until they were like glass, then rubbing in my special brew of linseed oil, varnish, and mineral spirits to bring out the grain. I wanted to listen to music with her on the little speaker I'd bought, the first worldly item I'd ever coveted and purchased just for myself and just for pleasure, and work on some project, something I was fixing for her, building for her, and smell the pretty woman-scent of her while she sat on the couch and knitted or read or …

Or nursed our baby.

I didn't actually know how married couples spent their time together Outside, other than my glimpses of Drew and Hannah's life, but that was how I imagined it. If it was something else? Drinking alcohol and dancing and … and whatever else they did? I wouldn't know how to do that.

All of that was why I'd been putting all my energy, ever since I got here, into getting ahead. I may have walked out of Mount Zion with nothing but my skills, but I could become a foreman myself eventually. I knew what it took, because I'd been watching my dad all my life, ever since he'd married my mum after the farm accident that had killed my father. It was having the knowledge, doing the work, and getting to that spot where the other men followed your orders not from fear, but from respect, because they knew you'd thought it through, and that you'd never ask them to do what you wouldn't do yourself.

I couldn't be a man out here, couldn't marry and have a family and a home, without a good livelihood and money saved, and building was the only way I knew to get it. It was all on you to do, if you wanted it, so there was nothing to do but to get stuck in and do it.

It was exciting, and it was terrifying. Nobody chose your wife for you, for one thing, and even if you did find a girl you liked, somehow or other, by yourself, and managed to ... ask her, because that was what you did here, she didn't have to marry you. She could say no, which meant you had to go find somebody else and try to like her that much.

And you had relations first, before you even asked her to marry you. That one, I still couldn't get over.

It wasn't like I didn't know it happened. Some blokes bothered unmarried girls at Mount Zion. It wasn't a good thing, though. It was a shameful thing, and if I'd seen it, I'd stopped it, because that was what any decent man would do. How could I bother some girl like that myself? Especially if she was meant to be the girl I would love?

It was called "having sex," here, or other things. It wasn't that I didn't know the words. I'd heard the others say them, even at Mount Zion. And since then? It was in those books, and even if it hadn't been—it was all some blokes ever talked about.

It wasn't something that was right to tell other men about, though, I was sure of that. You didn't describe a girl's body like that, or talk about the things you'd done together. The things you'd done *to* each other. Or the things you wished you could do. I didn't want to have those thoughts. The problem was, when the others talked, the pictures stayed there in my mind, even if I tried to shut my ears.

Oriana was still focusing fiercely on her driving. She looked pretty as a flower garden in midsummer, as always, in loose trousers like a bell-shaped skirt and a gauzy buttoned shirt that outlined her figure in a way I tried not to notice. She'd been the prettiest girl at Mount Zion, with the sweetest smile, the prettiest mouth, the softest skin, and the nicest ... curves, and she'd had the gentlest hands with the babies, too. When I'd looked at her even then, I'd known I had to stop looking, or I'd be having lustful thoughts. And now? Now, it was worse.

Before she'd run away, I'd hoped that when the Prophet chose her husband, he'd choose me, and had known he wouldn't. Even though I wasn't really her cousin, it was still too close to wrong. She was soft and sweet, though, and she needed a husband who'd be kind to her. Or maybe that was the Devil talking and that was just my excuse, because I wanted her.

Now, she'd be the one choosing, which was right. I could see that. Marriage made too big a difference to a woman, and forcing them to be with a cruel husband, or a careless one, had never sat right. Girls didn't choose out here, though, until they were older. Until they were nearly thirty, or even older than that, whereas a woman in Mount Zion would have six or eight kids already by then, and her husband might have become one of the Elders if he had mana enough. When he'd be running his own construction crew, no certificate or school necessary, because he'd been doing this work for twenty years now, and he knew how.

And when he'd be going to bed every night with his wife, undressing in the dark and hearing the rustle of cotton as she did the same, then pulling back the blankets and sliding in beside her, feeling her hand come out to touch him on the shoulder, to tell him that she was glad to be going to bed, too.

Kissing her lips.

There the thoughts were again, no matter how I tried to push them away. Oriana said, "It's in here," and pulled into a brightly lit drive. *Emergency,* the sign said.

"Thought this was for broken legs and all," I said, because I needed to say something.

"It is," she said. "And for this as well." She was pulling smoothly into a carpark, slotting herself neatly in between two larger cars. Oriana was good at physical things. Cooking. Sport.

Dancing.

We'd had music nights sometimes at Mount Zion, for a treat. The married couples would dance together, but not too close, because intimacy was private, and the girls would dance with their friends and laugh and look pretty.

The boys and unmarried men? We'd watch.

When I climbed out of the little car, I saw that I hadn't been successful on the non-blood-dripping. There was heaps of blood now on my shirt and trousers, and blood on the seat, too. I said, swallowing to keep the sick down, "I should've asked for a towel. I'll clean the car for you tomorrow."

"Gabriel," she said, and laughed. A little breathlessly, and all the way sweetly. "It's not your fault that you cut yourself. I'll clean it for you."

I would have answered, but I was getting a bit wonky.

She said, "Are you all right?" Then, more sharply, "Gabriel! You're weaving. How much blood did you lose?"

"I ... I'm all right," I tried to say. "I don't ... like blood. Sometimes. Normally, I'm ... fine. I'm fine now. Fine."

This could not be happening. I wasn't going to pass out because I'd cut my hand on a *can!* What was she going to think?

"Here." She was beside me, pulling my uninjured hand

across her shoulders. "Lean on me, and you'll be all right. Only a few steps. Nearly there."

She walked beside me, her arm around my waist, all the way into A&E. When we got there, she sat me down in a chair and marched off to the desk by herself as if she did it every day, and then she came back with a towel, wrapped my hand in it, held it above my head, heedless of the blood she was getting on her pretty pale-green shirt, sat beside me still holding my hand up, and said, "I heard you've been studying at night to get your certification. That must be hard work. Going to classes, too. Is it ... all right, the classes? I always feel left behind at school, honestly, because it's all things I haven't learnt. The things the rest of them already know, I mean. You're so clever at building, though, so maybe it's not the same. You probably know more than all of *them*."

She made me feel, somehow, like things had tipped back the right way again, and I was the man I wanted to be. Strong. Sure. She was pressed up beside me to hold up my arm, and looking me straight in the face for once, her own pretty face, with its gentle brown eyes, the honey-colored skin and soft mouth, the faint spatter of freckles on her cheekbones and nose, open and innocent and trusting.

I thought, *Stop it. She's not yours, you can't ask her to be, and there's nobody else you can ask for her, either.* And wondered once again—

How did you do this, get a woman to like you enough to marry you, when it was all down to you?

How?

21

NEW ROAD, NEW RULES

ORIANA

I delivered Gabriel to his flat after a long wait in Emergency, during which I helped him hold up his hand and ignored how my own arm was aching. He'd gone mostly quiet again, so I had, too, until I'd given him a lift home close to midnight, his hand stitched up and wrapped in a white bandage.

I was driving carefully past a group of laughing, shouting students, some of them waving bottles around and all of them stumbling off the pavement and into the roadway, and thinking, *I can't imagine that being me. I need to imagine it, though, if I want to live here, if I want to have more friends, because it's what people do.* I asked, maybe in order not to think about that, "Do you need me to come back and take you to Matiu's for your ute tomorrow? And when do you get the stitches out?"

"I'll walk," he said. "And not for ten days or so. I won't be really fit to work until then, either. Cutting my palm ... it couldn't be worse. I'm useless."

He sounded so bothered that I wanted to put my hand on his, but I didn't, of course.

"Won't Gray understand?" I asked, a little timidly. This was men's business, but who else was he going to talk to? He could ask his dad about it, but not tonight, because it was late. Wouldn't he lie in bed and worry? I was here, and it was too sad and too lonely not to have anybody to share your fears with.

He didn't answer, so he *didn't* want to talk about it, and I tried not to be bothered by that and found a carpark outside the block of flats he directed me to. At least two kilometers from Matiu's grand house on the hill, and nothing like it. Even in the dark, I could tell it was pretty shonky, or maybe I was just comparing it to Gray's houses, which were so beautiful, you barely wanted to leave them.

He didn't move to get out. He said, "Yeh, Gray's a good boss. But I don't like to leave him shorthanded."

"It was an accident," I said.

"It was careless." He sounded so angry, I flinched.

"Sorry," he said. "Sorry." He ran his uninjured hand over his face, and I thought that he wouldn't say more, that he'd climb down and go inside. Instead, he said, "I need him to think I'm reliable."

"Gabriel." He was the one who jumped this time, hearing his name. He looked so tired, and so ... bothered, and I missed the sweetness of that day when we'd cared for Drew's kids together, and the way he'd smiled when he'd given me my sewing machine.

He felt stupid, I suddenly realized. Just like I did, so often. I said, "He knows you're reliable. He said so."

He dropped his hand. "He did?"

"*Yes*. He says you're an awesome worker. I should know," I added when he still looked dubious. "I live with him. Anyway, how could you not be? You were always the best. Everybody knew that." I was glad it was dark in the car, so he couldn't see me turn red. I went on, though, because he needed to know this. "You should hear how kind he is to us, and especially how kind he is to Daisy if she's tired or has had a bad day. He knows how hard she works, that's why. So I'm sure he'll be kind about you as well."

He said, "It's not the same."

"What isn't?"

"It's different, with your wife. Or it should be. Your wife isn't—" He broke off. "I don't know. She's not one of your workers. He should notice, and help. Dad noticed, with Mum, and she did with him as well. Wasn't your dad like that with your mum?"

"No," I said, and felt a pang of longing for my mum that was like a blow to the chest. Small and brown and gentle and quiet, she'd never walk out the gate of Mount Zion, even if five of her children had. She'd been in there too long. And I'd never see her again.

Gabriel asked, more quietly still, "Was he cruel?"

My breath caught. I could tell he was looking at me, even though it was dark. I said, "I don't ... know. I don't know how men are supposed to ... be."

He said, "Not like that." After that, he stirred, said, "I should go in," and opened the car door. "Thank you for driving me. And for the, uh, talking."

Was that sarcastic? I couldn't tell. I said, "I was glad to drive you. Glad to help. And I know I ... that I talked. But women are meant to talk, Outside, and I'm trying to ... to fit. To learn how to fit."

He said, "I was glad you talked." And just sat there, which made a glow start up low in my belly and travel up my throat. I was so agitated, I was nearly trembling, and I didn't know what to do. It was like that night with the sewing machine, but it was even worse.

Finally, he said, "Well, goodnight, then." He got out and went to slam the door, then caught it, stuck his head inside the car, and said, "Drive safely. It'll be even madder out on the roads going home, I reckon. Alcohol and all. And Oriana?"

"Yes?" I could barely get the word out.

"Thank you for taking me," he said. "And holding my hand up and all. I liked it." And slammed the door.

Gabriel

Two things happened the next day. Well, two things other than my thinking for much too long about how I'd said, "I liked it." What? I'd liked her holding up my hand and getting blood on her shirt? Probably losing the circulation in her arm? I needed to learn how to talk to girls. It should be easier the better you liked somebody. Instead, it was harder.

Other than that, the first thing was that my dad rang the doorbell at seven-thirty in the morning.

I was awake. The flatmates weren't. Somebody yelled, "What the *fuck*," as the doorbell rang again.

I ran down the stairs to open the front door. It was my dad. Not entirely surprising. Who else would ring your doorbell at this hour on New Year's Day? He looked at me, then looked at my hand and looked at me again, and I said, "Yeh. Cut it. Come up," tried to feel less stupid about it, and led him upstairs to the flat.

When we got inside, Rowan was just coming out of the bathroom to the sound of an emphatic flush. He glanced at us and said, "Keep it down, will you, mate? It's bloody New Year's, and I just got to bed bloody three hours ago," shambled back into his bedroom, and slammed the door.

My dad gave me what I'd call an expressive glance, and I shrugged and said, "Yeh. Well. The rent's cheap, and they're pretty good blokes." Rowan had lent me his power drill a couple of weeks ago to put a cupboard door back on after it had come loose from its hinges—the landlord was pretty useless—and when I'd gone on to replace a faulty electrical outlet, had actually decided to fix the tap on the kitchen sink himself. So he *did* have skills, which was interesting. Last week, we'd both helped Duncan transport a new mattress home with the aid of my ute, and he'd bought pizza for all of us. So—not so bad.

Unfortunately, when I led my dad into the kitchen, I realized that (A) my hand was bandaged, and (B) the washing-up wasn't done from last night, or yesterday morning, for that matter, which meant the sink was full of dirty dishes, and it wasn't going to be easy to clean them. I said, "I was going to suggest a cup of tea. And breakfast, because I haven't made mine yet. Reckon I could fasten a plastic bag around my hand and give it a go."

My dad didn't say, "I'll do it," which wasn't a surprise. He also didn't say, "Let's go to a café," which either of the flatmates would've said in a heartbeat. Instead, he said, "Come home with me. Your mum will fix you breakfast."

I wanted to say the "café" thing myself, because honestly, it made me a bit uncomfortable to have my mum cook a separate meal for me, but ... it was my dad. So we went downstairs, and I said, "Oh. I forgot that the ute's at Matiu Te Mana's place. You could drop me there, afterward."

"Why?"

Ah. Why, indeed. I climbed into his car, he put it in gear and headed out through the oddly deserted streets toward his own flat, and I said, "I went to his house to have him stitch me up, but he wasn't there. Oriana drove me to hospital instead, as I was bleeding pretty badly. I thought it would be best to collect the ute this morning, so she drove me home afterward."

Dad said, "Is it serious?"

"No. Cut it on a can lid. Ten days until the stitches come out." I may as well tell him the truth. What else was I going to say? "I was practicing with my chainsaw"?

Dad grunted. I wasn't sure what that meant, and I didn't have anything cheerful to say about the ten-day thing, so I was silent. Always my go-to move.

My mum said, "Oh, dear," about the bandage, and, "You

look thin," in general, after which she and Patience produced a breakfast of eggs, bacon, baked beans, fried tomatoes and mushrooms, and toast. They'd have done sausages as well, but I asked them not to. I wasn't sure if I'd ever want to eat sausages again. As I was getting outside of all of it, Dad asked, "Why did Oriana drive you to hospital? What was she doing there, at that house?"

Mum stood up and told Harmony and Patience, "Come help me with the washing," and I thought, *Ah. Here we go, then.* I said, "The answer's not a secret, Mum. You can hear it."

She said, "Men's business," and headed out of the kitchen with the girls.

Dad said, when they were gone, "Why are you questioning your mum?"

I didn't answer for a minute. I needed to gather my thoughts for this. I said, "We do live here now. I'm trying to adapt."

"Adapt in your home," he said. "Not in mine."

"Fair enough," I said, and, when he looked up sharply again, "I'm a man. I'm going to answer you as a man, not a boy." Half of me wondering, inside, why I was pushing this, and the other half saying that I had to. I added, "Oriana was minding the kids while Matiu and Poppy were out. Prudence—Priya—was with her, so Oriana left her there with them and took me to hospital, as I was bleeding pretty freely. She sat with me in the ED, and then she drove me home."

He stared at me, brown eyes on blue, and I looked back at him and willed myself to be calm. He said, "That's what I came to talk to you about, but this puts a different complexion on the matter."

My heart had started to thud again. Stupidly. I said, "What was, exactly?"

"Relations between the families," he said. "Gray asked if we'd like to come to a New Year's barbecue today. Heaps of people, he said, not just the family."

"Time to try again, he reckons?" I said. "Now that we've settled in, got used to things? He wants family relations between us for Daisy's sake." That wasn't hard to suss out. The house we were working on, from early morning to night, six days a week? It was for Gray, but really, it was for Daisy. I didn't know that because she was involved. I knew because she wasn't. She'd said what she wanted for the bath and kitchen, and Gray had said the rest would be a surprise, but that it would be the best.

That was why we were the crew, my dad had told all of us. Because we'd give Gray our best.

"Yeh," Dad said. "About the family thing. Reckon he's right at that. Family's more important than ever, out here. Those girls are our family as well, and what example do they have, without us?"

That was one way to look at it. I'd bet it wasn't the way Daisy was looking at it, but I wasn't about to say it. I said, "A barbecue sounds good." Cautiously.

"Second thing," Dad said. "He wants me back on the university job as soon as the rest of the crew gets back from their holidays. That means we need a new foreman at the house."

I waited. It was hard to breathe. Dad said, "I'd like you to do it."

I said, "OK," and couldn't think of anything to add.

"Your hand being injured isn't ideal," he said, "but a foreman's not just working with his hands. He's working with his brain, and his judgment. Can I trust your judgment?"

"Yes," I said. "And I'll do everything I can with the hand, too." Wanting to jump. Wanting to shout.

"It won't be a rise in pay," he said. "Gray wanted to pay you more. I said—not until he shows he can do it. Show us for the next couple of weeks, and then we'll see about that rise in pay. My guess is that Gray will pay you the extra for the time before, so you won't be hurting, not if you come up to standard. Thirty days to get it all done. Thirty-first of January. That's the deadline."

"I know the deadline." My heart was beating like it wanted to jump out of my chest. "We'll meet it."

"Good," he said. "Then I'll take you back to get the ute. Unless you want to do anything first, since you don't have two good hands. Shopping. Like that."

He was willing to take me *shopping?* I wouldn't have guessed he'd even know where the store was. "Well, uh ... yeh. That'd be good."

"Then let's go," he said, and stood up.

I put my dishes in the dishwasher first. He looked surprised. I told myself again, *My choice.* After that, I said, "I appreciate your trust in me, making me foreman. I won't let you down."

"I know," he said. "That's why I did it."

22

THE KNICKERS BIT

G*ABRIEL*

I was at Gray's again, and so was Oriana. I'd seen her as soon as I'd parked for the barbecue.

Well, of course she was here. She *lived* here. At the moment, she was with the kids, helping the littlest ones play cricket. She'd stand behind them and help them swing the bat, then run with them afterward and pick them up if they fell. Making it not scary to try, and making it fun.

She wasn't wearing shorts today like most of the women, or a long dress like the women from my family, except Glory and Patience, who were wearing *almost* long dresses. Oriana was in what they called a "sundress" instead. It had wide straps over the shoulders, big red buttons down the close-fitting front, and a full skirt that ended well below the knee, and it was patterned with strawberries. She had some kind of elaborate plaits in her hair, and she was pretty as a picture. I'd never seen her arms and legs and upper ... chest revealed this much, and once again, I stared.

Pity she wasn't staring back.

I was cooking steaks on the barbecue for Gray's mum, Honor, during all this staring, because that was something I could do with one hand. I couldn't carry tables—well, sheets of plywood on sawhorses—or set up sunshades, but I could cook steaks, and the fish I'd do next, too. Cooking on the barbecue was something men did Outside, for some reason, even if they didn't cook anything else, and it was the only kind of cooking I was somewhat confident about. The flats had a barbecue, outside, and I'd been using it, as it felt marginally more sanitary than the cooker in the flat, and you could do vegies on it as well as meat. I'd taken to cooking for the others sometimes, too, as they were even worse than me. Hard to believe, but they were. There was microwaving as well, of course, but that didn't really count. I wasn't even sure you could actually call it "food."

I saw Gray coming across the grass toward me, looking serious, and didn't drop my gaze. I had to face this, and it wouldn't get any easier.

Oh. What if it wasn't just about the hand?

Then face it and be honest.

He got there at last and said, "Your dad says you injured yourself last night." About the hand, then.

"Yeh," I said. "Ten days at least, the doctor says. Stitches, eh."

"All right?" he asked. "How are you managing for yourself?"

"I'm fine. No worries."

"A cooking accident, your dad said," was the next comment. "Reckon that's tough, learning how. Knife slipped, eh."

"No. I did it opening a can."

He grinned. "Nah. Seriously? Embarrassing, eh."

It was so unexpected, I found myself grinning back. "Embarrassing, yeh." And then, for some reason, went on, "Especially as Oriana had to give me a lift to hospital. I went to see Matiu for the stitching, but I didn't realize they'd all go out for the holiday, and ..." I explained the rest as best I could.

"Should've gone straight to Emergency, I reckon. Oriana was working."

Gray stood there a minute in silence, one hand in his pocket, looking over the fruit trees and the garden, then up the hill to where Oriana was still playing cricket, and said, "She's your cousin." Neutrally, but not.

"My step-cousin. Aaron's my stepdad. My dad died when I was a baby."

I shouldn't have said anything about Oriana. That was just borrowing trouble, and Gray wasn't even my foreman. He was the boss. You didn't bring your problems to the boss, or reveal yourself to him, either. You talked to your mates, at least that was the idea. I didn't have mates like that, though, and even if I had, I couldn't imagine telling them this. They couldn't understand in a million years, because they hadn't grown up in Mount Zion.

I could've told my brothers, I guessed, but that would be odd, too. They were married, but their wives had been given to them.

Gray was Daisy's partner, though, and Daisy was Oriana's sister, which meant that Gray was the one person who might actually understand. Even though Daisy never seemed one bit Mount Zion anymore.

"Ah," Gray said. "And you looked stupid to her. Cutting your hand on a can."

"Yeh. Also, I'm not fond of blood. It didn't ... go well. I should tell you that. Just in case."

"In case you become a foreman on a big job sometime," he said, matter-of-factly. "Though that may not be for me."

It hit me like a punch. No matter what Oriana had thought, he was thinking of sacking me because of the injury. Because of my carelessness. "Oh," I said. "Right." And stared down at the steaks, poking them with the fork, pretending I was checking them for doneness when I knew they weren't done.

"Gabriel." He laid a hand on my shoulder briefly, being

kind. Yet he was still talking about this here, with close to forty people around, and I needed to school my face so they wouldn't know how the earth had opened beneath me. "I'm telling you that," he went on, "because loyalty doesn't work the same out here. Not the same lifetime commitment, eh. Some bastard is going to try to poach you from me anytime here, and against my better judgment, I'm telling you that you're free to go if you think your future lies somewhere else. I hope you'll stay, though. You've got a future with me, too, and I'll take care that it's a better one. Good men aren't easy to find, and you're a good man. If a bit careless with the can opener."

The relief was almost too much. I controlled my face with an effort and started turning the steaks. My hand wanted to shake, but I wouldn't let it.

"And my new foreman on the house," he said. "Time to prove yourself, eh. And if you're not fond of blood, you arrange ahead of time for one of them to take over for you if blood's involved. Everybody has some weakness. But last night, you … what? With Oriana? What didn't go well?"

I swallowed. "Nearly passed out on the way from the car to Emergency. She had to, uh …"

He was grinning again. "Let me guess. She had to hold you up."

I smiled. I wouldn't have thought I *could* smile about that. "Yeh. She did."

"Mate," he said. "She loved it."

"No, she didn't. How could she?"

"It's Oriana. Soft heart. Kind heart. Don't tell me she didn't try to make you feel better."

"Well, yeh," I said. "Kind heart is about right."

Somehow, I was looking at her again, in front of Gray. Taking her own turn to bat now, skirt and all. She hit the ball a mighty *crack*, it spun and flew like she'd put some power behind it, and then she was running, and laughing. Playing.

Gray said quietly, "She's not a child. None of those girls have been kids for a long time. They're babes in the woods, and they're the last thing from it."

Once again, I was frozen. I wasn't sure what he was saying.

He said, "I could've seen this one coming, I reckon. I thought you were cousins. Does your dad know how you feel?"

I knew I was flushed red. "He guessed, I think. He doesn't approve. The ... her ..."

"Her what?" Gray's face was set in harder lines.

No choice but to say it. "That they're more worldly, I think. Daisy's sisters. But we're out here in the world now, aren't we? Changing some things doesn't mean changing everything, but we don't always seem to agree on which things matter, my dad and me."

"Hmm," Gray said, his face relaxing some. "Does *she* know?"

"No!" I lowered my voice and said again, "No. I wouldn't know how to tell her. I don't think I *should* tell her. She's seventeen. That's one of the things that should change, I think, how she thinks about her future, but Dad thinks ... maybe the opposite. I'm not sure."

I was being so disloyal here, I was sweating, and I wasn't explaining myself well at all. Why had I said any of this?

Gray was quiet a minute, then said, "No dating at Mount Zion, obviously. When you're notified that your marriage has been arranged, what happens then? How do you get to know the girl?"

I stared at him. "How do you mean? You don't. Not until you're married. But you know who she is, of course."

"No ... picnics? No, uh, ice cream? Courting in the parlor? I'm trying to think how dating used to work. I can't imagine, it seems."

He was still the boss, and yet I was asking, maybe because he was about as worldly a man as I was ever likely to know, other than Drew. "How does it work Outside, then, finding a woman? Is it that? Picnics and all?"

He laughed. "You're asking the wrong bloke. I was a sportsman. How dating works for a sportsman, when he's young and stupid, is: 'easily.' You meet her in a bar, and you go home with her. Sad to say. And then I met Daisy, of course, and nothing was easy. Hang on, though. I know who we can ask."

He took off toward the yurt, and I thought, *No,* and also, *You go home with her? When you've just met her?* Unfortunately, I was trapped here by my steaks, because Gray was coming across the grass now with his mum, Honor, who was smiling as if she were looking forward to this.

She said, "Gray says you have a question about dating. And you're not burning up my lovely steaks, are you?"

"No," I said.

"To which?" she asked. "Dating, or the steaks?"

"Uh ... both." I could have thrown down the meat fork and run, I guessed, except that I couldn't. Rude, humiliating, and pointless.

She wasn't smiling when she said, "You know that it doesn't work the same out here. That girls get to choose for themselves."

"Yeh," I said. "Better, I think."

Her eyes searched mine. "You do, eh."

"Yeh," I said again, then couldn't think what else to throw in there.

"So this would be," she said, "getting to know a girl. One you liked. Or one whose knickers you wanted to get into, maybe."

"No!" The second time I'd answered too loudly. "No," I said more quietly. "I don't, uh ... want ... plan ... to do that."

More searching gaze. So far, this was about the worst barbecue I'd ever been to. "You don't want to," she said flatly.

"Mum," Gray said. "I think what Gabriel's trying to say is

that he wants to do the, ah, knickers bit later. Once they're ..."
He glanced at me. "Fill in the blank here, mate."

"Married," I said desperately. "Once we're married. How do you—well, get to know a girl enough for that, though? To ask her and all, and for her to say yes?"

"In the old days, you mean," she said. "When some people *did* wait for the knickers bit." She laughed. "I like that. The knickers bit. Seems to me you probably met her family, and invited her to meet yours. When you go to see her with her family, they know you're serious, and so does she. And after you have dinner with them, maybe you invite her for a walk. It's a start, eh. Lets you see whether she likes you, too. And you do little things for her to show her you're thinking of her. Bring her something you made for her, maybe, or fix something she's having trouble with. That's good. You think of what a good husband would do, and you do those things. Like a male bird showing the female he knows how to build a nest, eh."

"Knew you'd have the answer, Mum," Gray said. "I wouldn't have thought of making her something."

"No?" his mum said. "And yet there you were after you met Daisy, spending your entire day off putting up alarms and cameras and a gate to keep her safe. Funny you don't realize that counted."

"Loaned her my car, too, though," he said. "And it's a pretty nice car. Also the yurt."

"Yeh," she said, "and yet I reckon it was taking the time on that gate that did the business. A man can say anything. Can buy anything, too. When he spends his time and his sweat—that means more. Making briquettes out of those steaks, are we, Gabriel?"

I jumped, checked them, and started piling them onto the platter. "Just done," I said. "Just now." I put them onto a platter, scraped the grill, and picked up the rack with the fish fillets. Fresh-caught wild king salmon, flaky and buttery as you like. I needed to focus this time, because fish was tricky that way.

I put the racks in place, and then I looked at Oriana again. I couldn't help it. She was bowling to the little kids now, her movements graceful, assured. She looked ... happy. I watched her applaud as a little boy with red hair hit the ball and ran, and then I realized somebody was watching me watch. Daisy, up on the terrace, and she wasn't smiling. I turned my attention to my fish again.

My dad had told me not to think about it. Gray seemed to be saying something different, but as for what Daisy would say ...

My heart? My heart knew what it wanted, and so did my body. Was that just lust, then?

Where does a man's loyalty lie? With his family? What part of his family? With his employer? Or with that one woman?

It's your job to lead, my father had said, *and you led her astray.* I'd assumed he was right. He was my father.

Therefore shall a man leave his father and his mother, and shall cleave unto his wife: and they shall be one flesh.

That was God. Not the Prophet; from the Bible itself. Genesis, which was the first book, and the foundation.

She's still seventeen, I reminded myself, or, possibly, the angel on my shoulder reminded me. *She has plans. She has a life to live.*

The demon on my other shoulder answered.

Why can't she live it with me?

23

THE BROKEN PIECE

Oriana

Gabriel didn't come to talk to me at the barbecue. Maybe that was because Daisy told me to sit with her and Gray, along with Frankie and Priya, and Gabriel was at a table perpendicular to us—I knew that word, because of maths—with his family. His parents, his sister, his brothers and sisters-in-law. And with Patience, who was sitting next to him and, as I watched, cutting his steak into pieces, because of his hand, and pouring more lemonade into his glass. Looking at him from under her lashes for a moment, then looking away. Touching her hair, which was curly, pale blond, and so beautiful.

My heart gave such a lurch, I felt a little sick. That was flirting, and Uncle Aaron was watching it, then exchanging a glance with Aunt Constance. Not a "she shouldn't be doing that" glance, either.

Daisy said, maybe noticing me looking their way, "Did Gabriel hurt his hand? On the job, Gray? Pity."

Gray hesitated a moment, then said, "No. Not on the job. Got some stitches, too, so he won't be able to do as much at work. He's going to be foreman for the rest of it, though, which should work out OK. It's good to give him the chance."

I wanted to say, "He is? How wonderful." I wanted to tell Gabriel ... I didn't quite know what. Congratulations, obviously. I glanced over there again. Everybody was laughing, his dad was lifting his glass in Gabriel's direction, and Patience was sparkling, smiling, and saying something. Probably something admiring.

Oh. Gray. He didn't look at me, and I had no idea whether he knew I'd driven Gabriel last night. Maybe Priya had mentioned it, or maybe Gabriel had. The knowledge was trying to burn a hole in me, and I could tell that meant it was a sin. I said, "He hurt his hand cooking. He came to Matiu's house looking to get it stitched, and I took him to A&E, as he was bleeding pretty heavily and wasn't really fit to drive himself."

"Thought you were minding the kids," Daisy said.

"Priya was there," I said. "With her phone. There were two of us while the kids were awake."

"Did you ring Matiu or Poppy?" Daisy asked. "That you were leaving?"

"No," I said. "I didn't think of it."

"That's a pity," Daisy said. "Matiu's my colleague. Remember, he's employing you partly as a favor to me, and watching those kids was your first responsibility. Also, Gabriel has parents. He has brothers. Why did you have to be the one to take him?"

Frankie said, "Probably because it's Gabriel, and he's so *hot.*" She didn't say it in an admiring way. She said it in a disgusted way, and she and Priya exchanged a look, like they'd talked about this already in the few hours since Frankie had come back from Wanaka for the long weekend.

"Matiu agrees with you, Daisy," Priya had to chime in, "because he said, 'Next time, just ring us and tell us you're leaving, so we'll know.'"

I didn't normally get angry. I got sad, and I felt guilty, but somehow, I never quite made it to "angry," not the way

Frankie did. I was angry now, though. That must be what it was when you felt the blood pulsing in your head like it wanted to get *out*. I said, "He did say that, and I said I understood, and I was sorry. Also, he said it because I told them I'd left. It wasn't a secret, and I had blood on my shirt. It was Matiu's department I took Gabriel to. I told them not to pay me for the hours I was gone, too. Gabriel was *bleeding*. He was unsteady on his feet by the time I got him to hospital. Yes, I should've thought to ring Poppy. Another time, I'll do better, but I had to decide, and I decided."

Daisy said, "That's fair, and you're seventeen. That's why teenagers aren't given adult responsibilities here, because you haven't experienced enough. You felt it was a crisis, you made a mistake, and now you've learnt. Just so you're not really thinking of Gabriel as a partner, in case Frankie's not just being silly. You're not in the same place, however it feels. He's full grown, and if he hasn't had sex yet, he'll be having it soon. He's extremely good-looking, and I'm sure he isn't short of offers. It's not Mount Zion. He's a quiet man, and maybe a conservative one, but even if he's looking for a wife and not just sex partners, he's not looking for a seventeen-year-old, hey, Gray. He'll want somebody who knows what she's doing, because he'll want to learn."

Frankie said, "Really? This has to be our conversation? About Gabriel's sex life? About Oriana's sex life? Pardon, her vague virginal sexual fantasies? Do I want to discuss sex? I do not. It's not that special anyway," she told me. "Not for a woman, it isn't."

"Well, yes," Daisy said, "it is. If it's with a man who cares enough about his partner, and knows what to do. Which is why Gabriel *should* find those women who are willing to teach him. That way, he may actually learn what to do himself. I can guarantee he doesn't know it now. He'll only know how to do what's guaranteed *not* to work, because that's what Mount Zion teaches you. Also, you'll look silly if you run after him,

Oriana, and that won't feel good at all. Last night was one thing. It felt like an emergency. Fine, although you could've rung me in that case, and I'd have come. But, please, don't make a fool of yourself. It's so hard when you have to look back on that later and cringe. I'm telling you that because I know. We didn't grow up like people here. We don't know how to date, or how to be cool. Wait until you're a bit older. Just—please wait."

I said, "I think it's unfair to talk about him like that. You don't know what he thinks. Would we like it if he talked about us?" I never said things like that. I never *thought* things like that. Somehow, though, I was saying, "He's kind. Why does he have to be a ... a man to you all the time, like that makes him evil, or so ... so different? Why can't he just be a *person*? A *kind* person?"

"Trust me," Frankie said, "that's not how men see themselves around women."

"Explain to them, Gray," Daisy said. "And that it's also not a wonderful thing if he pities her, which he will, because he *is* kind."

Gray didn't look rattled, but then, Gray never looked rattled. He said, "Oriana's right, and she's wrong. You're right, Daisy, that young blokes are going to think about sex, and that they may especially think about it around her, because she's a very pretty girl. But then, I suspect young women think a fair bit about sex, too. But I don't think you're giving the man enough credit. I think he goes deeper than that. I also think that this isn't really my business, or any of ours, come to that, other than Oriana's. I don't see that she did anything really wrong, and it's not like he's taken any kind of advantage of her so far, or like she's asked for our advice. Maybe we should let it go."

"I'm responsible for her," Daisy said. I didn't often hear her being cross with Gray, but I was pretty sure she was now.

"And you've done a good job," Gray said, "helping her

navigate her way through all this newness. Some things, though, you have to learn for yourself, mistakes and all. Not sure where the middle ground is for a seventeen-year-old between Mount Zion on the one hand, everything controlled for you, and where you were when you got out, trying to support yourself and get educated and all with nobody to help you. Oriana's been pretty sensible so far, though. How much do you have in your bank account now?" he asked me.

"Nearly six thousand," I said.

Frankie said, "You're joking. In a *year*? How?"

"Because I don't have to pay rent," I said, "or for my food, so I can save for when I do have to." I was better at saving than either Frankie or Priya. I made my own clothes, and I didn't buy treats. For that matter, I was better at *earning*. Shouldn't that count?

"You paying rent won't be happening for a year and a half at least," Daisy said. "Not until you're done with school and ready to get serious about your future. But until then, while you're living here? Yeh, I'm going to be offering my advice. There's no reason you should have to learn everything the hard way, like I did."

I could have argued, but I wasn't good at arguing. I hadn't had enough practice, maybe, except that Frankie'd had even less practice than me, and she was excellent at arguing. So I decided to just be glad that we weren't talking about Gabriel anymore, and got up to get my strawberry and lemon curd tart out of the fridge.

Gabriel didn't come over to talk to me after that, either, and I was sorry despite myself. I'd worn my prettiest dress today, and when I'd put it on, I'd imagined him telling me I looked nice, and me telling him that I'd made it on his sewing machine, and him getting that warm look in his eyes. The only thing that happened, though, was that Aunt Constance came over to me where I was serving out the sweets, picked up a knife, began to cut a hummingbird cake into slices, and said, keeping her voice low, "What do you think your mum would say about that dress?"

You're not in Mount Zion anymore, I reminded myself. "I hope she'd think it was pretty," I said, "and that she'd be proud I made it."

"On the sewing machine that Gabriel bought you," she said. "That was kind of him, wasn't it?'

"Yes. Very kind." I was stiffening up all over. Why was she saying this?

"He's a good cousin, and a good brother, too," she said. "A wonderful brother to Harmony, especially. He'll be married before too long, I think. Long past time, really. He'll be a Godly husband, like his dad. As long as he has a wife who's glad to let him lead, who puts his happiness before her own."

I was putting a piece of tart on a plate, but my hand slipped and it broke in half. She said, "We all want happiness for Gabriel, don't we?"

Gray was, somehow, in front of me. He said, "I'll take that one. Broken or not, Oriana's sweets are the best. And, yeh, we all want happiness for Gabriel. Just like we want it for Oriana."

24

FIVE NEEDLES

ORIANA

On the Friday night after the barbecue, I was babysitting again, sitting on the front steps outside Laila's house with Long John lying beside me, both of us taking advantage of the summer warmth. I was babysitting because Laila was out on a date with Lachlan, her neighbor, who'd also been at the barbecue. Laila was always so composed, it was hard to know what she was feeling, but I thought that she may have been nervous. It was their first date, and "first dates" were a thing, if people actually did dating. Which, apparently, they did. Just not people in high school.

I wished ... well, I wished for too much. Like a high-school girl, probably.

Time for forget it. Time to sit out here on the not-church steps, enjoy the warm night and everything else there was to enjoy, and knit. I thought better when I knitted. If I could knit during class, it would be so much easier. I'd have an excuse for looking down, for one thing.

I had one of the flat's huge wooden front doors propped open, so I could hear the girls in case they woke up. They'd taken some effort to settle tonight, Amira popping up again and again, always with another question. The latest had started, like the others, with, "Oriana?" spoken in a deceptively soft little voice from around the corner, as if she didn't have ten times the determination I did. And this time, she'd brought Yasmin with her.

I'd heard them in their bedroom, talking and giggling. They were twins, of course, but I knew about talking and giggling with your sisters. We'd whispered to each other, daringly, from our bunks late at night, when our parents were asleep, and in snatched moments during the day, too, taking in the washing from the lines or washing dishes together in the kitchens. My sisters had been my constant companions, the holders of my secrets, and I'd been theirs.

Now, though, would they ever understand my secrets again? Would I understand theirs?

That was why I hadn't shushed the girls, probably. Besides, I was used to little kids asking me for things. I *liked* little kids asking me for things, in fact. Better than adults asking me for things, especially if that was, "What can you tell us about the abolition in the European nations of the global slave trade from Africa, Oriana?" Another thing I hadn't heard of before this year, and that I still wished I didn't know. At least I'd been wise enough not to ask about this one when the topic came up in class, and had done my usual instead: looked it up on the Internet.

The world was full of horrors, more than I'd ever known. The problem was, Mount Zion had horrors, too. I'd seen too many of them. Which horrors were worst? I didn't know. The ones at Mount Zion just seemed to be on a ... a smaller scale. And there was no higher authority to appeal to, nobody to step in and stop the evil, because the only authority was the Prophet.

And your husband.

As long as he has a wife who's glad to let him lead.

Was I? I wasn't sure anymore. On the other hand, I wasn't

one bit like Daisy, so confident in every situation. I wasn't Mount Zion, and I wasn't Outside.

You can learn. Just keep your mouth shut so you don't make a fool of yourself. Daisy's right.

Amira's question this time had been, "Why do horses have long tails, but rabbits have short tails?" Which was a much better topic.

In the past, I would've said, "Because God made them that way." This time, I said, "I don't know. Why do you think?" Everybody said it was good to ask questions, and besides, I really *didn't* know, other than the "God" thing. And if God *had* made rabbits that way—why had He done it? There must have been a reason.

I'd never thought that way before. It would've seemed like questioning God. It was a bit heady to do it now. Exciting.

Amira put her head on one side and hopped on one foot a while as if it would help her think, and had just opened her mouth when Yasmin said timidly, because Yasmin was so much like me, "So they can swat flies? My mummy says that's what they're doing when they're swishing them like that. Keeping the flies away."

"Yes," I said. "They *do* use them for that." And she beamed.

"But don't rabbits have flies on them, too?" Amira asked. "And I was going to *say*, Yasmin."

Yasmin, for once, shut her mouth and looked stubborn, so I said, "Yasmin knew first, though, so of course she gave the answer." Timid girls got to speak up, too, under my rules. That way, they might not be so timid. And I should put them to bed right now, of course. Instead, I asked, "Where do rabbits live? Where's their home?" Because—wait. I actually *knew* this, for once. I thought I did, anyway. You learnt some things growing up around farming that people didn't necessarily learn in school.

Amira hopped on the other foot a few times, clearly thinking furiously, but again, Yasmin said it first. "In a sandbank, underneath the root of a very big fir tree. That's where Peter Rabbit lives."

That was a story, I knew now. I'd read it to the girls. "Yes," I said, getting a bit excited myself. "A burrow in the ground. And what does a stoat like to hunt?"

Amira and Yasmin looked at each other, then Amira asked, "A what?"

"A stoat," I said. "Like a weasel. It's long and thin and eats other animals. What does it hunt?"

"*I* don't know," Amira said. "I never heard of it!"

"Rabbits?" Yasmin asked.

"Rabbits," I agreed. "But rabbits are very fast, and they have heaps of tunnels in their burrows to help them escape, so if the stoat is behind the rabbit, trying to grab it, and the rabbit is hopping away very fast …"

Both girls were jumping now. "The stope can't grab its tail!" Amira shouted.

"And catch it!" Yasmin said. "And eat it!"

I laughed, and they did, too, and then I remembered and shushed them. "Yes, but now that we know, you both need to go back to bed. And go to *sleep.*"

I'd failed completely at child-minding, because they both hopped around the lounge instead, being rabbits themselves, thoroughly wound up and not likely to fall asleep anytime soon, and it was almost *nine.* What if Laila had come home early and found out? After the thing with Poppy, where I'd left the kids to take Gabriel to hospital?

Also, what would have happened to me if I'd been out of bed at nine? Or to my oldest sister, if she hadn't got me back into it?

Nothing, because I wouldn't have *been* out of bed, that was all.

Now, both girls were asleep at last, it was close to ten o'clock, and I was alone. Well, other than Long John. I was pretending, maybe, that this was my flat, and they were my girls. That I'd cooked them dinner—which, in fact, I had—in a cozy little kitchen and not in a long, low, always too-hot extension to the dining hall, hurrying along the row of cookers and fridges manned by a dozen women, the sweat dripping down our backs under our heavy cotton dresses, pooling between our breasts. That I'd tucked them in and sung to them and read a book about make-believe animals doing almost-human things—which wasn't right, because humans were created in God's image and animals weren't, but the stories were too nice not to read—and kissed them goodnight, and then I'd taken my shower and taken down my hair and changed into my nightdress, and ...

My imagination screeched to a halt there the way it always did, except when I was lying under the duvet in the dark with the visions playing across the screen of my closed eyelids, refusing to be banished.

It was as if my body had woken up, since that night watching the movie with Gabriel, or it had come to life, maybe. I'd seen too many photos now, had watched too many films, even the Disney ones, with that breath-holding moment before the first kiss. I'd heard too many songs. I had all these ... these *feelings* in my body, and I couldn't stop noticing them. Was it the Devil tempting me, or was it just that I should be long married by now, so I could share those feelings with my husband? I didn't know, and I didn't know how to ask.

I thought some more about make-believe animal stories instead and whether there was actually anything wrong with them, watched my cheap bamboo needles flashing in and out of my dark-blue knitting in the lamplight, and concentrated on my pattern. I was doing cables and ribs, which would make it warmer for ...

"Oriana?"

The voice was low, but I jumped anyway and dropped a stitch. Long John jumped to his feet—a bit clumsily, because of the missing leg—and started wagging his tail.

It was Gabriel. Standing at the foot of the steps, dressed in his usual work trousers and long-sleeved shirt, looking so much like Mount Zion, I froze. As if he could read my thoughts. *All* my thoughts. As if I'd conjured him up like summoning the Devil.

He said, "Can I come up?"

"You don't have to ask," I somehow managed to say.

"I do have to ask," he said. "There are still rules here. They're just different rules."

I felt the heat rising into my cheeks and hoped he couldn't see it. He meant that men asked here, or maybe that I didn't know the right rules. I said, "Come up, then. Please." And tried to stop my hands trembling as I picked up my stitch.

He sank down on the step beside me. Long John started in with his usual overenthusiastic greeting, but when Gabriel said, "Lie down," he did. Even though Gabriel's voice hadn't been harsh, or even loud.

The church porch was wide, because of those double doors, and Gabriel wasn't touching me, but it felt like he was. I said, "Why are you ... Were you out walking, then? Or going somewhere?" And immediately thought, *Why are you asking him his business?*

He didn't seem to mind, because he said, "Yeh. Out walking. It gets a bit warm in my flat. A bit ..." He moved his hands restlessly, one over the other, then clasped them. The left one still had a bandage on it where his stitches would remain for a few more days. The white cotton was grubby, and my own hands itched to change it, to check and clean the wound. How could he do that well enough with one hand?

They were capable hands, big and broad, the knuckles scarred. His face was as beautiful as the archangel he was named for, and so was his body, so tall and strong. His hands weren't. They were battered and calloused and imperfect, like they were the real parts of him.

I said, "It feels small, maybe. The flat." Like most places in

Dunedin, the flat wasn't far away, but you measured not by distance here, but by elevation. The church was on a bit of a hill. Poppy's beautiful house was at the *top* of a hill. And Gabriel's flat was on no hill at all.

I wondered if he liked living there. I wondered if his new life was worth what he'd given up for it. His place in the world. His friends. The life he'd always thought he'd have.

I wondered how I'd ever ask.

"I don't mind small," he said. "I mind dirty, but I don't get much choice about that. Flatmates, eh."

"Oh," I said. "Is it lonely, too? It's lonely sometimes for me," I somehow went on, "even just being with my sisters. If I had to live with other people, and not people who ... who understood what it's like, being the way we are, I don't think I could bear it."

He cleared his throat and didn't answer for a long moment, and I said, "But you're not me, of course."

"No," he said. "I am." Then hurried on, "Why are *you* here, though? Alone at night, at a church. In front of a church. Is something wrong?"

I was still struggling to pick up my stitch, and I'd known how to do that since I was *six*. I got it at last and explained, "It's not really a church. It's Laila's flat. My employer, who was at the barbecue. Poppy's friend. And Lachlan's house, too, the man who came with her that day. They're out on a date tonight, and I'm babysitting Laila's girls."

"Oh," he said, and was silent.

"Oh!" I said, and jumped. "Not that he ... not that it's the *same* flat. I mean, his flat is in here, too. In the building. Separately."

"Oh," he said, and I wondered a little wildly how much both of us had said, "Oh."

I sneaked a peek at him. He was grinning, and suddenly, so was I. Grinning, and then laughing. "You have to *explain* so much," I finally managed to say. "That people are ..."

"Having relations," he said, "or not."

"*Yes*. And half the time, you don't even *know*."

You'd think it would be odd, talking about this, but it wasn't. Every kid at Mount Zion knew about having relations. Sex within marriage wasn't a shameful thing, it was the most important thing, what men needed from their wives and the way women served both their husbands and God. It was holy, at least that was what we were told. What I'd seen had never looked all that special, and from the snatches of conversation I'd sometimes overheard, it didn't always seem to feel lovely, either, even though the Prophet said it was, and Daisy had said it could be wonderful. Gabriel would have grown up hearing and seeing his parents having relations in the dark the same way I had, but maybe he knew more about it. Well, he probably did. He'd have been outside all day, and, well—animals.

The thought was making me hot again, even though I'd just been thinking that it couldn't really be that nice. Looking at Gabriel, though, and thinking about his hands … the night was cooling, but still, it was as if I were wearing too many clothes. Which I definitely wasn't.

I was wearing another dress I'd made myself, in fact. It had a print of glorious yellow and purple flowers, and the flowing fabric nipped in through the bust, down to the waist, and below, then flared gently from my hips to below my knees. It had oversized, round purple buttons that I adored, plus little sleeves. Cap sleeves, they were called, which meant that my arms and legs were bare again. I could sense Gabriel looking at them, and at my hair, which had grown past my shoulders since I'd first had it cut, and tended to wave even more now that it didn't hang to below my knees. I'd taken it down after the workday, which he might think was sinful. And it wasn't anything like Patience's pale-blond glory. My hair was brown, not even near-black like Daisy's and Frankie's. It was ordinary, like me.

My skin got hotter. He didn't look much different than

before, and I did. What if he didn't approve of that? What would that mean to me?

I didn't know the answer, but a rebellious part of me was saying, *I like my dress, though.* Even though I still wore an apron when I worked in the kitchen, I was making them now in different colors and patterns. My aprons had ruffled trim, contrasting waistbands, and wide strings that tied in a bow. I loved them, even if that was vanity, and I didn't want to go back to the white ones I'd worn all my life over long-sleeved, ankle-length, shapeless sacks of dresses.

With all the beautiful colors in the world, the orange and blue butterflies, the pink and red and purple flowers, the rainbow hues inside a shell at the beach, the shining blue-black of a tui and the emerald and russet of a kereru, flashing overhead with that distinctive rustle and whirr of wings as you walked through the bush, why would God only want people to wear brown?

Gabriel asked, "What are you making?" and I jumped, because I'd thought at first that he'd said, "What are you thinking?"

I concentrated on the chunky yarn beneath my fingers, the heathered indigo of it contrasting with the paler colors of my dress. Bulky, hand-dyed alpaca was much too dear to use for something I wouldn't sell, but I'd wanted the best for this project.

"It's a hat," I said.

"I see that," he said, with a smile in his voice. "Not for you, though, surely. You'd do something prettier. White, maybe, and with flowers on. You always have flowers on your clothes now, every time I see you. It would be made of something fluffier, too. Angora, maybe. That's not for summer, either, though. A winter hat for Gray? A bit early to be knitting it, surely, in January."

I couldn't lie. I couldn't tell the truth either, though. "No," I said. "And I started early because I'm doing a jumper to match next, and I want to be sure I have enough time." And prayed, *Please don't ask me.* Except that I should want him to. How else would I get his measurements? Because, yes, it was for him. I was doing exactly what Daisy had said. Making a fool of myself.

I could assume he and Gray were about the same size, but I wanted it to fit perfectly. If he was feeling alone, there in his flat, shouldn't he know that somebody was thinking about him, wanting to do something for him? It could just be admiration, couldn't it? Respect? He didn't have to know how I felt.

I could bring the jumper up casually, maybe. *I thought you might like a hat,* I'd say. *The wind's so cold in winter. And I'd like to try knitting a lovely top-down raglan jumper anyway, the kind you can wear every day. Maybe with leather patches on the shoulders and elbows, so it wouldn't wear out even if you were working in it. Carrying things, boards and so forth, over your shoulder. If you think you'd like it, if you'd wear it ...*

I thought about the way he'd looked carrying those boards, always with a heavier load than the others, his big hand steadying the load and his biceps straining, showing under his shirt, and got a bit breathless. A bit *more* breathless.

"Oh," he said, sounding completely different than before. "You're making it for somebody else." Worried, maybe, that it *was* for him. How could I ask now?

"Yes." I went on, seizing on the first topic that came to mind, "Laila thought it was odd, once she knew about Mount Zion, that I didn't care that she lived in a church."

"The building, you mean." He still sounded different. Remote, almost. Had he guessed, and now he was trying to put me off? Please, no. "Did you tell her that there's no church, the way she thinks, at Mount Zion?"

"Yes," I said. "A bit. That the dining hall was where the Prophet preached, and that purpose-built churches are idolatry, constructed for man's pride and earthly desires and not for love of the real Word of God, so they don't count as holy places. That the Prophet said so, I mean," I hurried to add. "I'm not sure I— But anyway. She didn't think that was as … as bad as other people do, maybe because she's not Christian, not even a little bit Christian, the way people usually are, Outside."

I stole a glance at him. What would I do if he thought this was bad? I didn't know, but somehow, I needed to find out.

Laila was good. I was realizing by now that "good" and "evil" weren't the straight lines I'd always been told, that there were all sorts of curves and twists to them, but surely, Laila was good, the same way my mum was. She was kind all the way down, not just on the surface. You couldn't have such kind hands, couldn't hold babies the way she did, as if she loved every one of them, and not be good.

I felt, normally, like I didn't know anything, but I did know about mothers and fathers and babies. And surely, *surely*, somebody so good couldn't be going to Hell, no matter what I'd grown up believing. "She's Muslim," I told Gabriel. "Like my friend Aisha, that you met. Laila *was* Muslim, anyway. She says she's not sure how much she's anything anymore. Same as me." And then I trembled, kept my fingers moving, the five pale, overlapping needles flashing in and out amongst the soft ropes of indigo, and waited.

The yarn caught on a rough spot, and I sighed. A small sound, but Gabriel must have heard it, because he said, "What?"

"Nothing. I need to sand this needle, that's all."

"You used to knit with metal ones," he said. "I remember."

"You do?" I sneaked another look. He was smiling a little, as if he hadn't even registered the "Muslim" thing. Not to mention, "Same as me." I believed in God. I did. But I was starting to believe that He wasn't the God I'd always heard about, and I didn't know if that was blasphemy.

Goodness. That was what I wanted to believe God was. He should be what you strove for, right? Which was goodness.

Mercy, and charity, and hope. If God was always angry, if He was so easily vengeful ... how could that be right?

"Yeh," he said. "Some women used the wooden ones, and others used metal. You went faster than almost anyone. As fast as the aunties."

"You can't go as fast with the wooden ones," I said. "But they're much cheaper."

"Oh. I see. You'd have more friction with wood, at least if the metal's smooth, and friction would slow you down." A pause, and then he said, "I envied you, in a way. Having my hands working ... that always feels better, but you can't sit around the table after dinner with your circular saw, eh."

I laughed, and he grinned again and said, "Could drive off your company. The noise, and the potential loss of a finger or two."

"Almost as bad as a can opener," I agreed.

I thought I'd gone too far, but he laughed again, the sound warm in the night. The skin crinkled around his indigo eyes, and he kept smiling at me and said, "You're changing, eh."

My heart, somehow, had started to beat much harder. "I'm not sure," I said. "I love my job for Laila, and living at Gray's is wonderful, of course. So comfortable," I hurried to add, in case he thought I sounded ungrateful. "Luxurious, really, when he had no obligation to house us at all, and certainly not to keep doing it. There are all those flowers and vegies in the garden, too, besides the animals, and I get to help with those as well. Which is all brilliant."

"But," Gabriel said. No judgment in his eyes, just interest.

"But I don't seem to be reacting the way I'm meant to," I found myself saying. "I don't want the right things. To do something important. To go far. My sisters want that. Four of us out here, and it's only me who's ..." I trailed off.

"D'you wish you hadn't left, then?" he asked quietly.

I couldn't answer. That was because I couldn't *find* the answer. "No," I said at last. "I don't think so. I know it's better.

Being able to choose for yourself, even though that doesn't always feel nice, and I think some things that happened ..."

Just go on, I told myself, when I wanted to stop. *He left, too. And the Prophet isn't here to find out.*

It was so hard to go on, though. "I think some things were wrong," I said, all in a rush.

"Hurting people," Gabriel said, still quietly. "Hurting kids. Hurting women." A pause. "Hurting your sisters."

I couldn't get a deep enough breath. I couldn't still the beating of my heart. "Yes. I think that's wrong. I think the Prophet is wrong to say it's all right. And to ... to force people. Not to let them out. Women, I mean, and making them get their husbands' permission for ... for anything. For everything. And not to pay people, so it's hard for them to leave anyway, because you need money for everything Outside." The first time I'd said any of that out loud. I hadn't mentioned birth control, of being able to choose for yourself when you had your kids and how many you'd have. A man *couldn't* be all right with that. Not if the woman was the one choosing. Not if the man was from Mount Zion.

Gabriel said, "So do I."

"You do?" I was still knitting determinedly, my fingers comforted by the feel of the needles and the silky wool.

"That's why I left," he said. "I just wish I ..."

"That you fit," I said.

"Yes," he said. "How do you know?"

I'd been so caught up, I realized, I'd gone straight past the point where I should have started to decrease, and I'd have to rip out. I set the needles in my lap and said, "Because I feel the same."

"Really?" he asked. "I'm glad to be out. Glad to ... see more. To do more. But I don't fit. If I had a wife, maybe it wouldn't matter. Or we could ... we could fit at home. Together. My wife and I."

He stopped. I couldn't breathe.

He said, "That's what I want. I'm working on it. Trying, anyway. To have a future to offer somebody, because it's what you said. You need money for everything. What about you? What do you want?"

He was my cousin, and he was confiding in me. I should be honored. I *was* honored. I said, trying for lightness, "I don't know. I keep hearing that I need to finish school, even though there's no rule that says you have to go through Year 13."

"I'd like to be done with that as well," he said. "Technical school, I mean, though it's been good to learn new things. New methods. But I'll be glad to have that certification, and more time to work. More opportunity to get ahead, so I can have a home."

I nodded, but my lips were too numb to say anything. He said, "You'll be wanting to get back inside. It's late," and stood up.

I scrambled to my own feet, and he said, "Gray invited me to dinner with you tomorrow evening. With all of you, I mean."

"Oh," I said.

Something odd crossed his face, but he said, "He should've asked you first, as I'm guessing you could be cooking it."

"Yes," I said. "I mean, yes that I'll be cooking it, not that he should've asked me. It's his house. He can invite whoever he likes, and I'm happy to cook. Happy to help. Do you ... have a favorite? Something you'd like me to make?"

Why was I asking it? And how was I ever going to give him a hat, let alone a jumper? He'd know how I felt then, surely, and he couldn't know. He was looking for a wife. *Planning* for a wife. If I were well past marriageable age now by Mount Zion's standards, what was he? He'd be asking Gray about it, probably, because men must ask somebody, mustn't they? You'd have to be introduced, at least.

"Set up," people said. You got set up for a date. That was probably why he was coming to dinner, to talk about that, because he'd never come before, not by himself. Or he'd already met somebody, maybe at his flat or at a café where he'd gone to dinner, and he wanted advice about how you moved along to getting married. Gray would have advice. He always did.

Wait. Patience. Cutting his meat at the barbecue, and what Aunt Constance had said.

Patience was only sixteen. You needed a Family Court judge's permission to marry before eighteen—I knew that well enough—and besides, Patience's parents were still in Mount Zion.

And you think Uncle Aaron couldn't get their permission? To marry Gabriel? *The one everybody wanted for their daughter?* If Gabriel married her, she wouldn't sin. She might be Outside, but she'd be safe.

Especially if she got married at sixteen.

Looking at him, then looking away. Touching her beautiful hair.

I heard Aunt Constance's voice again. *He'll be married before too long, I think. Long past time, really. He'll be a Godly husband, like his dad. As long as he has the right wife, one who's glad to let him lead and puts his happiness before her own.*

She certainly hadn't meant me. She'd meant, *One who grew up in Mount Zion and has the right attitude, and no worldly sisters.*

"I like most things," Gabriel said. He hesitated, then added, "I know you're brilliant at sweets. Maybe you could do something like that for after, if it's not too much work. I miss those, the kind we used to have, the way they tasted so ... special. With the fruit and all."

"Of course," I said. "If you like." I'd give the hat to Gray, I guessed. Even though it didn't match his eyes.

Gabriel said, "Right, then. I'll see you tomorrow. Be careful driving home. Friday night, eh." He smiled a little. "Feels like I'm always saying that. Cousin, though." And left.

25

THE THRILL AND THE SHAME

G*ABRIEL*

I left Oriana at the church and walked home, feeling even more confused than I had when I'd started out. It was nearly ten-thirty, I'd worked over ten physical hours today, and I needed to go to bed.

I'd started work at seven this morning, and I'd be at the jobsite—at Gray's—at the same time tomorrow, Saturday or no, because we were in an all-out push to finish the job now. This was my future, and if Oriana didn't want me, when she was done with her schooling and whatever else she needed to do, I'd …

I'd find some other way to have a life, however it felt now. It was one thing to be content with the path somebody else laid out for you, hard as that had seemed at times. It was another thing entirely to find a path for yourself, and stay on it. But I'd chosen to be here, and my path, my way forward, was with Gray.

"He'll be doing this for Daisy," Dad had told me again when he'd handed off the responsibility. "That means he'll care more. Don't let them cut any corners, however close that deadline comes, and don't be tempted yourself. A man who doesn't give his best isn't much of a man."

"I won't let you down," I'd repeated, and so far, I was pretty sure I hadn't, but it wasn't easy. I wasn't the oldest man there by a long chalk, and they all knew it. The crew was my brothers, two of our other cousins, a couple of unrelated blokes, and me. All of them from Mount Zion, and a motivated lot, as most of them had families to support, and everyone had come out the same way I had: with nothing. We'd all been put to work by Gray, but for the first time in our lives, we were earning a pay packet for it.

Tomorrow, I'd be setting my alarm for five-thirty, as usual, so I'd be sure to be on the job before seven. The foreman should turn up first. The others wouldn't be far behind, though. Saturday meant overtime, and every man here wanted overtime.

We had the bones of the interior in place now, and I had half the crew putting up drywall, refinishing the wood floors, and laying down underfloor heating in the bathrooms. As for me, I was doing the new wiring with frequent detours to check in with my brothers on the cabinetry. There was nothing as satisfying as finish carpentry, working with the grain of the wood to create something both functional and—well, beautiful, because surely there was nothing sinful about using your God-given skill to craft something beautiful, whatever the Prophet had said about vanity. Pity that Uriel was having to do too much of it this week, after I'd hurt my hand. I'd wanted it to be me. More vanity, maybe. I did as much as I could anyway. If you want men to follow you, you'd better be going in the right direction.

I'd learnt something else, too, talking through what Gray wanted with my dad. I'd learnt how people used a kitchen, and a bath, too, and what all those drawers were for. Where Daisy and Gray needed more room to move about, and where they wanted everything within an arm's length. Where we could create a higher benchtop workspace in the kitchen to suit Gray's height, because Daisy worked all shifts as a nurse in Emergency, and they took the cooking in turns.

I might not know how to cook many things, but I knew streets more than I ever had before about how families lived.

But—there you were. Gray *had* worked out the design of the house to suit Daisy. When the house was done, the three girls would surely stay in the yurt, because Daisy and Gray were wrapped up in each other, and couples Outside wanted to be alone. How long would Gray keep wanting all that extra family around? There was still another sister, Dove, in Mount Zion, and all the brothers, too. Brothers with families of their own, and Gray hadn't been raised this way. How long before they were spilling out of the yurt and the caravan and moving into the house?

Frankie wouldn't stay long, I suspected. Whenever I'd seen her, she'd seemed confined by her ever-present family, by her past. Restless, needing to spread her wings after having them so ruthlessly clipped by her father and her husband. Frankie wore the clothes Oriana didn't: the tight jeans, the short skirts, the little shirts with scoop necks, and she wore them with defiance, like she was daring anybody to make a comment. She didn't talk much to men, but not in the way Oriana didn't. Oriana still looked down. Frankie looked straight through them. But they looked at her.

I wasn't easy in my mind about Frankie, but I knew it wasn't my business, even if I was her cousin. Not anymore. She might be Daisy's business. She wasn't mine.

Frankie would be moving in with flatmates as soon as she finished school, I was sure, and blazing a path through university, because she was clever, and as driven as her elder sister Daisy. She'd get a scholarship, and she'd leave. Fierce, I'd call the two of them, as if they burned to make up for the time they'd lost, the ... the *personhood* they'd lost, and nobody was going to tell them what to do ever again. The desire all but pulsed out of them. You could see it. You could *feel* it.

But for now, it was home life for the other two girls. At night, anyway, because they were both working. I'd see Oriana out the window from time to time all the same, coming and going in the dawn light before she left for the day or, sometimes, after she came back from her job, carrying a bucket or a trug or a basket of eggs, doing her chores. This morning, I'd seen her again. She'd been headed for the garden in overalls, but she was so obviously Oriana, whose backside would never look like a man's.

I'd watched her for a moment, then turned to see my dad's brother's eldest, Valor, staring as well. And I didn't care for the look on his face.

I asked, "Getting that drywall up?"

He didn't jump. He held my gaze a moment too long, then said, "Yeh." With a smile at the corner of his mouth that I didn't like at all.

Who was she making that hat for? I hoped it wasn't for him, but I'd seen him talking to her twice before, and her looking flushed and uncertain, or maybe just excited. Both times, I'd gone over and pulled him back to the job. Maybe that was wrong, but I'd done it anyway. I was in charge, and we didn't have time to stand about and chat. That was my excuse, though I wouldn't be examining it too closely.

I didn't know why Valor had left Mount Zion, but whatever the reason was, it probably wasn't entirely good. He was as eager as any of us to earn money, but as for what he spent it on, I wouldn't have liked to guess. Almost the only man on this job besides me who wasn't married, he was good-looking in a dangerous sort of way that could be attractive to a girl who'd been brought up the way Oriana had. A gentle girl who expected a man to order her about. A girl named Obedience.

Thinking about it as I trudged along with the bag of groceries I'd bought on the way home—I was back to the microwaved packets again, thanks to the hand—I ran said hand through my hair, wished I had time to get it cut before dinner tomorrow night, wondered why Gray had invited me, got a good throb from my stitched palm, and sidestepped to avoid a woman who was looking down at her phone.

She looked up, laughed, and said, "Whoops!" and I recognized her as a girl who lived in the same block of flats I did. The next flat down, in fact, with a couple of flatmates of her own. They tended to be loud, like most uni students. I hadn't worked out yet why young people were so loud Outside. Must be some combination of the freedom and the drink, plus the influence of the music, which they played so loudly, you had to scream over it.

"Sorry," I said, even though she'd been the one nearly running into me. I said it because she'd stopped.

"Katie," she told me, taking the earbuds out of her ears. They were tidy ears, with long, swinging earrings hanging from them, fully visible beneath the ragged edges of her haircut, as short as a man's. She was pretty, too. A student, maybe, a few years younger than me and looking not one bit like Mount Zion.

"Gabriel," I said.

"I know," she said. "I looked at your post on the table, sorry. Wanting to know your story, or at least your name. Your post isn't all that interesting. That's all I know so far." She laughed again. "Saturday night, eh. Coming back from your night out?"

"Yeh." I added, because I wasn't sure of the etiquette here, "You?"

"Going for more beer for the party." She waved the fabric bags she was carrying. "Come give me a hand, carrying it home? You could come to ours, afterward. We'll have to stand up in the crush, the greedy bastards will probably have scoffed all the pizza, and the music could be a bit rubbish, but we can pretend to dance anyway. Bounce up and down, more like."

She was looking at me. At my face, but mostly at my body. I felt the tingling rush of that look, and then, as usual, confusion. I'd grown up careful not to stare lustfully at girls. Outside, the girls seemed to be the ones staring lustfully. Saying hello. Introducing themselves. Even women well over thirty, who must have kids by now. What was I meant to do about that, except pretend I didn't notice?

"Cheers," I said, knowing I should help her and wondering why one of the "bastards" from the party hadn't, "but it's been a long day. And I ..." I stopped.

"Ah," she said. "Partner?" Her head on one side now, studying me, not one bit afraid to ask.

"No," I said, feeling tongue-tied. "Not, uh ... not yet."

"Well, I didn't think so," she said, "because I've never seen you with anyone. Want to hand me your phone? I could put my number in, in case the not-yet-partner doesn't work out, or in case you want to wind down after one of those long days. We could get a beer without the noise. Sit down for it, maybe. You could tell me why you work so hard, and I could tell you why I don't work hard enough. Shameful, eh."

I could feel my face getting hot, even though her tone was still cheerful, and nothing like any of the Prophet's warnings about Scarlet Women who lured men onto the rocks. "Uh, I don't ..." I said, and then had no idea whatsoever how to go on. "Thanks," I decided to say, "but I think I'm good."

"Oh, well," she said. "You know where I live." Still perfectly cheerfully. She left, and I watched her go, thought again that she was pretty, and also thought, *If you saw the state of my ute and my kitchen, you might not be so keen. Not to mention that I don't have the first idea how to have sex.*

It wasn't that I didn't want to. I wanted to, at least part of me did, and it was a pretty insistent part.

I'd hit two x's one after the other one night this week on my phone by mistake, as if the Devil really *were* guiding my hand, and things had started appearing on the screen. Things I couldn't believe. Tiny videos I could still see as if they were burned into my eyes, titled with names I could still remember. *Girl in white dress getting ...* I didn't want to finish the sentence, even to myself.

I'd gone on and watched them, to my shame. I'd spent hours when I should have been sleeping watching them, in fact, and had ended up with every part of me hot and aching, feeling as dirty as I'd been told I would. Also bleary-eyed and heavy-limbed at work the next day, with those images still in my head.

I'd learnt something, I guessed, but I was even more confused now, everything stirred up together inside, the thrilling excitement mixed with the shame, and I didn't know who to ask about it. Not Gray, because what would he think of me? He'd be rescinding that dinner invitation pretty smartly. And the thought of asking my dad made me go hot in the face. Who else was there?

One thing I knew, though. Whatever other men and women did Outside, I couldn't be rough with a woman. I couldn't push her around, even if that was what she expected. I'd seen too much roughness and too much pain already. The last thing I wanted was more of it.

But the rest of it? The kissing, and the touching, and ... everything else?

I wanted that.

26

OUT ON A LIMB

G*abriel*

I lay awake too long that night, thinking about those videos I'd seen, my hands and my body itching to watch more of them. Thinking about Oriana, and trying not to connect the two.

Finally, at one o'clock in the morning, I sat up in bed and *did* watch videos. Not that kind. Another kind. And the next afternoon at three, once the shorter Saturday workday was done, I sent a text, then drove to the top of Maori Hill, where I rang the bell on an anonymous white gatepost and got buzzed in. I still knew the code, but I'd never use it, not now that I wasn't living here anymore.

As the ute chugged up the drive, Jack shot out of the house, then slowed to an amble as if he'd remembered it wasn't cool to be excited, especially once you were ten. He was the one who'd explained "cool" to me, too. When I got out of the ute, in fact, he just said, "Hiya."

"Hiya," I said back. "Here to see your dad."

"I know. He told me. D'you want to play basketball afterward, though?"

I started to say, *I don't have time,* because I needed to take a shower, shave, and change before I headed back to Gray's, but instead, I said, "Sure. I've got fifteen minutes, anyway. I'll come find you when I'm done, OK?"

"OK," he said, but looked a bit anxious, like I might not do it. The family had just got back from Wanaka, I knew, as the Super Rugby preseason was starting soon, and the team would be back in training. Drew's family had been living in Dunedin only a couple of years, and I wasn't sure how many good mates Jack had here. Jack could be a bit guarded. He tended to observe and think before he spoke, like me, and also like me, he had an odd family, people were too interested in it, and he was old enough now to notice.

He said, "Dad's in the back garden. Come on. I'll take you."

When I got there, it was to see the little girls in the sandpit, building roads. Grace was talking a mile a minute, making up a game, while Madeleine listened, round-eyed and enthralled. As for Drew, he was walking circles around the garden in a determined sort of way, carrying baby Peter, who had a fist in his mouth and was grizzling. Drew said, when I caught up with the circling, "Hi, mate. Good to see you. I'd shake your hand, but …"

I said, "No worries. He's got a tooth coming in, maybe."

"Yeh," Drew said. "Second one. We were up and down with him all night. Hannah's got a cold as well, so she's taking a nap, and the rest of us are headed to New World in a bit for some grocery shopping, then gearing up to make something exciting for dinner. It's a thrilling life, eh. Aren't you sorry you moved out, and weren't over here hoovering with me today instead?" He grinned when he said it, though.

"Sometimes I am," I said. "When the grease in the kitchen gets too bad. Doubt my flatmates even know what a hoover is."

"Offer's still open," he said.

Oh. He thought I was fishing for another invite. "No, thanks," I said. "I'm working on my independence and all."

"Mm." He studied me out of appraising gray eyes. Peter began complaining more loudly, and Drew started the walking again. "What happened to the hand? Work accident?"

I explained again. The stitches were coming out in a few days, and I'd be glad not to have to tell this story anymore.

Drew smiled, but he didn't laugh. "Well, they say most accidents happen in the home. Unless you're a rugby player, of course. Ute still running OK?"

"Sweet as," I said, pretty proud of knowing the right slang. "Actually, though, the question I need to ask you ... it's a bit awkward. Why I came in person. I need to tell you first that you can say no."

His eyebrows rose, but he said, "Go on and ask. I know how to say no." Calm as always. "Are you asking to borrow money? Is that it?"

"No!" It came out too forcefully, and I lowered my voice and repeated, "No. I'm wondering if I can borrow your shed for a bit again, though. And your tools. On Sundays, it would be. Maybe four Sundays. I need a workshop to do a project, and I've still just got the flat, and not all the tools I'd need. It isn't much, not like fixing the ute. Drill. Dremel. Vise grip. Like that. I'd ask somebody else," I hurried on when he didn't answer, "as you've already done so much, but I wasn't sure who."

The gray eyes were shrewd. "Still not going well, then, with Gray's family? Sorry, I guess they're your family, not his. With the two families, and all? Even though you're all working on his house?" Drew and Hannah invited me to dinner every few weeks, and somehow, Drew always got the truth out of me.

"No," I said, "that part's going OK. I got made foreman, in fact, for the rest of it. It's a small job, of course, and just for the month, but ..."

"But it's a bloody good start," Drew said. "Good on ya. What's the problem, then?"

"Well, I, uh ..." *Harden up.* "I don't want to presume, and I don't want to hang about there when I'm not working, unless I'm invited. There are reasons." He waited, and I went on, hopelessly far out on that limb, "I know I'm presuming with you, too. I understand that. It was Jack who put the project into my mind, actually. The jewelry rack."

"Good of you to help him with that. Not sure it worked out too well, though. First try at love, I guess."

"Yes," I said. "You know that I don't have much experience with that. But I ... there's somebody I ..." *Just say it.* "Somebody I want. Somebody I've wanted for a long time. And I'd like to make her something to let her know I appreciate the ... the way she is. I know what, and I can do it, but I need tools."

Drew kept up his pace around the flowerbeds, like Fastest Baby Walker was a sporting event, and I walked along with him. Jack was digging at the sand beside his sisters in a half-hearted sort of way as if he were too old for this, clearly wishing for that basketball game. Finally, Drew said, "Could be better, as you're not nine, to let her know you want her first and see how she feels about it. Not sure how well the jewelry rack worked in terms of return on investment, eh. Ask her for a coffee instead, maybe. Take her to lunch. Or breakfast. I took Hannah to some pretty memorable breakfasts, back in the day. Of course, I had to fish her out of the sea first."

"What?" I was confused.

"Yeh," he said. "Some men are born romantic, some achieve romance, and some have romance thrust upon them. I fished a drowning mermaid out of the sea. You could call that having romance thrust upon you. You're a pretty good-looking bloke, though. More than that, Hannah says. I'm guessing the girl may say yes without needing the heroics."

"I'm doing that," I said. "That is, I'm having dinner with her tonight. Well, with her family."

Drew's brows rose again. "Good work. But—wait. With her family? How old is this girl? It's not Mount Zion out here."

I opened my mouth, then shut it again, and he said, "Explain." Still mild, but it was pretty clear I needed to do it.

"She's eighteen in June. And I know," I went on, when the expressive eyebrows rose again. "That's too young, out here. But she's not from out here. She's from Mount Zion."

"Oh." Drew walked a minute more, thinking, and I waited until he said, "How does she feel about you?"

"I don't know." There it was. "She's a bit shy. And I realize she has to finish school and all. She has a job as well, and that's good."

"I can only judge by Daisy," Drew said. "I barely know her, but I'd say she's pretty independent. Maybe more independent because of where she came from. Not sure she'd have been keen to get involved with somebody from the cult after she'd escaped it."

This had been a bad idea, coming here. Or being with Oriana was a bad idea, but it didn't feel that way. I waited a moment myself, but when nothing brilliant came to me, I said, "Giving her this ... it doesn't mean she has to want me. It doesn't mean she has to take me. But I need to know I tried. There'll be other blokes—there *are* other blokes who are interested, and there'll be more, but it's for the wrong reasons. That she's pretty, and she's soft. She could be hurt, because it would be so hard for her to say no. Women aren't allowed to say no at Mount Zion. And I know it sounds wrong to say, but I know I'm the right man for her, and I'm sure she's right for me, too. If I try, though, and she does say no, because I'll take care she knows she can, what have I lost? A few Sundays, that's all."

And my heart, I didn't say, because it wasn't the sort of thing you *could* say. But then, my heart had been lost long ago.

I should tell him it was Daisy's sister, but for some obscure reason, I didn't want to. Or maybe not for an obscure reason. Because of the "cousin" thing. Because Gray *was* my boss, and my job mattered more to me than almost anything, which was why pursuing Oriana was the last thing I should be doing. Yet here I was, doing it anyway.

"Can't argue with that," Drew said, "as that was how I felt when I met Hannah. If you aren't going to give it everything you've got, you may as well not even lace up your boots. Sure you don't just want to get laid, though? Or are you doing that already?"

He didn't ask it in a joking way. He asked it the way my dad would've.

I was starting to sweat now. It was as if he'd seen me watching those videos. As if he knew. "No," I said. "There've been some girls. Some women, who've, uh ..."

Drew didn't help. He just looked at me.

"Who seem to be interested," I said. "In me. Because of how I look, obviously, because it's not for my money and sophistication. I could get one of them to ... to teach me, but I know what I want, and it's not that. I've waited twenty-five years to have sex, and, yeh, that's old. I can wait longer, though, until it's right. I'm not ready to be married yet anyway, because I have to be able to give her more than I've got now."

Drew said, "Fair enough. So you need the shed. You've got it. Anything else?"

I longed to ask, "Is the way people have sex on the Internet the way it really works, Outside? And if it isn't, what is?" How could I, though? Instead, I said, "No. Thank you. If there's anything I can do for you, for Hannah, for the kids, while I'm here, you know you only have to ask. Doing that shopping, maybe, Jack and me. Jack's a fair hand at shopping. I'd offer to cook, but ..."

Drew laughed. "Yeh, nah. I've heard stories about the cooking. If Hannah gets another cold, though, I could take you up on the shopping help, especially with the season starting in a couple of weeks. Four kids is heaps, it turns out. Dunno how those Mount Zion people have twelve. Maybe just play some basketball with him for now, eh."

"I will," I said. "And thanks. I'll take care with your tools, and I'll keep the place clean."

"I know you will," Drew said. "Or I wouldn't have said yes."

27

UNEXPLORED TERRITORY

ORIANA

On Saturday afternoon, I finished folding my laboriously pitted sweet-tart pie cherries carefully into the almond cake, then scraped the batter gently into the springform pan, smoothed the top, sprinkled on the sugar-dusted slivered almonds, slid the pan into the oven, and set the timer.

There. That was the first part done. I had about five more things to make and not quite enough time to do it, because I'd helped Iris at the farmer's market today. That had meant getting up at five, and I'd only just got home in time to take a quick shower and change into a dress and apron. That was all right, though, because I had Priya to help me, and it wasn't a special occasion.

I'd be very calm tonight. Very adult. I was cooking dinner for my family, and Gabriel was part of my family, that was all. Anyway, however much I'd like it to be, life Outside wasn't any more like a Disney movie than life in Mount Zion had been, and I wasn't a princess. I was like anybody else now, going to school, working at a job, and contributing what I could. Which, today, was dinner, because Daisy was working the day shift, and weekends were busy in Emergency. Frankie, of course, was still in Wanaka. Priya texted with her, I knew, but Frankie seemed to be glad for the distance from the rest of us. Gray? He was working, too, weekend or no, because the university projects were on as tight a timeline as the house.

I was happy to feed them. I was *proud* to feed them. They were my family.

And then there was Priya, who was sitting at the kitchen bench, mincing garlic and ginger,. None too quickly, because she was half-swiveled around, watching a film on Gray's big TV. Something she did as much as possible.

I needed to talk to her about that. The TV.

Then do it. Here we were, after all, just the two of us.

I could ask Daisy to do it instead. I could tell her the problem, and …

It's not Daisy's problem to handle. It's yours. You want to be adult? Time to start.

I resisted the urge to begin separating eggs for my custard sauce, reached for the remote instead, and turned the TV off.

"Oi," Priya said. "I was watching that."

"I know," I said. "And I think you watch too much." Then felt a bit sick. I was good at telling little kids what to do. Not so much with people my age.

Priya scowled. Like Frankie, she'd shed Mount Zion's rules like taking off a coat. I was envious, honestly. "Why do you get to decide that?" she asked. "How is it your business?"

"Maybe it's not my business here," I said. "But at Laila's, it's my business. I know you take the girls into Laila's bedroom and watch TV in the afternoons. We can hear it."

"So?" Priya said. "If she thinks I shouldn't, she can tell me."

"She did. She told you the things she'd like you to do with the girls. Play with them. Read with them. Draw with them. Take them on the bus to the beach. Take them to the park. Heaps of things you can do, that she *asked* you to do."

"She can—" Priya started again.

"She can't," I said. "It's not like Mount Zion. She doesn't trust that you'll stay if she cracks down, because she knows you don't have to obey the rules. There are only a few weeks left in the school holidays, and how's she going to find another babysitter for that time? She knows that she's stuck with you. And she's working as hard as she can to feed those girls, to pay her mortgage, to pay *us*. She doesn't need another worry."

"She's rich, though," Priya said. "She has a *house*. With her own cooker, and her own bathroom!"

Had I ever been like this? Yes, I had. I'd been worse. "No," I said. "She's not. I know it's hard to see, but she's supporting those girls on her earnings, and she's got a leak under the kitchen sink and mildewed caulk all around the bath. Her windowsills need scraping and painting, her lino is peeling, and so many other things. She doesn't have time to fix all that, or money to hire somebody else to do it."

"How do you know?" Priya asked, because unlike me, she'd always press you.

"I don't," I said. "But I know she tracks her expenses, and there's a way she frowns when she's going through the props, and a way she's grateful when I can make some of them, or even when I offer to hem the cloths. Anyway, when you say that ... don't you hear how it sounds? Like she deserves to be taken advantage of, or like you aren't obligated to do your best? And I'm the one who brought you in. When you don't do the job well enough, it reflects on me, too, and I love my job. I *need* my job."

"I like my job, too, though," Priya said. "You act like I don't care. I like the girls. I take good care of them, too. The last person drank alcohol and had holdovers!"

"Hangovers."

"Whatever. Besides, they love to watch TV."

I hesitated, then said, "You know ... not everything they told us at Mount Zion was wrong. At least it doesn't seem that way to me."

"You *left*."

"Yeh, I did. But ..." I struggled to get the ideas out. I'd never been asked for my ideas, and I'd had no practice expressing them. "Some of the things that are important here in order to be ... to be respected, are the same as at Mount Zion. Working hard, for one thing. Doing what you say you will. Doing your job well, so people trust you. That's what Daisy does. It's what Gray does, too. He's working again today, after working so hard every day this week. He works harder even than people at Mount Zion. And that's why he's hired the men from there, too. Because they know how to work hard. Look at ... look at Gabriel." I felt the red creeping up my cheeks, and went on anyway. In for a penny, in for a pound. "He's in charge of the job, even though he's not the eldest. That's because of the way Uncle Aaron is, and the way *he* is."

Priya flashed back, "I know you're madly in love with Gabriel, and you think he's perfect. Everybody knows. It's obvious. That's why you're so nervous about making dinner, isn't it? Because he's coming?"

"I don't ..." I tried to say.

"All the girls at Mount Zion looked at Gabriel, any time they could get away with it," Priya reminded me, as if I could've forgotten. "Everybody hoped they'd be joined with him, because everybody knew it was past time. We all wondered what the Prophet was waiting for. *Who* he was waiting for. For somebody to turn sixteen, but who? Well, that's obvious now, isn't it? Patience. Why else would Uncle Aaron have taken her to live with them? For Aunt Constance to train her to be his wife. It may not work, though, because I think girls here must wish the same thing, and they don't have to wait to be joined. They have relations with men all the time and dress in sexy ways and talk to them and *ask* them to have relations, probably, and you don't do any of that. So he's got Patience, and he's got sexy girls, and he gets to choose whoever he wants now. Why would you be in love with somebody who doesn't want to marry you? What's the point?"

I was trying to answer, and I couldn't. My face was burning, and so was my neck. My mouth was dry, and all I wanted was a glass of water.

So get one.

I grabbed a glass, poured the water, drank it, and took some breaths. Then I put the cool glass against my cheek and tried not to cry.

Priya said, her voice sounding not nearly so sure, "Obedience?"

"Or-Oriana," I managed to say.

"Sorry. Oriana. Are you OK? Sorry. I ..."

I nodded and tried to smile. "Yeh. You just ... it made me feel bad. I know it's true, what you said. I know it. And it ..." I hauled in a breath and felt the hot tears pressing at the backs of my eyes. "Never mind." I tried another smile, and this one worked better. "It's OK. I know it's true. Anyway. What were we saying?"

I wasn't Daisy, that was sure. I didn't have her command, let alone Gray's, or her toughness, the way she fought back. Maybe you got more of that as you got older. I hoped so, because I didn't seem to have any at all. Also, I needed to make this custard sauce. I still had to go down to the garden for the vegies, and ...

I was thinking it, and then my hands were busy again. Pulling down the bowl, separating the eggs, one in each hand, into a bowl, then rocking the cracked portions back and forth in my hands until only the yolks remained, orange and glistening, after which I dumped them into their own metal bowl and took out two more eggs to repeat the process.

I might not be good at command, but I was good at eggs. I was good at gardens, too, and good at babies. Surely that gave me *some* authority.

Priya had her elbows on the benchtop, watching me. Now, she said, "Are you sorry you left?"

My hands paused, then resumed their motion before I added the cornflour, then grabbed the whisk and started to beat the yolks. "No," I finally said. "Gabriel asked me that, too. Maybe he asked because I'm only good at Mount Zion things, and I only *like* Mount Zion things, so why would I leave?"

"I think he asked," Priya said, "because you're more like Mum. You know. Obedient. The way people there think is good, and nobody Outside does. But all that about hard work —are we meant to keep on not having any fun, then, because women don't deserve to rest? I thought that was the point, that we get to do fun things, and not just have fourteen babies and barely get to hold them, because they're in the nursery and we have to work all day in the laundry instead. What should I do, then, if I'm not meant to watch TV with the girls? And why not, anyway? Why is it bad?"

My hands still wanted to shake, because this was still a confrontation, and confrontations did make me shake. Fighting wasn't allowed between women at Mount Zion, but it happened anyway, just more quietly, all hissed words and poisonous glances and bitterness expressed behind somebody's back, and I hated it. It made me sick inside. I turned on the stove, got out milk and sugar, and began to beat them together in a pan with my whisk, and that helped. And then I ventured into that unexplored territory. "Well," I said, "if they were your girls, would you want somebody watching TV with them, in the middle of summer, for two or three hours a day? I mean, really? Would you?"

"I ..." Priya said, then stopped.

"Why do you watch TV with them at all, besides that you like it? I like it, too, but how does it help them?"

Priya's own cheeks were a bit flushed now. "Because when they're tired and Amira is being naughty, it calms them down.

When they're watching, they're quiet, and Laila likes them quiet!"

"But why are they quiet?" I asked. "Because they're thinking? What are they thinking?"

Priya opened her mouth, shut it again, opened it again. And shut it.

I said, "When I watch TV, it's because I don't want to think."

"Everything's so different Outside, though," Priya said. "It's so much easier just to watch TV." Exactly what I'd thought myself, much too recently.

I tried to think what to say next, and Priya said, "And what else would I do with them?"

I said, "Maybe do some housework for Laila? You could teach the girls to sort the washing, and to fold their clothes. You could wash the sheets and have them help you put them back on the beds. Some ... some little task like that, every day. If you're there all day anyway, why not?"

"That's your brilliant suggestion? That we all work *more*?"

"Well, it's one of them." I wasn't Daisy, so positive in every situation, and I definitely wasn't Gray, who was the boss and always seemed like it, but I knew some things. I knew this. "That's how you get to be the babysitter she wants for *next* school holidays. I try to think, what can I do to help her? And I do that. It makes me happy, too, because I know I'm doing the right thing, and she appreciates it."

My mind was working as fast as my whisk now, and my thoughts were coming together along with the custard. I poured the milk mixture slowly, a pale, thin ribbon, into the rich yolks, whisking all the way, then put the bowl over the water that was barely simmering in the double boiler and kept stirring. "Work doesn't have to be just ... grueling," I tried to explain. "It doesn't have to be horrible. Hanging out wet sheets and towels, ironing in the heat until your hair's dripping wet under your cap and your scalp is itching. Chopping three dozen onions that make you cry. Scrubbing rows of awful men's toilets. You could scrub *one* toilet, then go to the supermarket for Laila, and start dinner for her. You could teach the girls how. It could even be fun. Because the way kids' lives are here ... I think it must be a little exhausting sometimes. They're always going places. Doing things. Having so much ... so much noise all around them all the time. It's nice to stay home sometimes, too, and do quiet things, and having playtime is more fun after you have work time. If you never *have* work time, doesn't playtime start to feel like work? Because I think it would."

Priya was staring at me like I'd grown an extra head. I felt a bit that way, too. Who knew I had all these ideas, when I couldn't come up with three sentences about the abolition of African slavery in Europe?

My custard was perfect now. Exactly right, smooth and just thick enough, and that pale yellow that looked as delicious as it tasted. I took the bowl out of the double boiler, stirred in the vanilla, covered it all with clingfilm, and popped it into the fridge, then checked the time on my almond cake. "You could make a timetable for them, maybe," I told Priya. "A calendar for the week, with work time and reading time and playtime and adventures. You could draw it on a piece of paper, and help the girls read it. If you do little pictures, Amira will be able to read it better, too. Then they'd know what they were going to be doing that day, and you wouldn't even have to tell them that they were going to watch less TV and have them be unhappy. I'll bet they wouldn't even notice."

"See," Priya said. "That's why you're good at this. You can *think* of it. Pity you can't hold the babies and babysit at the same time."

"Yeh. But I can't." I finished putting the dishes in the sink and wiping down the benchtops. "Thanks for letting me say."

"Sorry I said the thing about Gabriel," she said, looking down at her cutting board.

"That's OK," I said, filling the sink to clean up the mess before I got busy on my starter and the mains. Which were easy. As long as my cake turned out, I'd be all good. "I know you're right."

We could fit at home, together. My wife and I.

"Besides," I said, "Daisy says it's better not to think about men until you're older. Until you're educated." I didn't say, *Do other girls' bodies feel so … so insistent, though?* Obviously not, because Daisy was *old*. She was over thirty! How could she have waited all those years if she felt like me? And Frankie, too, who didn't care about men.

I was sinful, obviously. That had to be it. I tried to make my mind do right, but I had a sinful body, and it kept betraying me.

I dried the double boiler and put it away, then looked at the time. Oh, no. It was five-twenty. I told Priya, "When you finish that, shell and devein the shrimp and put them in this bag with the marinade, would you? The recipe's just here. I need to go get the vegies." And ran out, grabbing a trug as I went.

I was coming back up again, my trug full of green stuff, thinking that I needed to start the fire under the barbecue, and that my cake was due to be done in less than ten minutes, so I'd better go test it, when I saw a man above me in the drive. Not that that was unusual, but …

He hesitated a moment, as if he were about to hurry away, then turned and seemed to catch sight of me, and my heart skipped a beat, because all that flashed across my mind was, *Mount Zion.*

Oh. It was Valor. Gabriel's cousin.

Wait. What was he doing here now? The other men were long since gone for the day, and anyway, Valor wouldn't have been the last man to leave. That would have been Gabriel.

He started toward me.

Wait.

28

SNAKE IN THE GARDEN

Oriana

I wanted to ignore him, to walk back into the yurt. How could I do that, though? Wouldn't he just come inside? Valor wasn't like Gabriel. He didn't think about how you'd feel.

He set ice prickling up my spine, and he always had, ever since we were kids. He'd teased the little ones back then, dropping bugs down the girls' backs and twisting the boys' arms until they cried. He'd done all that to me, too, but he'd also cornered me outside once, when we'd been in the orchard picking up windfalls.

I'd been four, and was searching in a far corner away from the other kids, because I wanted to bring back the most fruit and have Sister Charity—who was my idol, so pretty and calm —exclaim over them. Valor came over where I was, but he didn't pick up fruit. He told me that we were going to play a game instead.

I can still remember, as clearly as if it's stamped on my brain, how he stood too close to me, there behind the gnarled trunk of an ancient pear tree, and how I wanted to run away. I didn't, because he was older, and he was a boy.

He unfastened his trousers, then, and took a wee on the

gray bark. I stared at the trunk as it darkened, at the stream of yellow liquid trickling down it and into the grass, and didn't want to look at him, especially not at that part of him that I'd only seen on babies, that I was only meant to see when it was my husband.

Most of all, though, I remember him telling me, "Now you do it." Standing so close, he was nearly touching me, and so much taller than me, which meant I had to do what he said. But how could I?

"I can't," I whispered, afraid to look around, to see if somebody was watching. If I couldn't see them, maybe they couldn't see me. "I'll get in trouble."

"Nobody's looking," he said. "Take down your undies and wee. It's a game, and it's your turn. That means you have to do it." He stood there, then, and stared at me until I was squatting on the ground, my undies around my ankles, holding up my skirt. Knowing it was wrong. Knowing that if somebody saw, I'd be punished, and I'd deserve it.

The heat of the urine against my skin, and the way I'd struggled to keep my balance and hold my heavy skirt up, terrified that I'd wee on my dress, because Sister Charity would be sure to notice the wet spot, and I was too old to have accidents. You got punished for that, and I hated being punished. I always wanted to run the moment my dad took his belt out of his trousers, even though it had never been me it was happening to, not yet. I weed in the dirt like nobody but an animal should do, heard that belt whistling through the air, and shook.

After that day, whenever Valor looked at me, he smiled as if he were remembering, too. The shame I felt every time he smiled like that, because he knew I'd sinned, and I was still so afraid he'd tell.

It got worse, though. Whenever he had to move past me in some tight place—and somehow, that always seemed to happen—his hand would brush against my breast or my backside. Especially once my flat chest had turned into buds, because when that happened, he touched me more.

The worst one, though, happened when I was twelve.

I was taking a cart from the dairy to the kitchens when I saw him coming the other way, but I opened the gate between us anyway, because I couldn't run back to the dairy. I'd get a slap or worse, and anyway, Sister Hopeful had sent me because I was reliable. I needed to keep being reliable.

I stepped to the side to let Valor go through the gate first, not raising my eyes to him, and then stood, confused, as he stepped the same way I did. When I muttered an apology and stepped the other way, so did he. Once more, until I finally stood still and he laughed. Teasing, the way he always did, in a way that made your skin feel prickly.

"Nah," he said, stepping aside and sweeping out an arm. "Just joking. Go on."

He shifted, though, as I came through behind the cart, and pressed me up against the post with his body. I stood stock-still, not wanting even to breathe, not knowing what to do, and he said, with a smile in his voice that scared me, "Who knew you'd get so pretty? Should I ask the Prophet to join you to me, do you think? Pity we can't do it sooner than sixteen, because I'd say you're ready. You're already bleeding, aren't you?" I felt his hand go between my legs, groping through the thick cotton skirt, and froze. That hand was closing over me, searching, touching, the rough rasp of fabric rubbing against tender parts I'd barely even touched myself as I gasped and tried to shrink away. "Now that I've touched you like this," he said, "and got you taking down your pants for me, too, you're already half mine. Who else will want you?"

I could still feel the shock, then the red tide of humiliation sweeping in. I could still feel myself stumbling when he'd finally stepped back and let me go, and see the smile on his face before I tore my gaze away, took my cart, and ran.

He couldn't really influence the Prophet, though. Yes,

Valor was the Prophet's grandson, but there were heaps of those. Besides, everyone knew the Prophet waited for divine inspiration to assign partners, because marriage was an eternal bond.

That was one reason, though, that I'd run when Frankie had asked me to go with her. However much I'd tried to stay out of Valor's way, however much I'd told myself that he would never dare to ask such a thing, I'd seen the Prophet the week before in the dining hall, looking at me and then at the table where Valor sat. And I was sixteen.

Some of the other girls had wished for him. Gabriel was the … the golden one, like the archangel he was named for. Quiet. Sober. Responsible. And so beautiful, you'd have to look away even if you didn't, you know, have to look away. Valor was dangerous. Exciting, at least that was what they said, with his flashing dark eyes and bright white smile. That was why they thought he might be joined early, even though men were usually at least twenty-three when they married their sixteen-year-old brides. For the wild ones like Valor, though, I'd heard the older women say, the joining would come sooner. "Settle him down," they'd say.

I knew Valor was more than just exciting, but I didn't tell. How could I, without telling what I'd done, too?

And now he was here again. He'd left Mount Zion a few months ago, but that had been after Gabriel's family had stopped visiting us, so I hadn't seen him much. The first time I'd come up the track for my car, seen him walking into the house pushing a dolly with boxes piled onto it, and realized he must be on Gray's crew now, I'd felt like he had me up against that fence post again. Shocked, and so ashamed. Wanting to run.

I could have told Gray, but how could I admit that a man had touched me so intimately? Was I even a virgin anymore, after what he'd done? And I'd been seductive, obviously. The Prophet said that men sinned when women tempted them with their bodies and their lascivious looks, and I'd always had the biggest breasts of any girl my age.

Keep walking. Walk into the yurt, I thought, but I couldn't. It was exactly like before, and I was frozen, the trug in my hand. Also, Priya was in there. I didn't want her to see Valor with me, to hear what he'd say. To me, or to her. It wasn't safe. He'd talked to me four times now, and he always seemed to be waiting for me to appear, the way he'd come out of the house so fast. After that, it would be the same as before. Teasing, and complimenting me, but not in a way that felt real. Telling me I was looking pretty, except for—something, always. My shoes, or my hair, which he said was old-fashioned and ugly, worn in plaits or knotted behind my head, or that I wasn't wearing makeup. He'd talk, and I'd look down and feel like my skin was crawling.

Now, he was four steps away, then three, and then he was standing in front of me. Standing a bit too close, just like before. Smiling again. I wasn't looking straight at him. I knew it wasn't forbidden anymore, but his eyes were like snake's eyes, and once I looked into them, I'd be trapped.

Again.

He said, "All by yourself, eh. The boss gone, and Chastity gone as well. Left you here all alone. Girls shouldn't be alone."

I wanted to say, "I'm not alone, because Priya's here," but how could I? I'd seen him looking at Priya, too, and I knew what was behind that look. I said, "Daisy. Her name is Daisy." My voice trembled, hard as I tried to stop it.

My cake. I needed to test it, or it could come out too dry. Would Priya think to check it? Gabriel had asked me for something sweet. Something special. There was only a minute, with cakes, between done and dry. I didn't have time to make anything else, except maybe stewed apples, and that wasn't special.

"That's right," Valor said, his voice an amused drawl. "Daisy. But it's really still Chastity. You know it is. And you're still Obedience in your heart, aren't you? The Prophet gave you your name for a reason. You can't just throw it away like that."

"The Prophet's not ..." My voice was still too wobbly, but I went on anyway. "Not in charge here. If you want him to be in charge, you need to ..." My throat was too dry to go on, because he'd taken another step toward me. I took another step back, and felt my legs hit the edge of the porch behind me.

"I need to what?" he asked, and came another step closer. "Go back? Maybe I don't want to go back. Or maybe I'm meant to be here. Maybe I've got a job to do. Did you think of that? Did you think, why would Valor have left Mount Zion, when he's the Prophet's favorite? No, because you don't think much, do you? You look after babies. That doesn't take many brains. Good thing you're pretty." He took something out of his pocket. A bottle, but a flat one. "Whiskey. Part of my wages. But I'll share."

"You ... you shouldn't be here," I managed to say. "Gray doesn't like people being here unless they're working. How did you get in?"

Valor had taken the top off the bottle and taken a drink. Now, he held it out to me, and I shook my head. "What Gray doesn't know won't hurt him," he said, not putting the bottle away. "I thought I'd have a proper look round for once without Gabriel shoving his sticky beak in, and now I have. All this for one man, just for playing a kid's game, and he's got another house as well, they say. Beggars belief. All sorts of ways to get rich, Outside, doing the Devil's work."

"Gray will find out you've been here," I said. "He'll sack you. And if you don't like him, why are you working for him?"

"Who's going to tell him? You? I don't think so. Because then I could tell him about you, couldn't I? How you took your pants down for me and let me touch you, because you're not nearly as sweet as everybody thinks, are you? Or you could have a drink instead, and we could keep our secret." He held the bottle out again.

No way to back up more. Nowhere to go. The bottle was next to my mouth, the sharp smell of alcohol choking me, and Valor's hand had come out to touch my hair, like he thought he had a right, because it wasn't covered. Because he thought that meant I was sinful. Fallen. From inside the house, I could hear the oven timer going off, the insistent *beep-beep-beep*, and I thought, *My cake. It's going to be ruined.*

Priya, I begged. *Don't come out. Don't look for me. Stay inside, away from him.*

And please, nobody see me. Please, nobody see this.

29

RUST SPOTS

G*ABRIEL*

I punched the code into the gate, waited for it to roll back with a clanking of steel, then headed down the drive feeling good. I'd showered, I'd shaved, and I'd changed, and at last, I had a plan. It only took courage, and I had courage. Or if I didn't, I'd get some.

I was also early, but that was all right. I could sit at the kitchen bench and watch Oriana cook, ask her what she was doing and why. I needed all the cooking help I could get, and maybe she'd like knowing more than me about it.

Around a corner, the loose shingle spattering against the tires, and I was frowning, because I saw a flash of white where there shouldn't be one. I slowed, looked, and there it was. Another ute, older than mine, parked behind the far garage, where it was nearly hidden. Rust spots on this one, too, and no attempt to keep the contagion from spreading.

Valor's ute.

What the hell?

I sped up, then, because I saw him. Next to the porch, in front of the yurt. Somebody with him. Too close.

Oriana, shrinking against the boards. He was crowding her, his hand in her hair, and he was holding something to her lips.

I was out of the ute, jumping down, and running. Behind me, I could hear more tires on shingle, but I was already there, grabbing Valor by the collar, pulling him off her.

Oriana, shaking. I barely saw her, because I had both my hands on Valor now, and then I was hauling my fist back, ready to hit him. The red mist was covering my vision, and all I could see in the center of that red tunnel was his face. Not smiling now. Shocked.

My fist didn't land. A hand on my shoulder instead, pulling me back, and a deep, urgent voice. Gray, with one hand on me and one on Valor, saying, "What the *fuck?*"

Oriana said, her voice high and breathless, "It wasn't Gabriel. It wasn't. It was Valor. He came ... he came ... and Gabriel pulled him off. He pulled him away."

Gray said, "What the hell is he still doing here?" His voice, for once, not controlled. A roar.

I said, nearly panting with anger and self-disgust, my hands wanting to reach for Valor, to beat him, "My fault. My fault. He must have stayed behind when we were packing up for the day. Or he fell behind, because I saw him get into his ute and start it up. I didn't pay attention, though. I didn't count everybody leaving, because I was in a hurry. My fault."

Valor didn't say anything. He just smirked, and I wanted to wipe that smirk off his face.

"Maybe," Gray said, "but he's the one who did it." He looked at Oriana. "Are you all right?"

She nodded, a quick jerk of her head, her arms wrapped around herself. In her pretty apron, all blue flowers, and her pretty yellow dress, the front of her soft hair twisted at the center parting, pulled back and fastened with neat holders, framing her white, shocked face.

The door banged, and Priya was on the porch, asking, "What's happening?"

Oriana turned her head and said, "It's fine. Go take out my cake. It's going to be too dry." Her voice was still shaking, but she was trying to make it stop. Not reacting like a child. Reacting like a woman.

Priya said, "I took it out five minutes ago, when it tested done. What's *happening?*"

I told Gray, keeping my voice controlled with what felt like the biggest effort of my life, "I need to help Oriana."

He let me go, though he still had a hand on Valor, and I took another step. Two, and I was taking the wicker trug from her and setting it on the porch, then putting my arms around her, because how could I do anything else? She hesitated a moment, then buried her face in my chest and clung to my shirt. I felt her shaking, knew she was crying, and thought, *How could I not have watched him to make sure he left? Why didn't I warn Gray about what he is?* And felt, for the first time since I'd left Mount Zion, despair. That in spite of all my care, all my effort, I'd failed.

Another car coming down the drive now. A cherry-red Mustang. That would be Daisy, home from work.

"Wait," Oriana said, pulling back, dashing at her eyes with the heels of her hands. "Gray, wait. I need to ... I need to tell you something."

Gray said, "If you've got something to say, I'll listen. Let me throw this arsehole off my property first, though."

Oriana

"No," I said. "I need to ... He has to hear, too. He has to know I said it. I can't ... I can't let him hold this over me anymore, or let it burn a hole inside me, and the only way is if I've told."

Gray looked at me, then at Gabriel, who was still holding my hand as if he were anchoring me, his body between mine and Valor's. Being kind, always. Being protective. Then Gray looked at Daisy, who was coming up the drive, then starting to hurry, as if her nurse's senses had picked up trouble.

Gray said, before Daisy even got there, "You don't have to tell us. I'll sack him anyway."

"No," I said. "I do." Before, in a place where we were meant to confess everything, I'd held the secret shame close, not even telling my sisters. Now, when I didn't have to tell at all, I needed to. I didn't want to, but I needed to, if that makes sense.

Gabriel said, "Whatever it is, it doesn't matter." Quietly, because Gabriel was usually quiet, but like he meant it.

I thought, *It will matter. But it matters now, too, inside me.* It had lain there, all these years, like a blot, ugly and dark. I wanted to scrub it out so badly, and this was the only way I could think to do it. However hard it would be to say it, and to know that everybody would know that about me.

We ended up inside the yurt. All of us, including Valor, sitting around the table as if we were about to have dinner. Gabriel sat beside me, and he was still holding my hand. After we'd sat, he'd picked it up again, then hesitated, looked at me, and said, "I won't hold it if you don't want me to. But I thought—"

"Oh," I'd said, flustered once more. "No. It's ... it's fine." It was more than that. It was an anchor.

Now, Daisy said, "Valor grabbed you just now. That's all I know. Why? Is there more to the story? Something else he did? What, exactly?" Sounding the way Daisy always did sound. Brisk. Efficient. Like she expected a straight answer, and would keep asking until she got it.

Valor said, "You want her to confess her shame? You want everybody to know that about her?"

Daisy whirled on him so fast, he flinched. She wasn't even as tall as me, but when she pulled herself up to her full height, she looked bigger. She said, "I don't care if the rest of the story is that you raped her. I don't care if it happened twenty times. That still wouldn't be her shame. It would be yours."

"Not hers, if she's spoilt for marriage?" Valor asked. "Not what a man will think." He glanced at Gabriel and smirked some more.

Gabriel was on his feet like a shot, and so was Gray, the two of them pinning Valor between them. I scrambled out of my chair in the opposite direction, because this felt bad. It felt violent, like when my dad had disciplined one of us, and the others had to hear. When you'd put your hands over your ears and squeeze your eyes shut, your lips forming the words to a prayer. At least, that was what I'd done.

"Shut up." That was Gray, and his voice was full of that violence. "Sit down and shut up."

"You have no authority over me," Valor said. "You're not the Prophet. You can sack me? Right, I'm sacked. And I'm leaving."

He turned, but before he made it a step, Gray's hand was on him, clamped straight down on his arm. Gabriel was still on the other side, and there was no getting around him. Gray looked across Valor at Gabriel and said, "Sit down. I'll hold him. And if somebody needs to bash him, I'll do it. I've wanted to bash the men of Mount Zion for more than a year now, and I've only managed to hit one of them."

"Gray," Daisy said. "You could get ..."

"Yeh, nah," Gray said. "It'll be worth it. Also, I was defending Oriana at the time. Keeping him off her."

"You aren't," Valor said, nearly spitting the words.

"Yeh?" Gray asked. "Who's going to tell them that, mate? You? I'm sure that'll go well. Sit down and shut up. Somebody more important is talking." Then he shoved him into the chair, stood over him, keeping a hand on his arm, and nodded at me. "Go."

What had I been thinking? How could I do this? Daisy,

though, had come to sit beside me, was taking my hand. Gabriel didn't have the other one anymore, but the way he sat, so squarely between Valor and me, it felt like he did. As for Priya, she looked gobsmacked. As if nothing like this had ever happened in her life, which was probably true. I didn't know anybody else it had happened to, so it must be me. My carnal self, again. But that still didn't make it all right for Valor to do, did it?

Too confusing.

I said, "When I was little, he made me ... he made me wee in the grass. And he touched me other times. Through my clothes. Down there." And blushed until it felt like my head would erupt in flames. My hand started shaking, and now, Gabriel *did* hold it. With his bandaged hand.

Everybody sat there, and I thought, *Why aren't they saying something?* Finally, Daisy asked, "Is that everything?"

"Yes," I said. "Except that he weed, too, that first time. On a tree."

"Which you watched," Valor said. "And when I told you to pull up your skirts and pull down your undies, you didn't say no, did you? What else did you do for me? Why do I know what you look like? All over?"

"You don't," I said. "You *don't!*"

I didn't see it happen. I didn't know it was happening. But somehow, there was a *thud*, the back of Gabriel's chair was hitting the floor with a clatter, and his hand was pulling back. And Valor was staggering, his nose spouting blood like you'd turned on the tap.

"She couldn't say no," Gabriel said. He was over Valor, had hauled him to his feet, was propelling him toward the door. "She wasn't allowed to, and she didn't know how anyway. You're not in Mount Zion anymore, though. Neither am I. So try it. Just try it. I'll be one step behind you."

"You?" Valor was trying to laugh, even though he still had a hand over his nose, and the blood was running down his shirt. "Think I'm scared of you? Know what we called you? Peter Pious. You're not going to hurt me."

Gabriel said, "I just did." After that, he opened the front door and put a boot in Valor's backside, and Valor flew down the stairs and landed hard before staggering to his feet, cursing.

It was terrible. Violent, like I'd thought.

But I knew I'd be reliving it tonight, after I went to bed. And I might even be smiling.

GABRIEL

Yeh. Well. That was a first.

I watched Valor to make sure he really left. I jogged up the road after his ute, in fact, took care the gate closed behind him, jogged down again, tried to get my breathing and my anger under control, and thought about what I could do. What I *should* do.

I couldn't decide, so I headed back to the yurt.

Oriana was in the kitchen, making dinner as if none of it had happened. If she'd cried again, and I'd bet she had, she'd done it fast and then mopped up, so nobody would see, and so she could get on with it. Gray and Daisy headed out the back to use the gym equipment, Priya helped Oriana with the cooking, and I sat at the island benchtop and didn't say anything, because I didn't know what to say, especially in front of Oriana's sister.

Almost the only thing Oriana said to me was, "Do you think you can do these prawns on the barbie for me, once it's hot enough? I didn't get it preheated soon enough, with …" She stopped, pressed her lips together, and handed me a tray piled with stacks of the things, shoved onto skewers and smelling of their marinade, which, Priya told me when she headed out to the barbecue with me, was made of ginger, garlic, and lime.

"Because it's Asian-inspired food," she explained. "I didn't know all the kinds of food there is. You try to make it all a bit the same, so it goes together. You'll see. And Oriana—" She stopped.

"What?" I asked.

She glanced toward the house, then at me. "Nothing," she said, and headed back in.

When I brought the barbecued prawns in on a tray, the table was laid, and dinner was nearly ready. That was how fast Oriana had moved. Her face was still shut down, but if her hands were shaking, I didn't see it. We sat, finally, and ate those prawns, succulent and fresh as the sea, because, Oriana said, she'd bought them at the market this morning. We ate leaves of salad wrapped around brown rice and mince flavored with more garlic and ginger, plus something crunchy and white called water chestnuts. There were tender new sugar snap peas, too, with more of those flavors.

Priya was right. This was nothing Oriana had learnt at Mount Zion. It was good, though. Better than takeaway food. So fresh, and so ... bright, somehow, like the flavors were bursting in your mouth. Nothing like those meals I cooked for myself in the microwave.

Oriana sat beside me while we ate, saying nothing. Daisy and Gray talked determinedly about the alpacas, about what was growing in the garden, about progress on the house, about Daisy's shift at the hospital and her study schedule. Finally, though, possibly after enough time had elapsed for calm, Gray asked about Oriana's job with the babies.

"Still seems a bit odd to me," he said. "I know everybody takes photos of their babies, but an hours-long photo session? Must be something special about them, though, or people wouldn't bother. Maybe show us some, Oriana, if you have any." Being kind, that was.

She said, "It's not like the snaps people take at home. It's so different, you can't think. It's ... Here. I'll show you." She pulled out her phone, scrolled a bit, and passed it to Gray.

"Nice," he said.

Daisy said, "Hardly supportive, boy."

He laughed. "Sorry. It's cute. How's that?"

"Not much better," Daisy said.

"Different if it's your own kid, I expect," he said, and passed the phone to me.

It was a baby. Well, obviously. A naked, sleeping baby, curled up like she was still in the womb, bum up and head turned to the side, nestled into the middle of what looked like an enormous pink rose, the fabric looking soft and slightly out of focus. The baby's hair was dark, and she was wearing a white headband with more pink roses on it, and transparent white wings that extended across her back. She looked like some sort of flower fairy.

I said, "It's beautiful," and Oriana's face lit up like the sun coming out from behind a cloud.

"It was my idea," she said, proud, but shy to sound it. "The prop."

"Yeh?"

"Yes. The rose. It wasn't hard, just trying different ways with the fabric, here at home, getting it to work. I've got ideas for other flowers as well. Laila's the one who knows how to pose the babies, though, and she knows how to do the lighting and all, too. You try to make the backgrounds not too complicated, so your eye stays on the baby. There's an art to all of it, and you have to be so careful moving them, because they're fragile. They're brand-new."

"I'm guessing you're learning, though," Gray said.

"Yes," Oriana said. "At least, I'm doing my best."

"Pity it's a totally stereotypically female occupation," Priya said, and Oriana flushed.

"What does that matter, if she likes it?" Gray said, and Oriana looked at him with gratitude.

"Doesn't matter anyway, as you'll have to leave when school starts again," Daisy said. "Work experience is always good, though."

Oriana didn't say anything, just got up and began clearing plates. I stood up to help her, because that was the right thing, surely. She didn't say anything but "Thanks," but when she served a cake topped with sugar-dusted cherries and accompanied by a pitcher of custard, she told me, "It's a fruit dessert. The kind you wanted, I hope." As if she'd made it for me.

I took a bite and sighed. The cherries were baked tender and juicy and surrounded by moist almond-scented cake, and the custard sauce was the real thing, rich and golden, not the stuff you got in bottles from the supermarket. "Yeh," I said, and smiled at her. "Thanks. It's perfect. It's what I've missed."

She smiled back, and this time, it wasn't tentative.

"I reckon it's good to be good at things," I said, even though we were in front of everybody. "Whether they're women's things or not. I'm only good at men's things, myself. Doesn't mean I can't do the rest, because I'm learning. Not one bit good at them, though."

"And you don't want to be," she said.

"You could be right." I laughed because, suddenly, that was how I felt. Because she'd made me that cake, maybe, and I'd finally had a chance to bloody Valor's nose and kick him down the stairs. Oriana'd got to say what she needed to at last? Maybe I'd got to *do* what I needed to. "Reckon we're both stuck in our ..."

"Your rigid gender roles?" Priya asked.

"Maybe," Oriana said. "Why not, though? I help with the garden, too, and the animals. Which are things men do, in Mount Zion," she told Gray. "Men do everything outdoors there, but I *like* being outdoors. I do the things I *like*. What's wrong with that?" Probably the most assertive speech Oriana had ever made in her life, and I was smiling. She looked at me and said, "What?"

"Nothing," I said. "I'm impressed, that's all."

"What's wrong with it is that you don't like anything that pays decently," Priya said. "Looking after kids and tending the garden and cooking and knitting and taking care of animals? You're going to have flatmates until you're *thirty*. You're going to be *poor*."

"I earn money," Oriana said, the set to her jaw a little less soft.

"Working with babies?" Priya asked. "Babysitting? I know what you earn. How are you ever going to move out of here and then keep up with the rent doing those things? You have to at least be a teacher to earn anything working with kids, and you need university for that. Or you could get married, I guess, but men don't want somebody poor, either. Anyway, I'm not going to get married until I'm thirty. I'm not going to be trapped with somebody awful just because I don't make enough money to leave."

"Money's not everything, of course," Gray said neutrally. "And Oriana's welcome to live here as long as she likes."

Daisy said, "I'd say, 'Said by somebody who's always had heaps,' except that you haven't."

"Gray's mum cleans houses," Oriana said, as if she hadn't heard any of that. "Is she not good enough, then, Priya?"

"She *supervises* people who clean houses," Priya said.

"Now she does." That was Gray. "Started out cleaning them, though, right enough." His brown eyes were level, and so was his voice, but you wouldn't want to cross him, and Priya was coming close. "We shared a house with another single mum, too. Never had much, and she'll tell you that's all right. Careful what you take from all this new you're seeing."

"Kind hearts are more than coronets," I said. "And simple faith more than Norman blood."

Daisy said, "What?" and stared at me as if the rocks had spoken. Or as if she hadn't realized I could read, maybe.

I shrugged. "Didn't you have that poem in school, then?" Mount Zion had been big on poetry of a certain type, Tennyson and Kipling and blokes like that. Poetry of the empire, they'd said, which had been explained to us as "the period when our British values and military might were at their pinnacle." We'd had to memorize them, and to recite them, too.

Oriana said, "I had that poem. I always liked it." As she was the living proof of the lines, I didn't doubt it.

When we'd eaten our cake—I had a second helping, it was that good—Priya said, "I'll do the washing-up," and hopped up to get started. Daisy said, "I've got some more, uh, working out to do myself. Something I wanted to ask you, though, Gray, about my form. In our room?" Upon which he said, "Course," and followed her there as if he were a magnet and she was the pole.

I glanced at Oriana. Pretty obvious what was going on with that. She looked like she knew it too, but she just said, "I'd like to have a look at your hand, Gabriel."

I blinked. "My hand? My knuckles may be a bit bruised, but that's all." I was meant to ask her to take a walk in the garden. That's what Honor had suggested, and *also* what Drew had suggested, so it must be right, and this was the time. Unfortunately, I had no idea what to say to her there. Did I talk about what had happened with Valor? Not talk about it? Talk about something else? *What* else?

She sighed and, for once, looked a bit exasperated. *"Gabriel.* I mean your *stitches."*

"Oh." I looked at the bandage. "What about them?"

"I want to see them," she said.

"Odd sort of desire, surely," I said.

She laughed, exasperated again, and said, "Just ... come into the bath with me."

Right, I thought. *Right.* I was completely confused by now. I wanted to go—of course I did—but I also didn't. I'd have said that Oriana felt the same way I did about having relations, especially after what she'd told us today about Valor. Now she didn't? Was it living with Gray and Daisy, then, when they weren't married? Had it been corrupting, the way the Prophet had always warned? Gray was as devoted to Daisy as any man I'd ever known, though.

In any case, we weren't in Mount Zion anymore, and the rules were different. And yet I was as confused as I'd ever been in my life when Oriana took me around the curve of the yurt and into the bath. I was following her, trying not to stare at her backside in that pretty apron, the strings meeting in a bow whose ends draped over her curvy bottom.

I didn't want to do this, and I did. And I didn't trust my better nature to win out. Not one bit.

30

NOT MUCH OF A VIKING

O~RIANA~

I headed into the bath with Gabriel behind me and said, "Close the door, will you?" That was because I'd heard Daisy say something. Or maybe *moan* something. I'd heard Gray's voice, too, low and hoarse and urgent, and I didn't need to hear any of that. Not with Gabriel standing right here!

He looked startled, but he did it. I reached around him and turned on the fan, and he made a move toward me, said, "I, uh ..." and stopped.

I stepped closer, did my best to ignore the hammering of my heart, and picked up his bandaged hand. He put his other hand on my shoulder, and I froze. I mean, I couldn't move. Not like with Valor. Different. I looked up at him, and he said, "I, uh ..." again, then, "I'm not sure how to do this. Also, I'm not sure about the, uh ... bathroom."

"What?" I stared at him. "This is where the supplies are, though."

"Oh." Now, *he* looked confused. "Do we ... stand up, then? And I don't have ... I'm pretty sure you're meant to have a ... a condom. So there's no baby. Or is that what you mean by supplies?" There were red patches on his cheeks, and he hadn't moved his hand from my shoulder. "I mean, I think we should think about that, decide about that, before we, uh …"

"*What?*" I took a step back, and so did he. I banged into the toilet, and he banged into the door. "I need to check your *hand.* I brought you in here to change your bandage!"

"Oh!" It came out a bit loud, and then he said, more quietly, "Oh," ran a hand over his face, and started to laugh. "Sorry, then. Sorry. I'm … I'm horrified. At myself, I mean."

I wanted to be horrified, too, but instead, I was laughing as well. Possibly hysterically, thanks to everything that had happened tonight. Valor. Gabriel hitting Valor. Gabriel throwing Valor down the stairs. My confession. This. It was all so terribly … unromantic. Every time I thought I was over it, I looked at Gabriel and laughed some more, until we were staggering, hanging on to the door, in his case, and the edge of the sink, in mine. In the *bathroom*. Where he'd thought I'd taken him to … have *relations?*

In the *bathroom?*

"You're … as bad as me," I managed to say at last, wiping my streaming eyes. "I know I don't know anything, but I'm pretty sure you're not meant to do it in the bath."

"Yeh, well." He was grinning. "Reckon you know now that I don't know anything, either."

I shouldn't say this, but I was saying it anyway. "Really? You mean you haven't had relations with girls? Sorry, I mean had sex. You haven't had sex with anybody, even though girls Outside …"

"No." He was still so beautiful, it was like looking into the sun. "It's never seemed right. I may not be much chop at being a worldly man. Also, I'm always embarrassed. I don't know how to do it, for one thing, or even how you get from a girl talking to you to the point of starting to do it, and I'm never sure … Don't you think it could hurt them? I mean, aren't you meant to have relations because you love somebody? Don't girls feel that way, then? I always thought they did."

"Yes," I said. "At least, that's how it feels to me, too. Like you should be ..."

"Married," he said. "Yeh. How it seems to me, too."

"So just because you look like a Viking warrior," I said, "you aren't one?"

"I look like a Viking *warrior?*"

"Well, not *now,*" I said, still wanting to giggle. "Now, you mostly look confused. But before, when you were hitting Valor and throwing him down the stairs, you may have done. And now you know what I got from my history class this past year. I know what a Viking warrior looks like, or what some artist thinks he did. They used longboats and raided Britain. That's about all I've got."

"I also don't know how to use a longboat," he said. "Or raid. And I don't like violence much anyway. I'd be a rubbish Viking."

"You did well today, though," I said, feeling shy again.

"Yeh," he said. "But that's because I needed to hit him." Now, he wasn't laughing.

"So it's not ..." I said, and stopped.

"Not what?" He took a step closer, and his face had changed again. "You can tell me."

"Not ... because of what Valor said?" I asked. "It didn't make you think that I'm ... fallen? That you came in here with me and thought that?" I couldn't believe I'd asked it, but I couldn't *not* ask it, either.

"No!" he said. "Of course not. It's just ... I can't tell what anybody means anymore. When you asked me to come with you, I thought— I thought, 'Oh. I got it wrong, then.'"

"But you wanted to," I said. Again, with a daring I hadn't realized I possessed. "I thought you just said you *didn't* want to."

"I do," he said, "and I don't. But it's nothing to do with Valor. Whatever happened with him ... I know it was wrong. Wrong for him to do, I mean, and what you didn't want. He thought he could follow you out here and do it again. He can't, because you told. Now, we all know, and we'll all be looking out for you."

There was a sort of warmth happening in my chest. Not embarrassment this time, or maybe embarrassment, but something else, too. I got out the Dettol, the gauze, the tape, and the cotton pads from the cabinet and said, "I'm going to pick up your hand and take off the bandage. And that doesn't mean we're about to have relations in the bath."

He laughed again. "Got it. Fire away."

I unwound the grubby tape, then went to peel the gauze off. It stuck a bit, but I got it off, too.

The stitches were black, and they were neat. The skin around them, though, was red, puffy, and angry-looking. Not as bad as I'd feared, but not good, either. I'd patched up the kids in the nursery enough to know that. I washed my hands with plenty of soap and asked, "How often have you been bandaging this?"

"Every day," he said. "Or most days, anyway. When I remember."

I began dabbing Dettol onto the stitched area, and he wasn't wincing, though it must have stung. "And how much have you been cleaning it?"

"Well … not," he admitted. "I don't have all the stuff, and it's a bit hard to do with one hand. It doesn't hurt much anyway. Except when I carry too much with it or whatever."

"Gabriel." I was dabbing on antibiotic ointment now with a cotton swab. "You have to *care* for it. Have you had a fever?"

"Uh—no. I'm fine."

"No," I said. "It isn't really fine. Maybe you can come see me before you go in to work, Monday, and I'll change the dressing for you and check it. You start at seven, don't you?"

"Yes."

"Then come see me first, and I'll do it for you." I was putting on a new layer of gauze, then taping it in place, taking care the wound had a chance to breathe. "There. I'll tidy up. But ..." I hesitated.

"Yes?"

I wasn't even sure where the next thing came from. "Can I cut your hair?"

31

NOT CHILLING

ORIANA

Gabriel wasn't looking at me, but he was. He was looking at me in the mirror, and I couldn't breathe. I still had his hand, too.

"Yeh," he said, and that was all. Then he smiled, and my heart turned over.

"Then bring in a chair," I said, doing my best to be brisk, like Daisy, "and I will." Meanwhile, I got a sheet from the cupboard. When Gabriel came back, I put him in the chair, wrapped the sheet around him to keep the hair off, and realized.

"Oh," I said. "My scissors are in the caravan. Would you ... if we go down there to do this, could you please *not* think that I'm inviting you to have relations?"

This time, he laughed. "Yeh. I could."

"Bring the chair, though," I said. "We'll need it. I'll bring the sheet."

For his haircut. It was just a haircut. I had to *stop* this.

When we were walking down the track together with the night-blooming jasmine scenting the air, though, he said, "This is what Honor told me to do. Take you for a walk after dinner."

"Honor?" I was so confused. "Why?"

"Because she thought I liked you."

I couldn't answer that. I literally couldn't think of anything to say, so I just said, "It's here," as if he couldn't see an enormous metal caravan in front of his nose, and opened the door.

It was so strange, standing with him beside the couch that turned into Priya's and my bed at night, that I couldn't quite believe it was happening. My mind hadn't caught up to my body, or something.

He said, "This is nice."

"It's just a caravan," I said, embarrassed. "I tried to make it cozy, though."

"It is. The way it looks like ... like you'd want to stop here, because it's comfortable, and it looks right, too. Pleasant, that's what it is. Homey. I'm not sure how you did it. My place doesn't look anything like it. Did you make this blanket?"

"Yes." That wasn't exactly brilliant conversation, so I went on. "The knitting wool came from our alpacas. From the first shearing, actually, which was this year. I know all their names, and which one gave each color, which makes it extra-nice." The soft, warm checked throw was made of big blocks of cream and brown and gray and black and fawn and white, and was perfect for curling up on the couch, when I had the time to do that. On the weekend, sometimes, when I'd look out the window, my fingers working the pattern automatically by now, and think.

Making plans, and discarding them, because I couldn't make any of my plans fit my life.

"I heard you named them," he said, and I couldn't tell what he thought of that.

"Yes. I felt silly doing it, or maybe ... sacrilegious. I know people Outside have animals as pets, and they sleep in their houses and all, but is it all right to love them? I don't know, but I do anyway. I always have. I love being able to help care for them now. And you know what's funny? Daisy loves them, too, as much as she hates everything else about Mount Zion. I've seen her down there, feeding them by hand after a hard shift, her hand in their fleece, because it's so soft, like curly strands of silk, and touching it makes everything better."

He said, "I can understand that. I think I might like a dog, in fact. In the house, even, though I can't have one in the flat, so it doesn't matter now."

"For later, then. When you're married, like you said." If I made myself face it, it wouldn't hurt so much. Or …

Because she thought I liked you.

"Yeh." He looked at me, and I lost my breath and couldn't look away. "And I know I shouldn't ask, but … you share a bed with Priya?"

"Yes." It felt too intimate, standing here talking about beds, even though we weren't as close as we had been in the bath. "There's another little bunk you can use, up on top, but it's nicer to share. I always feel cold, otherwise, even when it's warm, without somebody to … to touch."

"Yeh," he said. "I know."

The moment stretched out, and I tried to think of what to say and couldn't.

"Anyway." He lifted the chair. "Still OK with cutting the hair? I know I could go to a shop, and I should, but I'd rather you did it."

I did it, though I'm not sure how. Holding the lengths of golden hair between my fingers as I scissored and combed. Standing before him when it was time to do the front of his hair and seeing him, beautiful and unsmiling and so broad, his shoulders and chest stretching forever. I could tell my face was getting ever pinker, could feel my hands wanting to shake, and my heart was beating so hard, I was surprised he couldn't hear it. And yet, when I was done and was sweeping up, when he'd run his hands over the neatly trimmed edges of hair and smiled at me, then gone and looked in the bathroom mirror, and had finally said, "I should go, I guess," I wanted all of it to go on for longer, no matter how uncomfortable it was. Just like that night in his ute, after our evening with Drew and Hannah's kids.

I didn't say so, of course. I just walked him to the door, which was about three steps away. He paused on the verge of opening it and asked, "Did you mean it, about dressing my hand?"

"Yes. Of course."

"It'll be before seven."

"I know. And I'll be here to do it. Come to the yurt, though. I have better supplies there. Besides, Priya's a bit slow in the morning, so she'll ..."

"Be getting dressed," he said. "Right, then. The yurt."

Three days of him appearing every morning, and me opening the door before he could knock. Taking him into the bath and peeling the tape away, exposing the wound, cleaning it, gentle as I could be, slathering it with antibiotic ointment and bandaging it again, and seeing his skin gradually lose the redness, the puffiness.

When he arrived on Thursday morning, though, knocking softly on a door I hadn't quite got to in time, he didn't come inside, just stood out there with his hands behind his back.

I said, "What?" Already laughing, because that was the kind of look he had on his face.

He held up his left hand, palm out.

"You got them out!" I took it by the wrist to look better. Boldly, but I'd been holding his hand like this for days now, so that was all right, surely. Even though I loved looking at his hands. They were big, they were calloused, they were strong, and they were everything I wanted. "It looks good." I smiled up at him, and he was smiling back. "Healed. What a relief."

"Yeh," he said. "Everything works, too. I just wanted to stop by and say ... well, thanks. And ..." He pulled the other hand out from behind his back and handed me what he'd been holding there.

They were flowers, wrapped in green tissue paper. Five blooms, set on short, twiglike stems, surrounded by glossy green leaves. Gabriel said, his voice coming out a bit halting, "I know you have flowers already. I mean, Gray has them growing, so you can have them in the house anytime you like. But I thought maybe ..."

"No," I said. "I love them. They're beautiful. Thank you." Startlingly white, the petals waxy, creamy, the pattern they made reminding me of roses, but with the tightly folded interior framed by a collar of outstretched petals. They were the loveliest flower I'd ever seen, and they smelled sweet and deep and rich as custard. "They're beautiful," I said again, holding them up to inhale the scent again. "I'll put them in the glass pitcher by my bed, so I can smell them as I go to sleep. What are they?"

"Gardenias. I was thinking roses last night, when I shopped for them, maybe because that's about the only flower I know besides lavender, but I saw these. I hadn't seen them before, and I thought maybe you hadn't, either. You can't grow them out of doors here. Too cold. I thought they were a bit like you, though, the way they're so simple and beautiful, and the way they smell. Not like roses. Not ... not usual. I'm glad you want to put them in the caravan. It's pretty there already, and these would make it prettier." He had those patches of red on his cheeks again. "They mean something, too, gardenias."

At this moment, Gray came out of the bedroom, fastening his belt, and said, "Heading over to work, Gabriel?" in a meaningful sort of way, and Gabriel said, "Yeh. Just going. Anyway ... thanks, Oriana. For the hand and all." And left.

I glanced back at Gray, who was still looking at me. Then I opened the door again and ran.

Gabriel was almost to the house already. Taking long

strides, moving fast. I called his name anyway, and he stopped on the porch. And turned.

I stood at the bottom of the steps, still holding my flowers, then had to step aside as Uriel and Raphael headed up them, carrying a wooden cabinet between them, casting me a surprised look along the way.

I said, calling it out, because Gabriel wasn't close, "I'm babysitting for Laila tonight after work. Until nine-thirty or ten." Uriel turned his head and grinned, but I didn't care.

"Oh," Gabriel said. "That's extra money, then."

"Yes. I'm saving everything I can." Idiotically, because what did he care? "Anyway. Have a ... have a good day. I'm glad you have your hand back."

"Yes," he said. "So am I." And smiled. Slow, sweet, and heart-melting.

I barely felt my feet on the walk back to the house.

Now, it *was* tonight. Nearly nine, the girls in bed, and Priya and me on the couch. I was knitting, but not on the front porch this time. I was on the couch in the flat instead with Long John curled up on the carpet at my feet, but I couldn't settle. I kept wanting to go sit on the steps for whatever was left of the night, just in case Gabriel turned up. I could be doing that for the next hour, though, getting cold and feeling stupid, and what kind of babysitter would it make me? How would it look to him, even if he did turn up? Like I was desperate.

Like a girl who'd had a crush forever.

Or just since she was twelve.

Oh. Texting. People would normally text, wouldn't they? You said something like, "Want to chill?" I didn't know his number, though, and he didn't know mine. We weren't used to texting, at least I wasn't. Also, I'd feel like a prize idiot texting, "Want to chill?" to Gabriel. Maybe because I *didn't* want to chill.

I wanted to *be* with him, to sit with him and look at him and walk with him and feel, deep in my bones, the person he was.

I'd asked Laila about seeing him, of course. I wasn't going to make that mistake twice. She'd said it was all right to sit outside with him, so that was good.

If he came.

Meanwhile, Priya was alternately watching TV and going through her schedule for the school year, when she'd be back in a classroom again. I had mine, too, but I hadn't paid it much attention yet. She said, "I didn't get French and have to take Spanish instead, but that's OK. I got Theatre, though. That's so cool."

"Really?" I asked, ripping out the row I'd been knitting and going back to pick up the stitches again, because I'd done the cables backward. I wouldn't have made that mistake when I was *ten*. "Why? I can't think of anything worse. Being up on stage with everybody looking at you?"

She said, "I thought it might help."

I looked up from picking up my stitches, because there'd been something desolate about that. "How?" I asked. "How would it help?" She flinched, and I said, "I'm not criticizing. I'm asking. You mean—help with adjusting? Because I have trouble sometimes with that." I didn't want to admit it, even though she'd already pointed it out. It was a sore spot, you could say.

She didn't pounce on it, to my relief. She said, "It feels like ... I'm already playing a part, most of the time. I'm looking at other people, studying how they seem to feel, how they act. How girls are around boys, for one thing, but really ... everything. And I thought, maybe if I learn about acting, I can ..." She trailed off, then said, "I don't know. It sounds stupid."

I set my knitting down. "No, it doesn't. It makes sense to me. I usually just get quiet, but ..."

I had to stop, because I'd just realized something. I got

quiet when I was unsure, and I stood back. Daisy, and Frankie, and Priya ... they worked to get into the same flow as other people instead, and they'd put a mask on to do it if they had to. They charged forward. They charged *in*. I said, "I think you should take the class and use everything you learn. Just don't let it ..." I stopped again.

"What?" Priya asked. "Don't let it what?" She wasn't watching TV anymore. She was watching me.

"Don't let it ... change you," I finally said. "Or that's wrong, because everything changes you. Going to school, being Outside, whatever—it all changes you. But I think you should try not to feel like the way you are inside is bad. Or wrong."

"Excuse me?" she said. "Of *course* it's bad. That's why we left! Having to do whatever a man says? Having fourteen kids? Never getting to decide anything? Daisy says that *all* that is bad, and that we should get to choose what we do! I *want* to choose what I do. Don't you?"

"Yes," I said. "I do. But ... isn't there part of you, the God-given part, that feels the *most* real? And if God made you that way, deep down, can it be bad?"

She said, "God doesn't work that way, on just one piece of you, inside. God says how *everything* is."

"I don't know," I said. "That doesn't make sense, if we *do* get to choose. I just know that when I do the things that matter most to me, even if they aren't the things other people like, I'm happy. That hasn't changed, so that must be the part of me that God made. At least, I think so."

"What if what made you happy was being horrible, though?" Priya asked. "Like Valor?"

"Oh." I had to think about it, though I didn't want to. I didn't ever want to think about Valor again. "I don't know. That's the Devil, maybe." Not a satisfactory answer, and there was a reason that it was easier to be in Mount Zion. You never had to try to sort out these things. The Prophet told you, and that was that.

I was seventeen years old. I was a girl. I'd had to work hard just to pass Year 11 maths. How did I know the answers?

That was when I heard a knock at the door. And dropped my knitting again.

32

THE POWER OF THE MOON

G<small>ABRIEL</small>

I'd taken a shower after work, shaved again to make sure, then dressed in clean work clothes and wished I had something else, something better. I'd cooked sausages and baked frozen chips in the oven, all the while wrestling with whether to go over there tonight.

Was it wrong? Should I go to somebody else first? To Daisy and Gray, that would be. It felt like I should be asking permission, but why? Wasn't the choice ours, under these new rules?

In the end, I went.

Not entirely true. I went because I couldn't *not* go. Not after Oriana had run after me and told me she'd be at Laila's tonight. Uriel and Raphael had laughed afterward, had given me stick, as I could have predicted, and I'd known my dad would be hearing about this and couldn't care. I'd smiled and said nothing, but my heart had felt like it was about to burst.

My heart still felt overactive, but in a slightly sick way. Oriana wasn't sitting on the steps, which made this visit not accidental, and not casual. It meant I had to decide whether to knock. I didn't even know that she was still here. I should've texted her, probably. If I'd had her number.

Harden up, I told myself. And knocked.

A burst of excited barking, first, and then the door opened. The dog, wagging his tail furiously, looking for a pat, and Priya. "Hi, Gabriel," she said. "What are you doing here?" Like most of her sisters, she had no problem looking me in the eye anymore. The only one who still had trouble with that was Oriana. So why was I so sure that Oriana was the right one for me?

I don't know. I just was.

"Came to see Oriana," I said. "She here?" My heart was completely out of control now, banging away like a freight train, because Oriana *was* here. In the doorway, in fact.

She was wearing trousers, but the loose, flowing kind she liked, which were black with a pattern of tiny roses today. Her pink shirt matched the flowers, her hair was tied up in a soft knot, and she looked like everything sweet and pretty in the world. She said to Priya, with all the self-possession she hadn't had when she'd cut my hair, "I'll sit outside with Gabriel for a few minutes."

Priya said, "You probably shouldn't." Her gaze going between the two of us, suspicious, or just curious, I couldn't tell. I could picture her going home and telling Daisy, but what did that matter, if I wasn't going to be doing anything wrong? And I wasn't. That, I was sure of.

Oriana said, "I discussed it with Laila earlier. She said it was all right."

"Oh," Priya said. "All right, then." She shut the door, but before she did, the dog shot through and came to stand beside me. Oriana laughed, dropped onto the steps, and gave the dog a cuddle, like she had so much affection, it had to come out. I thought about the times I'd seen her from the window, down in the paddock with the alpacas, feeding them out of her hand, stroking their sides. I sat beside her and said, "You don't get tired of it, then, being so ..."

"Being what?" she asked. Still composed.

"Taking care of the babies, and then babysitting. The animals and all, too. Caretaking, I guess."

"No," she said. "I don't always know how to go on with adults. I know with kids and animals, though, and the babies are nothing but dear. How could anybody not love holding them and caring for them? I know I'm soft," she went on, as if determined to say it, "but somebody has to be soft, don't they? Don't babies need somebody like that, at least?"

"Everybody needs somebody soft," I said. "I know I do."

"Oh," she said, and that was all.

You'll never get anywhere if you don't begin, I told myself. I had a hand on the dog's back, and Oriana was rubbing his ears. He was the chaperone, I guessed, sitting between us like it was his job. He and Priya. I asked, "Did you look up about gardenias?"

Now, she looked startled. "No. Was I meant to?"

Oh. She hadn't. I tried to remember what I'd said about it, and couldn't. Saying more now felt like a leap into the dark, but I took a breath and took that leap. "I hoped you would, but maybe I didn't ask you clearly enough."

"I could look on my phone, I guess," she said.

I laughed, though I didn't exactly feel like it. "No. It's OK. I'll tell you. They're meant to be, ah … purity. A pure soul, maybe. That's what the woman at the shop said. And joy. And …" The hardest one. "A secret love."

She sat absolutely still. She was silent for so long, in fact, I thought I'd overstepped. I thought I'd misinterpreted. I thought everything. Then she said, "Really?" and clasped her hands between her knees as if they weren't entirely steady.

I wanted to take her hand, but I couldn't, because I still didn't know for sure. I said, "I wanted to ask the Prophet for you, back in Mount Zion. I knew he'd say no, though, because you're my cousin, and because asking would be setting myself above his wisdom. But you're not my cousin, not by blood, and I've been in love with you for ages. For years. I couldn't help it. If you'd been promised to Valor, I was going to ask you to …" *Now or never.* "To run away with me," I finished. "I couldn't think of any other way to keep you safe."

She put her hands to her face, and I realized they were shaking. I said in alarm, "Oriana. No. If you don't want it, if you don't want me, if you can't love anybody from Mount Zion, if it's too soon, and you're too young, and you want to … to do the things young people do here. Whatever it is, you can tell me. I know you're too young, Outside. I know people here don't do it like this, and I don't know when the right time is, or how to ask, but I need to ask anyway. That doesn't mean you have to say yes. Both people have to choose each other, or it doesn't work."

She turned her face to me, then, and said, her voice shaking all over the place, "Of course I choose you. Of course I do."

It took a moment to sink in, and I knew why she'd had her hands over her face. I couldn't control my own face, and I also felt like I could float away.

"Really?" I asked, feeling tongue-tied. Feeling stupid.

"Yes," she said. *"Yes."* And smiled her radiant smile. She was the sun, and she wasn't. She was the moon, because her light would always be gentle, but the power of that gentleness could pull the tides.

"Oh," she said. "Except that I don't know what you're asking. I mean, I realize it may not be about … about marriage, like I thought. It may be going out. Being my … my boyfriend. Or whatever." She tried to laugh, and then she had her hands over her face again. "This is so embarrassing," she said from behind them. "So … so scary. I don't know whether I can … what to hope for. Or how to do things. How to be a girlfriend."

"Oriana. No." Now, I did take her hand. I took it away from her face and held it, and she turned into me like a sunflower. I put my arm around her, the same way I had on that evening with Valor, and completely differently. Now, it wasn't just protection I was offering. It was love, and I could give it, because she wanted it. Her head was on my shoulder, her hand was still in mine, and there was almost too much feeling there to speak. I said, "I want to marry you. I want to make you happy. Being with you, having you make a home for us, the way you do—that would be everything. That would be all I could want. I don't know how, either, on any of it, but I reckon we can try."

She nodded against my shoulder, then pulled away and looked up at me, her eyes shining, and said, "That's what I want, too. And I don't believe it's wrong to want that. I don't. If it's not wrong to wait to get married until you're thirty, and to have relations with different people before that, how can it be wrong *not* to do those things? Why isn't it just a different choice?"

"It is," I said. "It can be. I'm bad at words, but I'm good at … at knowing. And I do know. I'm sure. You need to finish school, I understand that, and you probably have plans after that, too. I can work with your plans. I just couldn't go any longer without asking."

"And I couldn't go any longer without telling," she said. "That I love you. If it's wrong, I'm wrong, and I'm going to stay wrong. I love you, and that's all."

33

FIVE FLAMES

G<small>ABRIEL</small>

I woke to the alarm at five-thirty the next morning, just like always, and I didn't. That is, I didn't roll out of bed immediately as I'd done all my life. I lay there a minute more, remembered that Oriana wanted me, too, and felt the spreading joy of that flowing like warm water through my veins.

That's not a good enough way to describe it, but I didn't have a good way to describe it. I just knew that when I'd gone to bed last night, my prayers had been different.

Gratitude mattered, but you couldn't thank God for pleasure without thanking him for pain, maybe. I'd gone through my life set on "medium," but ever since I'd walked through Mount Zion's gates, I'd been set on five flames. It was like my senses had sharpened, or maybe like I'd walked through life before this half-asleep. It wasn't comfortable living on five flames, but it was definitely living.

Right. If you don't get up and get to work, though, you're going to be living without your job. I threw my bright-green sheets and light-purple duvet off me and rolled out of bed, then stopped stock-still, because what I'd just flashed on ... it wasn't my bedroom, with its dingy not-white-anymore walls and its terrible metal window frame. It was that blanket Oriana had knitted out of alpaca wool. The six colors of it in big, contrasting blocks, all of it ready to be pulled over you when the night got chilly. When you were in bed.

I always feel cold, otherwise, even when it's warm, without somebody to ... to touch, she'd said. After that, she'd cut my hair, her face a mask of concentration, her clever hands wielding comb and scissors as if this mattered. Standing in front of me, between my legs, because there was no other way for her to reach me, and I'd been looking at her breasts in that yellow dress, at the curve of her waist and the swell of her hips. I couldn't have avoided seeing them without closing my eyes, and I wasn't closing my eyes. I'd had to fold my hands in my lap, and it had been all I could do to control my breathing.

Best haircut of my life.

Get dressed. I did, and I made breakfast, too, in the not-quite-as-dirty kitchen, since I'd been able to do the washing-up properly at last once the stitches were out. And then I washed up the frying pan, hoped the others would wash it after they used it, knew they wouldn't, climbed into the ute, and went to work.

Saturday. A short day. Done by three. My dad was helping us today, because we were only a couple of weeks from that deadline now, and I didn't see how we'd get it done without more help, now that Gray had sacked Valor. I could come in tomorrow, on Sunday, to finish the wiring, but ...

I'd wanted to kiss Oriana last night. I hadn't, partly exactly because of Valor, who'd touched her when she hadn't wanted it, and partly because she'd said, "Laila will be home any minute," in a distracted sort of way, and I'd guessed that meant, "And it wouldn't be right for her to find me out here with you when I'm supposed to be watching her kids."

After that, though, she'd said, "I'm telling you that because I want you to kiss me. I'm afraid I may be ... fallen. Maybe Gray and Daisy are sinning, *really* sinning, after all. Maybe that's why I have too many thoughts. I need to say it, because you need to know it." And looked up at me, even though I could tell it was costing her an effort. In her pink shirt, with her soft hair and soft mouth and that tremble under the surface of her skin.

I'd wanted her so much, I'd thought I'd burst into flames.

I'd said, "I have thoughts, too."

"You do?"

"Yeh. About you, and about … I've seen some things now. I'm not sure how real they are. I've tried not to put you into the stories, but sometimes, it happens anyway." It was confession time, apparently.

"You mean …" Her cheeks were pinker now, and she had her hands up by her face again. "It's a sin, though. For both of us."

"Yeh," I said. "I know. Porn. I saw it by accident at first, but then I watched. I promise I won't watch anymore, but I did. I saw. You haven't, though, I guess. Girls don't, it seems. Or maybe they do, but they don't say."

She shook her head, though her hands were still pressed against her face as if she were holding herself together. I thought, *Why did you tell her?* And answered, *Because she has the right to know, and because it feels so wrong not to.* I wondered, though, how I'd feel if this was how I lost her.

Like a fool, that was how. Or a sinner.

She said, finally, "I haven't … watched. I wouldn't know where to watch. I have thoughts, though, and they're always …" She heaved a breath all the way from the bottom of her lungs, and the next words came on that exhale. "About you. They're always about you."

I'd touched her hair, because I'd wanted to kiss her lips, and then I'd wanted to kiss her more places. I ran my hand along that soft, shiny hair, put up so neatly, wished with everything I had that I could take down her hair and take off her clothes and feel her trembling hands undoing my buttons, too, her hands on my body, that we could learn about it all together. I said, "I want to do all those things, but I want to do them with you." She caught her breath, and I went on. "I know we need to wait until we're married. I don't want to do the wrong thing. I don't want to hurt you. But ... I hope it can be soon. I'm saving for my own flat, and I'll work as hard as it takes to make this happen."

"I want it to be soon," she said. "And I'm saving, too. It won't just be you."

"You're still seventeen, though," I said. "Daisy will say it's wrong, and I think Gray will, too."

"I know. And I should probably care." Then she started, grabbed her knitting, jumped to her feet along with the dog, and said, "That was Lachlan's car. I need to go inside."

Now, I thought, *We need to sit down with Daisy and Gray and tell them, and make a plan.* That was what mattered, not my out-of-control imagination. I pressed the buttons for the code on Gray's gate and wondered if he'd invite me to dinner again. Was it wrong to eat at a man's table when you were planning to take a seventeen-year-old girl away from her family?

Well, yeh, almost certainly. I might not know much, but some things didn't come from experience. Some things came from inside you. I heard the gate closing behind me, headed down the hill with more of that shingle-spatter, and tried to refocus on this. On today, and what each man needed to do in order to finish the job. If I let Gray down and didn't finish on time, he wasn't going to think much of me.

Last week, he'd told me that he was giving me that rise in pay. "But don't be thinking your check will be the same after this week," he'd said. "Some of that's for the time you've already been foreman." All the same, the number I'd seen on my check yesterday had made me sweat a bit. It put me that much closer to changing my life. If we finished on time, and if I showed Gray and Daisy my account balance? Wouldn't it help?

I stopped thinking about it, because somebody's little car was already here, parked in the spot I usually took. Only two of us with the gate code: my dad, and me. He'd already be at the house, then. I checked my watch. Six-fifty. I was five minutes late. I parked beside his car, checked my phone to make sure nobody else needed to be let in, jumped down, and went inside to find him.

He was standing in the middle of the kitchen, in which the cabinets were half installed, but he swiveled to meet me when I stepped through the door.

"Getting closer," he said. "Paint job's not bad. Who did it?"

"Raphael," I said. "As he's the most meticulous. And if you'd take over installing the cabinetry today, working with Uriel, that'd help. We're behind on the third bath, and I want to do it myself, so the stone's perfect." It was for the ensuite in the master bedroom, it was marble and was going to be more beautiful than I'd ever imagined a bath could be, and I needed to lay it myself. Gray would know if it wasn't right, and what was worse—I would.

A *ding* from my phone, and I checked it and buzzed my brothers through the gate. Dad said, "I'd like you to come home after work."

"OK," I said. I knew he meant, "to his house," not to mine, even though I'd never lived in the flat. Had he heard, somehow? Or guessed? Had Raphael or Uriel told him, maybe?

The sound of the door opening, another *ding* that was another member of the crew arriving, and I was going out to meet them. And seeing Oriana out the window, walking up the track and headed toward the yurt with a basket on her arm. Eggs and fruit, maybe, for Daisy and Gray's breakfast. She turned her head to look at the house, or, probably, to look at the arriving workers, but it felt like she was looking at me. I went to the doorway and raised my hand, and she raised hers and smiled. Shyly, and so sweetly, and I got another rush of emotion. Five flames again.

That was all, except for a text in early afternoon, when I was holding up an oversized slab of marble with my cousin Diligence, slotting it into place with absolute precision. I heard the chime, remembered how Oriana and I had finally exchanged phone numbers last night, just before she'd dashed into the house with Long John, and told myself it would be one of the flatmates. Rowan, texting, *Out of loo paper,* or something like that, as if it were easier to tell me than to go buy some.

Somehow, I'd become the wife in my flat, or possibly the mum. There was a thought for you. *Don't do that, when it's the two of you,* I reminded myself, and got a kick of excitement in my gut at the thought.

When the stone was secure, I told Diligence, "Lay the cement for the next one," then pulled my phone out of my pocket and glanced at it, even though it was a terrible example to set.

It wasn't Rowan. It was Oriana, saying, *Come for dinner? I didn't ask yet, but I'm cooking it. Daisy's on day shift, so she'll be there. Maybe come by at five-thirty, so we can talk first. Meet me?*

My heart gave an almighty leap that was either excitement or dread, and I texted *OK,* tried to breathe, and picked up the next slab of marble.

My parents, then Daisy and Gray. What could go wrong, other than everything?

34

BURNING IT DOWN

Gabriel

I found out.

I left work after my dad, of course. After everybody. I'd learnt my lesson. And when I got to my parents' flat, Harmony opened the door to me, looking ... something. Excited, or something else.

I said, "What? Something happen? Is it school?" I knew she was nervous about starting, even though Patience would be starting along with her. Yeh, the look was worry, and I gave her a cuddle. No shower for me yet, and I probably didn't smell the best, but what could a brother do, when it was his youngest sister and she was looking like that?

She didn't seem to care that I was sweaty, because she buried her face in my chest for a minute, then stepped back, gathered herself, and said, "No. I'm fine. It's just ... Mum and Dad are being odd." The last part in a whisper. "And I think it's about you. Dad's in the shower, and Mum's in the bathroom with him, talking."

"Oh." Another lurch in my gut, and I said, trying to joke, "This feels like one of those times when people have a beer first. Pity we don't do that."

Patience was out here now, too, and she'd heard that, because she asked, "D'you want a lemonade?"

"Yeh," I said. "Thanks."

My mum came into the kitchen while Patience was pouring it, gave me a quick cuddle of her own, and said, "Your dad says it's going well, on the house."

"We'll get there," I said. "Could be some long nights, though, pulling it all together. The baths, especially, though they're going to be beautiful. I never knew bathrooms could be beautiful."

"Marble, Dad says," Mum said. "Which is vanity."

"Yeh," I said, "but is it, really? It's a natural stone. Made by God, eh." She glanced at me sharply, but my dad came in, then, and she didn't say anything, just stood and poured him his own glass of lemonade, though the pitcher was right there. For that matter, Harmony and Patience were right there.

Both my parents sat down after that, and Dad told me, "Sit down," then told the girls, "Go to your room, please." Harmony cast me a speaking look, and Patience cast me a sparkling one, and they went.

I didn't say anything. That was because I couldn't think of anything to say, so as usual in that situation, I shut up. Dad said, "I've been giving some thought to your future. Talking it over with your mum as well, which is why she's here."

Mum nodded, but was quiet, her hands folded in her lap. I took a sip of lemonade, because my mouth was dry, and said, "My future feels pretty well sorted at the moment. Just depends on me, eh, but I'll be giving everything I've got."

Dad said, "Time for you to be married, though. Well past time. Paul says, 'It is better to marry than to burn.' Young men burn, and burning leads to sin. You're twenty-five."

Oh. Here we went. I said, "I agree," and put my own hands in my lap in case they shook.

Dad looked surprised, but recovered himself and went on.

"Patience is a good girl, but she needs a husband to set the standard for her to follow."

I got that sinking feeling in my gut again. If this kept up, I'd be seasick. I said, "She's barely sixteen. Looking forward to starting school, surely."

Dad said, "That school has boys in it, and she's ready to sin. If it's wrong for a man to sin, how much more wrong for a girl? She needs leadership. I'm not talking about a heavy hand. I'm talking about a *just* hand, a hand she can obey, because she'll know it's coming from concern for her soul."

He glanced at my mum, and she said, "She's been looking at magazines in the shops. I found one under her mattress two days ago. I got her a job at the knitting shop, and she spent the money she earned on that? It's for teen girls, yet half the articles are about sex. One of them's about ..." She lowered her voice. "Abortion rights. Not just birth control. I've used birth control myself. I'm not keeping that a secret anymore. But *abortion*? There was something else under there as well. Two skirts that can't reach her knees, and three T-shirts. In size small, which means *small*. Where is she wearing those things, and when? If she isn't brought under control now, I don't know that it'll be possible."

"Why are you telling me?" I was gobsmacked, but I was something else, too. Angry, I thought it was. "Why aren't you telling Glory? She's her sister. Or why aren't you talking to Patience, for that matter?" Patience hadn't looked one bit abashed when she'd greeted me, which meant they *hadn't* talked to her. What, they were going to present our marriage to her like it was done? I thought that was why we'd left!

"It's not Glory's place to say," my dad said. "Patience had the right to walk out of Mount Zion, but she walked out because all of us were here, and her parents will need to know that she's properly settled. That's why we took her in with us, because Uriel and Glory can be—" He stopped.

"And now you want to ... what?" I took a drink of lemonade. Somehow, my hands weren't shaking anymore, because I knew what.

"To give her to you," Dad said. "You need a wife. After that? She can finish school if she likes, if you agree."

"She's not yours to give," I somehow said. "She gets to choose what she does, and I don't want an unwilling wife."

My dad's face darkened, and my mum looked shocked. Dad said, "She wants you. Anybody can see that, not that it matters. She's not capable of making a right choice. Her head can be turned by anything. She needs direction."

"Then," I said, "she's not ready to be married."

"So you're saying," Dad said, "that you refuse."

I breathed in, and then I breathed out. "Yeh. I refuse. Because it's not right for her, and it's not right for me. I have somebody else I want to marry. I've found the right woman."

My mum said, "Oh, no." Faintly, as if this were her worst nightmare.

"Don't worry," I said. "She's from Mount Zion. It's Oriana."

If I'd expected a thunderclap, it didn't come. Nothing at all came for a long minute, in fact. Mum said, "You realize that Patience is probably sitting on her bed right now, hugging her pillow and wishing for you."

I said, "I thought she wasn't capable of making a right choice."

My dad shoved himself back from the table so abruptly, I nearly flinched. He was a deliberate man. That's where I'd learnt it. Not now, though. He stood, leaned forward with his hands on the tabletop, and said, "You forget yourself."

Somehow, I'd stood, too. The table between us, and more than the table. A gulf. "No," I said. "I know myself, and so does Oriana. She knows herself, and she knows me."

"She's seventeen," Dad said. "And you say you're worried about Patience's age, that she doesn't know what she wants? What's the difference, other than lust?"

"Love," I said. "From both of us. That's the difference." I was sweating. Sweating more, because I'd already sweated heaps today, laying stone in the summer heat. I didn't want to do this. I wanted to go home, take a shower, and go see Oriana.

You need to do this first.

"There's another difference, too," I said. "Oriana knows what she wants. She's not just ... not just dreaming and hoping. She's not looking for somebody to tell her what to do, either. She's been working since she got out. She's got ideas, and she's got plans, and she's got ..." I tried to sort out what it was. "Potential," I finally said. "A whole future for herself, not just the one she wants with me. It's exciting."

"That's not the way life works," Dad said. "Two people who want different things, have different goals? What is that but guaranteed conflict in the home, and raising a woman to a place she doesn't belong? Marriage wasn't created to be a battle. Husband and wife are meant to be one flesh. The husband loves his wife as if she were his own body, protecting and providing for her, and a wife offers her ideas to him in a spirit of giving, and submits to his authority out of the respect she holds for him. That's God's way, because that way leads to contentment and peace in the home. Have you forgotten your Bible so quickly, then?" He quoted, 'Wives, submit yourselves unto your own husbands, as unto the Lord. For the husband is the head of the wife, even as Christ is the head of the church: and he is the savior of the body. Therefore as the church is subject unto Christ, so let the wives be to their own husbands in every thing.'"

I would have spoken, but he held up his hand and went on. "'Husbands, love your wives, even as Christ also loved the church, and gave himself for it. So ought men to love their wives as their own bodies. He that loveth his wife loveth himself.' That's not tyranny. It's leadership."

I said, "It sounds right, because I've heard it all my life, and

I know it's what you and Mum believe. But it's not what I believe. Oriana's *not* myself. She's *herself*." *I doubt it's what Uriel believes, either,* I didn't say. *And I can guess what he and Glory will think of this plan when they hear.*

"It's not a matter of thinking," Dad said, "out of your limited knowledge. Your *worldly* knowledge. God's word is perfect, given to us as a path to follow."

"And where does it say," I asked, "that a father chooses his son's bride? Where does it say that a leader chooses a woman's husband? A woman who isn't even his child? Or call Patience what she is. A girl."

A silence so loud, it pressed on my ears. My dad's face across the table. My mum sitting rigid. Horrified.

"Get out," Dad said.

I'm not sure how I walked to the door. My legs felt stiff, and when I got to the ute, climbed in, and shut the door, I started to shake. *Adrenaline,* I thought dimly. *It's just adrenaline.*

It was more than that. It was setting fire to my family, to the life I'd known for twenty-five years. I'd walked out of Mount Zion's gates, and somehow, I'd ended up on this road.

I'd thought I was walking the right path, but I'd tossed a torch behind me, and now, I was burning everything down.

How could this be right?

How could it not be?

35

NOT DANCING WITH A LAWYER

ORIANA

Unfortunately, when Gabriel rang the doorbell that afternoon, we didn't get a chance to be alone and talk things over the way I'd planned. Priya was sitting at the kitchen bench with an exercise book, working on the maths problems Frankie had sent her, the exact same way Frankie was always doing, and Daisy and Gray were in the shower after their extra-long Saturday run on the beach, because to Daisy and Gray, if you didn't hurt afterward, the exercise hadn't been hard enough. They took the longest showers in the world when they took them together, and I was starting to suspect that you *could* have sex in the bath.

How, though, if there was no way to lie down? Gray was big, and Daisy wasn't, so … did he hold her up? Against the shower wall, maybe? That was the only way I could imagine it working, but it was so much more exciting than thinking about being in bed, under the duvet. If you were both naked, and wet, and kissing each other …

Stop it. How did I just *look* at Gabriel, and start thinking all these things?

Priya said, "Hi, Gabriel. You're here again, eh," and looked at me in a meaningful sort of way. "I hope you really are going to have the house done by the end of the holidays," she decided to add, "because Frankie's coming home in two weeks, and she is *not* going to want to live in the caravan with Oriana and me. She says she isn't sharing a room again, and someday, she's getting her own flat. I can't imagine living all by myself, can you? It sounds so lonely."

"Yeh," Gabriel said. "To me, too." And smiled at me.

I'd been chopping up cabbage for coleslaw. Now, my knife faltered. I heard the bathroom door open and Gray say, "So much for my self-control." Daisy said, "I like you without self-control," and he laughed. Then there was the sound of the door shutting, which meant they were in their bedroom and getting dressed.

I could tell Gabriel had heard. He raised his eyebrows at me, and I thought, *How do people wait to do this? How?* I said, knowing my voice wasn't the steadiest ever, "I brined these chicken thighs to make them tender and juicy, but I've never made this recipe before, so who knows. Will you cook them on the barbecue for me? Seven or eight minutes on each side, and after that, I have watermelon to do as well. Just a minute on each side for that, at the very end. It sounded like a good dinner for today, because it was hot, and you've been working so hard."

"Watermelon on the barbecue," he said. "Sounds different. But good."

"I brined the chicken in beer, actually," I said, handing him the platter. "Along with other things. The alcohol cooks away, but you may smell it, so ..."

"No worries," he said. "You're not too sinful for me." And looked like he knew exactly how sinful I wanted to be.

I said, "Let me cut the watermelon, and I'll bring it to you. The grill should be hot enough, but you may want to check it." My *face* was hot, that was sure.

"Yeh," he said. "I'll do that."

He went outside, and I rested my palms on the benchtop and tried to breathe. Which was when Priya said, "Want me to slice the watermelon?"

"No," I said. "I'll do it right now. Could you lay the table, please?" I'd arranged anise hyssop and bee balm in a vase, all purple and blue and pink, and the flowers' fresh, sweet scent wafted to me on the breeze from the open windows. I wished we had a tablecloth and cloth napkins, though. That would be so much more festive. When I had my own flat, or ... if *we* did, I'd make those, using the right fabric, so it would drape and have some interest. Seersucker, maybe, for summer.

Pleasant, Gabriel had said. *Homey.* A bright yellow table with a vase of flowers in the middle, all of it sunny and cheerful. I could do that.

Priya said, "You're extremely obvious, if you want to know. Patience is pretty sure Gabriel's going to marry her, by the way, so ..."

I thought, *He isn't, though.* "Oh?" I asked, and kept slicing watermelon. "How do you know?"

"Because Aunt Constance keeps talking about what he likes, like she's training her to be her daughter-in-law. Patience and I went shopping today while you were at the farmer's market and she was on her lunch break, because she's working Saturdays at the knitting shop now. She asked me to keep the things she bought in our closet, though, because one of the dresses is really short, and Aunt Constance wants her to keep wearing long ones with barely any pattern. Patience doesn't even want to wear *medium* ones. I told her to remind Aunt Constance that she'll be in school in a week, and her skirts aren't going to be long then. Though the uniform is still pretty awful."

"What did she say to that?" I asked. "Also, do you think you should be hiding her clothes?" I needed to go outside and talk to Gabriel, but I needed to hear this first.

"Of course I should," Priya said. "They're trying to keep

her in prison, like she never left Mount Zion! Besides, she said that what Uncle Aaron and Aunt Constance don't know won't hurt them, and once she's married to Gabriel, they aren't going to be able to tell her anything."

"Doesn't she want to go to school?" I asked. Patience was like Frankie, except without the anger. I couldn't imagine her *not* wanting to go to school. *She* wasn't going to have any trouble participating.

"She thinks she can be married *and* go to school," Priya said. "I tried telling her that *nobody's* married when they're in school, but she just said, 'Then I'll be the first. What else am I going to do? I can't stay locked up here, getting *watched* all the time and criticized for everything I do. Uriel and Glory don't want me, not now that they have their baby. Their flat's tiny, and they're having relations constantly. In the *daytime*. As soon as the baby's asleep, Glory told me, they're doing it again. In every *room*. How could I live there with them having relations all over the place?' Which is a fair point. She said they had wine in their fridge, too, last time she was there, and Glory asked her not to tell Uncle Aaron. As if she would. They let her taste it, and she said it was lovely. It was white wine, and she said it tasted like fruit, or maybe like flowers. Last time she babysat, they went to a club and went dancing, and Glory wore a short dress. It was *red*. Uriel had a cocktail, which is even *stronger* alcohol, but Glory couldn't, because she's not eighteen yet. Also, she's changing her name to Georgia, and Uriel's changing his to Usher.'"

"Oh," I said. "That's ... a lot to change."

Priya went on as if I hadn't said anything, as if all of this was bursting to get out, which I reckoned it was. It was heady stuff for a girl from Mount Zion. "Patience says that Glory says that her name sounds like an old lady, and Uriel's sounds like urine, and she's not going to be married to a man whose name sounds like urine. Uriel's an *archangel,* and that's still what she said. Patience said that Uriel just laughed and said that Glory's pretty naughty, especially for a mum, so she'd better be called something less holy. Patience wants to change her name to Peyton. That doesn't even sound like a *girl*. She wants to be a lawyer, so she can wear suits and be all cool and argue with men."

"That doesn't sound like wanting to marry Gabriel," I said. "That sounds like a different life altogether."

"Same thing," Priya said. "Marrying Gabriel, and then having a different life altogether. She says, can you imagine how hot he'll be when he's actually dressed well? And not being a builder? Uriel's going to try for a job in sales. You can make heaps of money that way, Patience says, because that's what Valor's doing now. He's selling farm equipment, and he says it's easy and he's already making more money than he was working for Gray." She hesitated. "I didn't say anything to her about Valor and you. I didn't know if it was shameful. I guess Gray didn't, either, because nobody else seems to know about it."

My knife stilled, and then I forced myself to keep going with my slicing and said, "It shouldn't be shameful, but it still feels like it. And I think it's still shameful to men from Mount Zion, so ... don't tell anyone, for now. Thanks for asking me first."

"It's so hard to know," Priya said. "It almost seems like shame is the opposite Outside. Gray and Gabriel seemed like they thought only Valor should be ashamed, but ..."

"Yeh," I said. "Others won't feel the same about me. I know that." I should probably discuss that with her, if I'd even known how, but it was the last thing I wanted to think about tonight, and then there was the whole question of what my aunt and uncle would think of me if they knew. I had a feeling they'd share the shame around more readily than Gray had. Or Gabriel. I asked instead, "So is Uriel going to sell farm equipment, too?"

"I think so. He says it's not the most exciting, but it's the thing he knows, and maybe he can move on from it and sell luxury cars or something like that. At least that's what Patience told me, and that maybe if he does it, he can get Gabriel to do it as well. Or be a model, she says, since he's so handsome. I never realized how handsome he was until I compared him to other people, but Patience says she always realized."

I didn't ask, "Does Gabriel want to be a model?" I was pretty sure I knew the answer, so I finished slicing the watermelon instead and took it out to him. Unfortunately, just when I was about to bring up talking to Gray and Daisy, Gray came out and started talking to him about the house instead, so I went back in and finished making my coleslaw.

At least Uncle Aaron and Aunt Constance would be happy about my marrying Gabriel, even if nobody else was. After all, I wasn't going to be a lawyer and wear suits and argue with men, or tell Gabriel he should be a model. I tried to picture Gabriel drinking cocktails at a club, dressed in tight trousers and pointed shoes and dancing with a lawyer, and almost laughed.

That would be half of our family happy, at least. Now I just needed to work out how to bring the subject up with Gray.

Not to mention Daisy.

GABRIEL

Oriana's dinner was amazing, as usual. I'd got the chicken just right, too, charred a bit on the outside and still juicy inside. We made a pretty good team. I wondered how much more it would cost to get a flat with a balcony, or maybe a patio, so you had a barbecue right there and could eat outside on summer nights, maybe with candles, and got a bit distracted at the idea. That could be because Oriana was wearing the sundress with the strawberries and the straps again, and she was so pretty. And because every time she looked at me, she colored up again, and I could see her breasts rising and falling under that dress.

It's better to marry than to burn. I hoped it was true, because if I didn't marry her soon, I was going to burn so hard, there'd be nothing left of me but ash.

When we'd eaten all the chicken and most of everything else, and Oriana had jumped up and brought over a rich golden cake that turned out to be full of apples, pears, and blackberries, not to mention the custard that went with it, Daisy said, "You're being especially quiet tonight, Gabriel. Either you're being mysterious, or you're worried about Gray's house. Since I've never seen you be mysterious in my life, it's probably the house. First, is there something wrong, and second, when do I get to see it?"

"When it's done," Gray said. "I told you. I have a plan."

"You always have a plan," she said.

"Mm," he said. "That's probably because I love to make you happy."

I had my mouth open to speak when Oriana jumped in to say, "Speaking of plans, Gabriel and I have one, too."

Daisy set her fork down, and the amusement was gone. "What kind of plan?"

My turn. I realized, at this least opportune of moments, that it would've been better to wait until the house was done and I'd hopefully had a chance to impress both Daisy and Gray, and to prepare. Not to mention bringing Oriana my gift. After what had happened at my parents' today, though, how could I wait?

Gray's phone rang. He picked it up and said, "Aaron and Constance are at the gate. Why?" and looked at Daisy.

She said, "No idea." Her eyes were wary, though. Watchful. I was guessing she *did* have an idea.

Gray said, "One way to find out," and hit the button to buzz them in.

I said, "Before they get here, I need to say this. Oriana and I have been talking, and we *have* made a plan. We're going to be married." Apparently, this was what happened when you didn't prepare, or maybe it was what happened when you'd had the kind of weekend I'd had. The kind where you thought, *There's no good way to say it, and nobody's going to be happy, so just go ahead and get it out there, whatever happens next.*

Gray said, "Ah. Not too surprising."

Daisy said, *"What?* And not now, you're not. Not anywhere *close* to now. Absolutely not."

Priya said, "I *knew* it."

Oriana said, "Yes. We are. Very soon."

The dog, Xena, lifted her head and cocked it, as if she sensed drama.

And my dad knocked on the door.

I said, "One thing's sure, Oriana. My mum and dad are going to learn all over again what a good cook you are, because this cake is choice. I'll get two more plates." And smiled at her.

She looked as determined as a soft woman could be, and as nervous, too. I stood to get those plates and told her, "We've got this."

Did we? I didn't know. But I knew I'd be fighting for it all the way.

36

PLANS AND DREAMS

O*RIANA*

The first thing that happened when Aunt Constance and Uncle Aaron got in the door was that I cut them some cake. We'd had a seminar in school last month about "Exploring Your Dependable Strengths for Career Fit," and making cake was one of my dependable strengths. You were supposed to "lean into" those, whatever that meant. At this moment, as far as I could tell, it was slicing cake.

Aunt Constance said, when she'd taken a bite, "Very good. Is there orange in it?" in a tight-lipped sort of way.

"Yes," I said, trying for the sort of composure that came easily to Daisy and not at all easily to me. "The zest and the juice both. Also vanilla bean. And brandy, to give a deeper level of flavor, but the alcohol cooks out."

Priya said, "You always say the alcohol cooks out. Are you sure?"

"Yes," I said. "It evaporates."

"Not a good idea to use it, all the same," Aunt Constance said. "It's a slippery slope that paves the road to Hell, and besides, you can't know."

"I can, though," I somehow said. "As long as you simmer

it, it cooks out. The alcohol molecules don't stick together as strongly as the water molecules do, so when you heat it up, more alcohol molecules fly off. It's chemistry. And so far, I haven't been tempted to drink any, so I don't see how it can be a slippery slope to Hell any more than using vanilla is. I don't like alcohol, unless it's in food."

Aunt Constance's lips got tighter, and I knew why. I was arguing. It didn't matter that I was right.

Shouldn't it matter, though? How else did anybody learn things, if nobody could bring up other information? Even if that person was a woman, and seventeen?

Daisy said, "It's an excellent cake. Deliciously full of brandy, too. Mm. I'd like another slice, please, Oriana. Also, Oriana and Gabriel were just bringing up a proposal." Daisy was normally so calm. It was being an Emergency nurse, maybe, or it was just Daisy. Tonight, though, she looked like she was quivering under her skin, and her eyes were locked on Aunt Constance's.

Wait. Maybe this meant she'd support us.

Wait again. Aunt Constance *would* support us. The combativeness would be because Daisy wanted to say, "Absolutely not." She *had* said, "Absolutely not," in fact.

I tried to brace myself. I couldn't quite do it. I felt something under the table, then. Gabriel's hand, reaching for mine. I glanced at him, and he said, "We were. Our proposal to get married, in fact."

Uncle Aaron said, "We already discussed this. I forbade it. Why are we still talking about it?"

Wait. He *didn't* like the idea? I'd thought he'd be thrilled. Did *everybody* think I needed to be a lawyer, or an accountant, or an airline pilot, or whatever terrifying job Daisy thought was important enough?

"If it's me," I somehow said, "that you think I'm not good enough for Gabriel—I'm probably not. I mean, I'm sure he can get somebody better, somebody who has all her education already and earns more money than I do, because he's wonderful. He won't get somebody who loves him more, though, or cares more about making him happy. He can't, because I feel both of those things with all my ... all of my soul. All of my *heart*." *And all of my body,* I didn't say, because that wouldn't help.

"How will he be happy," Aunt Constance said, "going against his parents, and against God's laws? You've been filling his head with your plans, your dreams, telling him they should take precedence over his."

"She hasn't—" Gabriel began.

"I never said—" I tried to explain.

"And here I am," Daisy said, "thrilled to hear that she actually *has* plans. A man isn't a plan," she told me. "A man is usually an excuse *not* to make a plan. Not that I have anything against you," she told Gabriel. "You're a fine person, and I'm sure you'll be a good husband to somebody, but you're eight years older than my sister, and that's not right. If she has plans and dreams, shouldn't she be allowed to pursue them before she's tied down?"

"What's not *right*," Uncle Aaron said, "is that she's putting her plans and dreams above his."

Gray said, "Hang on, now. Let's talk about this. I know what you think," he told Daisy, "and I understand why you think it. I know what Aaron and Constance think, too. What we haven't heard is what Gabriel and Oriana think. Shouldn't we let them tell us? It's their life, after all."

"I didn't do all this to—" Daisy started to say.

Jumping in felt like leaping into a pool of sharks, but didn't I have to answer that? I said, "I know why you did this. You got us out because what happens at Mount Zion is wrong, and you wanted something better for us. I appreciate it so much. You saved Frankie, and you saved Priya, and I'm realizing that you saved me, too. But I *have* something better. I'm doing all the things I want to do, and I'm so ..." I was choking up, and I didn't want to cry. I clutched Gabriel's hand tighter and said, "I'm so grateful to you, and to Gray, and to Uncle Aaron and Aunt Constance, too, for helping. But does *everything* about my life, about how I am, have to be wrong, just because I'm more … more like Mount Zion? You keep saying I should have plans and dreams, but it feels like they have to be the same as *your* plans and dreams. Can't I dream of something different?"

"They don't have to be mine," Daisy said, still sounding stiff. "Of course they don't. I just want you to get an education and have a good career. I want you to have the freedom to create your own life, and you can't have that when you're weighed down too young with marriage and babies. And you're *seventeen*."

"I'm almost eighteen," I said.

"In four months," Daisy answered. "If you're measuring in months, you're not old enough."

"If I don't marry Gabriel soon, though," I said, "we're going to have relations, and that *will* be a sin. We aren't going to be able to help it. I can hardly help it now."

GABRIEL

That brought the conversation to a halt.

I said, "Oriana's right. About all of it. We don't want to have relations outside of marriage, but it's getting hard not to."

Gray said, "I've never tried not to, but I can imagine."

He was the only one here who didn't seem rattled, and I did my best to imitate his calm. "My parents want me to marry Patience," I said, because didn't I need to explain this? "And Patience *is* too young. You want me to marry her *because* she's too young," I told my parents. "To influence her. To control her."

"To guide her." My father's eyes were burning with

controlled fury again, and I hated defying him. What was the choice, though?

"I don't want to control anybody," I said. "I never have. I want to marry Oriana and be her partner. The things she loves are the same things I do. We're not complicated," I tried to explain to Gray, who wouldn't understand this. "We're simple. We want to work hard and have a loving home. We want a quiet life with ... with each other."

Oh. I'd better check. I glanced at Oriana, and she nodded, so I went on. "I'm pretty sure we both want babies, too, but what's wrong with that? I don't want her to have them before she's done with school, or to have twelve of them, to get that tired and not able to do her ... her business, with the knitting and all, and her job."

"You want her to do her job *and* take care of the house and the kids and you," Daisy said. "That's not freedom. It's the opposite."

"No," I said. "I don't. I know how to clean. I know how to do the washing, too, and how to shop for groceries. I don't know how to cook very well yet, it's true, but I can make breakfast, and I'm learning. I can learn to look after kids, and I'll be working all the hours God sends to take care of my family. I can promise that now and know I mean it, because I've already proved it."

"You're twenty-five," my dad said. "You haven't had a chance to prove it."

"Why did you make me foreman, then," I asked, "if you don't trust me to give everything? I *will* give everything. I *want* to give everything. To the job, and to Oriana. We just want a *life*."

"How much have you saved for that life?" my dad asked. "You'll support your family on what?"

I was about to answer, but Oriana spoke up again. "I've saved over ten thousand dollars. I know how to work as well. I know how to save. We just want to do it together."

Wait. Ten thousand *dollars?*

"You can't have," my mum said.

"School, though," Daisy said.

Oriana said, "Two more years of it, according to you. And for what, exactly?"

Daisy stood up. "I can't talk to you about this. If you don't even understand that, how can I ..."

Oriana said, "All right, I'll *go* to school. I just want to be married, too!"

"Well," Daisy said, "you'll need the Family Court's approval to do it before eighteen. What do you think the judge is going to say when you tell him you've just come out of Mount Zion, and you're sure you're old enough, because everybody's always told you that you need to marry an older man as soon as it's legal and then obey him in everything?"

"What do we have to do," I asked, "to convince you?" I looked around the table. "All of you?"

"You could just wait until Oriana's eighteen and get married anyway," Priya decided to point out. True, but not exactly diplomatic, because everybody but Gray erupted at that.

My dad said, after a fair amount of heated talk back and forth between him and Daisy, fury on my mum's face, and Oriana looking miserable, "I'm going to have to pray about this. I thought leaving was the right thing to do. Now, I wonder. If it leads my children into these kinds of disobedient paths ..."

"Wait until you find out what Uriel and Glory are doing, then," Priya said. "Oh, sorry, Usher and Georgia. They even *sound* glamorous now. Raphael and Radiance are still pure, though, as far as I know, so there's that. One out of three, eh. Or two out of four, if you count Harmony, but who knows?"

My mum said, *"What?"* Her face had been going red. Now, it went pale.

My dad said, "That's enough. We're going. Gabriel?" He

stood up and looked at me in that expectant way that means, *You're following my lead.*

I said, "I'll stop here a bit longer, thanks. I'm pretty sure Gray and Daisy have more to say to me."

My dad said, *"I have more to say to you."*

"And I'll listen, later," I said. "But Daisy is Oriana's sister. I have to respect that. Mostly, though, I have to respect Oriana." I thought of something, discarded it, and then, somehow, said it anyway. The thing I'd thought weeks ago. "Therefore shall a man leave his father and his mother, and shall cleave unto his wife: and they shall be one flesh."

"You can't pick and choose like that," my dad said, "after you rejected the word of God at my kitchen table this morning."

"Everybody picks and chooses," Gray said. "Or searches for the most important lessons, maybe, because there's contradiction all over the shop in every holy book known to man."

"Blasphemy," my dad said.

"Reality," Gray answered. "I don't see many of Jesus's teachings in the Prophet's ideas. Very Old Testament, I'd say. Or, rather, very much what serves the Prophet's interests."

My parents were still standing. So was Daisy. Gray wasn't. He and my dad locked eyes, and finally, my dad said, "That's enough. You're still my employer, and I'll respect that. I'll take your orders on the job. I won't take them in my home, about my family."

"You forget," Gray said, still calm as glass, "that you're not in your home. You're in mine."

My dad had nothing to say to that, because he clearly *had* forgotten, and within about thirty seconds, my parents had left.

Oriana sat there and trembled, her hand cold in mine. And I thought—*We did it.* And then ...

What have we done?

37

NO TURNING BACK

GABRIEL

At three o'clock the following afternoon, Drew's front gate was swinging open once more, and I was steering the ute up the hill to the big white house made up of cubes. Jack met me at the door and, instead of saying hello, blurted out, "After we do Step Two on the project, can we play basketball?"

Hannah appeared behind him, holding Peter. "We need to offer Gabriel something to drink before you two head out to the shed," she told Jack. "He looks hot."

"Cheers," I said, stepping inside and getting out of my work boots. Peter gave me a wide, gummy smile, and I said, "That tooth came in at last, eh, after all that trouble." He had a second little square of white in the middle of his lower jaw, and he was losing the bald look, too, as his hair came in as flaxen curls like his mum's. "Getting big," I told him. "You'll be crawling soon, I reckon." He chuckled as if he couldn't wait to break the bonds and make a mad dash for it, and I took hold of his dimpled hand with two fingers and a thumb and thought, *This is going to be me, before too long.* A rush of excitement at that, despite the limbo Oriana and I had been left in last night.

Some things, there are no easy answers to, not when you have less than two weeks to finish renovating a house and it already doesn't feel like there are enough hours in the day. Especially if you lose any more of your crew, or your dad isn't willing to lend a hand anymore, because you've infuriated and defied him. Most especially if the man who's given you that opportunity, *every* opportunity, is teetering into war with your dad, which will only hurt both of them, and it's your fault. That was why I hadn't pushed it harder last night, at least I hoped it was.

Drew was in the kitchen, and he stood up when I came in and clasped my hand. Hannah went for a glass of water, even though she was still holding Peter, and I said, "I'll get it, if that's all right," and did. I'd started noticing how often women poured things for me to drink, and it felt a bit ... symbolic, maybe.

Drew said, "You're later than I expected. Busy day?"

"Yeh," I said. "Put two coats of polyurethane on the cork floor in the kitchen. Only chance to do it, with all the cabinet hardware still to go on and the benchtops and backsplash to install. Worked on the ensuite bath some more in between."

"Working seven days a week, then," Drew said.

"Getting it done," I said, and drained the glass. "Cheers on the win last night."

"Thanks," Drew said. "Preseason, that's all, but we'll take a win."

"They won by two tries," Jack said. "That's heaps, so it means they're much better than the other team, not just a little bit better, and it probably means they'll have a good season, too."

"Nah," Drew said. "Just means we were better on the night. You can't judge the season until you've played all the games." He looked at me more closely. "Everything all right?"

I wanted to tell him, but I didn't really have anything to tell, not yet. My season, too, had barely started. So I just said,

"Ask me in two weeks, after the job's done. Ready to give me a hand, Jack?"

I had more than a deadline now. Finishing the job would mean there was no reason anymore to hold off on addressing my parents' wishes. And then it would be crossing the Rubicon.

No turning back.

OR MAYBE I'D already crossed the Rubicon, because when I got to Gray's on Monday morning, Uriel and Raphael were outside the gate, waiting for me. They followed me through and down the hill, and when we all got out, Raphael looked at Uriel, Uriel looked at Raphael, and neither of them spoke.

I said, "You're early. That's good. We can measure again for those benchtops to be sure and then cut the stone today. Moment of truth, eh."

Uriel said, "Moment of truth is right, but not the way you're thinking." They both stared at me some more, and I said, "Let's go inside."

Dad had told them, then. Told them what, exactly? Neither of them looked happy, but why not? Oriana was nearly as old as Radiance and Glory, and Raphael and Uriel didn't seem to have any problem being married to *their* wives, even though those marriages had happened when the girls were barely sixteen. Besides, from what Priya had said yesterday, Uriel was veering even further off track than I was. So why?

Ask them and find out. I opened the door, went inside, and said, "We're walking in socks in the kitchen until Friday, when that polyurethane's cured. And let's have it. What?"

Uriel said, "Just that Dad told us he's going to be renting a house and we'll all be moving in together, that's all, because of whatever it is you're being disobedient about, which I'm guessing is marrying Patience, or rather, *not* marrying her. It's pretty obvious that's what he wants, and I don't see you doing it. And that Patience told Priya what Glory and I told her about our plans, and Priya told Mum and Dad, which you must know, because you were there, and Gray denied Dad's authority over his family, which set Dad off. Now he's saying he's not sure he can keep working for an ungodly man, which means *we* aren't going to be allowed to work for an ungodly man. That isn't what I walked out of Mount Zion for, living with my entire family and having my dad tell my wife and me what we can wear and drink and *do*. Why the hell won't you just go on and marry Patience, so she stops stirring up trouble? That girl needs to be married, and she wants to do it with you, so why not do it and make it easy on all of us? She's pretty enough for any man, and she'll follow your lead except when she doesn't. She's looking for adventure, bro, and that's the best kind of wife. Just marry her and have fun and be Peter Pious again outside of the bedroom and get Dad off our backs. What are you waiting for?"

"You're the one who wants to kick over the traces, though, Uriel," Raphael said. "Not Gabriel. I agree about not moving back with Dad and Mum, but you don't want to be a builder anyway, so what does it matter to you whether we keep working for Gray? And I don't like hearing you curse." Uriel looked angry. Raphael just looked unhappy. He was the gentlest of us, and the happiest, too, normally. A bit like Oriana, though it was odd to think that a man could be like a woman.

"This job's for losers, is why," Uriel said. "Who's the one with the big house? Wait, with *three* big houses? It's not us, that's certain. Valor says—"

I said, "How do you know what Valor says?" Sharply, because I was startled.

"Because I had a beer with him the other night at the pub," Uriel said, "and he's making good money selling farm equipment, with no experience needed except the kind we've got.

All it takes is being able to talk. Upselling, it's called, finding out what people want and then talking them into wanting even more. That's how you make the big money."

"Talking people into things they can't afford," I said. "That's what *I'd* call it."

"Everything's financed," Uriel said, "so why not? So they pay a bit more each month, and have to make those payments for another year. They're getting more for that money, and you aren't ruining anybody's life. If they can't pay, the bank takes the thing back, that's all."

"That's usury," Raphael said, looking unhappier than ever. "And Valor is—"

"Obviously you don't like him," Uriel said. "Because he's got his own ideas, is why. And I know Gabriel doesn't like him. He told me you nearly broke his nose and got him sacked, just because he flirted a bit with Oriana," he told me. "He's better off, he says, and you did him a favor, in the end, but she's not your wife or your sister, and we're not in Mount Zion. She's allowed to talk to a man, and what do you care anyway? Don't tell me you want Oriana when you could have Patience. She's pretty as she can be, yeh, and she's got a body that was made for a man to get his hands on, but *she's* not looking for adventure, and she's not any kind of challenge. Her sisters, now ..."

I pretended a calm I didn't feel. The look of Oriana, pressed up against the porch. The way she'd cried when I'd held her. The shame on her burning face when she'd told us what Valor had done. I said, "My life isn't your business. I'm not telling you what to do, am I? Go sell farm equipment if you want to, but Valor's not a good man, even if he was your mate growing up. And stop talking about Oriana like that." I wished I could say more, but this was Oriana's story, not mine, and to my brothers and my dad, it would be her shame, too. I couldn't put her in that spot. "If you're relying on Valor to help you," I went on, "you're looking for help in the wrong place. Valor's never done anything that doesn't benefit himself. Patience left Mount Zion because she was going to have to marry him!"

Uriel said, "So? She *isn't* marrying him, is she? Not until he's actually earning that good lolly, anyway. You don't like anybody who wants to have a good time, that's all. Fun is sinful, and all that. Well, Glory and I think differently. We're not moving into a house with Mum and Dad, but Dad's already looking anyway."

"Why?" I asked. "Didn't you tell him how you felt about it?"

"Of course I didn't," Uriel said. "In less than two weeks, we'll be done here, and I'll be back working for him. I'm not burning my bridges. It's better to have a year of work history before you make a move. And not to get sacked."

"What about you?" I asked Raphael.

He looked uncomfortable. "Radiance and I don't want trouble," he said. "With Dad, or with anybody else. We're happy here, and I'm happy working for Gray. I'd have said you were, too. What's this all about, really?"

I said, "That I do want to marry Oriana." How long would it take for them to find out, once Priya talked to Patience? "Dad's against it because her family's too worldly, and Daisy's against it because our family isn't worldly enough. Everybody's against it but Gray, and you know he'll back up Daisy."

"And you don't want to lose your job," Raphael said.

"No," I said. "I don't want to lose my job, and neither do either of you. So for now, let's just *do* the job. We'll finish this the very best we're able to, and when we have, I'll talk to Dad again. It's twelve days," I told Uriel when he would have said something. "He isn't going to find that house to rent in twelve days."

"What's going to magically change in twelve days?" Uriel asked.

"I don't know," I admitted. "But I'll think of something."

38

THE WAITING GAME

Oriana

At seven-thirty Thursday night, my phone lit up with a text.

Aisha. It wasn't the usual half-complaining thing, but instead, *WE'RE HOME!!!!! Ring me!*

I went outside first, to a garden bench where I picked up my knitting and started a new row on my circular needles before I hit the button. That was because Priya was in the caravan, which meant there was no privacy. I *did* like having other people around me, but sometimes ...

"Why?" Aisha said when she picked up. Not "Hello," like most people, or even, "Oriana, hi!" No, just, "Why?"

"Why what?" I asked, my fingers already working. I'd started Gabriel's jumper on Sunday. I would have started it Saturday night, since I hadn't got to sleep for hours, but the light would've woken Priya. It was a top-down knit, so I didn't have to pay much attention. Stockinette stitch was about as easy as knitting could be, and I was done with the increasing and was knitting the chest now.

I'd started it, because I'd finally measured Gabriel for it. Down in the caravan, after that confrontation. *Without* Priya, for once, because Daisy had said, "Help me with the washing-up, Priya," and given me a meaningful look. Of course, the look probably wasn't, *Here's your chance to put your hands on Gabriel!* More like, *Here's your chance to tell him goodbye, because this is all wrong for your future and is causing so much unhappiness to everyone,* but for once, I wasn't being guided by anything but my own sinful stubbornness, and I'd measured him instead.

I'd done his arm length first, concentrating hard so I wouldn't get flustered, and had got flustered anyway. He'd smelled clean, like cotton and soap, and his shoulder had been hard with muscle under my hand. I'd managed, though. I'd even managed when I measured his chest, though I had to get closer for that and felt like I could burn to cinders, feeling him so close to me. As for him? He was standing stock-still, barely breathing, and I wanted to think that was because of me.

Gray asked us to wait to decide anything, I reminded myself. *At least until the house is done, because that makes everything so complicated. Which is better than what everybody else wants. The least we can do is go along with that.* I said, "One hundred seventeen centimeters," a little breathlessly, and turned away to write it down.

It isn't like you didn't know his chest was broad. Stop it.

His hand on *my* shoulder, then, and his voice saying, "Oriana." With something in it I hadn't heard before.

I said, "Let me ... let me get your waist." And wrapped the tape around him again. Standing close. Looking down.

He said, "I can't," and I jerked my hands away. Unfortunately, I forgot that I was holding the tape measure, because I pulled him into me.

His hand on my shoulder again. His other hand at the back of my neck, and I couldn't breathe. I lifted my eyes to his, and the measuring tape dropped to the floor, because what I saw in his blue eyes was ...

Hunger.

I was still watching when he lowered his mouth to mine, but when he touched my lips with his, my eyes closed, and my own hands came up to hold his shoulders. I needed to, or I'd have fallen. It was a brush of lips, and that was all, but it was like being touched by fire. I jumped, and then I burned, and he kissed me again. Longer this time, and still soft, but the arm that had gone around my waist to pull me in didn't feel soft at all. He was standing rigid, holding himself back, and the knowledge of that purled through me like warm candle wax and melted me in exactly the same way. I was holding *his* head now, pulling it down, feeling all of my body pressed to his, and that other thing, too, that Aisha had called an "erection." I felt it, and I shuddered.

I didn't know how long it took. I just knew that when he raised his head, it was too soon. He said, "We can't," but he didn't step away.

I said, "I know," but I didn't step away, either. He was in his usual kind of shirt, soft cotton with a button front, and his skin was warm through the fabric. I pressed my palm against his chest, and it was solid, so I turned my head and kissed him there.

"Oriana." His voice came out strangled. "We can't." Finally, he took a step back, then ran his hand over his neatly trimmed hair and tried to smile, but couldn't. "Not when Gray's been so …"

"Reasonable," I said. "Kind. But Daisy will be sending Priya down in a minute, and …"

"And I'm in no fit state to receive visitors," he said with a wry grin, and we were both laughing. Slightly hysterically once more, until we were laughed out, exhausted by emotion, and he was holding me, my head on his shoulder. He said, "And here we are again anyway, with our hands on each other. We can't. I should go."

"I need to measure you, though," I said, stepping back like there was an outgoing tide dragging at my feet.

Another smile. "Reckon you could've done that already. Sorry. It's nothing I can help."

"Not *that*." It was all I could do not to giggle. "Your *waist*."

He bent down for the measuring tape and handed it to me, then stood still while I did it. "Eighty-one," I told him.

I expected him to say ... what? "I do have excellent proportions"? "I wish I could stay and kiss you some more"? "I'd love to get married right now"? Instead, he said, "What I feel, when we do that ... do you feel anything like the same? I don't know who else to ask," he went on when I must have looked shocked, or shy, or however I felt, "and anyway—I reckon I should ask you, because you're the one who matters. Or is it just more ..." He seemed to be groping for a word. "Nice? Because to me—it's like fire."

"That's it," I said. "Like fire, but with aching. It almost *hurts*, and it's ..." Could I say this? *If you want to marry him*, I told myself, *how can you have these kinds of secrets? If you want him to touch you and kiss you, don't you have to say?* "I get wet," I finally managed, feeling my cheeks flame. "From inside. And so hot and ... and tingly. That's how it feels. I never knew my body could feel this much. Not something that isn't pain, I didn't. If it feels this good just to kiss you, what will the rest of it feel like?"

He groaned. "I'm trying not to think about that. And I need to go, or I won't be able to."

Oh. Whoops. That had been Saturday, and it was *Thursday*, and I was meant to be talking to Aisha. "Sorry," I told her. "What did you say?"

"Excuse me," she said, "why you've barely texted me?"

"Oh. I haven't? I thought I had. What else was I meant to say? Besides, you were with your family. In Pakistan, and Australia, and ..."

"I know where *I* was," she said. "Where were *you*? You've got a full-time job helping somebody photograph babies, and you love it. That's random, if you like. You've done heaps of babysitting and worked at the farmer's market. I did heaps of babysitting, too—staying with my aunt and uncle in Sydney was awesome, except for that—but it isn't what I wanted to talk to you about! Because it's *boring*."

"Oh." I blinked. "OK. So what *did* you want to talk to me about?"

"Well," she said, "how about everything? I could tell you about the hot guy who talked to me at the beach three days in a row, for one thing. His name was Graham, and he was blond and had that surfer body, you know? And that surfer hair, too, a bit messy? He had his board, and I got to watch him surf. I don't know how good he actually was at it, but he looked good to me. He stood up on the board and caught the waves and all. That is, I watched him until my little brother told my mum about him, and she decided we should take the kids to the zoo instead. Zoos are cruel! Also, I had to push my little cousin's pushchair all day, and an old lady asked me if he was my baby! Excuse me, I'm seventeen? How did I go from hot guy at the beach to having a baby, with none of the good part in between?"

"Oh," I said. "That's a pity, about Graham. Maybe he'll text you, though, if he has your number."

"Yeh, well, he did once," she said, and sighed. "But of course he didn't after that. He's nineteen, and done with boring school, and by the way, he's in *Sydney*. I can't wait to go to university, that's all. My parents think they can tell me not to date. Ha. They are *so* wrong. They won't *be* there. At least I know you didn't have any romantic adventures either, so that's cheering. Has it been dread, having to work while everybody else was having lovely holidays?"

"No," I said. "It's been good. I've babysat heaps as well—oh, I said that—and I worked for Honor, cleaning, but you know that, too. I've made some lovely dinners, and my knitwear business has really taken off. Well, summer, you know, with the tourists, but still. I'm going to ask Frankie if she can make me a website when she gets back. You can sell from there and ship all over the world. I probably won't sell very much at first, but if I have the website on the labels, and have business cards made up, and tell every customer at the market that there's more on the site, don't you think they might tell their friends, who *didn't* come to New Zealand, to check me out once they see my lovely things? That's what I'm hoping, anyway. Maybe I could even try lace shawls, the kind that are like cobwebs. If I did them in a silkpaca blend, for a bridal wrap, in ivory, or in a pink so pale, it's barely there ... People like luxury, and the more beautiful a piece is *and* the more you charge for it, the more they like it."

Did I feel guilty for not telling her everything? Maybe, but ... Gabriel wasn't some fella I'd met on the beach, and I didn't want to talk about him as if he were, if that makes sense.

"You're going to make a website so you can earn more money, which you won't spend, because you never go anywhere or do anything," Aisha said. "And knit shawls. And make lovely *dinners.* For your *family.* You need to go back to school and get a dose of modernity again."

"I have modernity," I pointed out. "Excuse me, website? That's modern and exciting."

"Maybe if you're in 1995," she said.

"Also," I told her, "I earned more than four thousand dollars after taxes this holidays. That's modern enough for me. And I have my full driving license, and Prudence changed her name to Priya and got her hair cut and is wearing jeans and short skirts. I got *her* a job, too, but she hasn't saved as much as me. She likes clothes too much."

"Really? Priya?" Aisha asked, her attention diverted. "That's a Hindu name, though."

"Yes," I said, "because my mum is. Was. And she's ..." I couldn't go on. I'd got one of those waves of longing again. I wasn't even sure why. My mum wouldn't have understood any of this.

She'd have held me, though, and her arms were so gentle.

"Wait," Aisha said. "Why haven't you told me that? That's kind of a big thing to leave out of your narrative."

So, yes, we had something to talk about, as I sat in the garden away from Priya's curious ears, knitting Gabriel's indigo jumper that matched his eyes. Just not the most important things.

Maybe when school starts again, I thought, *I'll have more to tell, or I'll feel able to tell.* Gabriel had said, on Saturday night, "Let me get this job done, because otherwise ... what if this blows up more, and my dad tells the others they have to quit? I can't do that to Gray. Let me get it done, and then we'll decide."

That was going to have to do for now. Meanwhile, though ...

I burned.

39

IMPORTANT RESEARCH

ORIANA

The next day, it was Friday, and that left one more week before the house had to be finished. Saturday night was the deadline, and the next day, Frankie was due home.

Saturday, January thirty-first. It felt momentous. It felt *huge*, because after that …

After that, I started Year 12. After that, we'd see. I hadn't seen Gabriel since that night in the caravan, other than to wave to him. He'd been working late every night, we both started work early in the morning, and there was no question of inviting him to dinner again, not right now. Not with Daisy so against us.

And I missed him so *much*.

Meanwhile … well, meanwhile, I was on my lunch hour with Laila, just done eating my sandwich and cleaning the studio in preparation for this afternoon's clients. Laila was playing one of her soothing music pieces over the speakers. This one was whale sounds, she'd said. It was a sort of hooting and moaning with a background rumble, mixed with some kind of bells. I wasn't sure if it was soothing. We hadn't had much music at Mount Zion, other than worship songs that I'd never liked much. A bit boring, I'd always thought, and not nearly as nice as birdsong. When I'd heard the loud music everybody seemed to play Outside, I'd thought that even more. Whales were an improvement on that, I guessed, though I still preferred birds.

Stop thinking about whales. Next Friday will be your last day on the job. You need to ask.

Finally, after I'd finished the mopping and had begun to sanitize the furniture, I did it. I asked Laila, "Can I speak with you a minute?"

"Of course," she said. Calmly, as always, like nothing ever rattled her. I wished I could be like that. "Cup of tea, maybe?"

"Oh," I said, and finished my wiping. "Yes. I'll get it, though. Would you like a biscuit?"

As I was waiting for the water to boil, I thought, *You can always ask her something else. About ... about other career opportunities, maybe.* While I was waiting for the tea to steep, I thought, *Except that you still have two years of school, and she knows it, so you'd be wasting her time.*

How can I wait two years? I can't. Why should we have to?

Finally, I was sitting with her, and she was drinking her tea and eating a biscuit.

Now. Ask her now. I said, "I'd like to hear about how you have sex."

She choked, spilled tea all down her shirt, and sprayed biscuit crumbs everywhere, and I jumped up and stammered, "Oh, no. Let me help you clean up. I'm so sorry," and thought, *Why did I think I could ask this? I should've asked Daisy instead. I knew it was private, and I still asked, and now she'll probably sack me! How am I going to tell Daisy I got sacked?*

I cleaned the studio all over again while Laila changed, and when she came back, I said, "I'm sorry. Please don't sack me. I know sex isn't appropriate to talk about with people, that it's private, but I didn't know who else to ask. My sister Daisy, of course, but she's so *sure* about everything, and ..."

"And you thought I wouldn't be," she said. "So you mean, not how *I* have sex, but .."

"No!" Oh, no. How could I have *said* this? "I mean ... I thought you *didn't* have sex. Now. Because you're a widow. Or ... Lachlan ... You went on two dates, I know, but ... but even if you aren't, you must have had it before, because of the girls, so ..."

"I'm not sure how helpful I can be," she said, putting me out of my stammering misery. "I was married, but I'm not an expert."

"Oh," I somehow managed to say, through my confusion. "I didn't know you could be good or bad at it. Well, once you know how to do it, anyway."

She sighed, or she came as close to sighing as Laila ever did, and said, "Let's sit down." I thought, *Now she'll sack me*, but instead, she said, "You haven't read any books, then. Or watched anything."

"No. You mean there are books that tell you how? Is that how people normally find out, then? Wait. Is it like school? Is there a ... class?" There was a class for everything else. Knitting. Cooking. Raising chooks from eggs. All the things I'd known how to do forever, that I'd been surprised grown people had to learn to do, so why wouldn't there be a class for this, too? It would be horribly embarrassing, of course, but as long as I could sit in the back row and just take notes, and you didn't have to participate ...

She didn't answer, just asked, "Is this about Gabriel? It looked like he was holding you when we drove by the other night, and as you'd said that he wouldn't touch you ..."

"No," I said. "I mean, yes, he has a bit, held me, I mean, and kissed me two times, but he ... we ... We want to get married."

She paused a minute, then said, her voice gentler than ever, "You do know that you don't necessarily have to be married to have sex, right? Or to kiss somebody, because you're right, that's a better place to start. You're seventeen, and I'm guessing he's not much older, and that's truly too early to be married. It's better to know the person first."

"But I *do* know him," I said. "So much better than I know anybody Outside. I know what kind of a person he is. How he is with his brothers and sisters, and how hard he works, and what his parents are like and how they've been with their kids, and just ... just everything. And he's twenty-five, so he's really not too young, even if I am, a bit, at least my sister thinks so. And Outside, you don't know any of those things about a person. You don't know anything that really matters."

"So if you know him," Laila asked, "what's the problem? Other than that you're even *more* too young, if he's that much older. I'm sorry," she said, her face horribly compassionate, "but that would be considered predatory by most people."

"He's not," I said, knowing my face was flushing and unable to help it. Why did everybody *say* that? It wasn't true! "He's just exactly not. He's ... he ..." I wanted to tell her about Valor, but how could I say that?

Just do it. "Somebody else is," I said. "That way." My face was flaming, and I couldn't quite look at her. "Or he was. When I was younger, and ... and recently. He's closer to my age, too, so I don't think it's really about the age. Besides, Gabriel hit him when he did that."

"And then kissed you," Laila said flatly. "And touched you. Oriana. Don't you see?"

"But he always *asked*," I tried to explain. "He's so ... he's so *careful*. And he's as scared as I am! He doesn't know how to do sex, either, and he doesn't want to hurt me. He wants to *marry* me. But shouldn't we know, first? I want to *know*. I know you kiss, and that the man ... I know how the main part happens. I've seen it, with my parents."

"With your *parents.*" She looked gobsmacked, but why?

"Under the blankets," I said. "So I know the position and so forth, like everybody does, but I don't know what I'm meant to do while it's happening. I thought I would just lie on my back, but I know now that some people make ... noises. Maybe because your kids aren't there. And if you're making noises, you're probably not just lying under somebody, at least I never heard noises before. The noises last longer, when I hear — when I know it's happening, and when I *do* see something in a film, it always looks like heaps more *is* going on, because they're doing things. Rolling around and so forth, and sometimes their ... their heads aren't together. I think they're kissing each other in other places, too. Sometimes you see that. Him kissing below her shoulder. Him touching her leg. And they're both all the way naked, too, so obviously, people take all their clothes off. Which is different, too, so I need to know."

"OK," she said. "Wow. How soon is this marriage planned for?"

"It isn't," I said. "Nobody wants it but us."

"And are you planning to be intimate beforehand?" she asked. "Or is this for after the wedding?"

"Uh ..." I wasn't sure what to say. "We don't want to do it before we're married, but we ... he ..."

She said, "You get to decide that, too. It's not just his choice. If you do want to, or you don't, tell him the truth. For every step of the way, because you don't go from zero to full sex all in one night, normally. You need two votes for a yes to move forward. If there's only one 'yes,' that means 'no.' This isn't Mount Zion, and both votes count."

"What if I'm not sure, though?" I asked. "I do feel like I want to wait until I'm married to have the real sex, I mean, have his ... his, ah ..."

"To have intercourse," Laila said.

"Yes. But people *do* other things, right? The kissing and touching and all, like in films? At least, Daisy and Gray seem to. They kiss and touch heaps in front of us, so in bed, I'm pretty sure they ..." I didn't actually want to think about what they did. I couldn't help it, maybe, when I heard them, but I didn't have to *talk* about it! "But they're having relations, of course. Intercourse."

"You do anything you both want," Laila said, "on any timetable you like. And if you're asking what *you* should do? Do what feels good to you."

"Like what?" I asked. "That's the problem. I don't know what there is! And I need to know how to please him, don't I?"

I was so embarrassed, I wanted to curl up and die. But how else would I find out?

She said, "If he's not experienced, either ... not experienced at all?"

"No," I said. "Only with me, but kissing was nice. For both of us. We've seen films and all now, though, and like I said ... Gray and Daisy. I know about kissing."

Laila said, "I'm guessing he's looked at some porn, too."

"Oh, no," I said. "That's such a sin. Well, one time, but he says he won't do it anymore, but is that how men find out, then? Is it like ... instruction?"

Laila said, "I'm pretty sure he'll look again. For one thing, he probably wants to learn at least as much as you do. But I don't think real sex is necessarily exactly like porn, so he could get some wrong expectations if that's how he's learning. If you want to do something past what you've done, you could see how the kissing goes and take it from there. Tell him you want to take it slow, and to tell him how you feel and have him tell you how he feels. There's kissing in various places—necks are nice, and then, uh, farther down, and touching each other's bodies, and ..." She stopped, then said, "Go slow," again. "See how everything feels. Tell him you'll stop when he wants to, and make sure he'll stop when *you* want to. If you do that, if you find out together? I reckon it'll work."

"Oh," I said. "Well, that's, uh ... perfect. Thank you." Even though it wasn't perfect. I needed to know *exactly*. How would I ever do it right, otherwise?

She seemed to know what I was feeling, because she said,

"You can watch that porn together at some point, if you like. That will give you an idea. Keeping in mind that it can be a bit ... outlandish. It's what you'd call the advanced level, and sometimes the 'ridiculous' level."

I asked, "Won't I go to Hell, though, if I do that?"

Her eyes were much too understanding. "I don't think that's really what people go to Hell for, do you?"

Oh. I had to consider that one. "I don't know. I always heard you went to Hell for immorality."

"Enjoying sex isn't immoral," she said. "No matter what you do, as long as you both want to do it. How can it be, especially if you're married? Who does it hurt?"

"Uh ... God? Because how my body feels when I think about those things ... doesn't that hurt God?"

"Why?" she asked. "Why would God make those things feel that good in our body if He didn't want us to do them?" I couldn't answer that, but I didn't need to, because she went on. "The best thing would probably be for both of you to read about how to have an orgasm. How a woman has one, that is, because a man's not much of a mystery. You can find heaps of articles, I'm sure. Especially if you've never had one."

"You mean spill seed?" I asked. "Women don't spill seed, though." Now I was more than embarrassed. I was completely confused.

"At Mount Zion," Laila said, "don't they talk about sex being pleasurable for women?"

"Not exactly. The Prophet says it's a woman's duty, because men have needs, and it's how you show your love and submission."

Laila looked ... something. Disgusted, maybe, and I thought, *I shouldn't have asked.* What she said, though, was, "Knowing what you know now, feeling what you feel, don't you think *women* have needs, too? It sounds like you're noticing that *you* have needs. Isn't that why you're asking?"

"I thought I was just sinful, though," I said.

"I'd say you're normal," Laila said. "All of that, what you're feeling? That's how a woman's body is meant to feel. Isn't it better, if it's how you show love, if you *want* to do it? If you enjoy doing it? If you *love* doing it?"

"Oh," I said again. "Maybe you're right, because that's how Daisy says it is, even though it hurt before, with her husband. She says it's lovely with Gray, though. I thought it must feel good, like eating something wonderful, or climbing into bed when it's cold outside, but it feels odder than that in my body even just to think about, sort of warm and tingly and sometimes even worse, and I can't even tell if it's a good feeling or a bad one. It's more like needing to sneeze, but not sneezing. Is that normal?"

She took my hand and squeezed it, so maybe it hadn't been so bad to ask her. "Women have orgasms," she said. "You don't spill seed in the same way, but it's every bit as much of an orgasm. The way your body's reacting is part of it. Sexual arousal, is what that feeling is. I'll find some articles for you, but tell him it's important that he reads them, too, because pleasure is easier for a man. When he puts his penis in your vagina, that rubbing feeling he'll get will make him have an orgasm, but it probably won't for you, not by itself. So I'll find you some articles. About female stimulation, and positions, and what he needs to do and so forth, so you can *both* have an orgasm, and get all the enjoyment you can out of it."

"You know so much," I said. "That would be awesome. Thank you."

She said, "Trust me. I really don't. But here's an idea. Read the articles together. If you're too embarrassed to do that—or to talk openly about birth control, by the way, and *arrange* birth control—you're not really ready to have sex. You may want to learn how to have an orgasm by yourself, too, because every woman's body is different. That way, you can show him what works for you, because you'll know."

"You mean …" I couldn't say this word, could I? *"Masturbation?* But girls don't do that!"

Yes. I said it.

That was when the doorbell rang. That would be Laila's next clients, so I jumped up to get ready, and I didn't get a chance to tell Laila that masturbation wasn't possible even if it were actually, you know, possible, because I'd go to Hell for sure.

If she gave me articles about sex, though, and I read about how a woman had an orgasm, or, worse, *watched* how, with naked bodies and noises and all … how was I going to stop myself from trying?

I had such a sinful body.

I needed to get married.

40

ONE SIDE OF THE RUBICON

G<small>ABRIEL</small>

At seven o'clock on Saturday night, Uriel and Raphael were still loading rubbish into the skip beside the house. As for me, I'd got out the industrial vacuum and was starting to get stuck in when I felt a tap on my shoulder and turned.

Oriana. Dressed in her overalls, with her hair in two plaits, because she'd been in the garden earlier. She was holding a platter of sandwiches and a pitcher.

I turned the hoover off, smiled at her, and said, "Hi." I wanted to kiss her, but Uriel had just come back into the house and was casting a knowing glance at us, so—no.

She said, "I know it's the last night. I thought you might have heaps still to do, so I brought sandwiches and lemonade."

I hadn't realized how hungry I was until I looked at those sandwiches. "Cheers," I said. "Uh ... put them in the kitchen, I guess."

"I will," she said, "and then go for the glasses." She looked around. "It's so beautiful, I can't believe it. It doesn't even look like the same *house.*"

"Yeh." I couldn't help being proud. It had taken two long, hard months, and so many hours from me, these past two weeks, scraping off every drop of spilled paint, lining up every cabinet handle perfectly, leveling every appliance and doublechecking the hookups on every piece of plumbing, but we'd done it. "It is. It's a good design, though. Good choice of materials, too. That was Gray."

I followed her into the kitchen, and she said, "It's just *lovely*. The benchtops ..." She ran a hand over them. "What is it?"

"Soapstone," I said, touching the deep-gray surface myself, because that soapy-smooth texture was so satisfying.

She said, "Are you trying to clean it all before Daisy sees it tomorrow? Is that why you have the hoover?"

"Yeh. It's better if it's clean, don't you think?"

She didn't say anything I'd have expected. She asked, "Can I help?"

I hesitated. "Everybody here's being paid to work. I can't—"

"I'd like to help," she said, "if you don't mind. I'd like it to be beautiful for Daisy, and I'm excellent at cleaning. Otherwise, how long will it take you? Please let me help."

That was how we ended up working until after eleven that night, the last two standing. My cousins left, and then my brothers did, and Oriana was still spraying down the shower in the master ensuite, then on her hands and knees scrubbing the floor as I hoovered up dust and more dust, because there was no dust in the world like construction dust. My body protested against sixteen straight hours of labor, and Oriana's must be feeling about the same, but she didn't stop until we were standing in the master bedroom and she was gathering up rags and spray bottles while I wound up the cord on the hoover. The outermost room on the uppermost floor, and we were done.

Around us, the house ticked over in the way that houses do

in the middle of the night, the overhead light gleamed on polished wood floors, and the heat pump came on with a low *whoosh*, because the night had grown cool. I said, "Thanks," then tried to think of something else to say, but I couldn't. Suddenly, I was bone-weary, and so dirty, I felt caked in grime. I blinked, and my eyes felt like sandpaper.

She said, "You were already here when I came out of the caravan this morning. You need to go home."

"Yeh." I tried to laugh, but couldn't. I ran a hand over the back of my neck. "I do. I should kiss you or something, say something romantic, but ..."

"Gabriel." She stepped close, put a hand on my shoulder, then rose on her toes and kissed my cheek. "No, you shouldn't. You should let me drive you home and then let me make you a cup of tea while you take a shower."

"You can't," I said. "How will you get home?"

"By driving," she said.

"The ute—" I began. Honestly, it was a bit hard to talk.

"I'll bring you back for it tomorrow," she said. "It's Daisy's and Gray's big moment. Gray didn't actually *say* to stay out of their way, but I know he wanted to. Frankie's coming home at last, it'll be mad, and ..." She shrugged. "I'd be glad to have something to do, that's all."

When she walked into the flat behind me, I didn't know what to say. When we found Rowan and Duncan playing video games, *they* didn't know what to say.

"Hi," Oriana said, as self-possessed as I wasn't. "I'm Oriana."

"Uh ... hi," Rowan said, his eyes going from Oriana, still in her dusty overalls but also still so pretty and curvy, and then to me, even *more* dusty and not at all pretty and curvy. I guessed that no matter how good Oriana was still managing to look, we didn't exactly exude waves of "just had sex."

I told Oriana, "I'll go take that shower, eh."

"You do that," she said. "And I'll make you that cup of tea."

I meant to be in the shower about three minutes, like usual. When the water hit me, though, then beat down on my aching back ... I put my hands against the opposite wall, bent my head, and let it run. It was probably ten minutes by the time I was toweling off—the current towel was bright pink and nearly threadbare—then putting on pajama bottoms and a T-shirt, bundling up my sweat-stained clothes, and going to dump them in my bedroom laundry hamper.

When I padded barefoot into the lounge, my flatmates had moved. Duncan was leaning against the kitchen bench, telling Oriana, "Yeh, my mum didn't like her much," and Oriana was saying, "Oh, what a pity," and pouring boiling water into three mugs of tea, then picking up the tea towel, because Rowan was doing the washing-up and she was drying.

I blinked. The shower had woken me up a bit, but not much, or maybe it was just that I seemed to have stepped into an alternate reality, one in which my flatmates cleaned. Oriana looked up, saw me, smiled, wide and sweet and glorious, and said, "You look a bit happier."

I grinned and ran my hand over the back of my neck. "Yeh. I am. You need to get to bed yourself, though."

She dried the frying-pan, which had served far beyond the call of duty by this point, and bent to put it in the drawer. "I do." She opened the fridge, sniffed at the milk bottle, made a dubious face, and said, "Maybe not."

Rowan said, "There's another one in a bag in the back," and went to get it.

Duncan said, "What the hell, mate. You hiding the milk away?"

"If it's mine, I am," Rowan said. "Otherwise, it's gone in a day." He dumped some into each of the mugs and told Oriana, "Have mine, and I'll make another."

She hung the tea towel neatly over the handle of the cooker.

"Thanks, but I need to go home. If I collect you at eight-thirty tomorrow morning, Gabriel, we could do breakfast in the caravan."

The boys looked even more surprised at that one, and I couldn't blame them. I told them, "With her sister," and told Oriana, "That'd be awesome."

"Then we could also peek and see if we can tell how Daisy likes her house," she said. "What d'you reckon Gray ran over there to check the minute you texted him we were done?"

"I wouldn't take that bet," I said. "As he's checked every day this week. I'll walk you out."

I shut the door behind me and leaned against it. Somebody walked by—it was Katie, the girl from the flat next door, dressed in a short skirt and more swinging earrings. Oriana said, "Hi," to her, and Katie looked almost as shocked as the flatmates. Oriana told me, "I'm so dirty," and smiled again. How did she somehow have all the self-possession I lacked?

"Yeh. You are." I smiled back, and Katie put the key in her lock and went inside. The fatigue was coming in waves, but so was the satisfaction. I'd finished the job, I'd given my best and done my all, and we were standing on one side of that Rubicon, waiting to cross. I told Oriana, "I want to kiss you again."

She didn't answer. She stepped into me, pulled my head down with both hands, and pressed her lips to mine.

Maybe you think it isn't sexy, kissing a girl in dusty overalls. You haven't kissed Oriana, though, with all her sweetness and all her hunger. By the time she stepped back and dropped her hands, my own hands were on her hips, I was breathing hard, and I didn't want to let her go.

"I'll come back tomorrow," she said. "We'll have breakfast, and we'll make a plan."

"To cross the Rubicon," I said.

She looked startled, but she'd had the same education I had, because she smiled again, kissed me once more for good measure, and said, "Yeh. We need to do that, but whatever happens—I'm going to marry you anyway. *Moea he tangata ringa raupa.* I learnt that, recently. It means, 'Marry a man with calloused hands,' a man who knows how to work and wants to do it, and that's what I'm going to do. See if anybody can stop me."

STILL TEETERING ON THE EDGE

Oriana

I went to bed on Saturday night feeling so ... confident. At least, I thought that was what it was, because I woke up that way, too. I lay beside Priya with the birds singing their hearts out in their dawn chorus and thought, *I was brave, and I did the right thing.* It was a new feeling. It was a *good* feeling.

Last night, I hadn't worried about what Daisy would say, or what Uncle Aaron would say. I'd seen the weariness in the men's bodies as they hauled out rubbish, looked at the clock, and thought, *They need something to eat and drink.* When I'd gone in and seen the dust on the windowsills, felt the grit on the benchtop when I'd set my hand on it, remembered Gabriel with rings of sweat under his arms and a dark patch of it on his back, wrestling with a huge hoover, I'd thought, *He needs my help.* And I'd *done* it. I'd met his flatmates, I'd done all the things that made sense to me to do, I'd kissed Gabriel and told him I wanted to marry him, and the world hadn't ended.

I wanted to tell somebody. The problem was—who would I tell? I could ring Aisha—well, when it got later, I could—but she wouldn't understand that this wasn't a crush, it was my life. I could tell Priya, but Priya had blurted out Uriel and

Glory's secrets. She hadn't been able to help herself, because it was all too exciting. I understood that, but I didn't want her blurting out mine. I could tell Daisy—well, no, I couldn't, obviously. That was out.

Or I could tell Frankie, since she was coming home today. Except that Frankie was even worse than Daisy about school and marriage, so, again—no.

I could tell Gabriel, that was who. *We could fit at home*, he'd said. *My wife and I.*

Could your husband be your friend? It was a ludicrous question, like asking if you could marry your cat, but … maybe it wasn't. He *understood*, that was all.

I stayed happy for hours. I did collect him from his flat. I kissed him at the door, in front of one of his flatmates—Rowan, the one who'd helped with the washing-up—and I brought him home with me. Like an adult. Like a regular person who got to choose for herself, because it was her life.

When we walked down to the caravan, Gray was in the garden, working with Iris and somehow managing to look expectant, like he was nearly poised on his toes, which meant Daisy was still asleep after her evening shift and nothing had happened yet. How was Gray managing to wait? *I* could hardly wait.

When we walked past, Gray said, "Gabriel. Hold on a sec."

Gabriel stopped, and now, the expectancy and tension were in him, too. Gray came up, put out a hand to shake, and said, "Awesome job, mate. How late were you there?"

"Eleven or so." Gabriel's face was wooden. That would be because he didn't want to betray how much this mattered to him. "Cleaning. Oriana helped. For hours, actually."

Gray looked at me, then. "Thanks," he said. That was all, but I could tell he meant it.

"You're welcome," I said. "It's a beautiful house. She's going to love it."

Gray ran a hand over the back of his head and looked a bit sheepish. "Is it that obvious?"

"Yes," Iris said. She'd been feeding the flowering plants. "Just don't go anywhere near the chickens, because you'll throw them off their feed. Just about throwing me off mine, aren't you."

Gray said, "I love you, too, Iris," and grinned, and she snorted. Then he turned back to Gabriel and said, "I trusted you to get it done and get it done right, and you justified my trust. Ready to go to work on the new job tomorrow? I know you should get a holiday after all that, and over Christmas and all, too. If you want it, I'll give it to you, but ..."

"I don't need a holiday," Gabriel said. "I'm ready." He hesitated a moment, then said, "My dad ..."

"I'm sure he'll have an opinion," Gray said. "But I didn't ask him. I asked you. Five days a week, and no overtime for a good while."

Gabriel cleared his throat, then said again, "I'm ready. And I'm still planning to marry Oriana."

"I don't blame you," Gray said. "These sisters are awesome, eh."

"Daisy won't think it's awesome." That wasn't Gabriel. It was me.

"Reckon you'll have to decide what to do about that, then," Gray said.

He wasn't smiling now. Then he looked back at the yurt as if he couldn't help it, and I told Gabriel, "Come on." They needed privacy for this.

Normally, on Sunday, I worked. In the garden, and on my knitting projects, and shopping for groceries and so forth. That morning, I didn't. I made tea, and Gabriel, to my shock, fried tomatoes and mushrooms and cooked eggs and bacon and toast, popping the things into the oven as he finished fixing them on the two-burner cooker so they'd stay warm.

When I'd pulled out the frying pan and he'd taken it from me and said, "I'll do it," I'd said, "You're joking."

"I'm practicing," he'd said, "or maybe proving a point," and smiled at me, and I'd lost a little more of my breath.

Priya didn't say much, but she watched, and I didn't care. Gabriel and I took our plates down to the bench in the garden, where the sun was drying the mist from the plants and the birds were still singing, and he said, "I'd like to have a patio or a balcony in our flat. It'll cost more, but I'd still like to."

"Yes," I said. "Me, too."

After that, he was quiet, and after a while, I took our plates back to the caravan and got my knitting, and Gabriel sat with his elbows on his knees and his hands clasped between them and was still. The birds sang, the bees hummed in the beds of pink and purple Agastache, the smell of mint wafted over to us from the flowers, and sitting beside Gabriel was ... peace.

That was where we were when Gray and Daisy came down the track, holding hands.

Daisy was the most practical, efficient, focused person I'd ever known, and I'd grown up in Mount Zion. Today, though ... today, I knew what "stars in her eyes" meant.

She asked, "Where's Priya?"

I set down my knitting and stood up. "In the caravan. I'll get her."

"Never mind," Daisy said. "I will." She did, and once we were all gathered together, she said, "We're getting married. Gray and me, I mean. Well—" She laughed and pushed at her hair. "Obviously Gray and me. And our bedroom has an ensuite. It's the most ... it's the most ..."

Gray put an arm around her and said, "She's always wanted an ensuite."

Gabriel said, "Congratulations. That's awesome, about the wedding."

Daisy focused on him, then. "You did it, Gray says. The marble in there, taking care to get it perfect. It *is* perfect, too."

"Yeh," he said. "I wanted it to be nice. It was important to him."

She smiled. "Thank you."

A phone warbled. Daisy patted herself and said, "No pockets. It's yours, Gray."

"I'm ignoring it," he said, and did.

Another warble. Mine. I pulled it out of my apron pocket and looked at it. "It's Frankie," I told them.

"Put it on speaker," Daisy said, and I did. And if you're wondering if part of me was thinking, *Maybe this is the time to bring up Gabriel and me,* you're right. But another part of me was thinking, *This is exactly the wrong time to bring it up. Let Daisy have her happy day.*

Frankie said, "Hi, Oriana. Where's Daisy?"

"Right here," Daisy said. "You're on speaker, and you're *almost* the first to know. Are you in the car? Is Honor with you?"

"No. Well, yes, about Honor," Frankie said, "but—"

"Put us on speaker, too, then," Daisy said. "And listen."

Frankie did, because I heard Honor's voice saying, "Daisy? What's happening?"

Gray said, "Hi, Mum. Daisy and I are getting married. Gave her the ring and all, and she said yes."

Honor said, "Lovely. Also no surprise at all. You must've finished the house, then."

"Yes," Daisy said. "He did. Well, Gabriel and the crew did. And it's so *beautiful.*"

"Like I told you," Honor said, "it's the male bird showing the female he knows how to build a nest."

"What?" Daisy asked. "I don't—"

"Oh, wait," Honor said. "I said that to Gabriel."

Silence for a minute, and Gabriel said, "I, uh—I'm here, too. This is Gabriel."

"Oh," Honor said. "Got that sorted, then, did you?"

"Uh ..." Gabriel said, and looked at me.

Frankie broke in, and I couldn't be sorry. "That's lovely and all, Daisy, if you want it," she said, which wasn't exactly screaming, "Congratulations!"

"Cheers," Gray said, with that smile in his eyes he got sometimes. "For that heartfelt endorsement."

"But I rang you for something else," Frankie said. "To tell you that I'm not coming back."

"Oh," Daisy said. "What? Why? Are we—"

"It's not you," Frankie said. "You're awesome, and so is Gray. But I want to stay up here with Honor."

Daisy said, "Oh."

Honor said, her voice as calm as Gray's always was, "Frankie thinks it may be easier, as the other pupils won't know her old name up here, or her story."

"Mount Aspiring is a good school, too," Frankie said. "And I need people to notice me and *know* me for something besides Mount Zion. I want to be *normal*. I want to learn how to be normal around men, especially. How not to care what they think, and how can I do that at a girls' school? Maybe you think that I should be able to do it better in Dunedin, because it's so much farther away from Mount Zion, but I can't, because everybody already knows. And—"

She stopped, and Daisy said, "And having all of us around reminds you."

"Yes," Frankie said. "Knowing you know everything that happened to me with Gilead, and that you're sorry for me. I hate it. And I can't take any more of walking by the men from our family and having them look at my clothes and think everything they do think. Or those family meals, with Uncle Aaron trying to tell everyone what to do, and him and Aunt Constance practically telling me out loud how unwomanly I am and trying to shame all of us back into submission. Sorry, Gabriel."

"No worries," Gabriel said. "Everybody's got an opinion. Sometimes, you don't want to hear it."

Frankie said, "Wow. What happened to *you?*"

Daisy said, "I ... I understand." Gray had his arm around her now, and for once, she didn't look poised and confident. I felt so bad for her, I wanted to cry, and when I glanced at Gabriel, his face looked as troubled as I felt. "Of course," Daisy said, her voice stronger. "You should do what you like, Frankie."

"I can help Honor by staying here, too," Frankie said. "With the cooking and cleaning and all. She says she doesn't mind having me."

"I don't," Honor said. "Happy for the company, and Frankie knows how to pull her weight."

"And, yeh," Frankie went on, "I don't exactly love cooking and cleaning, but it's not nearly as bad if I'm not doing it for any men, just for Honor and me. I can have a job here and save for university and study without any distractions, because you know I need a good scholarship."

Priya said, "We wouldn't be a distraction, though. There's a whole separate bedroom in the yurt for you! Or you could live in the caravan, maybe, if you don't want to be close to us, and then you wouldn't have to clean for *anybody.* And Oriana will cook, so you don't need to. What am I going to do without you? That was the whole plan!"

Frankie said, "You'll have Oriana."

Priya said, "She's not—" then closed her mouth again.

"I know she's not academic," Frankie said, "but she loves you, and she'll help. She'll ride the bus with you and eat lunch with you, too, until you make friends."

I'd got so cold inside, my arms had started to prickle. I tried to think of what to say, but all I could think of was, "Excuse me." I picked up my knitting, left the phone on the bench, started up the track, then remembered and turned to say, "Congratulations, Daisy. And Gray. And Frankie, you should do what you want. What makes you feel better. Everybody's not the ... everybody's not the same." I wanted to say more, something like, "We all still love you," so I could pretend that what she and Priya had said didn't matter, but I knew I'd cry, and I didn't want to cry in front of all of them.

I'd felt so confident, earlier, but I wasn't. I was soft, and I got hurt no matter how much I tried not to. I couldn't stand to let them see it, though, not anymore. So I did what I always did. I ran away.

42

WORTH EVERYTHING

GABRIEL

I should have stayed and said "congratulations" again to Gray and Daisy, maybe. I couldn't. I was so angry at Oriana's sisters, I didn't trust myself not to lash out. I was a deliberate man, and an even-tempered one, but not right now.

I followed Oriana.

I saw the back of her disappearing into the caravan, and I sped up and walked straight through after her. Again, I should've knocked, and I didn't.

She turned at the sound of the door, her hand already at her face, because that was how fast she'd started to cry. She was wearing the yellow dress again, the one she'd worn on the night when she'd cooked dinner for all of us and Valor had cornered her and hurt her. Now, she'd been hurt again.

Why did so many people think that just because somebody was kind and gentle and wouldn't hit back, they could go ahead and say whatever they wanted? *Do* whatever they wanted?

I didn't stop, and I didn't think. I took the two steps across to her and took her in my arms. She started to say something, and I said, "I don't care how good Frankie is at maths, or how strong anyone says any of them are. What they said was cruel, and it's not true. You're worth more than that. You're worth everything."

"I'm not—" She was in my arms, but she still had both hands over her face. "I'm not worth anything, not to them. The things I want to do, the things I'm good at doing—they don't *count*. Why can't they count? Why can't I ... why can't I *count?*"

"You can," I said. "You do." I ran my hand over her hair, then down her back, covered by a pretty dress she'd made herself. I wished I had the right words. Watching her cry was making me even angrier. "They don't see," I said. "Maybe they can't see, but I can. Gray can, too. You're as brilliant as your sisters, don't you see that?"

"I'm *not*," she said, and it was almost a wail.

"You are," I said. "Just at different things. Have any of *them* started their own business and grown it already, the way you have? What do they know about growing vegies or caring for animals or handling newborn babies or cooking brilliant meals or all the other things you've learnt to do? To say that looking after your family doesn't matter, and then say in the next breath that Frankie wouldn't have to worry about cooking, because you'll do it, like it's nothing—that's cruel, and it's wrong. Of course it matters! They say that women from Mount Zion are oppressed and belittled, and then they belittle you the same way. It's *wrong*."

She was still crying, but maybe she'd slowed down a bit. "Daisy just ..." She sniffed. "She just wants what's best for me, I know, but—"

"But it's not what's best for you," I said. "Come on. Let's sit down."

There weren't many places to sit, not together. Just on the couch, so I sat there, and I pulled her into my lap. She still had her hand over her nose, and she tried to laugh and said, "I need tissues."

I reached for the box on the little shelf beside the bed and handed her some, and she wiped her eyes and blew her nose, then said, "I was feeling so good, before. Like I finally *knew*. Like I was finally ..."

I kissed her. How could I help it? I kissed her sweet mouth, and I brushed back her soft hair, and I tightened my arm around her waist. I was going to say, "You are," but somehow, I didn't, because she had her hands around my head and was kissing me back, and then she had her hand on my chest again like that other night, when she'd kissed me there. Her mouth opened under mine, and I put my tongue in there. I'd read that it would feel good, and it did.

We kissed like that for a minute, or for five, and then my mouth was dragging across her cheek to her ear, her neck. Oriana had a beautiful neck, graceful and smooth, and when I kissed her under her ear, she shuddered, her hands tightened on me, and the excitement in me ratcheted up another notch, if that was even possible. Her head was thrown back, her bottom was pressed into my groin, one of her hands was in my hair ...

I wasn't going to make it.

ORIANA

When Gabriel had first kissed me, I'd thought, *How can you want to do that? I'm so messy, and I've just been so weak.* When he *kept* kissing me, I stopped thinking it, because his tongue was in my mouth, his hands were urgent on my body, and I could feel his erection pressing into my hip. I was getting that hot/wet/tingly thing again, and it was so bad, it was burning.

And then he started kissing my neck. I heard something, and realized it was me. I was making noises. *So this is why*, I thought dimly, and then I couldn't think anything, because his hand was at my waist, and then it was moving up my body.

And then it stopped. I lay back into him more, and then I did it. I took his hand and put it on my breast.

Oh. That was how that felt, then. Like even more of everything.

He didn't grab me. He held me there, and then his hand traced up, his thumb brushing along the place where the neckline exposed my skin, and I was gasping into his mouth, because he was kissing me again.

This was why Mount Zion wanted you to cover up, because surely, this was sin. This was fire, and it burned. His thumb against my skin, the barest touch, as if all my nerves had concentrated there. His tongue moving in my mouth, the strength of his hand around my head, then the brush of his sandpaper cheek against mine. It was so alien, so different from being kissed by my sisters, by my mum, and my whole body was trembling.

Priya's voice, then, saying, "Oh." The sound of the caravan door banging shut. Gabriel's hand left my breast, but he didn't stop holding me.

I turned my head. It was hard to do.

I'd never drunk a glass of alcohol. I'd never taken any drugs, but this must be how it would feel, like your blood had been replaced by something hotter and thicker. Like time had slowed down, and you were molten.

Priya said, "Sorry. I'll go ..."

I expected Gabriel to say, "I was just going," or something like that. Instead, he said, "Yeh. You'd better."

She backed out and the door banged shut again, and I said, "*Gabriel.*"

"What?" He had his hand—not on my breast, but almost. The tips of his fingers, now, just inside my neckline, and it was hard to focus on anything else. He said, "All I want to do is to keep doing this, and to hear you make those noises again."

"No. We shouldn't." It wasn't the strongest protest I'd ever made, though.

His hand stilled, and I thought, *Wait. We should.* He said, "You're right," and dropped his hand. "You feel too good, that's all."

"To me, too," I said. "Oh, and—I have something I want to share with you. I'm scared to share it, but ... I want to, too."

"If it's a video of you doing some porn thing," he said, "it's going to be too much to take. I may explode." He was Gabriel again, because he was smiling, and then we were both laughing, until our foreheads were pressed together and our arms were around each other and we were kissing again.

"It's almost that," I said, when I could manage it.

He stilled. "Seriously?"

"No! Well ... hang on. Let me get it." I got up off his lap—it wasn't easy, because it felt so good there—and picked up my backpack from its hook, then fished out the stapled sheets of paper. After that, I stood there like an idiot, clutching them to my chest, thinking, *Can I really do this?*

He said, "I'm trying to think what this is, and I can't. So I'm just going to say—I love you, and I want to marry you, and whatever it is—your application for a school or a job or whatever—you can show me. I'm not your family. I'm going to love you anyway."

I let out a breath I hadn't realized I'd been holding and sat down again. Not in his lap, because if we started up again, I was afraid we *were* going to have relations. Maybe he'd be able to stop. I wasn't sure I could. So I sat beside him, and then I took a deep breath and handed over the papers.

GABRIEL

Well, *this* wasn't what I'd expected. But then, kissing and touching Oriana like that had already been a whole new world.

I said, "Oh."

The top batch of papers was called, *Getting Off: 5 Types of Orgasms and How to Get There.*

The smaller headlines below said,

Your Clit and You.

The Elusive Vaginal Orgasm.

And finally, *What About the Anal Orgasm?*

I turned to the second page. Blended orgasms. Erogenous zone orgasms. Who knew?

Oriana, apparently, now. Which meant I'd better learn.

She said, "I know it seems a little ... sinful. And selfish, that I'm demanding something, when relations are meant to be more ... for men. Laila said, though ..." She trailed off.

I said, "Laila? Your boss? She gave you these?"

Outside could be so confusing.

"Yes." Her hands were in her lap, her fingers twisting, and her cheeks were flaming. "Because I asked her about how ... how you did it, because it seems like it's ... different, Outside. And she said that men, uh, men can have ..."

"That they can have orgasms pretty easily, maybe," I guessed.

"You *know* that?"

She looked so shocked that I had to laugh. "It happens in your sleep," I explained, "especially when you're a kid. A teenager. And then, well ..." Somehow, I was still grinning. Maybe because she'd surprised me, and touched me. How embarrassed must it have made her to ask about this? But she'd done it anyway, because she wanted us to have a good sex life, and not just for me. Because she burned, too. "I know masturbation's a sin at Mount Zion," I said. "It's not a sin Outside, and I've been thinking about you, and ... So, yeh, she's right. It happens pretty easily. Trying to slow it down—that's the main thing, for a bloke. That's how it seems, anyway, but it's also what I've read."

"You've read *articles*," she said. Half-shocked and half-amused, like me. Well, and also more than half-aroused, if she *was* like me. That was too many halves, but ... there you were.

"Yeh," I said. "Because I want to be good at it, too. For you." I held up the two sheets of paper. "I'll read these, OK? And then—well, we'll practice, I reckon. Practicing doesn't sound too bad."

She reached out a hand and tugged at the second batch of papers. "OK. That's enough for one day, though. We shouldn't ..."

I held onto the paper. "You got this, though. You read it."

"Yes, but it's—"

"Oriana," I said. "Let me *see.*"

She had her hands over her face again, the same way she'd done when she was crying, but I wasn't worrying this time. I was reading.

8 Positions Guaranteed to Make Her Come

"This is, uh, good," I managed to say. "With the diagrams and all." Should a few line drawings and some technical description make you hard as a rock? Well, if you'd been hard as a rock for about an hour, and you'd felt her bottom against you and had her breast under your hand and your tongue in her mouth, they did. "Can I keep this, too? And then we can ... talk about them, or something?"

She still had her hands over her face, but was peeking out from between her fingers. I smiled at her—it wasn't easy, because I wanted to try every one of those positions right now, not to mention that licking thing, because I *really* wanted to do that—and said, "It's OK that you showed me. It's *good* that you showed me. How else am I going to learn?"

She moaned a little. "I feel so ..."

"Dirty?" I asked. "Naughty?" Suddenly, I wanted to laugh. "Reckon I like you that way, because do you know how this makes *me* feel?"

"No," she said, but she took down her hands.

I smiled out of my whole heart, and into hers. "Lucky," I

said. "That's how." I kissed her one more time, because how could I help it, folded the paper into fourths, and then folded it once more, because letting Gray or Daisy see it probably wasn't going to help our case any, and pushed the whole thing into my back pocket. "You start school again tomorrow," I said.

"Yes," she said, and didn't look happy at all.

"But you're eighteen in four months."

"Also yes," she said. "And I know I should care about what Daisy says, but …"

"But what we say matters more. What we *want*. We're not asking anybody to fund us, and we're not hurting anybody. We want to live our lives, that's all." I stood up, because if I didn't go now, we'd be sinning, but I stopped at the door and turned back. "Also, birth control."

"Birth … control?" She opened her mouth, then shut it again, like she was afraid to have an opinion.

"Yeh," I said. "We should talk about it."

"Oh."

I waited, but she didn't say more, so I said, "I think babies should happen when the two people want them. But I don't know what you want."

"You mean you wouldn't mind?" For once, she didn't look embarrassed. She looked gobsmacked.

"Isn't that for me, too?" I asked. "How often the kids come?"

"Oh." She considered. "I never thought of it that way."

"Daisy gave birth control to women at Mount Zion," I said. "I just found out about that. Secret, eh."

"Yes," Oriana said. "She did. That's why Frankie didn't have a baby. But men don't—"

"Heaps of women there asked her for it," I said. "*Dad* asked her for it. Anyway, it doesn't feel like a sin to me. I'll love every baby that comes, no worries. I just don't want them to come so often that we can't …" I wasn't quite sure what I meant. I thought about my project, close to done now and waiting for me at Drew's. About Drew and Hannah and their four kids, from ten-year-old Jack to baby Peter, and the look of Drew walking Peter around the garden. How he'd said that four kids was heaps. "I want us to be able to care for them," I finished, "and I don't want it to be ... too much." It wasn't exactly what I meant, but I wasn't sure how to say what I meant.

"I do, too," Oriana said. "I want to have a baby, but I want other things, too. You get tired when you're pregnant, and when a baby's small. If you've just had one and you get pregnant again ... I watched my mum do that. I watched *every* mum do that, and I want to enjoy our life." She got up from the bed, came over to me, pulled my head down in the way that made my heart pound, and kissed me. "I wish it could start now."

"So do I." I'd never meant anything more.

"Your flatmates were surprised," she said. "That you brought a girl home."

I laughed. I had both arms around her again, somehow. "Yeh. They were. They said, '"How'd you get somebody that pretty, you ugly bastard?"'

"No, they didn't," she said, but she was laughing, too. "You're prettier than I am anyway."

"They did," I said. "And you're not meant to tell a man he's pretty."

"I'll tell you you're beautiful, then," she said.

A knock at the door, behind us. Tentative, more like a bird tapping. I opened it and told Priya, "Just going."

She said, "I live here too, Oriana. Also, Daisy and Gray are moving things back into the new house, carrying their bedroom furniture and all that out of the basement. Daisy says she wants to sleep there tonight."

"I'll come help, then," I said.

"So will I," Oriana said. "I'll just get changed first."

Priya hesitated, then said, "I didn't mean to— It's not *bad* that you're here. It's just—"

"Yeh," Oriana said. "I know. School tomorrow, eh. Frankie's right. It's better to have somebody to ride the bus with, and to eat lunch with." And then she stopped.

It was the least forgiving speech I'd ever heard her make.

I was pretty bloody proud, to tell the truth.

43

NOWHERE CLOSE ENOUGH

G*ABRIEL*

Daisy didn't say anything else about Oriana and me, at least not when we were moving furniture, and Oriana didn't press it. She told me, when I said goodbye to her by the ute later that morning and kissed her, too, even though Daisy was probably watching, "I know you probably think I should've said something about us, but I didn't want to spoil Daisy's day. I'm going to invite you to dinner, though, from now on. Friday and Saturday night both, don't you think? That's what people do, right? They have dates. That can be our date, and how can your family or my family object to it, if I'm cooking and we're eating with them?"

I said, "They can't. Well, other than the fact that it's still Gray's house." Oriana and Priya were moving back into the yurt tonight, but it didn't matter much, because all three places —house, yurt, and caravan—belonged to Gray.

Oriana said, "His and Daisy's now, he says. They want to be married soon. Next month, maybe, or as soon as she can get time off and he can leave work. She wants to go on honeymoon to the North Island, because she's never been. They're going to spend it tramping and kayaking and surfing and scuba diving and probably doing some kind of adventure race, for all I know, because she's been talking about wanting to train for one that's three days long. You barely *sleep.* You just race. That's not what *I'd* want to do for fun, but they're mad that way."

"What *do* you want to do?" I asked. "On a honeymoon? I'd better find out." She was still in my arms, and now, I kissed her again. I could see that Daisy was indeed looking, and so was Priya, and I didn't care.

"I'd like to go somewhere," she said, rubbing her cheek against mine in a way that raised my pulse rate even higher, then kissing the spot under my jaw. "Neither of us has ever been anywhere."

"Neither of us has ever had a holiday," I pointed out. "Reckon we won't know what to do with ourselves."

"Oh," she said, "I reckon we will." She kissed my neck some more and ran her hands over my shoulders, and … yeh. I was going to have to get straight into the ute the moment I let her go, and then I was going to have to do some deep-breathing exercises just to get home. "I wish it could be now," she said, "but if it can't, I'm still going to cook you dinner."

Two weeks like that, then three, of eating Oriana's dinners—gloriously tender steak, succulent lamb curry, salmon baked with thin-sliced potatoes and courgettes in parchment, and so much more, and, always, a sweet—doing the washing-up with her afterward, and then walking with her in the garden. Kissing her down there, too, away from her sisters' judgmental eyes, and beginning to touch each other, trusting to the flowers and the sky and the wind not to betray our secret.

Her hand under my shirt, stroking up my side, exploring my back and my chest, leaving a trail of fire behind it. The evening when we sat on our bench and ended up with her in my lap again, when my hand went up her leg, then inside her dress. That night, I got my hand on her bare breast for the first time. I kissed her neck while I did it, she moaned, and I felt that taut little nipple under my hand, wondered what color it would be, thought, *Somebody could come down here any minute and see,* and it didn't matter, because that thought didn't have a hope of stopping me. In fact, I was pretty horrified to discover, that thought just made it all that much more exciting, and if I could've got away with driving off with her in my ute, I couldn't have answered for what would've happened in there, because all I wanted in this world was to be inside her.

Three weeks of being close, and nowhere close enough.

So far, my dad hadn't said anything more about not working for Gray, though he'd started to invite his sons and their families to dinner on Sunday nights, and it wasn't optional. On the plus side, that was three nights a week I wasn't eating sausages. On the minus side, Patience was always there, pretty and lively and smiling and asking me admiring questions about my work and my flat and my life, and I was always sat next to her and feeling bad that she seemed to like me so much, and also not bad, because—did she even *know* me? Why exactly did she want me, then?

Because I had a future, maybe, though I wasn't sure how excited she really was about building. More likely because I was that thing people said. Beautiful.

Patience was beautiful, too, but how much did "beautiful" really matter when the years passed and you were sitting on the couch together, waking up next to her in the morning, picking your baby up out of its cot and bringing it to her to feed? Didn't it matter more how you felt doing all that? Or more like—didn't it matter more that those things were enough for both of you?

Uriel and Glory were always there, too, of course, though they didn't say much. The first dinner felt like we were all sitting on a block of ammonium nitrate and somebody was about to add the fuel oil, and the third dinner didn't feel much different. If it was meant to be a family-bonding exercise, it wasn't working. We weren't like most people, who've grown up eating dinner with their family and having family conversation. We'd grown up eating dinner with our community and listening to the Prophet talk, and all this felt was—awkward.

Oriana, of course, was back at school now. As for me, I went to work every morning on Gray's new job, which was building a shopping center. To my surprise, Gray put me in charge of one of the crews and coached me on what to do, patient as you can imagine. It hadn't just been about the house, then. He'd meant it. I was on the road.

My dad was still the foreman on the entire dormitory project, which was nearing completion now. Raphael was still working with him, but Gray moved my cousins and Uriel to the shopping center with me. The week that happened, my dad's face was stern and set at our family dinner, and my mum's lips were tight, but neither of them said anything about it, and the rest of us knew better than to bring it up. Besides, if there was one thing people at Mount Zion knew how to do, it was to follow orders.

I worked, and I finished my project over at Drew's and played basketball on Sundays with Jack and didn't give Oriana her gift yet, because, somehow, the time didn't feel right. I missed seeing her out the window in the mornings, coming up the hill with her basket over her arm, full of some delicious thing she wanted to offer to Daisy and Gray. I missed her when I woke up, and I missed her most of all when I went to bed and tried to sleep.

We could fit together, my wife and I, I'd told her once. She hadn't known I'd meant her, but I'd always meant her.

Always.

Oriana

My life had never been busier or more full of joy, and still, the weeks dragged.

My first day back at school, Aisha was waiting for me at lunchtime. Her eyes widened at seeing Priya's hair, which Priya had cut even shorter and spiked, for this occasion, so parts of it stood straight up in an almost-accidental manner. A teacher would tell her to wash it out later that afternoon, because she'd see that Priya was testing the limits on her very first day. Priya was wearing earrings, too, because she'd got her ears pierced with some more of her holiday earnings, and was now busily collecting things to put in them. When Aisha commented, Priya said, "You can only wear plain studs to school, though. I have some that are skulls, and some that are angel wings. Or bird wings, but I think they look more like angels, all snow-white and feathery. They'll drive my aunt and uncle mad when they see them. Sacrilege, eh. I can't wait. I have some that look like ribbons, and heaps more besides, but I can hardly *wear* them."

Aisha said, "I wish my mum would let me wear things like that."

"That's the good part about your mum not being there," Priya said, and I thought, *How can you say that?* and didn't respond.

"So did anything else exciting happen over your holidays, Oriana?" Aisha asked. "Wait, nothing exciting had happened when we talked, full stop. Did anything even mildly thrilling happen since, other than that you both stopped working at last? When, yesterday?"

"Friday," Priya said.

"We're still working, actually," I said. "On the weekend days until the middle of the month, because Laila—my boss—her assistant isn't back until then."

"With the babies," Aisha said.

"Yes," I said. "Priya's going to be minding her kids." That was all, because ... what else could I say? "How about you?" I decided on.

"Excuse me," Priya said. "Nothing exciting happened?

Other than that you and Gabriel told Daisy and Gray that you want to get married, and they shot you down, but you're still kissing Gabriel every chance you get, and he's practically taking off your *clothes*, and I had to leave the caravan so I wouldn't have to watch? Oh, and that his family and our family are nearly at war, except that everybody's unfortunately still working for Gray? It's like *Romeo and Juliet*—which I know about, by the way, because we have to read it for English, and I got a head start, as I've never read anything like that. School's so *interesting*, Outside, and I've just started."

Aisha had a palm up, and Priya stopped talking. "Excuse me?" Aisha said. "That you *what?*"

My hands stilled on my knitting. I was still working on Gabriel's jumper, because, well ... I was. It made me feel closer to him, handling the silky-soft wool that I'd dyed myself to be the color of his eyes, and seeing the jumper take shape, *his* shape, because I'd measured him.

I'd measured him, and he'd had to kiss me.

I said, "That we're getting married."

Aisha said, "You're *seventeen.*"

"I know," I said. "That's why we're not already married." Oh. My yarn was running out. I pulled out the next ball and prepared to switch over.

"Don't you want to finish school and go to university?" Aisha asked. "And where's your ring, if you're—what, engaged?"

"What does any of that have to do with being married?" I asked.

Priya told Aisha, "See? This is what I put up with!"

"So if you're working every weekend," Aisha said, "that probably means you're not going to be able to come over."

"Not for a while," I said. "You could still come to dinner at the weekend, though. I can give you a lift home afterward, so your mum doesn't have to drive you, or you could sleep over. Gabriel's going to be there Friday and Saturday nights, and

I'm cooking, so you could come on either of those nights. Gray says it's all right for me to invite people, and your parents will like it, because there's no alcohol. Well, Gray sometimes has a beer."

"Ooh," Priya said. "Extreme fun for her, watching you and your boyfriend not notice anybody else in the room. Not to mention Daisy and Gray, because *they* just got *engaged. Really* engaged. *With* a ring. You can come talk to me," she told Aisha. *"Somebody* has to."

Aisha did, and after that, she spent as much time with Priya as with me, and started helping her with Shakespeare, too. I was sad, and I wasn't. They liked the same things, and maybe Frankie was right. Maybe I needed to find friends who liked talking about the things I liked, animals and gardening and knitting and babies and flowers.

Wait. I *did* have friends like that, or I almost did. I had Iris, for one. Her conversation wasn't exactly ordinary, but it was interesting and funny and brutally honest. I had Laila, for that matter, who loved babies exactly as much as I did, and had her own business, too. I wanted to learn things, and Iris and Laila knew so many things.

So—yeh. School. I went through my days like that, ticking off my classes like numbers on a calendar. They were better this year, because in Year 12, you didn't have compulsory subjects other than English and were meant to study for the career you wanted. I was doing Textiles, Food and Nutrition, Business Studies, and Photography. I already knew almost everything in the textiles and food classes, to my disappointment, but I still had hopes for photography. I wanted to take better photos of my knitwear. So far, it was mostly things I'd learnt from Laila, but hopefully there'd be more later.

The business studies course was more about corporate structures than about setting up your own firm and keeping the accounts, though, and I didn't care much about bigger things. I wanted to learn about *small* things, so I read ahead in the book and looked up bookkeeping online and found software you could use for it, and wished there was a way I could just study that.

Instead of biology and maths, though, I was doing Digital Technology, because you could learn to make a website. I needed a website, now that Frankie wasn't going to be here to do it. I knew that none of my studies were likely to lead to university, and Daisy could see that too and wasn't best pleased, but there wasn't much I could do about it.

The talk swirled around me before every class—none of which Aisha shared, because needless to say, *she* wasn't studying Textiles and Food and Nutrition—and I knitted until it was time to start, listened to chat about boyfriends and films and shopping, and didn't feel lonely and embarrassed anymore. Going to school was a job, that was all. I'd done heaps of jobs, and learning to create a website wasn't working in a communal laundry for ten hours a day. I read ahead in the book in that class, too, and asked the teacher questions and practiced, and felt like in this, at least, I was getting somewhere.

I was alone in my bedroom of the yurt now, too, because Priya had wanted her own room, and I lay in a too-big, too-empty bed every night and missed Gabriel so much, I hurt. I knitted, and worked in the garden, and cooked dinner, and did my homework, and sold my work at the farmer's market, and

…

Waited.

For three weeks.

In the fourth week, everything changed.

4 4

HIS OWN MAN

G̲ᴀʙʀɪᴇʟ

The last Sunday in February dawned bright and hot. I went to the beach that afternoon with Hannah and the kids—Drew was on a two-week trip out of the country with his team—and played with the older kids in the water while Hannah held baby Peter and splashed in the shallows. Afterward, Hannah went for a long swim despite the frigid water, and I made a sandcastle with the girls and kept Peter busy with his own separate pile in hopes that he wouldn't knock the castle down, which he seemed oddly determined on. Not so much a builder as a disruptor, Peter.

As for Jack, he sat beside me, ignored the sandcastle, and told me about his rugby team, and how people thought you'd be as good as your dad when you weren't. I knew how that felt, so I tried to tell him.

"You can't convince people with words, not really," I finally said. "You just keep doing your best and don't say too much, and people will eventually find out who you are and judge you for it."

"Judging me is what I *don't* want, though," he said. "That's what they always *do*."

"Mm," I said, helping Madeleine overturn a little bucket to create a tower. "What would you call it, then, when you watch and listen, the way you and I both do?"

"I'm *thinking*," Jack said.

"About what?" I asked.

He was silent for a long minute, then said, "I guess that's judging?"

"Yeh," I said. "It is. And it's OK. People will misjudge you sometimes, too. They may think you're dull when you're just quiet and responsible. They can think so. Some people probably thought your dad was dull when he was a kid, too."

"No, they didn't," Jack said. "Everybody thinks my dad is awesome. They did a film about him, even, and how good he was at rugby and school and *everything* when he was a kid. How he was Head Boy and all."

"D'you think everybody's telling the truth about how they felt back then?" I asked. "D'you think they even *remember* the truth?"

Another long pause, and Jack said, "You mean because he's famous now and everybody likes him, so they don't want to say how they felt before. Maybe they think they'll look jealous if they say that."

"Yeh," I said. "See? You understand that, because you're a good judge."

"Daddy *is* awesome, though," Grace said.

"Yeh," I said. "He is. Because he's his own man, and he does the right thing." I wanted to say, *It's not easy to be the son of a man like that,* but I didn't, because I thought Jack might be figuring that out on his own.

Afterward, I went home and took a shower—after scrubbing the bath, because Rowan and Duncan's moment of housekeeping responsibility had begun and ended with Oriana's midnight visit—thought about touching Oriana on our bench last night and how she'd started kissing *my* neck now, and wished I'd been at the beach with her. I wanted to see her naked, but seeing her in her togs would work, too.

It would probably work a bit too well, based on how my body was reacting to the thought of it, so I got dressed, climbed into the ute, and went over to Dad's.

Patience opened the door to me, as usual. The flat smelled good, like meat, but not as good as Gray's house had last night, after Oriana had cooked chicken breasts marinated in lemon and lime juice in the kitchen I'd built. She'd served the chicken with a sort of relish made of avocado and mango, plus green beans and little tomatoes from the garden. The sweet had been a chocolate pavlova spread with cream cheese and topped with cherries and blueberries that had been cooked down a bit to make them tender. I'd eaten too much of that, probably, but it had been hard to resist.

Oh. Patience. She sparkled all over her face and said, "Hi. You're the last one. I was afraid you weren't coming, but luckily, here you are! Can I get you something to drink? It's so hot."

I said, "I'll get it, thanks," felt stiff and—well, dull—as usual, decided that that was better than sparkling back at her, if I'd even known how to sparkle, headed into the kitchen, and stopped short.

There were one too many people around the table. Mum and Dad, Raphael and Radiance with their baby, Uriel and Glory with theirs, Harmony ...

And Valor.

My face felt like it had frozen. His hadn't. He smiled at me—mockingly, which I could see clear as day, so why couldn't anybody else?—and said, "There you are, cuz. Thought you weren't going to turn up. Off with somebody more interesting than us, maybe."

"Yeh," I said, and couldn't think how to go on. What I wanted to do was hit him, and then kick him down the stairs again, but I couldn't, not in my father's house. He was still smiling. Not calling me "Peter Pious," because Dad was here, and Valor always had a different face when he was looking at authority. I thought, *Jack, if you saw me now, you'd realize how I know about people thinking you're dull,* and just ... stood there. Being dull, or controlling my temper.

Dad said, "Reckon we can finally get started, then. Go on and serve us, Constance."

Mum and Patience did, and then they sat down, pressed even closer than usual with so many around the table, so I felt Patience's thigh against mine and her shoulder against my arm.

I thought, *This has to be because Dad's got the house, which means there's no more putting off telling him where I stand,* and looked at Raphael. He shrugged a bit and raised his eyebrows, so he probably didn't know for sure, either. As for Uriel, he looked like he was barely holding himself back. Excited or angry, I couldn't tell which, but probably angry. It probably *was* the house, then.

So why was Valor here?

The usual stilted conversation as we ate. When we'd finished, though, Dad cleared his throat and said, "Valor says he has something he'd like to share with us."

If it's a get-rich-quick scheme, I thought, *I'll pass.*

Valor said, "The Prophet is going to be making big changes at Mount Zion, and he asked me to let all of you know first, as he values you so highly. Uncle Aaron, of course, but the rest of you as well. He doesn't much care that Daisy and her sisters are gone—good riddance, really—but you're different."

Dad asked, "What sort of changes?"

"He received a revelation," Valor said, "that it was time to reorganize. Time to open Mount Zion to the outside world."

He could have said, *Time for Hell to freeze over,* and I wouldn't have been any more surprised. He kept talking, though, and I thought, *What?* And then, as he went on, *No.*

I would never have thought I'd do this, but I was doing it

anyway. I reached into my back pocket for my phone as inconspicuously as I could, then started typing under the table, cursing my big hands.

Gray's number, because I didn't know whether Daisy was working today. *Come to Dad's now,* I typed. *Bring D & girls.* I thought a minute, then typed, *Urgent,* and hit the *Send* button. Patience glanced at me, and I was sure she could tell what I was doing, but I knew she'd never question me. She wasn't allowed to, and suddenly, I was filled with such fury, my hands actually started to shake. I set my phone on my thigh, tried to control my breathing, and waited.

Valor was still talking, of course. "It was the right thing, before, to set Mount Zion apart from the sins of the world, but now, it's time to be that shining city on a hill, an example to follow. Wages will be paid, also, which you'll all be glad to hear, as you were so worried about that."

"I don't think we're the only ones," Uriel said.

"Quiet," Dad said. "Go on, Valor."

"He'll be opening Mount Zion to visitors, too," Valor said, "encouraging them to ask questions and learn more about us. There's no shame in what we do, and there should be no secrecy, either. There's going to be a gift shop and a tearoom, and tours of the alpaca processing sheds and the lavender and honey operations. A chance to see the community at work, so everybody can see the happy kids, the smiling faces of the women, and know that this is no slavery, it's the contentment of people who know they have a place in this world, and in the world to come, too. We'll have men's work for sale as well, instead of just women's. Cutting boards, boxes and bowls, kitchen tools, and so forth, all made of New Zealand woods, showing what real craftsmanship looks like. It's a growing place, Wanaka. A popular place. There'll be classes in knitting and woodworking at the weekends, taught by experts, and paid for on that basis. You'll like that, Aunt Constance. Instead of a few women coming to an out-of-the-way knitting shop on a Saturday, you'll have a roomful of them every day, learning our ways, God's ways. If we get tour buses, and we will—how much more will that bring in? Enough not only to pay those wages, but to attract new brothers and sisters to our community. Here, I'll show you his plans. Uncle Aaron—the Prophet asked me particularly to show you the plans for the new buildings. He hopes you'll join him to make all this happen, because nobody can do it better than you." He pulled out some sheets of paper and passed them around. To the men, naturally, not the women.

"Suddenly," Raphael said. "All of this. Because of a revelation." He said it skeptically, which more than surprised me. Raphael normally waited for Dad to speak, and "skeptical" wasn't exactly his middle name.

"At the beginning," Valor said, "the community needed to close ranks against hostility and husband its resources. Now, we're nearly six hundred strong, and strong in our faith, too. We can afford to invite the world in. There are heaps of people everywhere who are sick of the diseases of modernity, people longing for quiet and peace and a return to structure, to traditional values and a community based around God's word. It's time to let them in—from all over the world—and to grow even more."

The others were looking at the papers, then at each other, murmuring things. The women, I saw with a quick glance, had their hands in their laps and their eyes downcast, except for Glory, who was looking at Patience. Saying what with that look, I couldn't tell. Dad stared at them both in turn, they dropped their eyes, and I thought, *All these months here, and it switches off just like that? At the very thought of going back, because what else is this all about?*

As for me? The paper was in front of me, but I wasn't looking. I'd say I didn't care, but I cared. I cared about my two sisters who were still in Mount Zion, with their husbands and their kids. I cared about Oriana's little sister, Dove, whom I knew she longed to see again. I cared about everybody who wanted to leave and was scared to, as scared as I'd been myself, because they didn't know any other way to live.

They could all leave easily now, you're thinking. The community was going to be open! You don't know, though, how being told you'll go to Hell for disobedience every day of your life can shape you, let alone hearing that torment described fully, almost lovingly, until you can feel the flames melting your skin and hear your own anguished screams. You don't know how it feels to know that the people you've left behind, the people you've loved most, aren't permitted to speak your name again, because you're damned for eternity. To be dead to your own mother and father? How do you think that feels?

Valor said, "You're surprised. I was surprised as well. I'd never have seen this coming, but the Prophet's wisdom is beyond ours."

Rap rap. A knock at the door. Not a soft one. An insistent one.

Dad looked up, startled, and everybody froze. I stood and said, "I'll get it."

I wasn't wondering how I'd fallen so far. I was wondering how I'd ever thought any of this was all right.

It wasn't all right anymore.

45

ALL THE WAY ACROSS

Gabriel

It was Gray out there, of course. With Daisy, and Oriana and Priya, too. How had they got here this fast? Gray must have driven like lightning. Or Daisy had, because she was out in front, her eyes like burning coals in her taut face. No makeup, her hair mussed, and dressed in shorts and a T-shirt and, I was pretty sure, no bra. She'd been asleep, maybe, after a night shift.

"What?" she asked. "What's happened?"

"Come in," I said. "You'll see."

When we appeared, Dad stood up fast and said, "This is a family meeting."

"You're always telling us that we're family," Daisy said, without a bit of deference. "Time to prove it. What's going on?"

Dad turned on me, then. "You did this."

"I did," I said. "They have a right to know, too."

Dad told Mum, "Leave us, please." She stood up, and the rest of the women did the same. Glory's mouth opened to say something, and Mum said, "It's not our place."

Uriel said, "It is—" until Dad stared him down, and Uriel told Glory, "I'll tell you later."

The women left. All but Daisy and her sisters, that is.

I didn't ask Valor to recap what he'd said. He wouldn't have done it. I just picked up my piece of paper with *Mount Zion Opening Plan* from the table and passed it to Daisy.

Dad told me, "Sit down."

"Thanks," I said, "but I'll stand."

Daisy had taken in the contents of the paper within about thirty seconds. She passed it to Gray, but she didn't address Dad. She told her sisters, "The Prophet's opening Mount Zion up to Outside. Paying wages, too. Paying women?" she asked Valor. "Or just men? Since I assume you're the messenger boy here."

"Or the right hand of the Prophet," Valor said. "And I didn't ask you to speak to me."

Gray looked like he wanted to hit him. I knew how he felt. Daisy said, "No? And yet I'm speaking to you anyway."

"This is my home," Dad said. He'd learnt that "private property" thing, apparently.

"It is," Gray said. "Gabriel invited us, but you're right that it wasn't his invitation to give. Are you asking us to leave?"

"If you're asking them," I told Dad, "you're asking me, too."

Everybody sat, frozen, and then there was a scrape of a chair, loud in the silence, and Uriel stood and said, "And me."

Raphael looked at him, at me, at Dad. And couldn't decide. He stayed sitting down. I didn't blame him. My heart was beating like a drum, and I felt sick.

It was one thing to turn my back on the Prophet. It was another to turn my back on my father.

Finally, Dad said, "You can stay. Oriana and Priya should hear anyway. I know you won't change your mind, Daisy, but you won't hold your sisters back from considering their options."

"That was the entire point," Daisy said. "That they should know they have options."

"Exactly," Valor said. "Everyone has options, and they always have. The gate is no longer closed, and nobody can spread lies about Mount Zion anymore or say that anyone's being held against their will. You should have known that already. How many times have you stood outside the gates and invited the saved to join you amongst the damned? If they didn't go, why not? The Prophet forgives you, though," he told Dad. "He sees that you were torn, maybe anticipating the need for this before he realized it himself. He admits that he's getting older, has become an imperfect vessel for God's word. He needs a worthy heir to take up the mantle. Maybe it's better that you've been Outside all this time. You understand this world and can work between the two places and make his vision a reality."

"How is it," Dad asked, "that he's not telling me this himself? He knows how to use a telephone. Why are you authorized to speak for him?"

Valor leaned forward, his brown eyes wide and trustworthy. He'd always had that ability to look straight into an elder's face and lie through his teeth. It had enraged me back then to see him get away with it, and it was enraging me now. He said, "That was my secret, mine and the Prophet's. I left Mount Zion to be his eyes and ears, to see what was happening out here. He feels a great responsibility for the souls cast into the darkness. Our God is a merciful God, and where there is true repentance, He forgives. If the Prophet couldn't do the same, he would be a poor messenger."

"He's a poor messenger anyway," Daisy said. "Or I'll say what I really feel. He's no messenger at all."

Valor said, "Well, I think we can all guess that *you're* not going back. You'll be glad to hear this one, though. And Oriana, of course." He smiled at her, and my fist needed to be in his face. "God has also revealed to the Prophet that he should wait to give women to their divinely appointed husbands until they reach the age of eighteen."

"A convenient revelation," Daisy said, her voice nearly a drawl, "now that they have to get the court's permission and not just their parents', since the new law's been passed. How many times has the court said 'yes,' I wonder? 'The Prophet's given me to a man eight years my senior, whom I've never spoken to, because he says that's God's plan,' doesn't sound much like, 'of my own volition.' And I should've guessed that was why you left. Being a spy suits you."

Valor's face reddened. "Oriana wants to go back, though," he said. "To be with her mum again instead of ... well, somebody like you. A sinner, who'll pay for her sins. Oh, and to find a husband, as I notice Gabriel's still as marriage-shy as ever. Why did the Prophet never give him a wife? Maybe he knows something the rest of you don't. You bet on the wrong horse there, Obedience, and who else are you going to get, damaged as you are? How old was Daisy before she found a man?"

Daisy would have said something, or I would have, but Oriana beat both of us to the punch. "Oriana," she said, "can speak for herself."

"Can she?" Valor asked. "Can she really, here in Uncle Aaron's home? The right hand of the Prophet, who is God's messenger on earth? Let's call the rest of the women in, shall we, while you speak for yourself? While you tell them everything?"

"Yes," she said. Trembling, and defiant. "Let's do it. Right now."

Oriana

This was the thing I'd worried about most. The thing I'd

sweated about. It was bad enough for Daisy and Gray to know, and even Gabriel. My aunt and uncle, though? *Everybody?*

What else was I going to do, though? I couldn't quite tell what was going on here—some people were going back to Mount Zion? Everybody was? Nobody was? I had no idea—and what about my brothers and sister and my cousins, who were still there? What would all this mean for them?

What would it mean for my mum?

Uncle Aaron left the room and came back with the women. They arranged themselves against the wall, their hands folded. My own hands wanted to fold, but I didn't let them. I felt like Joan of Arc, standing there, as vulnerable as if I'd been stripped bare.

I didn't wait for anybody else to talk, for Valor to explain … whatever it was he was going to explain, or for Uncle Aaron to do it. I said, "I don't know what's going on here, but Valor's still threatening me, even though last time he did it, Gabriel nearly broke his nose and kicked him down the stairs so he fell in the dirt. I don't know why he'd ask for more of that, but he is, so I'm going to tell you that he touched me, when I was a girl. Over and over again, and I'm guessing he did it to other girls, too. And you know what?" I was breathing hard, suddenly. Not out of fear. Out of fury. "That's a crime, and I'm going to the police and reporting it. If the Prophet is opening Mount Zion to the outside, let the police find out how many girls that happened to. I don't think I was the only one, and I don't think Valor was the only one, either."

"He wasn't," Gabriel said.

"Shut up, arsehole," Valor said.

"Be silent," Uncle Aaron said. Not to Gabriel, and not to me. To Valor. "Is this true?" he asked me, his face troubled.

"Yes," I said. "I've told Gray and Daisy and Priya and Gabriel already. Valor wants to say it's my fault, that I invited it. That doesn't work when the girl's four years old and the boy is ten, or when she's twelve and he's eighteen. I *couldn't* consent. Gilead raped Frankie and Daisy, they told the truth about it, and he's in prison. What's going to happen to you, Valor, now that Mount Zion is opening up? What else have you done? When the light shines on the community, what's going to be revealed, back there in the shadows?"

Valor was trying to say something, but I wasn't done. "And when the light shines on you at the end of your life, when God examines your soul, how can you think he won't see your sin? You can say anything you like. A snake has a clever tongue, too. A forked tongue. That tongue's not going to save you. Not anymore."

Patience said, "He did it to me."

Now, the others weren't staring at me. They were staring at her. Glory took her hand, and Patience's chin wobbled, then rose. She said again, "He did it to me."

Valor said, "You little *bitch.*"

"Are you willing to go to the police with me?" I asked. "I know I haven't ... that maybe you want Gabriel, too. I know why. Because he's not just beautiful, he's so much more. But somebody hurting little girls ... shouldn't that matter more?"

"It matters," Patience said, and that was all.

Priya said, "Anyway, I don't think Gabriel's ever going to be a model, Patience. Or even sell cars."

Gabriel said, "What?"

Priya said, "She thought you'd want to make more money, since you're so good-looking."

Valor was still standing there alone, looking alternately furious and like he was trying to think of a charming thing to say that would get him out of this. Everybody else, though, was looking at each other in confusion. Gabriel said, "I'm, uh ... not going to be a model."

Gray said, "I should bloody well hope not. That would put me right off, seeing you up on a billboard in your undies. Especially if you're my brother-in-law."

I said, "What happened to the job selling farm equipment, Valor? Thought you were going to get rich."

I was never nasty. *Never.* I was clearly doing it now, though, because Valor's face reddened, and he said stiffly, "I was looking for something to do while I did the Prophet's work, that's all. It didn't suit me."

Uriel said, "They gave you the sack for lying to a customer, you mean. An *important* customer, who saw straight through you. I was going to do it myself," he told Gray. "Changed my mind. I'm not going to stay in building, though. Glory and I are taking computer classes at night. That's where the money is, if you're clever, and you don't have to lie to anyone for it. It'll take a wee while to learn anyway. A year or two, most likely, but I'll give you notice before I go."

Gray said, "Oh. Well ... fine. Cheers." Sounding bemused, like his head had whipped back and forth so many times, it was aching by now. As for me, I was just thrilled that the spotlight was off me, and wondering—would I really go to the police?

Yes. I would. Daisy had done it, and Frankie, too, and told stories so much worse than mine. Besides, I had to do it for Patience, didn't I? And whoever else it had happened to. Some other twelve-your-old girl, trembling in her bed at night, hoping nobody would discover her sin.

Though how Patience had thought Gabriel would ever want to be a *model* ...

That was when Gabriel said, "Funny that the Prophet's just had this revelation now. I'm guessing it may be because God also told him that the Employment Court has granted Diligence and Truthful an emergency hearing, and he imagines that others will follow. Others like you," he told Daisy and her sisters.

"A hearing for what?" Uncle Aaron asked. "And you've known this, and not told me? Why?"

"I knew they were considering doing it," he said. "As

they're on my crew, and they wanted to talk to me about it. In confidence. They were worried about the rest of their family that's still there, but four of the others have joined as well. Some of those who are suing are still inside the community, which is a bad sign for the Prophet. That's the reason for the emergency hearing, because three of those others are Diligence and Truthful's sisters, and they've said they don't feel safe now that they've come forward. It wasn't my secret to tell, so I didn't, but now, it's out. We've all been classed as volunteers all our lives, and we weren't, were we? Nobody asked me if I volunteered to work all hours when I was six, or when I was sixteen. Nobody *ever* asked me. Did anybody ask any of you? Did anybody ask Daisy, or Priya, or Oriana? Or Mum, or the rest of the women? If the Prophet's talking about paying people now, of opening Mount Zion now, it's because he's scared of what will happen if he has to pay everybody the wages he owes them. The *back* wages. There are only six people asking for that relief now. What happens when there are six hundred? How many new recruits will he need to make up that difference? And what happened to the money, anyway? Hundreds of people donating their labor for decades. All those products going out the door for so many years. Where's the money?"

It brought down the house.

FINDING HOME

Oriana

Everything had changed, and nothing had changed. Gabriel and I left his parents' flat together, driving off in his ute. He didn't take me home, though. Instead, I asked him to stop short of the turning to the house and park at the Tunnel Beach carpark, where we walked through the waving grass along the clifftop track, down the steep steps, and through the concrete tunnel, coming out on the sand at last, amidst the wave-tossed boulders and the wheeling seabirds, with the waterfall splashing down across the little cove.

I stopped at the exit from the tunnel and told Gabriel, "I haven't been back here since Gilead kidnapped Frankie. It happened here, right in this spot. I looked around, and she was gone. I never even noticed. I had Hannah's girls, and we were paddling in the water, but Jack looked back and saw. That's the only way we knew what had happened."

Gabriel had my hand, but he wasn't pulling me along toward the water or anything like that. He was just standing there and listening. He said, "Jack's a good wee man. Like his dad."

"Like you," I said. "I couldn't have told everybody about

Valor without you. It's not holding me prisoner anymore, though, and I don't want that other bad memory to hold me prisoner here, either, and keep me away from this place. Daisy left, and Frankie left, and *I* left. I don't want to give Mount Zion the power to ruin good things for me. I don't want to give the Prophet the power. The Prophet isn't God, and what he says isn't anything like what God is, not to me. In fact, I don't think he's a prophet at all."

Saying it felt like a dam bursting. I'd never dared even to think it before, not all the way.

Gabriel said, "I agree with you," and that was all, but Gabriel didn't say most things with words. He said them with his body, and with his actions. With the hand that was holding mine, and the will that had carried him out of his father's house, not even staying for the discussion that would be happening there, because his decision was already made.

I said, "Let's walk," and we did. The wind had picked up after the heat of the afternoon. It was blowing from the southwest, and there'd be clouds building out there. Rain tonight, I thought. It would be good for the fruit trees, and I loved the comforting sound of rain on the fabric roof of the yurt.

The sea had roughened, too, the waves higher and flecked with foam, the water tinged with green. I hadn't grown up with the sea. I'd never even seen it until the week Frankie and I had run across the bare ground of Mount Zion, toward the fence and freedom. I told Gabriel, with the rhythmic sound of the waves in my ears like the beating heart of your mother, the smell of the salt in my head, the power of the wind against my skin, "It doesn't seem real, Mount Zion opening the gates. It doesn't seem possible. The night Frankie and I ran, it was so dark. We followed Daisy, and she took off her track pants to run, because they were Gray's and kept tripping her up, and my dad was chasing us. She was half naked, and it was her *bottom* half. I was so shocked by that, even while we were escaping." I tried to laugh, but I couldn't, because the memory was there, powerful and frightening as any giant in a story.

Gabriel's hand tightened, and then he threaded his fingers through mine so he could hold me better. He wasn't looking at me. He was looking out to sea, and the sand was firm under our feet. He said, "She was brave, eh."

"So brave. Gray, too. Frankie fell, and he carried her. He ran, and he still carried her, but my dad was catching up. My dad and your dad, because he was with him, trying to stop us."

Gabriel's feet faltered and stopped. "I didn't know that."

"I'm not sure Daisy knows. It was dark, and she was in front. I haven't wanted to tell her. Should I not have told you?"

"No," Gabriel said, "you should've told me."

"Let's walk," I said, and we did. The wind loosened the strands of my hair from its knot, and I put a hand up and tugged out the pins, dropping them into my pocket and letting the wild wind take my hair.

A loose woman, I thought, *with bare arms and waxed legs and her hair blowing everywhere.* I said, "Gray probably knows. When we got across the fence, Daisy pulled up the stakes, and the fence caught her under the arms. I don't know how many times she was shocked, but I had to half-carry her and Frankie to Gray's ute. When I looked back, Gray was holding up a shovel by the handle. Threatening them, obviously. He'd just met Daisy that night, and he did all that. But your dad ... he knew who Gray was when he met him again. He had to have known. Why did he go to work for him? Do you think ... you don't think it's like Valor, do you?"

"No," Gabriel said. "That's not who Dad is. I think he ..." He stopped and looked out to sea before he continued. "I think maybe he ran with your dad because that's how he was raised. And I think he must have regretted it, because afterward, he *did* help Daisy."

"He helped her before, though," I said. "He's the one who

told her Frankie was in trouble, so she came to get us that night. You don't think—" I stopped.

"What?" Gabriel asked.

"That he was with my dad *because* of that? That he was sort of ... watching out for Frankie?"

"It makes sense," Gabriel said. "Especially since he doesn't like your dad, even though they're brothers."

"Wow," I said. *"Wow.* He was like the Resistance. We learnt about that in school last year. The people who helped fight against the Nazis during World War II. They had to be undercover, because it was so dangerous."

"If he was doing that," Gabriel reminded me.

"Are you going to ask?"

He thought about that a minute. "Yeh. I am. And then I'm going to go my own way. Maybe he can only go so far, after forty-eight years in Mount Zion. That doesn't mean I can't go further. Maybe he'll move along the road some more, and maybe he won't, especially after everything comes out that I think is going to come out. Same with Mum. They aren't going to cast me off, though, and even if they did ..."

My heart was beating so hard now, it was a wonder I couldn't hear it, even over the sound of the waves and the wind.

"Even if they did," Gabriel said, "I'd still choose you. You're everything I want to come home to."

I HAD school the next day, of course, because I always had school. On and on and on. In Food and Nutrition, the teacher was talking about the nutrients in different vegetables, and what they did for your body. I took notes like always, and tried not to think about Gabriel yesterday, after we'd taken off our shoes and he'd rolled up his trouser legs. How we'd run into the sea together, and then how he'd picked me up, spun me around in the water, and carried me out of it. How he'd kissed me, there on the shore, with the thunder of the waves in my bones and my hair flying around us both. How he'd held my head in his two hands and kissed me like it was all he wanted to do, and then lifted me under my bum so he could kiss me better. And how we'd touched each other in his ute when he'd taken me home.

Parked behind the shed, where he'd parked when he'd worked on the house, but not getting out. Our tongues dancing together, and the cold of the window glass against my head, until he'd put his hand there to cushion it. His hand on my thigh, under my dress, cold against my heated skin, then sliding higher as he kissed my neck, dragging his cheek across my skin. The nearly unbearable thrill of that kiss, and his thumb stroking up my inner thigh, toward that place I'd only touched myself under the blankets, in the dark, when I hadn't been able not to anymore. My darkest sin, and my deepest desire, swirling me down into its depths until I'd be gasping, trying not to cry out, biting my lip to keep quiet so Priya wouldn't hear and know.

When he did it ... I wasn't going to be able to keep quiet.

I had my own hands on his shoulders, his back, and I wanted to feel him, but I wanted to feel this more. He was pulling me up higher against the glass, and his hand was at the fastening of my dress now. He said, his breath hot and quick in my ear, "I want to unbutton this. I want to touch you. I want to kiss you here."

I shuddered. Hot, deep, and convulsive. It felt like I had my hand on myself, even though I didn't. I said, "Yes."

The feeling when he worked that first button through the buttonhole, like there was no going back. And then the second one, and his hand sliding inside my bra. My skirt was nearly up to my hips, and his forearm muscles were tight under my hand when I grabbed him there. My other hand was around his neck, feeling that roughness of late-afternoon scruff, and then he freed my breast and bent his head to it.

I practically levitated off the seat.

When his hand left my breast, shoved up under my skirt again, and touched me outside my undies, where I was wet, where I was *soaked*—my hips started to move, and I was calling out. He wasn't saying anything, because his mouth was busy, and so was his hand. Rubbing me, then sliding under my waistband, and his fingers found me.

Oh.

I didn't realize I was saying it until he said, "Tell me if you don't ... ahh ... want me to do it." Not sounding like deliberate, careful Gabriel at all. Sounding like he couldn't stand it. Like he couldn't *bear* it.

I couldn't answer. I grabbed his head and pulled it to my breast again, he started sliding his hand over me, and ...

And it happened. The way it had in bed, under the covers, and so much more.

So.

Much.

More.

I was wailing, and he was doing it harder, keeping it going. All I could think was, *Don't stop. Don't stop. Don't STOP.*

"Oriana?" Ms. Christie asked. "Did you have something to share?"

My head jerked up. I said, "Uh ... no. No, miss. Sorry."

I'd made a *noise*. And I was wet again! In *school!*

Valerie Stewart, who sat beside me, was staring at me. So was the girl on my other side, whose name was Stephanie. I smiled weakly, knew my face was flushed red, and thought, *This is such a sin.*

And I couldn't care.

I had lunch next, fortunately. I stopped in the toilets first, splashed water on my face, breathed in and out, dried my face and hands with paper towels, looked in the mirror, and thought:

How can I go to Hell for this, when it feels this good? Doesn't God want me to feel good? I know I'm not married, but I want to be married! Doesn't that count?

I can't remember what I learnt the rest of the day.

SINS OF THE FATHERS

GABRIEL

I paid attention at work on Monday. I had to, or I was going to have another accident like the one with the can opener, and Gray wouldn't trust me anymore. I needed him to trust me, because I needed to keep earning a good wage. I needed that flat with a balcony, or a patio, so Oriana could have herbs and vegies in pots. I needed a good kitchen for her, so she could make the dinners she wanted to cook for us.

I needed a good bedroom, too. With a big bed.

I wanted to go see her after work. Instead, I went to my dad's.

Harmony and Patience were still doing the washing-up when I got there, because I'd eaten something quick from the microwave and driven straight over. They looked up when I came through the kitchen, but Patience didn't sparkle at me nearly as much as usual.

I stopped and asked her, "Doing OK?"

"Yes," she said, and tried to smile.

"You were brave yesterday," I told her. "Good on ya."

She bit her lip and looked down, and Harmony asked,

"Does a man ... does he mind, about things like that? Does it make him ..."

"It makes him furious," I said. "It makes him filthy. It makes him want to kill the bas— the man who did it. If it changes how he feels about her, though, he's not much of a man."

Patience asked, "Are you going to marry Oriana?"

"Yes." I wanted to add something else, but I couldn't think what. Finally, I said, "Some good man's going to love you like mad someday. He's going to be lucky." I hoped it was the right thing to say. I hoped it was enough.

Dad asked, "Are you here for a reason?" I couldn't tell what he was thinking, or what he was feeling.

It doesn't matter. You're here to tell him what you're *thinking.*

"Yeh," I said. "To talk to you. D'you want to take a walk?"

His eyebrows rose, but he said, "All right." It was raining again, but tonight, I felt like the walls couldn't hold me.

He waited until we were walking, then said, "I assume this is about Oriana."

"It's about everything," I said. "But, yeh, it's about Oriana. I'll marry her as soon as we're able to. I'd like to have your blessing, but I'll marry her anyway."

Dad said, "I wonder that you came to tell me, then."

"Because I respect you," I said. "And I trust you. You were the best man I knew, growing up. You still are. I know it's hard, changing. It's been hard for me, too, but I have a guiding light I've followed all my life, and it's you. I may disagree with you. I *do* disagree with you, but you'll always have my loyalty. You and Mum."

"But Oriana will have more," Dad said.

"Yeh," I said. "She will. That's how it's supposed to be, and even if it weren't—that's how it is."

He said, "You've never made me anything but proud, so I'm going to trust your choice."

The lightness I felt in that moment ... it was like the biggest backpack in the world sliding from my shoulders. I could swear I stood taller. I said, "Thanks," and couldn't go on for a minute. Dad gripped my shoulder, then released it, and we walked like that for a while until I asked, "Are you going back?"

"No. Your mum and I talked it over last night. It may seem to you that I—" He stopped, then went on. "That I don't respect her the way you feel a man should respect a woman. I do. But the old ways—they hold fast, sometimes. For both her and me. Doing it the other way doesn't feel right. I don't know that it ever will. But I've talked over every decision I've made with her. Sometimes, she disagrees, and she tells me so, and usually, she's right. If we do it in private ... well, that's our way."

"Fair enough," I said. "So why aren't you going back?"

"It's what you said about the money. And this goes no further, not now."

"Understood," I said, my heart starting to beat harder.

"I handled everything," he said, "except the books. The Prophet is the only one who sees those. I don't know why I didn't connect those dots sooner. Maybe because I couldn't see what he'd be saving it for. I still can't. He's not a young man. He's got nowhere to spend it. Why would he hoard it? It's foolish, and it's a sin."

"'And again I say unto you,'" I quoted, "'it is easier for a camel to go through the eye of a needle than for a rich man to enter into the kingdom of God.' It's vanity, maybe."

"Maybe," Dad said. "Reckon they'll find out when the tax authorities get hold of those books, because that's coming. It's going to come crashing down, I fear. My place is to be here, ready to help the brothers and sisters when it happens."

I had to stop, right there on the pavement, and turn to him. I said, "I'm proud to be your son." That was all, because the rest of it, everything in my heart, was choking me.

My dad had never held me, and he didn't hold me now. He

took my shoulder and clutched it, I took his, and we stood there like that, in the drizzle of an early-autumn rain, unable to speak.

Finally, we were moving again, and I said, "Oriana told me something yesterday. That you were with her dad, chasing her and Frankie and Daisy on the night they ran. I didn't know that." I tried to make it neutral. I couldn't keep this secret. I had to tell him I knew, but despite everything I'd said, I was afraid of what I'd hear next.

He said, "I was." A long, long silence, and then he sighed. "He's a hard man. Too hard. He shouldn't have let the Prophet give Daisy to Gilead, and he shouldn't have let him give Frankie to him, either. Even more, by then. After Charity died—"

"Gilead's second wife."

"She hanged herself," Dad said, and I stopped again, from shock this time. "From a showerhead, when she was in hospital after having their baby. So he wouldn't be the one to find her and cut her down, I always thought. Maybe so no man from Mount Zion would ever touch her again, even in death. She was sixteen."

I had to swallow, I felt so sick.

"Dove," he said. "Oriana's youngest sister. She's theirs. Oriana's mum's—Blessing's—baby was stillborn. Her twelfth, eh, and she was well over forty. The Prophet made the switch, and I didn't say anything. That's my sin. When he married Frankie to Gilead, I did say something, but I didn't say it strongly enough. Another sin. Gilead had learnt his lesson, I hoped. To drive a woman to suicide ..."

"But he didn't," I said.

"No," Dad said. "He didn't. That was why I had to help Frankie. She's not a Godly woman, but maybe I understand why. That's why I started to help Daisy, too, to come in and give the women birth control. It was a selfish reason, maybe. I couldn't bear another suicide on my conscience."

"I'm not sure it matters why you do something," I said. "Who has a pure heart? If God sees ... surely He knows. Was Dove adopted, then?"

"No," he said. "It was all done quietly, the switch. Wrong, I know now."

I tried to think how to say the next thing. I couldn't, so I just said it. "I may use that information."

He said, "Why do you think I told you?"

ORIANA

Tuesday went by, and then Wednesday did. Gabriel had classes for his trades certification on Wednesdays. I knew he couldn't come see me, but it didn't stop me wanting him to. We texted, but it was more *Good night* and *Good morning* than anything I wanted to say. I didn't want to talk to him over a phone, either. I wanted to *be* with him.

Friday night, we'd have dinner. Friday was soon enough, even though it didn't feel nearly soon enough.

On Thursday, my phone rang at school.

I was eating lunch with Priya and Aisha at the time, about to go wash my hands and start on my knitting as they talked about clothes. Aisha was showing Priya something on her phone, Priya was showing Aisha a photo of a necklace, and I was answering my phone.

It was Laila.

"Hi," she said. "Lunchtime, at school? Or d'you want to call me back from home tonight?"

"No," I said. "Now's good. D'you need babysitting? *I wanted to make Gabriel something good for tomorrow night, though,* I thought. *And have him take me for a drive afterward and stop somewhere. Somewhere dark and quiet.*

Well, I wouldn't be able to, that's all. We both wanted to wait for marriage, at least the top halves of our brains did. The dark parts, though, deep inside? They wanted to be in the ute again, with the windows steamed up and his hands under my clothes.

And my hands under *his* clothes.

If we wanted to wait, we shouldn't be in the ute at night.

"No," Laila said. "Well, yes, probably, but that's not why I'm ringing up. D'you know anybody from Mount Zion who might want to interview with me? A woman, though I shouldn't say that, but still—you'd only know a woman, surely. For this circumstance."

"For what?" I was confused.

"To be my assistant. You know babies so well, and obviously, there are heaps of babies at Mount Zion. A mum, maybe, who's come out of there and needs a paycheck. It's better than cleaning, though it doesn't pay better, I realize."

"I thought your assistant was coming back on the fifteenth. Isn't she there, then?" My breath was coming short, and I wanted to hush the chattering, echoing room full of girls so I could hear. So I could concentrate.

Oh. "Hang on." I walked out of the room, leaving my things behind. When I was standing in the passage, I said, "OK. I can hear now. Didn't she come back?"

"She did," Laila said, "but she's decided she wants to stay home longer with her baby, which is her right, of course, but … I haven't had much luck finding somebody else. You said other women had left. Surely there must be somebody."

Radiance, I thought, with her gentle voice and gentle hands. If she wasn't going back to Mount Zion. I said, "This is a regular job? Not a temporary one?"

"Yes," Laila said. "Regular as can be."

"Can I, uh …" I tried to think. "Can I ring you back tonight?"

"Of course," Laila said. "Any leads you can offer, truly. I'd appreciate it."

"Tonight," I said. And rang off.

48

WILLING TO WORK FOR IT

GABRIEL

Oriana texted me on Thursday afternoon, *Can you come over tonight? I'll make dinner. 6?* Not an invitation I was ever going to refuse, and if I thought more about what we'd do *after* dinner while I was driving over there, well ... Sunday felt like a long time ago.

When I drove up, she was standing on the porch waiting for me. Looking nervous, I thought. I kissed her hello, and then I kissed her again, lifting her up this time, because I loved doing it.

By the time I set her down, I didn't want dinner. She said, "I didn't make anything flash. A venison and Guinness pie, that's all. And I want to explain this before I say everything, but ... but maybe it's better if I just tell you when I tell everybody, so you can see what you think."

It didn't make much sense to me, but I said, "OK. Are you all right, though?"

She laughed, but it sounded breathless. "Yes. I think so."

"Good," I said. "Because I have something to tell you, too. You, and Gray, and Daisy. I was going to tell you tomorrow, but tonight works."

"All right, then," she said. "Come inside."

The pie, of course, was magical, full of dark brown gravy and tender chunks of meat, with carrots and onions embedded throughout and a flaky pastry on top. I wasn't sure how she did that, but I wanted her to keep doing it for me.

Daisy said, when she'd finished her slice, and the rocket and pear salad that Oriana had fixed to go with it, "That was delicious. Thanks. I'm going to skip pudding and go take a nap before my night shift."

She'd already half stood up when Oriana said, "Could you wait a minute, please? There's something I'd like to talk to you about."

Daisy lowered herself again, but the expression on her face was cautious. All she said, though, was, "Go ahead."

I thought, *Same thing I talked about with Dad. She's clearing the air.* And got ready for it.

What Oriana said, though, was, "Laila needs a full-time photography assistant again, and I'd like to do it."

Daisy looked at Gray. He raised his eyebrows at her and said nothing. She said, "You're in school, though."

"Yes," Oriana said. "I am. I'm taking classes to prepare me for my business, which is what you're meant to do, but they're not preparing me fast enough. I'm wasting time that I could spend *doing* my business, and learning what I want to learn in the evenings, or from Laila, about photography and business and making a website. I've made my own set of books for the knitwear already. I have questions still, but I have Gray to answer them. He's answered heaps of them already."

"I have," Gray said. "And glad to do it. You're a good businesswoman with a fine sense of how to product-test and where to allocate your resources. I can teach heaps of things, but I can't teach judgment, and I can't teach drive."

Daisy said, "Whose side are you on?"

"Yours," he said. "And your sisters'. Oriana has a gift. So do you. They just aren't the same gift."

"I've got a website set up, too," Oriana said. "It's not perfect yet, either, but it will be, because I can ask Laila. And if I ring her up and say yes, I think I'll have a job. A full-time job."

Priya said, "I can't believe you'd do this."

Oriana said, "What? Stop school? I'm nearly eighteen. I'm not going to university. I'm going to keep working with Iris and learning more, and working with Laila and learning more, and working for myself and learning more. I don't have to get permission to stop school, but I want Daisy to understand why."

"And this doesn't have anything to do with Gabriel," Daisy said.

"It has heaps to do with Gabriel," Oriana said. "I want to marry him and live with him. I have nearly eleven thousand dollars in the bank now."

"And I have over twenty thousand," I said. "And a ute." I pulled a piece of paper out of my back pocket. No, not the sexual positions one. That, I'd already memorized. This was a printout of my bank balance, and now, I unfolded it and slid it across the table to Daisy.

"Twenty thousand," Gray said, without expression.

"My flat's cheap," I said. "And I haven't bought much of anything. I've saved, and Oriana's saved, and this is what we've been saving for. To have each other. If leaving Mount Zion has taught me anything, it's that life is … it's too precious not to do the things that are right for you. I spent nearly twenty-five years having somebody else dictate my every move, and try to dictate my every thought. I'm not spending another year that way."

"So you want to …" Daisy said.

"To take the job," Oriana said. "And to marry Gabriel."

"You'd need a judge's permission." That was Gray again.

"I know," Oriana said. "I looked it up. I printed out the forms and filled them in, but I need to wait until I'm sure

Laila's going to give me the job, so I have the right thing to put on the "Occupation" line. Full time will look better. Then I file them with the court, and they have a hearing for me, and maybe Gabriel. They may ask you to say something, Daisy, and I hope you'll give your approval, but even if you don't, I'm asking. I don't think the judge will say no. I don't see why he would."

"Neither do I," Gray said. "Daisy?"

She raised her hands, palm up, then let them fall. "It's not what I would have wanted, but it's what you want, and honestly? I don't see how you'd have a better husband than Gabriel."

Oriana said, "Really?" Her face was naked with joy, and in that minute, she *did* look seventeen.

Daisy smiled. "Really."

Oriana let out a cry and jumped up so fast, she nearly knocked the chair over. She threw her arms around Daisy, who laughed and cuddled her back, and then she cuddled Gray and Priya, too. Finally, she looked at me. "I guess I should have told you first," she said.

I was laughing, too. "Nah," I said, "you should have counted on me, and you did."

After that? I stood up and kissed her, and then I picked her up and swung her around and kissed her again. "I don't have a ring, though," I said, when I'd finally put her down. "They do a special ring, Outside."

"I don't want a ring," she said. "Not until we're married. And if you're thinking of kneeling down or something—I don't need that, either. I just want you."

"Good," I said. "Because I want you, too." My heart was so full, it was going to overflow.

I was going to be married.

Oriana said, "Will you take me for a ride, after this?"

"Yeh," I said. "I will." I'd take her for a ride, and I'd do everything we both wanted to do, too.

Well, almost everything.

She said, "Oh! I made a plum tart. You like that."

"I do," I said, and then remembered. "But I have something to give you first, and something to tell all of you. I warn you—it isn't quite as nice."

ORIANA

I forgot about that last bit, because Gabriel said, "I need to go get the bag out of the ute."

"OK," I said, trying to be normal, trying to keep track of what was going on around me instead of just floating away on a cloud of happiness. "I'll start the washing-up."

Gray laughed. "On the night you officially get engaged? No. Priya and I will do the washing-up."

The dishes had barely disappeared from the table, though, before Gabriel was back, carrying a plastic shopping bag. He said, "If everybody would just sit down a minute."

My heart was beating hard. It was something about the look on his face, or the tension in his body. He tried to smile at me and couldn't quite do it as he said, "I've been working on this for a while now, at Drew's. I made a box, but you'll probably have a better way. Something you sew, with individual pouches, and then roll up and tie. I saw some ideas online, but I can't sew, so …"

Daisy said, "Gabriel. Would you just *give* it to her?"

He laughed a little, but said, "I'm nervous."

"We see that, mate," Gray said. "Give it to her anyway." He was smiling, and he was holding Daisy's hand.

It was like the pink cake with the candles, and it was so much better than that. It was like everybody singing that birthday song for you, but it felt like the angels were doing it.

Gabriel pulled a wooden box out of the bag. It was no larger than a big hardbound book, and was made of speckled rewarewa, the brown spots curling and swirling in a beautiful pattern on the buff background. I ran my hand over the gorgeously smooth, barely oiled surface, knew how hard he must have worked to get it that perfect, and said, "It's beautiful."

Gabriel said, "That's not the gift." He looked like he was trying to smile, but he couldn't quite do it. "Open it up."

I did. He'd fixed a brass clasp onto the lid, and I unhooked it, then held the two sides in my palms, took a breath, and opened the box with my thumbs.

It was lined in blue velvet.

And filled with knitting needles.

I picked up the first one. Two brass-colored metal needles attached to a blue cable, the points barely blunted. Two millimeters in diameter, maybe. Lace weight, and the smoothness and sharpness exactly what you needed to work with a yarn as delicate and fine as gossamer. Mohair and silk, and I could see the shawl now. I ran the needles through my hands, noticing how carefully he'd smoothed the ends, where he'd attached the cable. How had he *done* that?

Priya said, "Don't just look at *one*. Show us all of them!"

He'd done eight sets, all the way up to nine millimeters. I pulled them all out and laid them on the table, and when I was done, I looked at Gabriel.

"You learnt to do this," I said. "For me."

"I did," he said. "That first night, on the steps at Laila's house, when you were knitting, I thought—anybody who's that good at something needs the best tools. I read about how to do it, and then I did it. If you want love, real love, I reckon you'd better be willing to work for it."

I said, "I love you." I was crying, somehow, and I couldn't stop. "I *love* you." After that, I was in his arms. Not kissing him, just holding on, laughing and crying.

He said, "An OK substitute for that ring, then?"

"Better," I managed to say. "So much better."

It took a long time to get around to serving my plum tart.

When I did, though ... it took even longer to finish it. Not just for me. For everybody.

GABRIEL SAID, "I have something I need to tell all of you, that my dad just told me. I wish it were a pretty story. It's not. It's about your sister, Dove."

He started to talk, and the forks went down like dominoes. First Daisy's, then mine, then Gray's, then Priya's. As for Gabriel—he never picked his up.

Daisy said, finally, "Bloody *hell.*" Blankly.

Gray said, "I can't believe it. That bastard. That *arsehole.* I wish I'd killed him."

"Who?" Daisy asked. "Gilead, or the Prophet?"

"Both," Gray said, and his face was grim. I didn't think he was joking.

Priya said, "So Dove is ..."

Oh. I said, "Does that make it ... not possible, Daisy? For you to want her with us? To love her, if she's Gilead's? What about Frankie? How's she going to feel?" I thought of something, then. I looked at Gabriel, then hesitated.

He said, "She can live with us."

I couldn't even say anything. I just held his arm and eventually said, "I love you," again.

Daisy said, "Of course it doesn't matter." She pushed at her hair, though, and looked so tired. "We're all Dad's daughters, and Dad isn't much better than Gilead, and I love all of you, don't I? I don't believe there's any such thing as tainted blood. I don't know Dove—she wasn't born when I left—but ..."

"She's like me," I said. "She's not like Gilead, and she's not like Frankie. She's like me, and she's like ... like Mum. Sweet, and soft, and kind." Suddenly, it was all too much. The tears were there in my eyes, wanting to spill over. I was getting married to the most wonderful man I'd ever met. Would my mum even know?

Gray said, "Of course she'll live with us when it's time, as long as it's all right with Daisy. We have the place, and we should know how to do it by now, after all this practice. Besides, Dove will have her other sisters to help."

He looked at Daisy first. Daisy nodded, I said, "Of course," and Priya said, "Of course we want Dove. She's the *baby*."

Gray went on, "I'm trying to think how this knowledge changes things. The situation, I mean, and Mount Zion opening up, if it really is."

"I think it does change things," Gabriel said. "I need to talk to a lawyer, though, to be sure."

"Luckily," Gray said, "we know some lawyers. What's your idea?"

Gabriel told us.

49

INTO THE LION'S DEN

Oriana

On Friday, I went to school and said goodbye to Aisha, hugging her and saying, "I'll still see you, if you come home with Priya."

"It won't be the same," she said, and I knew it was true. Aisha and Priya would go to university, would become airline pilots or accountants or lawyers, and I'd be glad to see it, but I knew what I wanted to do, and it wasn't that. I told a couple of my teachers I was leaving, registered their disappointment or their unsurprised resignation, and didn't feel a bit bad.

After that, I waited outside the building for Daisy and Aunt Constance. When Daisy's car pulled up, Patience opened the back door of the car for me to climb in, and we drove to the police station and made a complaint against Valor. It wasn't fun, but Daisy held my hand. Besides, I kept thinking of Frankie on that day when we'd rescued her, lying on an examination table, bruised and battered and nearly broken, having her most private areas photographed and examined and *sampled,* and giving the statement that jailed Gilead. She hadn't even been as old as me that day, and she'd been through so much worse than this.

I made my statement, and when the woman officer gave it to me to read and sign, my signature didn't wobble.

Afterward, Aunt Constance said, "We could go to our flat for a cup of tea and lunch," and looked shaken. Her expression had been horrified when Patience had given her own statement, and I could feel her wondering, *Did this happen to Harmony, too? Should I ask her?* I thought, *You probably should*, but didn't say so. Patience would talk to Harmony, and if there were something there, I had a feeling it would come out. You couldn't always rush things. You had to give people time and space to make their own journey through the darkness. They had to believe that there really was light out there, and that they could find it.

Daisy said, "I have a shift," and looked like the last thing she wanted was to talk about sin. Valor's, Gilead's, hers ... who knew? The breach between the families was healing, maybe, but it wasn't healed yet.

I said, "Thanks, but I have heaps more things to do today," and Daisy and I dropped them off and drove home.

I took off my school uniform for the last time in my bedroom in Gray's yurt, with flowers that I'd cut this morning scenting the room from the cut-glass pitcher I'd bought with my own money, and then I sat down and filed the forms requesting an exemption to the waiting-until-eighteen rule for marriage. I pressed the button that said "Submit" three times in a row and didn't worry about the number of people who'd told me that it was already March, and my birthday was in June, and why couldn't I just wait? Then I went down to the garden and helped Iris with the animals and told her about my plans. She said, "Reckon you know best," and I thought that a person who'd been brought up knowing she was a woman but with everybody telling her she was a man might understand how it felt to be me.

I asked, forking up dirty chicken bedding from the floor of

the coop, "Is this what it was like for you when you told your family you were a woman?"

She said, "Worse. But I reckon if you do a thing that everybody's telling you is wrong and mad, half the world wants to hurt you for it, and your parents chuck you out of their house for it, and all you feel after all that is relieved, and like there's no choice and there never was—that's the right thing for you to do. Grab that wheelbarrow and help me shift this compost."

On Saturday night, I looked at flats online with Gabriel after dinner at the table in the yurt as Priya sat at the kitchen bench and did her maths homework. An hour later, I lay across the bench seat in an old ute with the windows steamed all the way over, got my first lesson in how to help a man have an orgasm, and thought, *I hope the court doesn't take long, because neither of us can stand much more of this,* and also, *I wonder how much a bed costs.*

On Monday, I went back to work for Laila.

Stepping into the studio, with its Gothic church windows, its cushioned posing table, and its baskets of props, felt like coming home. I'd worked here for barely six weeks, but they'd been the best six weeks of my life. And when I held the first baby of the day, a brand-new girl with golden skin and black curls, and felt her body melting into mine, when I bent my head to smell her baby scent, when her arms waved without direction before her fist closed around the collar of my shirt and held on, I knew this was where I was meant to be.

There's a difference between telling yourself you're lucky and *feeling* lucky. The difference is joy, the kind that seeps all the way into you like warm honey, that makes the sky look bluer and the birdsong sound sweeter.

The difference is getting to be yourself, and being loved for it.

On the next Sunday, we went back to Mount Zion.

Gabriel

It was nine o'clock, as always, when I climbed out of the ute with Oriana in front of that gate. The rest of them were climbing out, too: Daisy and Gray and Priya, my mum and dad, and, to my surprise, Frankie, whom Daisy and Gray had collected in Wanaka.

The yard wasn't empty today. What looked like all of Mount Zion was lined up there, in rows. Women, children, and men—hundreds of them. I heard a grinding sound, and the steel gate slid open on its track.

The crowd parted, and a figure came through, leaning on a stick. The Prophet, who'd always been a lion of a man, his gait now halting and uncertain. A stroke, maybe.

Hard not to see it as the wrath of God.

A man walked beside him, offering an arm, and another followed after. Valor, accompanying his grandfather, and Oriana's father following behind. Loyal Worthy, a short, stocky man with broad, hard hands. The flat stare from Loyal's pale-brown eyes didn't change one iota on seeing four of his twelve children for the first time in months.

The little group stopped a few meters from the open gate. The space between us loomed like no man's land, the zone between two entrenched combatants in a bitter war, and that was how it felt.

I didn't want to step through that gate.

The Prophet said, "The doors are open." His speech was as loud and confident as ever, and I found myself wondering whether his mobility was actually impaired, or if this was a bid for sympathy in the trials he had to see coming.

An old man, they'd say. *No point putting him in prison. What harm can he do?*

The harm had never been in his body. It had been in his twisted mind and his clever tongue and his absolute conviction.

Dad said, "So you've said. Are you paying people as you've promised, too?"

"We're starting to," the Prophet said. "Working out the accounts now. It's complicated."

"It's not complicated." That was Daisy. "There's a minimum wage. Timekeeping forms. Payroll firms. Gray could show you how to do it in a day."

"I don't require help from infidels," the Prophet said. His own blue eyes were flashing, and, no, nothing much had changed. "I need help from my blood, from the man I've trusted most. I assume that's why you're here, Aaron. Come in and see what I'm doing. There are no secrets here. There never have been."

Dad said, "That's what I'm here to see and discuss, yes."

"Just you and Constance," the Prophet said. "And Gabriel." His hooded eyes landed on mine, their stare nearly hypnotic. "Who will be at my left hand, if he returns."

I caught the look on Valor's face at that and thought, *Yeh, mate, it'll probably be you in the end. Good luck with that. I hope you're looking forward to prison.* This was my cue, though, so I said, "And Oriana. We're going to be married, and where I go, she goes."

"As it should be," the Prophet said. "'And Ruth said, Entreat me not to leave thee, or to return from following after thee: for whither thou goest, I will go; and where thou lodgest, I will lodge: thy people shall be my people, and thy God my God.'"

I wanted to say, "I meant into the compound for this, not making her be bound by my choices all her life," but I didn't, of course.

Daisy said, "We'll all come."

"No," the Prophet said. "This is still Mount Zion property, and I choose who steps onto it. The four of you, then." He turned and stumped away.

My mum could come, because she'd always follow my

dad's lead, and the Prophet knew it. And Oriana could come, because he thought she was exactly the same.

He was wrong.

Crossing over the metal track of the gate was almost the hardest thing I'd ever done. Harder than walking out of Mount Zion, and harder even than the last time Oriana and I had been here, when we'd rescued Priya. That day, we'd been driven by nerves and adrenaline and the idea of Priya held back. Held prisoner.

"*Screw your courage to the sticking-place,*" Oriana whispered to me, "*and we'll not fail.*" It was from Shakespeare, said by a woman to urge her husband to a heinous deed.

Regicide.

I stepped through the gate, and Oriana stepped through right beside me. I was wearing my usual clothes: brown work pants—actually, the ones I'd been wearing when I'd first walked out of here, because those things wore like iron—and a blue work shirt with braces. I looked hardly a bit different, and neither did Dad. As for Mum, she was in a long skirt and top, so not much difference there, either. Her hair was uncovered, but in its usual knot, and I could tell that she wished she weren't showing it. Her face was the face of a martyr facing judgment.

Oriana? Her hair wasn't in a knot. It was loose. She was wearing wide-legged, dark purple trousers, thicker ones than those she'd made for summer. Their wide fabric belt emphasized her curves in a way that Mount Zion had never allowed, and her pale-yellow top showed her collarbones and hinted at the unstructured bra beneath. It would have showed her arms, too, but she was wearing a cardigan she'd knitted. The body of it was lilac, like my duvet cover, and the sleeves were stripes of all the colors she loved so much, the colors of flowers: yellow and sky-blue and lemongrass-green, pink and red and deep purple. The cardigan had pockets and a striped hood in the same colors, and as she walked through the sea of brown, she looked like pure, bright life force.

Like defiance.

The Prophet led us to the administration building, someplace I'd been only when accompanying my father, and where Oriana and my mum would never have been at all. The only women allowed here were the Prophet's wife and daughters, and only to clean, restock, and serve. We went through one door and down a passage, ending in a sort of reception area where I'd sat and waited for my dad on those occasions. The Prophet told Valor, "Wait here," and Valor looked like he wanted to argue, but didn't dare. "The women, too," the Prophet added.

"No," Dad said. "They need to hear as well."

I was holding my breath. For all of it, but especially for that. How would the Prophet believe we were coming back if Dad was insisting on bringing Mum and Oriana into this sanctified place?

It was a standoff. The Prophet, with his hooded, penetrating eyes, and Dad, with his open gaze and set jaw. And Oriana's father, Loyal, not looking at her. Not *seeing* her. I could feel the tremble in her as if I were touching her. How hard was this for her? Or how impossible?

Not impossible at all, I thought, *because she'll do it.*

In the end, all six of us went through the door I'd only seen from the outside and into the Elders' Room. It wasn't what you may have supposed. No paintings or fine leather chairs or rosewood table, just a simple oval one made of fine-grained, pinkish-brown tawhai, the ubiquitous silver beech we'd used for almost all the furniture here, easy to obtain and easy to work, and seven straight chairs. One for the Prophet, and six for the Elders.

It wasn't seven in order to break a tied vote, or whatever you may be thinking. There were no votes. The Elders advised. The Prophet decided.

The Prophet took his seat at the head of the table and said, "Sit down." My mum hesitated, maybe knowing that a woman had never sat in these chairs, but Oriana sat down even before my dad and I did. Before her *father* did. At the bottom of the table, but still. The Prophet glared at her, and I could tell she wanted to drop her gaze, but she looked back at him instead, and I sat beside her and took her hand under the table.

My dad, at the Prophet's right hand, the same place he'd probably sat for years, with my mum beside him. Oriana's father, Loyal, who shut the door silently and then took his seat at the Prophet's left. And Oriana and me.

No windows. No witnesses. In the lion's den.

Time to do this thing.

50

BEGIN AGAIN

Oriana

I felt as trapped as a rabbit in a snare, and as frightened. I forced myself to breathe and willed my hands not to tremble.

Just listen, I reminded myself. *Uncle Aaron will start. Don't look at Dad.*

Actually, the Prophet started. "So," he told Uncle Aaron, "you've decided to come back and help me."

"I'd like to hear you lay out your plan first," Uncle Aaron said.

The Prophet talked. Nothing we hadn't heard before, because it was everything on the list Valor had handed out. Open gates. New recruits. Wages for everyone. The gift shop. Aunt Constance giving master knitting classes, Gabriel giving woodworking classes, and Uncle Aaron running it all. Brochures showing it, too, and I could just imagine. Gabriel in a work shirt and braces, shoulder muscles straining, doing something manly with tools. He'd end up as a model after all if he came back here, I thought, and fought an insane urge to giggle.

The Prophet didn't include me, but then, he didn't know what I could do.

Uncle Aaron waited through all of it—it took a long time—and then said, "And the tax authorities?"

"The community has always paid taxes," the Prophet said.

"So they haven't come around asking for more documentation?" Uncle Aaron asked.

"They've asked," the Prophet said. "The accountants and lawyers are answering. Harassment, that's all."

"And the emergency hearing with the Employment Court?" Uncle Aaron asked. "What do the lawyers say about that?"

I could swear that the temperature in the room dropped. The Prophet asked, "How has that knowledge come to your ears?"

"It hasn't," Gabriel said. "It's come to mine."

The Prophet swiveled his gaze onto him, and Gabriel sat even taller. I was so proud, I wanted to marry him right then.

"False witness," the Prophet said. "Persecution. Everyone here has willingly given their labor. You can attest to that, Aaron."

"Mm," Uncle Aaron said. "What provisions are you taking to deal with sexual abuse in this new world? Child abuse? Spousal abuse? What about the abuse in the past?"

Silence, and the gooseflesh rose on my arms.

"There is no abuse here," the Prophet said. "Only men and their wives living according to God's law, and raising their families." Then he quoted that same thing Uncle Aaron had, that thing I'd heard all my life. "'Wives, submit yourselves unto your own husbands, as unto the Lord.'"

Uncle Aaron said, "That isn't what the law says. It says that a wife has sovereignty over her body, and so does a child, to a lesser extent. To the extent that a parent can't lay hands on them in anger. How will you address that?"

"We will fight," the Prophet said, "as we have always fought. Are you with us?"

Uncle Aaron didn't answer, not quite. He said, "Dove Worthy."

The air was so cold, I shivered despite my cardigan. The Prophet said, "What about her?"

Uncle Aaron said, "Her sisters want to take her home with them, and they want to talk with their mother."

"Impossible," the Prophet said. "She's barely fourteen. She stays with her parents."

Loyal spoke for the first time. "Who are you, *brother*, to take my child from me?"

Gabriel said, "She's not your child. Her mother is dead and her father's in prison, and we all know it."

The Prophet's eyes flew around the table. Everyone stared back, and everyone, I was fairly sure, trembled somewhere, even if it was deep inside.

Gabriel said, "My father may be loyal. I'm not. Oriana and Priya and Frankie and Daisy will all bear witness to their abuse at the hands of their father, and I'll testify to what I've seen. Oriana and Patience Trueblood laid complaints two days ago against Valor for sexual assault, going back to the age of four and ending with an attack I witnessed myself, and Oriana is still only seventeen. How many more girls will there be, once the police start asking questions? How many more men will join Gilead in prison?"

The Prophet said, "False witness," again, but his jowls were quivering.

I would have said I was frozen solid. My feet to the floor. My hands to each other, in my lap. My lips most of all. Somehow, though, I said, "How many little girls will it take? How many little girls do you think there are? Gilead drove his wife to suicide, and you took her baby and put her in a household that was almost as bad. I'm sure Charity thought that at least her baby would be taken away now, that she'd be safe. Instead, Charity died for nothing but escape. Sixteen years old, hanging herself in hospital, where she should have finally been safe, because she'd known so much despair that she couldn't even hope anymore. Do you want the world to hear that story?"

"Blackmail," the Prophet said. "The Devil speaking through an ungodly woman."

Well, probably true. I probably *was* an ungodly woman at this point, and when we'd consulted the lawyer, the woman named Victoria who'd also helped hatch the plan to get Frankie out, she'd said it might be blackmail, too. "But if it works," she'd said, "it'll definitely be easier, as long as you're willing to take the risk."

"Public exposure?" Daisy had said. "He won't want that. That's a very nasty secret. I think it'll work."

Now, Uncle Aaron said, "Not blackmail. Justice. I was there, remember? I'll take my share of the blame for that shameful act. I'm expecting to. I won't be part of it anymore, though. You can have Dove taken from here and put in the care of her sisters, or you can have all of us telling that story."

The Prophet's face sagged, and his shoulders did, too, like air going out of a balloon. "What do you want?" he asked.

"What I said," Uncle Aaron answered. "Dove brought to her sisters, and allowed to leave with them, with permission signed over by Loyal and Blessing, making Daisy her guardian. And Blessing brought to see her daughters without Loyal there."

"No." That was my dad, and the word was an explosion. He was out of his seat and halfway around the table, and despite myself, I jumped up and shrank back. I heard that belt whistling down, and the sickening sound it made when it met flesh. I felt the burn of it, and the humiliation.

Gabriel stood up fast, blocking Dad's way, and told him, "Try it. Try to hurt her again. Try to hurt any of them again. I'll just hurt you. They'll destroy you."

"If I do this," the Prophet asked, ignoring my dad, "will you reconsider?"

"Yes," Uncle Aaron said.

It wasn't a good word to hear.

WE STOOD JUST inside the gate this time, in a little row once more, and waited. Daisy and Gray, Uncle Aaron and Aunt Constance, Priya and Frankie, Gabriel and me. I could feel the presence of the gate behind me like a menace, and I was guessing the others could, too. My legs felt weak, all of me felt shaky, and I couldn't control my face. It had been ten minutes. Were they just going to leave us here, then? Was the Prophet going to call our bluff?

Had it been a bluff? My part wasn't. What about Uncle Aaron's?

We waited, and the crowd opposite us waited, too. No children were as silent as Mount Zion children. They didn't squirm, and they didn't protest. They stood.

A door opening behind them. The door from the kitchens. Two figures moving toward us, one taller than the other, one thinner than the other.

The short, thin one wasn't Dove. It was my mum.

I looked at Frankie, and her face was working. I looked at Daisy, and her face was frozen. I looked at Priya, and the tears were rolling down her cheeks.

Twenty meters away. Ten.

I broke and ran.

When my mum's thin arms came around me, I wept. I cried for all the times she'd comforted me, for all the sweetness she'd carried in her body along with all of us, for all the words she'd never been allowed to say. I cried for the lullabies she'd sung to the little ones in the dark hours of the night, and most of all, I cried for everything she'd lost. Her children, and her freedom. And in a minute, I realized the others were there, too, which meant I had to step back and give them a turn.

Once I did, I had to hold Dove.

She clung to me and asked, "Do I really get to go with you? I'm not sixteen, though. Do I really get to come?"

Her eyes, alone among the twelve of us, were bright blue, her hair a paler brown even than mine, and with a strong curl to it that none of us had. I held her hand and said, "You really do. Today. You get to share a room with Priya, and go to school and learn about everything, and help with the animals, and never be hit again."

"Not even when I'm married?" she asked.

"Especially not when you're married."

"What about Mum, though?" she asked. "If I go, she'll be alone."

I looked over her head, because I was still taller, and there my mum was, with a trembling smile on a face that was wet with tears, holding each of my sisters' faces in turn, kissing their cheeks, murmuring to them. I said, "Mum. You don't have to stay. You can come, too. We're all there, and Aunt Constance is there. Dorian is there, too, and more of them will come. You can leave now."

She shook her head, but she was still smiling. "It's going to be open here," she said. "The Prophet has promised, and this is my home. You'll come visit me, and bring your children."

"But, Mum," Daisy said, sounding anguished. "We *want* you. I have a house for you. You can live with Priya and Dove in your own house and help me take care of them. You can cook if you like, or not cook, and knit with Oriana and Aunt Constance. There's work for you to do if you want it, but it's our turn to care for you now."

"*Meree betee,*" Mum said, stroking Daisy's cheek. *My daughter,* that meant. What she'd always called us. "I have a place to stay. I chose it. But you come see me. Come every month, the way you've been doing, but sit with me this time. Tell me your secrets and your fears. Let me be your mum again. That's the life I want."

"We'll be here," Daisy said. "And asking every time. Mum

—this place is going to go down, eventually. It's going to be destroyed."

"And if it does," Mum said, "I'll decide what to do. For now, my answer will be the same. I've chosen my path, and it's mine to walk. Watching you walk yours—that's my blessing."

Behind me, I heard Gabriel asking Uncle Aaron, "Did you mean it, that you'll reconsider?"

"Yes," Uncle Aaron said. "I don't say things unless I mean them. I've reconsidered. The answer is still no. I've had enough of this place. Let's go."

I waved out the back window of the ute until the tears blurred my vision, until Gabriel took the turn in the road and she was lost to view. My tiny, stoical little mum, whose heart was half of her. Her hand in the air and a brave smile on her face.

Waving goodbye.

51

ORIANA TAKES CHARGE

GABRIEL

Oriana cried half the way home.

How did you love a woman like this enough? How did you deserve her?

When I finally reached Gray's place, she turned into me, held me tight while I held her and wished for something to say to ease that pain, and finally said, "I need to ... I need to help Dove now. I've always been the closest to her. She won't understand Daisy or Priya, the way they want to change so fast and leave it all behind. She needs somebody to help her adjust."

I ran my hand down her back and up it again, over the cardigan she'd designed and the clothes she'd sewn on the machine I'd bought her, and said, "Yeh." Thinking about that first night at Drew's, wearing the wrong clothes, trying to get to sleep in the too-big bed, with my back on fire and everything I'd ever known in the rearview mirror. About the next morning, trying to cook myself breakfast, trying to hold back the panic.

She said, "If I don't see you for a few days ... are you OK

with that?" Sitting back, now, and looking anxiously into my eyes. Worrying about me, and not wanting to leave me alone.

I said, "I know you love me. Do what you need to do."

"Friday night," she said. "If not sooner." She started to open the door, then turned back to me. "I think school, for Dove. Don't you? It isn't the start of term, but ..."

"Yeh," I said. "Always better to have somewhere to go and something to do. Something to focus on. Something to learn."

"I think so, too," she said. "You're very wise."

I had to smile. "No. Just lost for long enough that I remember how it feels."

She put a hand behind my neck and kissed my mouth, then pulled back and said, "I can't wait to marry you," climbed out of the ute, and headed up the stairs to the yurt where, I was sure, she'd be making lunch for everybody. Making tea. Making it better.

Had anybody ever had the strength of these girls?

It wasn't Friday, in the end. It was only Tuesday evening when she called and said, "I got a notice from the court. I have a hearing next Wednesday on the marriage thing. That was ... that's fast."

What did that mean? I couldn't tell. I asked, "Too fast?" and wished I wasn't on the other end of a telephone line.

"No," she said. "Oh—I found two flats that don't look bad. D'you want to go see them with me tomorrow at six? That's when I can get in. I read that it's better to view before the weekend, when everybody goes."

"Yeh," I said. "Definitely."

Neither of the flats worked. One of them was as bad as my current situation, and the other was so dark, you'd want to put in brighter bulbs and keep them on all day. Not even Oriana's warmth could have fixed that.

She said, "Never mind," and told the estate agent, "If something better comes up, would you ring me first? I'm better at cleaning than anybody I know, and Gabriel can fix anything."

The agent, a middle-aged lady named Monica with poufy blond hair that didn't seem quite natural, looked at Oriana, then at me, and said, "You're, er ... pretty young for that."

Oriana said, "Oh. Are you not allowed to ask personal questions? That's OK. I'm seventeen and Gabriel's twenty-five, but I'm petitioning the court to marry him before June, when I turn eighteen."

"Oh," Monica said. "That's, uh ..." and looked more nonplused than ever.

"We left Mount Zion," Oriana told her. "That's why we seem different. You may recognize Gabriel from that thing they did on TV the day he walked out and we rescued my sister, because he's so beautiful. I was there, too, but I'm not as exciting. I work as a photographer's assistant. Newborn photography. It's brilliant." She reached into her purse, pulled out a card with a bare-arsed baby on it, and handed it over. "Laila Drake. She's the best. Oh, and I also have my own business." Another card, with a white lace scarf spilling over a black background, a sprig of lavender in the other corner, and the name, *Lavender Hill Farm Knitwear,* in the middle. "Gabriel doesn't have a card, but he works for Gray Tamatoa. The All Black. My brother-in-law. Gabriel's a team leader for Gray already, because he's so skilled and so responsible. I have eleven siblings, and he's the eldest of six, so you see ..."

The estate agent looked like she didn't know what had hit her. To be honest, I felt a bit that way myself. I just hoped Oriana wasn't going to throw in "Sir Andrew Callahan." I said, "I'm not ..."

Oriana said, "You are. I'm just telling her so. It's the truth, because not telling the truth would be a sin. We're young, but we're not. We don't have parties, we don't drink alcohol, and we don't play loud music. We're neat, we're clean, we're about to be married, and we both have heaps of money saved, just waiting to pay our bills. So—if anything comes up? Also—what's your favorite cake?"

I'd swear the woman's mouth was still hanging open when we left.

This time, I laughed all the way home.

ORIANA

My hearing was two hours of waiting and five minutes of talking.

The Family Court judge was an older lady, businesslike and brisk, and I studied her for those two hours as I sat on a bench with Gabriel on one side and Daisy and Gray on the other, tried to gauge her prejudices, and failed. I'd have said she was bored, but she wasn't. She listened, she decided, and she moved on.

I'd never be like that. Good thing I wasn't going to be a lawyer.

Finally, a man said, "Petition of Obedience Worthy," and I bounced up like a jack-in-the-box, climbed over Gabriel's legs, stumbled a bit on my way out of the row, and held up my hand to swear the oath.

It's all right, I told myself. *What you told that estate agent lady was right. Not telling the truth is a sin, and you don't sin.*

Well, other than taking your soon-to-be husband's penis in your mouth, and having him lick you where you'd never imagined anybody licking you, I didn't. But that was the whole *point.*

The judge read over my papers as I sat in the chair and felt much too conspicuous, and then she took off her reading glasses, scrutinized me in a way that convinced me she knew about the licking, and said, "You're a … a refugee from Mount Zion. Is that the term you'd prefer me to use, or is there a better one?"

"No," I said. "Refugee is fine. Though it wasn't really as bad as that for me, because of my sister, Daisy. I had somewhere to go and heaps of help from her, and from Gray Tamatoa, too. He didn't know us, but he helped us escape and let us live on his land." I didn't say, "In his house," because I'd discovered that people tended to think that meant he and Daisy were having relations, and they hadn't been, not back then.

The judge blinked, looked down at the papers, looked back at me, and said, "Explain to me in what way you're not being influenced by Mount Zion's values here."

Well, *this* wasn't what I'd expected to be asked. I had my hands tucked under my thighs, I was so nervous, but I cleared my throat, tried to organize my thoughts, and said, "I am, I think. I mean, I think we're always influenced by the way we grow up. So I ... to me, being married now doesn't feel early, because I've been doing things that people here, Outside, think of as married things for most of my life. Cooking, and cleaning, and caring for babies. I've learnt so many more things now, though. Gardening, and caring for animals—mostly bees and alpacas, especially the alpacas, and that's men's work at Mount Zion—that I didn't know before. I've been to school, and I've met all sorts of people. But I ... there's just nobody who's better than Gabriel. I've known him all my life, and he's ..."

"Your cousin," the judge said flatly.

"My step-cousin," I said. "And—are you thinking we've had pressure to get married? We've had pressure *not* to get married. My sisters are all going to university, or they've already been. That's what *they* think is the right thing for a woman, not starting up a knitwear business and helping with newborns. No, I want to marry Gabriel because I ... because I want to marry *Gabriel*. You should probably talk to him, and then you'll see."

"He's brought character witnesses of his own, I notice," the judge said, looking out over the courtroom. "Even though he's not the one who needs them. Gray Tamatoa. Sir Andrew Callahan and Lady Callahan. This is a simple proceeding, not a defamation hearing or a media circus."

"Well, I can't help that," I said. "People like to take their photos. That's why they have locked gates at their houses. But they wanted to come today in case you had questions about Gabriel. That he could be a predator, I mean."

I thought the judge might be trying not to smile. I shot a look at Gabriel, and he smiled back, so he wasn't worried. The judge said, "Why do I have the feeling that if I began calling character witnesses, we'd all be in the news tomorrow morning? You seem like a levelheaded young woman, so I'll just tell you—don't have babies before you're ready."

"Don't worry," I assured her. "We haven't even had relations yet. That's why we want to get married. Anyway, my sister Daisy's studying to be a nurse practitioner. She gave me that birth control that you put in your arm. We can have it taken out at any time, but we're not ready for babies, not for a while. We don't even have a flat yet. Well, we do, but it won't be available for another two weeks, so ..."

The judge's mouth twitched, and she said, "Permission granted," and banged her wooden hammer.

I said, "You mean that's it? I can get married?"

"Yes," she said. "I think you'd better." After that, she stood up and said, "The Court will take a fifteen-minute recess."

As she left, I thought she might have said, "I need a drink."

Probably not, though. She was a *judge*.

THE GREATEST OF THESE

Oriana

I wore a pink dress to my wedding, the way I'd always wanted to. It was the most beautiful dress I'd ever seen, of sheer chiffon appliqued with flowers. The skirt reached the floor, and the underskirt didn't. My shoulders were bare, too, and I had a tiny bit of cleavage showing. All of it might be sinful, but the dress was so gorgeous, I hadn't been able to help it. The moment I'd put it on, I'd felt like I was floating. Like life really could be this beautiful.

Daisy wasn't wearing pink. Her dress was white, form-fitting, elegant, and sequined, all of it showing her body and all of it the very last thing from Mount Zion. She'd said, when we'd shopped for the dresses with Priya and Dove, that she didn't want to be reminded, but I remembered those wedding days differently, maybe. The extra-good food the women had made, the special sweets, and the way they'd decorated the Joining Hut with flowers.

And the bride in a pink dress, excited to be starting her new life. You could say it was brainwashing, but those things were what I felt, so …

We did it in the garden, on the Sunday ten days after my

hearing. Gabriel and I had gone to get the license as soon as we'd received a copy of the court order granting permission, and Gray and Daisy had already had theirs.

"Let's do it together," Daisy had said, "if you want to, Oriana. That'll make it easier."

It had taken me a moment, but then I'd got it. Because she *had* worn that pink dress before, and then had sex in the Joining Hut. Sex that had hurt so much, she'd cried. For her, that day hadn't been a dream. It had been the start of her nightmare.

Today wasn't that day, though. Today was something entirely different.

The garden was full of people. Some of Gray's old teammates, who were his investors now. Drew and Hannah Callahan, who'd helped us get Frankie out and then had helped Gabriel, and their kids. Matiu and Poppy Te Mana and theirs, and, of course, Laila and Lachlan and Laila's twin girls. Aisha, sitting with Priya. Gabriel's family, and mine. It was an entire garden full of flowers and babies and sunshine. Even Iris had come, though she was sitting at the back and scowling. Never mind. I appreciated the effort.

Gray's mum, Honor, puffed up the track and said, "They're ready for you. Should I tell Victoria to start the bride music?"

"Yes," Daisy said, clutching her bouquet to her. It was roses and dahlias in shades of cream, burgundy, and peach, and it was lovely. You might think mine would match, but it didn't. Mine was all creamy white and green, because mine was gardenias.

A pure soul, Gabriel had told me. *Joy. And a secret love.*

Not secret any longer, because here we were, stepping into the sunshine.

Wait. Daisy's bouquet was shaking. I heard the music drifting up to us, coming from Victoria, the lawyer who'd helped us with Mount Zion both times, because she'd also agreed to play her cello for the ceremony.

The people who help you most aren't always the people you think, because there are more kind hearts in the world than you can count.

Now, Honor was beckoning us on, but I stopped and turned to Daisy, and then I took her wrist.

It was shaking, too.

I asked, "What is it?"

Victoria was halfway through the song now. *Marry Me*, it was called, and Gabriel had found it. The crowd was turning our way, looking for us. I ignored them. Victoria could play the song over again, that was all.

Daisy said, "What if I'm not good enough at being in love?"

GABRIEL

I'd heard this song first on the radio in the ute, driving along beside the sea, with the sun sparkling on the blue water, the windows down, and the wind in my hair. A year ago, that had been, before I'd got the nerve even to speak to Oriana, when she'd been sixteen and the whole thing had been impossible.

And I'd known anyway. I'd heard that song and thought, *That's how I feel.* I'd seen her walking down the aisle to me in my mind, and today, she'd do it for real. I had her ring in the pocket of the first dress trousers I'd ever owned, and she'd have mine on her thumb. "So I don't lose it," she'd said yesterday, during our final dinner as single people, sitting around the table in the yurt with her sisters and Gray on a night when it had taken every bit of willpower I had in me to get into the ute and drive away from her.

The problem was—she wasn't coming. I glanced at Gray, and he looked back at me, his eyebrows raised. I looked the other way, at the celebrant, who was slim and elegant and always looked a little amused. His name was Hayden, and he was married to one of those teammates of Gray's, to my surprise. I'd never known a gay man before. I hadn't imagined one being a bulky, bearded rugby player with two cauliflower ears and a smashed nose, let alone one who sat as stolidly as any man from Mount Zion ever had, his meaty hands clasped in front of him and his expression unreadable as he stared at his husband.

"The world is full of strange and wonderful things," Hayden had said earlier today, when he'd caught the surprised look on my face on meeting Luke Armstrong. I'd laughed and said, "Yes, it is," and I'd meant it.

Victoria paused at the end of the song. Up the track, Gray's mum, Honor, made an exaggerated circular motion with her hand. *Do it again,* I guessed that meant, because Victoria got her bow moving and did it.

There was no way the delay was Oriana. Oriana would walk to me barefoot if the ground were paved with thorns, and I knew it. I asked Gray, "Do you want to go see?"

"No," he said. "Either she'll come or she won't." He didn't look comfortable, though.

Was it too good to be true, then, this life we'd all planned?

ORIANA

I held my sister's hand and said, "You're good enough at being in love. You're good enough at *love.* How could anybody be better at it than you?"

Daisy said, "I'm not. I get overwhelmed sometimes. I go quiet. I need too much time to process. Sometimes I get annoyed."

I said, "That's not the definition. How much more love could there be than what you've done? You've risked everything, over and over again. You've walked into danger. You've been hurt, and you've come back anyway to help the people you love. Why wouldn't Gray want a woman like that? How could he do better?"

Daisy said, "I'm damaged." It was a whisper.

"So am I," I told her. "So is he. We're all damaged. That's the point, don't you see? That's what love does. It knits our wounds and heals our hearts. Don't you want to do that for him?"

"Yes," Daisy said. "I do." She'd moved forward to see around the corner, and I moved with her.

Handsome, smooth Hayden, the celebrant, standing with the leather folder that held the marriage service. And beside him, two men. One dark, and one fair. Gabriel raised his eyes, they met mine, and a thrill went through me like electricity. As for Gray? He was looking straight at Daisy, and I heard the breath catch in her throat.

"Then marry him," I said. "And heal his heart."

She said, "I need to do that."

"Yes. You do." Her hand was cold in mine, but it wasn't shaking anymore. I asked, "Ready?"

"Ready," she said. And started to walk.

Gabriel

Oriana walked to me the same way she'd walked through everything. Holding her sister's hand, and supporting her, because Oriana was love.

Beside me, I could see Gray's hands shake where they'd been clasped. He'd thought Daisy wouldn't come, because when you'd had enough things go wrong, it was hard to believe they could go this right. That you could ever get that thing you wanted most. That she'd walk to you and take your hand and promise you everything.

She came, though. They both did, but I only saw one.

Oriana, shining like the moon, a smile on her lips and in her eyes, walking to me like destiny.

We held each other's hands as Hayden talked, and we waited to make the promises. We'd say the words today, and we'd mean them, but the most important thing, we'd already done. We'd promised in our hearts.

"When I was a child," Hayden read, "I spake as a child, I understood as a child, I thought as a child, but when I became a man, I put away childish things. For now we see through a glass, darkly; but then face to face: now I know in part; but then shall I know even as also I am known."

A pause, and I looked into the eyes of the woman I'd always wanted. The woman who was mine, body and soul, the same way I was hers. Face to face. Knowing everything.

A man couldn't be this happy, but I was.

"And now abideth faith, hope, and love, these three," Hayden said. "But the greatest of these is love."

53

NIGHTS IN WHITE SATIN

GABRIEL

Around us, the barbecue went on. Kids ran on the grass, and babies cried. My mum kissed Oriana, and my cousins shook my hand.

How long did we have to stay?

I looked at Oriana, and she looked at me. I asked, "Do you want to get out of here?"

She said, "Yes."

The B&B I'd booked for tonight was only a few streets from the sunny flat, with its deck and its view over the hills, where we'd be moving in another week. After our honeymoon, that is, which we were spending in a bach at the northern end of the South Island, near Abel Tasman National Park. I wanted to swim in the Mermaid Pools and out in the sea, with its warm water and golden sand. I wanted to walk on the forested track and hold Oriana's hand. I wanted to start to see the world.

And then I wanted to take her home and see everything.

When I made it up the drive to the historic stone building that was the B&B and found a carpark, though, Oriana didn't open her door. She looked at me, twisted the gold band on her hand, and said, "I'm nervous."

"Me, too," I said, and waited.

"But I want to do it," she said.

What did I do now? The only thing I could think of was to take her hand and say, "I love you. I'm never going to hurt you. We'll do it together, and we'll go as slow as you need to."

"What if I'm not good enough at it, though?" she asked.

"You'll be good enough," I said. "No worries." And then I kissed her. In broad daylight, in my ute. *Our* ute.

Married.

My hand in her hair, and my other one close to the neckline of the pretty pink dress that I could see through. Sweet and sexy and soft, just like Oriana. I kissed her neck, and her hand tightened in my hair. I whispered in her ear, "I get to take off your clothes," then kissed her neck some more while she made a noise and I knew she was getting wet.

Was it going to be as good as I'd imagined? I had no idea. I only knew one thing.

I was never going to quit trying to make it better.

Oriana

I had a pretty nightdress for this, all white satin with cutouts of lace. You got ready in the bath, I'd read in a story, and came out scented and adorned and glamorous. When Gabriel stopped outside the door of our room, though, turned the key, then lifted me into his arms and carried me across the threshold ...

I couldn't think about any of that.

He didn't put me down before he kissed me. His tongue was in my mouth again, and my hand was around his head, pulling him in.

He set me down on the bed. It was big, with four posts, and it was dressed in white. Gabriel dropped the key, then pulled his phone and a little speaker from his trouser pocket and set them on the table. He turned to me, his eyes shining impossibly blue in his face, and asked, "OK?"

"Yeh," I managed to say. "O ... OK." I still had my sandals on—they had wedge heels and a pattern of roses on the leather, and were the prettiest, most delicate shoes I'd ever owned—and now, I reached to take them off.

"Don't," he said. "Let me." With something in his voice I'd never heard before.

He pushed buttons on the little speaker, and on his phone, and a song came on, slow and dark and moody.

"Nights in white satin," a man sang, and I shuddered. Gabriel said, "Ever since I first heard this song, you've been all I can think of when it comes on. Seeing you like this, on my bed. Waiting for me." He reached for one of my shoes, and I held my breath as he unbuckled it and dropped it to the floor, and then while he did the other one. He was kicking his way out of his own shoes, and I was on my knees on the bed, unbuttoning his shirt, running my hands over his broad chest and the ridges of muscle below it.

I'd touched him here, in the dark. In a cramped ute, our breath steaming up the windows. Now, it was day, he was here, and he was glorious. He was on his knees, too, his hand in my hair, pulling a bit. Pulling my head back. He was feasting on my neck, and I'd stopped thinking about his shirt.

His hand behind me, then. Searching for the zip, and finding it. And his hand stilling.

"Turn around," he said. "Please."

I did.

There was a mirror on the opposite wall.

He was behind me, one hand pulling my hair away from my neck, the other lowering my zip. I could see it happening, there in the mirror. My knees splayed apart, my hand behind my head, reaching for him.

He drew his hand down my bare back, and I shivered. He pulled the dress over my shoulders, it dropped to below my waist, and I looked at my pale-pink bra in the mirror, at his hand on my shoulder, and shuddered.

He said, "I'm going to take your clothes off," and I had to close my eyes. The music was swelling around me, all aching voice and soaring strings, and I opened my eyes and watched my dress coming off. Then Gabriel was kneeling behind me, his hands under my breasts.

Watching in the mirror.

He said, "You're beautiful."

I couldn't answer. He reached behind me and unhooked my bra, and it was falling, too. I was in a thong, the first one I'd ever worn, in the same pale pink. It should have been pretty, but all it was—was sin.

I watched his hands on my breasts. I watched them slide down my body and back up it again. I watched his thumbs and forefingers close over my nipples, and I was panting.

He said, "Look at you. Look at you. My wife."

His hand went inside the front of the thong.

I watched him give me that entire slow, rolling orgasm. My hair around my face, his bare shoulders and chest behind me, his hand inside my thong. My face starting to contort, and my head going back against his shoulder.

Urgent male voice, wailing out the words. Swelling music, and Gabriel's blue eyes staring into mine. Gabriel, watching himself do it to me.

My husband.

GABRIEL

I never wanted to stop watching her.

By the time she was shuddering under my hand for the second time, I was thinking, *I'm never going to make it.* And when I pulled her down, got her thong over her legs, and she took a breath and slowly opened those legs for me?

I knew I was going to.

I don't remember getting rid of the rest of my clothes. I do remember kissing my way down her body and back up it again. I remember taking her breast in my mouth, playing with the other one, and the sounds she made. I remember how that music sounded, desperate and aching.

I remember turning Oriana over, too, pulling her hair aside again, and kissing my way down her spine. The silk of her skin as I caressed her bottom, her thighs, as if my hands had a mind of their own, and their greed was endless. Petting the outsides of her thighs and, finally, the insides, my thumbs brushing over her but not quite getting there, not this time. I remember her turning over herself, her own greedy hands moving down my chest, my belly, then taking hold of me, and the agony of that moment. I remember her rising on her elbow, her other arm around my hips, urging me forward.

I thought, *Wait. I need to do this to her first. I need to ... on her back. I need to ...*

I couldn't think anymore. My hands were around her head, and many long, torturous minutes later, I was gasping, and then I was calling out.

I got to the part with her on her back, eventually. I got to the part where my arms were around her thighs, holding her up and holding her open as I drank her in. I remember the sounds she made then, and the anguish in her voice.

And when I still had my arms around her legs like that, but I was rising up her body, taking her mouth again—I remember that. I was kissing her, and then I found the spot and slid inside.

I froze.

She gasped out, "It doesn't ... hurt. Don't ... stop."

I said, "I ... I have to. I have to ... feel this."

I remember the way she threw her head back when I did it slowly, and the way her head started moving back and forth when I did it a little harder. I remember the feel of the backs of her knees against my elbows, and of her upper arms under my hands, because I was holding her there, and her arms had gone over her head. I remember the way her eyes closed and the way her mouth opened. And most of all, I remember the impossible pressure when she began to tighten around me. When the shudders were taking her and she was crying out, her hands twisting the white sheet, pulling at it. The gold of her wedding ring against that white, and the explosion in my body.

I married Oriana, and I burned.

Nights in white satin.

And days, too.

All our lives.

Forever.

GET THE LATEST NEWS, members-only content, and a FREE BOOK by joining my mailing list, www.rosalindjames.com/newsletter

Read Daisy's story: KIWI STRONG

Read Laila's story: KIWI GOLD

Turn the page to Explore More about the places, things, and recipes in this book!

A KIWI GLOSSARY

A few notes about Maori pronunciation:

- The accent is normally on the first syllable.
- All vowels are pronounced separately.
- All vowels except u have a short vowel sound.
- "wh" is pronounced "f."
- "ng" is pronounced as in "singer," not as in "anger."

across the Ditch: in Australia (across the Tasman Sea). Or, if you're in Australia, in New Zealand!

agria potatoes: floury potatoes that are excellent roasted, mashed, baked, etc.

agro: aggravation

air con: air conditioning

All Blacks: National rugby team.

ambo: paramedic

Aotearoa: New Zealand (the other official name, meaning "The Land of the Long White Cloud" in Maori)

Aussie, Oz: Australia. (An Australian is also an Aussie. Pronounced "Ozzie.")

Babygro: onesie

bach: holiday home (pronounced like "bachelor")

backs: rugby players who aren't in the scrum and do more running, kicking, and ball-carrying—though all players do all jobs and play both offense and defense. Backs tend to be faster, leaner, and more glamorous than forwards.

barney: argument, fight

bench: counter (kitchen bench)

berko: berserk

Big Smoke: the big city (usually Auckland)

bikkies: cookies

billy-o, like billy-o: like crazy. "I paddled like billy-o and just barely made it through that rapid."

bin, rubbish bin: trash can

binned: thrown in the trash

bit of a dag: a comedian, a funny guy

bits and bobs: stuff ("be sure you get all your bits and bobs")

bollocks: rubbish, nonsense

boofhead: fool, jerk

booking: reservation

boots and all: full tilt, no holding back

bot, the bot: flu, a bug

box of birds: everything's fine (this is more of a rural South Island saying)

box of fluffy ducks: everything's even finer

Boxing Day: December 26—a holiday

braces: suspenders

brekkie: breakfast

brilliant: fantastic

bub: baby, small child

buggered: messed up, exhausted

bull's roar: close. "They never came within a bull's roar of winning."

bunk off: duck out, skip (bunk off school)

bust a gut: do your utmost, make a supreme effort

A KIWI GLOSSARY

caravan: travel trailer
cardie: a cardigan sweater
chat up: flirt with
chilly bin: ice chest
chips: French fries. (potato chips are "crisps")
chocolate bits: chocolate chips
chocolate fish: pink or white marshmallow coated with milk chocolate, in the shape of a fish. A common treat/reward for kids (and for adults. You often get a chocolate fish on the saucer when you order a mochaccino—a mocha).
choice: fantastic
chokka: full
chooks: chickens
Chrissy: Christmas
chuck out: throw away
chuffed: pleased
cinder: gravel
collywobbles: nervous tummy, upset stomach
come a greaser: take a bad fall
cooker: stove
cot: crib (for a baby)
crook: ill
cuddle: hug (give a cuddle)
cuppa: a cup of tea (the universal remedy)
CV: resumé
cyclone: hurricane (Southern Hemisphere)
dairy: corner shop (not just for milk!)
dead: very; e.g., "dead sexy."
dill: fool
do your block: lose your temper
dob in: turn in; report to authorities. Frowned upon.
doco: documentary
doddle: easy. "That'll be a doddle."
dodgy: suspect, low-quality
dogbox: The doghouse—in trouble

dole: unemployment.

dole bludger: somebody who doesn't try to get work and lives off unemployment (which doesn't have a time limit in NZ)

Domain: a good-sized park; often the "official" park of the town.

dressing gown: bathrobe

drongo: fool (Australian, but used sometimes in NZ as well)

drop your gear: take off your clothes

duvet: comforter

earbashing: talking-to, one-sided chat

electric jug: electric teakettle to heat water. Every Kiwi kitchen has one.

En Zed: Pronunciation of NZ. ("Z" is pronounced "Zed.")

ensuite: master bath (a bath in the bedroom).

eye fillet: premium steak (filet mignon)

fa soifua: goodbye (Samoan)

fair go: a fair chance. Kiwi ideology: everyone deserves a fair go.

fair wound me up: Got me very upset

fantail: small, friendly native bird

farewelled, he'll be farewelled: funeral; he'll have his funeral.

feed, have a feed: meal

firie: firefighter

fizz, fizzie: soft drink

fizzing: fired up

flaked out: tired

flash: fancy

flat to the boards: at top speed

flat white: most popular NZ coffee. An espresso with milk but no foam.

flattie: roommate

flicks: movies

A KIWI GLOSSARY

flying fox: zipline
footpath: sidewalk
footy, football: rugby
forwards: rugby players who make up the scrum and do the most physical battling for position. Tend to be bigger and more heavily muscled than backs.
fossick about: hunt around for something
front up: face the music, show your mettle
garbo: sanitation worker
garden: yard
get on the piss: get drunk
get stuck in: commit to something
give way: yield
giving him stick, give him some stick about it: teasing, needling
glowworms: larvae of a fly found only in NZ. They shine a light to attract insects. Found in caves or other dark, moist places.
go crook, be crook: go wrong, be ill
go on the turps: get drunk
gobsmacked: astounded
good hiding: beating ("They gave us a good hiding in Dunedin.")
granny flat: in-law unit
grotty: grungy, badly done up
ground floor: what the U.S. calls the first floor. The "first floor" is one floor up.
gumboots, gummies: knee-high rubber boots. It rains a lot in New Zealand.
gutted: thoroughly upset
Haast's Eagle: (extinct). Huge native NZ eagle. Ate moa.
haere mai: welcome (Maori; but used commonly)
haka: ceremonial Maori challenge—done before every All Blacks game
hang on a tick: wait a minute

hard man: the tough guy, the enforcer

hard yakka: hard work (from Australian)

harden up: toughen up. Standard NZ (male) response to (male) complaints: "Harden the f*** up!"

have a bit on: I have placed a bet on [whatever]. Sports gambling and prostitution are both legal in New Zealand.

have a go: try

have a nosy for... : look around for

head: principal (headmaster)

head down: or head down, bum up. Put your head down. Work hard.

heaps: lots. "Give it heaps."

hei toki: pendant (Maori)

hiding: beating ("give him a good hiding")

holiday: vacation

honesty box: a small stand put up just off the road with bags of fruit and vegetables and a cash box. Very common in New Zealand.

hooker: rugby position (forward)

hooning around: driving fast, wannabe tough-guy behavior (typically young men)

hoovering: vacuuming (after the brand of vacuum cleaner)

ice block: popsicle

I'll see you right: I'll help you out

in form: performing well (athletically)

it's not on: It's not all right

iwi: tribe (Maori)

jabs: immunizations, shots

jandals: flip-flops. (This word is only used in New Zealand. Jandals and gumboots are the iconic Kiwi footwear.)

jersey: a rugby shirt, or a pullover sweater

joker: a guy. "A good Kiwi joker": a regular guy; a good guy.

journo: journalist

jumper: a heavy pullover sweater

ka pai: going smoothly (Maori).

kapa haka: school singing group (Maori songs/performances. Any student can join, not just Maori.)

karanga: Maori song of welcome (done by a woman)

keeping his/your head down: working hard

kia ora: hello (Maori, but used commonly)

kilojoules: like calories—measure of food energy

kindy: kindergarten (this is 3- and 4-year-olds)

kit, get your kit off: clothes, take off your clothes

Kiwi: New Zealander OR the bird. If the person, it's capitalized. Not the fruit.

kiwifruit: the fruit. (Never called simply a "kiwi.")

knackered: exhausted

knockout rounds: playoff rounds (quarterfinals, semifinals, final)

koru: ubiquitous spiral Maori symbol of new beginnings, hope

kumara: Maori sweet potato.

lifestyle block: A rural section (piece of property) for urban dwellers (the "lifestyle" isn't that it's fancy; it's the opposite—that it's a place you can own animals and do a little farming. It's the Kiwi lifestyle.)

littlies: young kids

lock: rugby position (forward)

lollies: candy

lolly: candy or money

loud-hailer: loudspeaker

lounge: living room

mad as a meat axe: crazy

maintenance: child support

major: "a major." A big deal, a big event

mana: prestige, earned respect, spiritual power

Maori: native people of NZ—though even they arrived relatively recently from elsewhere in Polynesia

marae: Maori meeting house

Marmite: Savory Kiwi yeast-based spread for toast. An acquired taste. (Kiwis swear it tastes different from Vegemite, the Aussie version.)

mate: friend. And yes, fathers call their sons "mate."

metal road: gravel road

Milo: cocoa substitute; hot drink mix

mince: ground beef

mind: take care of, babysit

moa: (extinct) Any of several species of huge flightless NZ birds. All eaten by the Maori before Europeans arrived.

moko: Maori tattoo

mokopuna: grandchildren

Moses basket: bassinet

motorway: freeway

mozzie: mosquito; OR a Maori Australian (Maori + Aussie = Mozzie)

muesli: like granola, but unbaked

munted: broken

naff: stupid, unsuitable. "Did you get any naff Chrissy pressies this year?"

nappy: diaper

narked, narky: annoyed

netball: Down-Under version of basketball for women. Played like basketball, but the hoop is a bit narrower, the players wear skirts, and they don't dribble and can't contact each other. It can look fairly tame to an American eye. There are professional netball teams, and it's televised and taken quite seriously.

New World: One of the two major NZ supermarket chains

nibbles: snacks

nick, in good nick: doing well

niggle, niggly: small injury, ache or soreness

no worries: no problem. The Kiwi mantra.

not very flash: not feeling well

Nurofen: brand of ibuprofen

nutted out: worked out

OE: Overseas Experience—young people taking a year or two overseas, before or after University.

offload: pass (rugby)

oldies: older people. (or for the elderly, "wrinklies!")

on the front foot: Having the advantage. Vs. on the back foot—at a disadvantage. From rugby.

op shop: charity shop, secondhand shop

out on the razzle: out drinking too much, getting crazy

paddock: field (often used for rugby—"out on the paddock")

Pakeha: European-ancestry people (as opposed to Polynesians)

Panadol: over-the-counter painkiller

partner: romantic partner, married or not

patu: Maori club

paua, paua shell: NZ abalone

pavlova (pav): Classic Kiwi Christmas (summer) dessert. Meringue, fresh fruit (often kiwifruit and strawberries) and whipped cream.

pavement: sidewalk (generally on wider city streets)

pear-shaped, going pear-shaped: messed up, when it all goes to Hell

penny dropped: light dawned (figured it out)

people mover: minivan

perve: stare sexually

phone's engaged: phone's busy

piece of piss: easy

pike out: give up, wimp out

piss awful: very bad

piss up: drinking (noun) a piss-up

pissed: drunk

pissed as a fart: very drunk. And yes, this is an actual expression.

play up: act up

playing out of his skin: playing very well

plunger: French Press coffeemaker

PMT: PMS

pohutukawa: native tree; called the "New Zealand Christmas Tree" for its beautiful red blossoms at Christmastime (high summer)

poi: balls of flax on strings that are swung around the head, often to the accompaniment of singing and/or dancing by women. They make rhythmic patterns in the air, and it's very beautiful.

Pom, Pommie: English person

pong: bad smell

pop: pop over, pop back, pop into the oven, pop out, pop in

possie: position (rugby). Pronounced "pozzie."

postie: mail carrier

pot plants: potted plants (not what you thought, huh?)

pounamu: greenstone (jade)

prang: accident (with the car)

pressie: present

puckaroo: broken (from Maori)

pudding: dessert

pull your head in: calm down, quit being rowdy

Pumas: Argentina's national rugby team

pushchair: baby stroller

put your hand up: volunteer

put your head down: work hard

rapt: thrilled

rattle your dags: hurry up. From the sound that dried excrement on a sheep's backside makes, when the sheep is running!

red card: penalty for highly dangerous play. The player is sent off for the rest of the game, and the team plays with 14 men.

rellies: relatives

rimu: a New Zealand tree. The wood used to be used for

building and flooring, but like all native NZ trees, it was over-logged. Older houses, though, often have rimu floors, and they're beautiful.

root: have sex (you DON'T root for a team!)
ropeable: very angry
ropey: off, damaged ("a bit ropey")
rort: ripoff
rough as guts: uncouth
rubbish bin: garbage can
rugged up: dressed warmly
ruru: native owl
Safa: South Africa. Abbreviation only used in NZ.
sammie: sandwich
scoff, scoffing: eating, like "snarfing"
sealed road: paved road
section: property (like a lot)
serviette: napkin
shag: have sex with. A little rude, but not too bad.
shattered: exhausted
sheds: locker room (rugby)
she'll be right: See "no worries." Everything will work out. The other Kiwi mantra.
shift house: move (house)
shonky: shady (person). "a bit shonky"
shout, your shout, my shout, shout somebody a coffee: buy a round, treat somebody
sickie, throw a sickie: call in sick
singlet: undershirt/tank top
sink the boot in: kick you when you're down
skint: broke (poor)
slag off: speak disparagingly of; disrespect
sledging: taunting, esp. in sports
sleepout: a modest cottage in the back yard. Typically no plumbing.
smack: spank. Smacking kids is illegal in NZ.

smoko: coffee break

snog: kiss; make out with

sorted: taken care of

spa, spa pool: hot tub

sparrow fart: the crack of dawn

speedo: Not the swimsuit! Speedometer. (the swimsuit is called a budgie smuggler—a budgie is a parakeet, LOL.)

spew: vomit

spit the dummy: have a tantrum. (A dummy is a pacifier)

sportsman: athlete

sporty: liking sports

spot on: absolutely correct. "That's spot on. You're spot on."

squiz: look. "I was just having a squiz round." "Giz a squiz": Give me a look at that.

stickybeak: nosy person, busybody

stonkered: drunk—a bit stonkered—or exhausted

stoush: bar fight, fight

straight away: right away

strength of it: the truth, the facts. "What's the strength of that?" = "What's the true story on that?"

stroppy: prickly, taking offense easily

stuffed up: messed up

supporter: fan (Do NOT say "root for." "To root" is to have (rude) sex!)

suss out: figure out

sweet: dessert

sweet as: great. (also: choice as, angry as, lame as... Meaning "very" whatever. "Mum was angry as that we ate up all the pudding before tea with Nana.")

swot: study; cram

takahe: ground-dwelling native bird. Like a giant parrot.

takeaway: takeout (food)

tall poppy: arrogant person who puts himself forward or

sets himself above others. It is every Kiwi's duty to cut down tall poppies, a job they undertake enthusiastically.

Tangata Whenua: Maori (people of the land)
tapu: sacred (Maori)
Te Papa: the National Museum, in Wellington
tea: dinner (casual meal at home)
tea towel: dishtowel
thick: stupid
throw a wobbly: have a tantrum
tick off: cross off (tick off a list)
ticker: heart. "The boys showed a lot of ticker out there today."
togs: swimsuit (male or female)
torch: flashlight
touch wood: knock on wood (for luck)
towie: tow-truck driver
track: trail
trainers: athletic shoes
tramping: hiking
trolley: shopping cart
tucker: food
tui: Native bird
turf out: kick out
turn to custard: go south, deteriorate
turps, go on the turps: get drunk
under the pump: under pressure
Uni: University—or school uniform
up the duff: pregnant. A bit vulgar (like "knocked up")
uso: brother or sister (Samoan)
ute: pickup or SUV
vet: check out
waiata: Maori song
wairua: spirit, soul (Maori). Very important concept.
waka: canoe (Maori)
Warrant of Fitness: certificate of a car's fitness to drive

wedding tackle: the family jewels; a man's genitals

wee: (1) small; (2) pee ("take a wee")

Weet-Bix: ubiquitous breakfast cereal

whaddarya?: I am dubious about your masculinity (meaning "Whaddarya... pussy?")

whakapapa: genealogy (Maori). A critical concept.

whanau: family (Maori). Big whanau: extended family. Small whanau: nuclear family.

wheelie bin: rubbish bin (garbage can) with wheels.

whinge: whine. Contemptuous! Kiwis dislike whingeing. Harden up!

White Ribbon: campaign against domestic violence

wind up: upset (perhaps purposefully). "Their comments were bound to wind him up."

wing: rugby position (back)

wobbly; threw a wobbly: a tantrum; had a tantrum

Yank: American. Not pejorative.

yonks: ages. "It's been going on for yonks."

ALSO BY ROSALIND JAMES

The *New Zealand Ever After* series
Karen & Jax's story: KIWI RULES
Poppy & Matiu's story: STONE COLD KIWI
Daisy & Gray's story: KIWI STRONG
Laila & Lachlan's story: KIWI GOLD

The *Not Quite a Billionaire* series (Hope & Hemi's story)
FIERCE
FRACTURED
FOUND

The *Escape to New Zealand* series
Reka & Hemi's story: JUST FOR YOU
Hannah & Drew's story: JUST THIS ONCE
Kate & Koti's story: JUST GOOD FRIENDS
Jenna & Finn's story: JUST FOR NOW
Emma & Nic's story: JUST FOR FUN
Ally & Nate's/Kristen & Liam's stories: JUST MY LUCK
Josie & Hugh's story: JUST NOT MINE
Hannah & Drew's story again/Reunion: JUST ONCE MORE
Faith & Will's story: JUST IN TIME
Nina & Iain's story: JUST STOP ME
Chloe & Kevin's story: JUST SAY YES
Nyree & Marko's story: JUST SAY (HELL) NO
Zora & Rhys's story: JUST COME OVER
Victoria & Kane's/Hayden & Luke's story: JUST SAY CHRISTMAS

Elizabeth & Luka's story: JUST ONE LOOK

The *Sinful, Montana,* series
Paige's & Jace's story: GUILTY AS SIN
Lily & Rafe's story: TEMPTING AS SIN
Willow & Brett's story: SEXY AS SIN

The *Portland Devils* series
Dakota & Blake's story: SILVER-TONGUED DEVIL
Beth & Evan's story: NO KIND OF HERO
Jennifer & Harlan's story: SHAME THE DEVIL
Dyma & Owen's story: DEVIL IN DISGUISE

The *Paradise, Idaho* series (Montlake Romance)
Zoe & Cal's story: CARRY ME HOME
Kayla & Luke's story: HOLD ME CLOSE
Rochelle & Travis's story: TURN ME LOOSE
Hallie & Jim's story: TAKE ME BACK

The *Kincaids* series
Mira and Gabe's story: WELCOME TO PARADISE
Desiree and Alec's story: NOTHING PERSONAL
Alyssa and Joe's story: ASKING FOR TROUBLE

ACKNOWLEDGMENTS

Ever since I wrote Daisy's story, I've wanted to follow up on her sisters. It's hard to imagine exactly how difficult it would be to leave everything you've ever known and take a step that you've been told all your life will lead to damnation. Where, along the continuum of living styles, do you end up? How much do the old ways pull you, and how much do you just want to throw off the shackles and reject it all? I'm guessing that the answers are as varied as there are people.

Thanks to my alpha read duo, Kathy Harward and Mary Guidry, for their advice and inspiration as they read along with this book.

Thanks to my husband, Rick Nolting, for reading also, and for asking his gentle questions.

Thank you to New Zealand for being its lovely self, and for never taking itself too seriously.

And finally, one big giant thank-you to my wonderful readers. I appreciate you.

Made in the USA
Las Vegas, NV
20 December 2022